INTRUSION

'Thoughtful, plausible and scary'
Sunday Telegraph

'*Intrusion* is a finely tuned, in-your-face argument of a novel . . .
MacLeod will push your buttons – and make you think'
SFX

'It's all so close to the bone it's almost painful . . . *Intrusion*
is a rather frightening vision of the road we are taking
with our smoking bans and our obesity epidemics
and our CCTVs. Particularly if you're a woman'
Bookbag.co.uk

'The message is powerful and the warning crystal clear'

BY KEN MACLEOD

INTRUSION
KEN MACLEOD

www.orbitbooks.net

ORBIT

First published in Great Britain in 2012 by Orbit
This paperback edition published in 2013 by Orbit

Copyright © 2012 by Ken MacLeod

Excerpt from *Existence* by David Brin
Copyright © 2012 by David Brin

The moral right of the author has been asserted.

A CIP catalogue record for this book
is available from the British Library.

ISBN 978-1-84149-940-6

Typeset in Goudy by M Rules
Printed and bound in Great Britain by
Clays Ltd, St Ives plc

Papers used by Orbit are from well-managed forests
and other responsible sources.

To Sharon

1

Concerning Hope

Like any responsible father, Hugh Morrison had installed cameras in every room in the flat. You bang them in like nails, the work experience had told him, and bang them in Hugh did. The internet said they transmitted to the police station. The bubble pack said they recorded. Hugh knew which to believe, and banged them in without a worry. You could only pick them up on the house wifi. The bubble pack said that too.

That March morning, the cameras in the kitchen recorded Hope. Hope Morrison, née Abendorf, sat at the kitchen table, staring into space. She wore wraparound glasses with clunky earpieces. Now and again she tapped her fingers on the table, typing, or moused the tip of her forefinger about. She had a job in China, answering queries to a help screen. She couldn't read Chinese. The query translations were automatic and most of the answers – all of them, if necessary – were also automatic, chatted out by a software module called Searle, but rewording the occasional answer did something positive to the site's traffic, so there you were.

Around about eleven the nursery called to say Nick had the sniffles, and could she *please* take him home before he infected the faith kids? Hope sighed and agreed. As she flipped the phone clip off she indulged a resentful thought that Nick had probably got the sniffles *from* the faith kids.

Hope toggled her screen-work to Searle, took off the glasses, and left the kitchen table. She kicked off her mocs and stepped into her Muck Boots, pulled an open-mesh wool jacket over her loose cotton top and long linen dress and a cagoule over the lot, olive green over shades of berry. She parted the sides of her hair over the front of her shoulders, zipped up and hooded, sidled past the hedge of handlebars in the hall and headed out into the rain.

Up the green, slippery, worn sandstone steps from her basement flat she went, treading carefully, to the pavement. Victoria Road, like (it seemed) half the streets in Finsbury Park this March, was obstructed by machinery: small JCBs digging out stumps, lorries carrying away felled trees, cranes and lifts steadying old trees as the chainsaws bit through their trunks, more lorries bringing New Trees to plant. In the hundred yards between Hope's front gate and East West Road she passed a dozen New Trees, planted as saplings in November and already sixteen feet high. God only knew what they'd be like in the summer. Each tree as she passed under it held off the pelting rain like an umbrella, making the last fall of leaves from the old trees slightly less slippery underfoot.

2

The nursery was a couple of hundred metres to the right along the southern side of East West Road. Hope crossed at the lights, dodging whirring cars and whizzing bikes whose smugly green owners thought the red didn't apply to *them*. Past the high plastic scenery-printed screens around the nursery, through the metal-detector and biometric-scan gate, and into the joyous uproar of indoor playtime.

Was it possible, Hope wondered as she looked for Nick's hurtling trajectory amid the skein, was it possible *at all* to tell the difference between on the one hand faith kids and nature kids (of which Nick was the only one here) and on the other the rest, those you might call, under your breath of course, *New Kids*? Were these a centimetre taller than others of their age, a glimmer brighter of eye, a syllable more articulate? A step ahead in the race, a pace more sure-footed? A decibel less loud?

At this moment, she couldn't tell. She scooped Nick up. He howled and stretched out his arms for the teacher who, three hours earlier, had had to prise him off Hope's leg. Hope inserted Nick's arms into the sleeves of his big yellow cagoule (several times), lifted his camo lunch box from a high shelf in the lobby and reminded him of what was inside it, waved goodbye to the teachers, and departed. Nick had the sniffles all right, sneezing into the crook of his elbow several times, and just barely amused by watching the rain wash the snot off the sleeve of his cagoule. He only brightened when he got inside and his toy monkey ran to meet him.

'Hello, Max,' said Nick, picking it up and cuddling it.

'Hello, Nick,' said Max, its arms curling around Nick.

Hope made Nick a GenSip and parked him at the other side of the table with Max on his lap and his lunch box open in front of him. She unfolded Mummy's Special Glasses That You Mustn't Touch and put them on. Searle had dealt with a score of enquiries, not all of them well. Hope sighed and got back to work. When she'd cleared the backlog, she warmed the kettle again and made herself a cup of instant coffee, and took a break by flicking to ParentsNet. She opened the Forums page and found it topped by a new thread with a slew of postings:

Nature Kids Now Illegal?

The incept story was a BBC item about a messy marital conflict. The couple were Iranian doctors, and (no surprise) militant atheists. The woman was six months pregnant. The man wanted her to take the fix. The woman, for reasons she refused to elaborate, didn't. She wanted a nature kid. If she'd claimed a conversion to one of the sects – Druze, Hassidic, Mennonite, Sedevacantist or even any old New Age Earth Mother nonsense, the sort of thing she could have made up on the spot – she'd have been covered by the conscience exemption. But she hadn't, and wouldn't. Her husband's insistence was equally stubborn.

And, to everyone's surprise, the judge in the family court had ruled in his favour. Or rather, as those on the judge's side of the argument kept insisting, in the future child's favour. Comments were already in the thousands – Hope tapped the Sense icon and watched a half-dozen animated talking heads summarise the main views.

She sat back, hands lightly clasped over her belly, and thought for a bit. Then she got back to work.

'Well I'm not bloody doing it,' she told Hugh, that evening after dinner and Nick's bedtime.

'That's fine,' he said. He didn't look or sound like he needed to say anything more. Hope, beside him on the sofa, head-butted his shoulder. It was like hitting a car tyre.

Hugh had taken off his work overalls hours ago, as soon as he'd parked his bike in the hall. He still smelled of wood, which Hope liked. She didn't like finding sawdust or tiny curls of wood-shavings snagged in the hairs of his chest or groin or head, which she sometimes did, even after he'd had a shower. She accepted the inconvenience, though, as part of the package. Hugh came as a package, all right, but what he didn't come with was baggage. What you saw was what you got, and what you saw was a big bluff guy with a shock of sandy (as well as sawdusty) hair already giving way to male pattern baldness that exposed, to close inspection, freckles on his scalp. The only reason he wasn't fat was that he worked so hard and so physically he turned every spare calorie to more muscle.

He'd grown up on a wind farm on the Isle of Lewis. Father an incomer, mother a native. Like his parents, Hugh and Hope had met at university, where Hugh was studying wind turbine engineering. When, halfway through his degree, the bottom had dropped out of that market, he'd calmly turned to carpentry.

He'd been doing that for a year when he and Hope had met. There was good money in carpentry, he'd explained, what with the China business and all the new kinds of wood. He took her on walks through whole forests of the stuff. His bike frame had grown in one.

Hope and Hugh. H+H. H2. H4H. That was what Hugh used to carve on trees. Maybe still did, for all Hope knew.

'So what are we going to do about it?' Hope said.

Hugh gave her a puzzled look.

'What *is* there to do about it?' he said. 'If you don't want to do it, nobody can make you do it.'

'Have you been listening to a word I said?'

'Yes, I have,' said Hugh. 'It's a decision, not a law. Nothing's been made illegal.'

(He said the last word with a slow lingual and a long nasal vowel, like this: ill-*lee*-gal. It was from the maternal half of his accent, which showed up now and then like a mitochondrial gene.)

'The point is,' said Hope, irritated at what seemed wilful obtuseness for its own sake, 'it sets a precedent. In effect the fix becomes compulsory.'

'In effect, yes. But only if someone sues.'

'Oh, come on. You know what'll happen to insurance, social services, and everything like that.' Hope waved her arms as if fending off midges. 'It all closes in. And then they'll make a law, like they did with pregnant women smoking and drinking.'

'Yeah,' said Hugh. 'There is that.'

He stood up and walked over to the stove. The air in the room smelled resinous for a moment as he opened the stove door and loaded some new wood in. He worked the lever that ejected a brick of soot, added the brick to the stack by the stove, and then sat down again.

'Well,' he said, 'I suppose that just means we'll have to break the law.'

Hope had been half-expecting him to argue, to suggest some compromise. He didn't share her opposition to the fix, and had now and again expressed some mild irritation at the succession of infant ills that its absence left Nick exposed to. He had once pointed out that the medicines to cure these ills were themselves very similar in principle and effect to the fix. Having found herself pushing at an open door, Hope stumbled and flailed.

'We could always claim we had a faith issue with it,' she said, half in jest.

'No, we could not,' Hugh said, folding his arms. 'I will not pretend to believe something just to get a conscience exemption. Because it would not be true, and because you would have to do more than claim. You would have to show evidence of practice, even if it was just muttering in front of crystals or something. And that would set a very bad example to the boy, if nothing else.'

'I wasn't being serious,' said Hope, hastening to reassure.

'I didn't think you were,' said Hugh. He opened his arms and smiled a little. 'I don't want to hear even jokes about that.'

'All right,' said Hope.

She knew that Hugh took religion very seriously, possibly just as seriously as had the Iranian couple whose case had brought about the whole new situation. And – all proportions guarded – for very much the same reason. He'd told her tales about the wind farms, in the wry tone of someone recounting things so absurd they were unlikely to be believed, but who insisted on their telling and their truth nonetheless. Neither old-time religion nor New Age woo-woo were, in his implacable view, deserving of any slack.

'Damn it!' said Hugh, vehement after a moment or two of pondering. 'Last week we were so happy that you're pregnant. Now we have to worry about this.'

He jumped up and prowled the carpet.

'There's plenty we can do,' he said. 'These parenting sites, there must be thousands of people in this position. There's all the legal challenges, there's civil-liberty groups and all that. It's not like it's all going to happen without a fuss. And it'll take longer than nine months, that's for sure.'

'Nine months is long enough for a lot of things,' said Hope.

'It is and all,' said Hugh.

Hope saw his gaze flicker to the whisky bottle on a shelf. She knew he wanted a dram, and knew he wouldn't take one because she couldn't. (Well, she could, but the monitor ring she wore on the same finger as her wedding band would log the violation with the health centre.) She wished she could persuade him, but knew from her earlier pregnancy that he would not be persuaded. For him it was a matter of honour, or maybe stubborn pride.

'But you're right,' she said. 'We can do lots of things.'

And there they left the question for the night.

Snow had fallen overnight, and likewise overnight the GenSip had worked its magic. Between them these phenomena made Nick eager for nursery. He didn't even clutch Hope's leg when she left him. She trudged home through another fall of snow, big wet soggy flakes that turned instantly to slush. She left her Mucks and cagoule to dry in the hall and padded in her mocs to the kitchen, where she tied on a floral-printed and ruffle-bordered pinafore apron in preparation for doing the housework. Hope had half a kitchen cupboard full of pinnies and half-aprons, most of them similarly retro regardless of their purpose or style or selling point: flirty, tarty, cheery, cheeky, Christmassy, shabby-chic, sophisticated, hostessy; pretty and practical; printed with flowers or sprigs or cupcakes or berries or heart shapes or vintage aeroplanes or Santa hats or polka dots or lipstick kisses or whatever.

The oldest of them, still there at the back, was a relatively plain floral-print Cath Kidston apron with matching oven gloves, which Hope's mother had given her the day she went away to university and to live away from home for the first time. Hope still recalled the sheer disbelief and feigned grati-tude with which she'd unwrapped the gift. For her mother, this sort of thing was 'ironic' (like that, with air-quotes). Her mother's generation, Hope had often thought, had tried on and played dress-up in their grandmothers' aprons as some kind of postmodern fashion statement, and left their daughters to find themselves quite unexpectedly stuck in the things, all wrapped and tied up with a neat bow at the back.

Hope resented it sometimes. It wasn't that she didn't like her aprons, or the working in and from home of which they were both a practical part and a clichéd symbol, but that they'd come to stand in her mind for a larger failing of her mother's cohort, who'd somehow let their guard down for a moment of post-feminist frivolity and found a whole shadow sexist establishment just waiting to pounce, to cry, 'Ah! So that's what you really wanted! We were right all along!' and before you knew it, the tax advantages of having one parent stay at home were so significant it was more than it was worth not to do it unless you were something like a lawyer – like, for instance, all those lawyers who'd dreamed up all the ostensibly child-protective legislation that had put so many workplaces outside the home off limits for women of childbearing age whether they ever intended to have children or not, which meant that nine times out of ten the parent at home was the mother.

For a moment she stood, hands behind her waist, fingers gripping the loops of the knot just tightened, and fell into a dwam as she gazed at the space in front of her. The main part of the flat consisted of the living room and the kitchen, united decades ago by the then-fashionable knock-through, an opening about three times the width of a doorway. The living room was at the front, facing the wall across a gap of about a metre or so; the kitchen to the back, facing the garden (or, as Nick called it, the back grass). Enough light came from the windows – the upper third of the front was level with the street – to give some cheering sun-shine to the living room in the mornings and the kitchen in the afternoons. Today the light seemed paradoxically brighter because of the snow. At other times, and in the evenings, the flat always seemed to Hope darker than it should be, in the cold, dim light of energy-saving bulbs and tubes. The flicker of flame from behind the mica plate of the closed-system stove in the living room helped a little, lending a few cosy wavelengths of natural light to the scene.

Likewise cheering touches were added by the paintings and drawings from her student days that Hope had framed on the walls, the far larger number of Nick's paintings from nursery tacked up all over the place; the tapestries and crochets, which Hope had made or bought, thrown over chairs and sofa, and the shelves and stacks of books: art history, cookery books, needlecraft books, textbooks from Hugh's and Hope's university days – more art history, engineering and science reference works – all decoration really, when you could summon their contents in an eye-blink, but good to have even if a pain to dust. You couldn't sell them, anyway: the second-hand book trade had collapsed under the dangers of fourth-hand smoke, with most of the stock sealed in vaults or incinerated. Hope's guitar, though also sadly gathering dust in the living-room corner where it stood propped, now and then lifted her spirits too, especially when she picked it up, blew the dust off it, and strummed a few bars or, on particularly bad or good days, sang at the top of her voice in the empty flat.

Hope washed the breakfast dishes, tidied Nick's toys – which got everywhere even in the hour between him getting up and going to nursery – and made the beds and tidied Nick's room. Max the toy monkey followed her around, picking toys up and offering them for her to play with. After a while he started to say 'Max hungry', so she set him to sleep mode and stuck him on the recharger. She made a coffee, hung up her apron, sat down at the kitchen table, opened her glasses and started working in China but not in Chinese. She took a break at eleven and checked the BBC. The nature kids issue had been knocked right off the front screen by a truck-bomb blast at a motorway intersection outside Munich: scores dead, hundreds injured, toll expected to rise. The atrocity had been claimed by the Neues Rote Armee Fraktion, a hitherto unheard-from local affiliate of the transnational insurgent franchise that everyone called the Naxals. Hope stared at fallen flyovers and mangled cars for as long as she could bear to listen. Then she shuddered and flipped to ParentsNet, where the nature kids thread had more or less taken over.

No new light there. Hope decided to skip the crowd-sourced wisdom of pseudonymous strangers and consult some real people. She wrote an email and fired it off to six friends, then got back to work. By lunchtime she had four responses.

Sheila: Hi Hope, Good to hear from you! Yes this is outrageous but remember it will go to appeal. Also legal challenge to faith exemption (i.e. need to extend it to non-faith conscience cases) has good precedent all the way back to that climate-change guy. Look up humanism for example, that's explicitly covered. So not to worry and obviously has no personal bearing on you because the machinery won't have ground out anything for a year at least. Best wishes re the pregnancy of course, you have morning sickness to look forward to ha-ha. xxx

Fatima: Yeah well, if you think ParentsNet has gone wild about this take a look at the British Persian sites!!! But seriously, have you thought about Nature Kids Network, it's a community for parents like you? Some woo-woo and anti-vaccers but mostly quite level-headed. They're the place to go for serious advice, and they've already got lawyers on board. Though to be honest Hope, I never did understand the objection, though I quite appreciate it's up to you and if what you're afraid of does come about I will be on the streets for you. Keep well.

James: Hi Hope, interesting points. Tricky one really. I understand your concern, but as a doctor, I see too many kids with congenital conditions or so-called childhood illnesses (which can have very nasty consequences even when minor) that could have been completely avoided had their parents agreed to the fix to be as gung-ho as you are about the parents' so-called 'rights'. It's like the tobacco/alcohol ban in pregnancy – lots of problems with that if you pose it as a 'rights' or 'freedom' issue, and there was a lot of fuss about that before the ban, and it was predicted to be unenforceable and all that, but when it came in it was

complied with except for the usual chav element, and the
medical benefits are plain in the stats and hard to argue with
if you've ever seen a case of foetal alcohol syndrome (which
I have, though not recently, I wonder why? No I don't).
Obviously I'm entirely sympathetic to *you*, don't get me
wrong, and I'll stand by you if they come for you (which they
won't) but as a doctor and as a friend my advice to you is to
change the problem by changing your mind and just taking
the goddamn fix.

Must dash but let's you and us meet up for dinner
sometime. Regards to Hugh.

Deirdre: Lovely seeing you the other day, with you all the
way on this one, let's have a chat over drinks oops coffee
soon. Bye 4 now!

What a great posse of friends I have, Hope thought. James in
particular annoyed her, but she knew it was just the medicine
talking. Doctors nearly always turned out like that.

She dismissed James from her mind, and mentally from her
Christmas-card list, and followed up Sheila's suggestion. A
search on humanism and a quick scan of the results left her
more despondent than before. For a start, the humanist organ-
isations and most humanist thinkers seemed entirely in favour
of the fix, though not at all for making it compulsory or even
hard to avoid. But what depressed her more was that she didn't
even agree with humanism. That there was no God was a
given, as far as Hope was concerned, and being nice to people

and making the most of your life struck her as a reasonable enough conclusion to draw from it, and in any case what she wanted to do. But beside the spires of theology and the watchtowers of ideology, it seemed a very shaky hut indeed, and not one that offered her much shelter or would stand up in court.

She couldn't see a way to make her objection to the fix a deduction from any body of thought. It came from a body of flesh, her own, and that was enough for her. She doubted that this would be enough for anyone else.

One p.m. Back to China.

2

The Science Bit

At the same moment, on the other side of town, another woman sat tapping a virtual keyboard. Unlike Hope, she was not working from home. She sat on a tall stool at a table in the corner of a laboratory on the tenth floor of the SynBioTech building in Hayes, Middlesex, where the EMI building had been. She was writing an article for *Memo*, the daily news site for people who read, if at all, on commutes. She was very pleased to be writing it, because she thought there was an important message to get across to the public (even the travelling public) and because it would earn her a hundred pounds.

Her name – her name can wait. What we are interested in, right now, is what she was writing. It was this.

Over the past ten years, synthetic biology – syn bio, as everyone in the trade calls it – has changed our lives in many unexpected ways. Now, with the Kasrani case, it looks like changing it again – and unexpectedly, again!

But first – what is synthetic biology?

One way of putting it is that it's like genetic engineering, but done by real engineers. Just as civil engineering doesn't mean building a dam by bulldozing soil from the riverbanks into some convenient shallow, syn bio doesn't take whatever happens to be there in the DNA and modify it. Instead, it builds new genes – and other biologically active molecules – from scratch, out of their basic components, and according to a detailed understanding of how they work.

The differences between this approach and the trial-and-error, suck-it-and-see methods of what used to be called 'genetic engineering' are immense. Synthetic biology has given us New Trees, which take up carbon dioxide twice as fast as natural trees, and endless varieties of other new plants, from the tough new woods to the ethanol fruits. Closest to home, it's given us the fix, a complex of gene-correcting machinery made up into a simple tablet which when swallowed during pregnancy fixes errors in the baby's genome, and confers immunity to almost all childhood ailments. Generations of animal testing and rigorous checking in software models run on the best supercomputers in the world have shown its safety and efficacy. For five years now, it's been freely available to all mothers in the EU (and, by the way, made available without patents to companies in the developing world). None of the major religions has any objection to it – no human material goes into it, and it doesn't add or take away from the human genome: it just corrects existing errors. Its effects aren't even hereditary – it's carefully designed not to affect the sex cells. The amount of pain and heartbreak and suffering it has already prevented is beyond calculation – and beyond dispute.

So why do some people refuse it? Well, some religious minorities are against it, as is their right. But what motivates people like Mrs Kasrani? Sheer stubbornness? Some deep-rooted doubt about 'going too far' or 'going against nature'? Or something else?

We don't know, because she isn't saying. But while anyone has a right to object to any medical intervention, however beneficial, the rest of us have a right to know why. That's why the judge ruled against her.

She read it over, decided it was too complicated for *Memo*, and ran it through an app called MyTxt4Dummies. It came out like this:

Syn Bio has made our world better. It cleaned the air. It gave us New Trees. It gave us the fix. The fix makes babies better before they're born. So what's with this foreign woman saying no to it? She isn't even a god-botherer. Time to put up or shut up, missus!

She sent it in, in time for the evening rush-hour version of

18

Memo. She was ashamed to have her name on it, but she needed the money. She wasn't employed by SynBioTech. She wasn't employed at all. She had a grant from the Institute for Science Studies at Brunel University, on a postgraduate research project on laboratory culture in advanced biotech dry labs. A social-scientific study of the culture of engineers, for whom 'laboratory culture' meant something that grew on a Petri dish under a warm lamp. Her name was Geena Fernandez, but that wasn't what her colleagues called her, behind her back.

They called her 'the science bit'.

3

Hugh

Hugh Morrison shook wet snow off his hooded Barbour jacket and hung it up in the cupboard in the hall just beyond where the bikes stood. As he did so he glanced at the shelf at the top of the cupboard. The frayed cardboard carton that he thought of as the suicide box – it contained a bottle of whisky and a pistol – was still there. The pistol was a high-power air-pistol replica of an automatic, and thus doubly illegal, but quite undetectable by sniffing for explosives. Hugh had no intention of committing suicide with it, or with the whisky for that matter. Hope didn't know about the contents of the box, and the carton itself was above her eyeline and she was unlikely ever to notice it. The cameras in the hall didn't see into the cupboard – Hugh had made sure of that when he'd banged them in – and there were no cameras in the cupboard.

He turned out of the cupboard and into the hall. Through in the kitchen, Hope looked at him over her shoulder from the sink, a smile just beginning. A little closer, Nick hurtled towards him, arms open, Max the toy monkey bounding in pursuit. A metre or so behind the boy and the toy, just below the eyeline between Hugh and Hope, quite solid, a stocky man with long red hair and a blue-dyed face walked at a diagonal across the narrow passageway. The hide pieces wrapped around his feet and strapped around his calves made a wet sound as his heels came up, and a faint, distinct thud as his heels came down. The fur of his sleeveless jacket was beaded with water, his check trousers soaked to the knees, but his hair and his arms were dry. He gave Hugh a sidelong glance a second before he stepped through the wall, and jerked his head a little to the other side, looking away, as if Hugh were an apparition he was aware of but did not care to face.

Hugh dropped to a squat, opened his arms and caught up the boy and the robot. He carried them both hugging and laughing through to the kitchen. As he stepped across the path the apparition had trod, he caught a distinct whiff of rank unwashed human mingled with the fresher smell of brine.

Hugh had grown up facing the new Atlantic, looking out at icebergs while wind-power blades beat the air overhead. Most of the people he knew were locals – the natives, they called themselves, the Leosich – but although Hugh had been born on Lewis, he knew he wasn't a Leosach. One day when he was about five years old he was playing with his toy spade in some left-over cement and sand at the edge of a new windmill site overlooking Cliff Bay. As usual in certain conversations at that age, he was talking about himself in the third person.

'So then he mixed them up like this,' he explained to Voxy, who was kneeling in her muddy skirt at the other side of the mess, 'and then with the other hand he picked up the water.' Hugh lifted a rusty paint tin full of rainwater. 'And he tipped it in and sort of stirred it, no I mean he shoved the spade under the mix and lifted and then turned it over as he poured the water on, skoosh, and—'

'Who are you talking to?'

Hugh felt a jolt go through him. The water splashed. He set the tin down, dropped the spade, and looked up. Murdo Helmand, a tall Leosach with a glass eye from the war, stood in bright yellow overalls and hard hat looking down at him. Murdo Helmand worked sometimes on the new windmills.

Hugh didn't know why he felt like he felt when he'd been caught doing something bad, but he did.

'Nobody,' he said.

Voxy gave him a hurt look across the mound of half-mixed concrete. She stood up. Hugh stared at the two wet patches where her knees had pressed on the thick woolly fabric wrapped around her legs and tied at the waist with some kind of hairy string. He couldn't look at her eyes. After a moment, he was seeing nothing but the trampled green grass and yellow flowers behind where she'd been.

'Nobody!' he repeated, angry this time, his eyes stinging as

22

he looked again at Murdo Helmand. He wasn't going to cry. He wasn't.

'Nobody?' said Murdo Helmand, teasing. 'So you were talking to yourself, were you?'

'Yes,' Hugh said, relieved. 'I was talking to myself.'

Murdo Helmand laughed. 'Only crazy people talk to themselves.'

He winked with his good eye (back then glass eyes showed only black and white) and strolled away to laugh with his mates on the site. Hugh felt hot. He didn't know where to look, so he looked down.

'He looked down,' he said, but not out loud, 'and he picked up the spade and went on mixing the cement, and it got sort of like mud and then he looked up but he couldn't see Voxy, and he felt really sorry because Voxy had been with him lots and was always nice, well maybe not always.'

With the back of his hand, splashed with wet cement and water, Hugh wiped under his nose. It felt gritty. He sniffed, and something stung inside his nostrils and he sneezed. He tried again with the opposite wrist, which was clean, and that was all right.

He stood up and looked around. From where he stood, on the side of the new site, he could see straight out to sea. The site was a hundred metres or so above the wide sandy beach, facing out on a bay between the two headlands: one all crags and cliffs, black with the white dots of gulls and gannets; the other rounded and green, a huge mound of grass-pinned sand, with a small cemetery on its slope. The breakers rolled straight in, crashing on the sand. Behind him the hill went up to a horizon a hundred or so metres away. He was forbidden to climb that heathery slope, because over the hill was a loch. He had, of course, climbed the slope, and nervously approached the loch's rush-bordered shore, then turned away and run back, muir-burned heather twigs blackening and scratching his legs. Hugh firmly believed, though he had never been told, that the dark waters of the loch covered a crashed fighter aircraft with the skeleton of the pilot still in its cockpit, and that an eel with a body as thick as a man's and of proportional length swam in it, and on occasion emerged from it to gulp down a stray lamb or unwary child.

On his left and a little below him was the windmill site, a broad flat excavation filled with concrete and sprouting metal rods and plates. Generators chugged. Lorries toiled up the slope from the road. The components of the tower were stacked like pieces from a kit for an enormous toy, around which a score of workers swarmed. Leosich and incomers, men and women were hard to tell apart in their yellow overalls, though more incomers than Leosich and more men than women wore the white hard hats of engineers and overseers. Down-slope from the windmill site was the local school building, Valtos Primary, due to reopen in August. Hugh knew he'd have to go there. He was quite looking forward to it, but he hadn't been able to explain to Voxy what it was all about.

'I don't see how you can learn things sitting inside,' she'd said. 'Only the new priests do that, and they don't know fuck all.'

Hugh had found this very funny, but when he'd swaggeringly repeated it to his mum, she'd frowned and asked him where he'd heard *that* sort of language and she hadn't been too pleased when he wouldn't tell her because he didn't want to snitch on Voxy.

Voxy! Hugh walked carefully around the perimeter barriers of the site, looking for her. He didn't call out – he knew he didn't need to. But he couldn't see her anywhere. All the time Murdo Helmand's taunt kept coming back to his mind, like he could hear it inside his head. *Only crazy people talk to themselves.* But he wasn't crazy and he hadn't been talking to himself. He'd been talking to Voxy. He'd always known that other people couldn't see Voxy, but it hadn't seemed important. It was just one of those things, like that other people couldn't hear things you said in your head (except Voxy, of course, who could). Now it seemed very important indeed, because it meant that if people saw or heard him talking to Voxy, they would think he was talking to himself, and only crazy people talked to themselves.

Hugh never saw Voxy again, and whenever he saw people that other people didn't see he didn't speak to them. Some of these occasions were more significant than others. Now and again he thought about Voxy, but fewer and fewer times as he grew up. The funny thing was, though, that whenever he thought about Voxy, he saw her in his mind as she would be now, if she'd grown up in pace with him. He could still remember her as she'd appeared when he was a little kid, and she was a slightly older and cleverer kid, but when he spontaneously thought of her, it was always as a girl, or later as a young woman, about the same age as himself. In his adolescence she featured sometimes in his sexual fantasies, but not often, and he came to turn his mind away from her as a figure in such fantasies – he became uncomfortable with it, not because he felt it was wrong, or thought of her as a sister or anything like that, but because she was in a sense too real, more real than the images of real girls he knew, or the women in the pictures he found on the net.

One evening, in his third year at university, he met her. She was singing in the Students Union bar of Aberdeen University. Hugh was standing at the serving hatch, waiting for a pint of bitter, when he heard a woman's voice and a guitar. Nobody sang in bars any more, not even in Students Union bars, so he turned around. The woman was sitting cross-legged on the bench at the rear wall, head down, strumming a guitar that lay across her knees. She wore tight blue jeans tucked into high brown boots, and a wool open-mesh jacket over a tight T-shirt. Her dark brown hair was piled in a loose knot, skewered by what looked like a wooden knitting needle, on top of her head.

'Twenty pounds,' said the bar person. Hugh handed over the coin and took the plastic glass, without looking away from the woman, and let the guy behind him move to the head of the queue. The woman was singing some English folk song. As she hit the chorus, she tossed her head back, and Hugh saw her face for the first time. He nearly dropped the glass. He actually splashed some of the beer, which at a pound a gulp was something he'd never done before.

She looked exactly like he'd imagined Voxy would look now.

His startlement passed. He took a sip and edged towards the rear wall, weaving around standing groups and Formica-topped woodchip tables and orange plastic chairs. The fluorescent lighting, dim but harsh, glared off the Union bar's white walls and colourful DrinkAware posters of vomit pools, car crashes, liver dissections and facial injuries. White noise and discords were just audible enough on the sound system to disrupt normal conversation and jangle the nerves, but not loud enough to drown out the woman's singing.

A small crowd, a dozen or so, had formed a semicircle around her, and elsewhere in the room heads had turned to face her, some with tentative half-smiles, some with looks of vague puzzlement, a few with frowns. Hugh elbowed into the semi-circle. The abstracted, unfocused gaze of the woman's big dark eyes snagged on the intensity of his look. He responded to the eye-locked moment with a quick, casual nod, as if she were someone he knew, which he felt she was. Her double-take became a triple, but it didn't shake her voice by a note.

She was into the final chorus and one or two of her listeners had joined in by the time Hugh felt a parting in the press of bodies behind him, then a nudge.

'Excuse me.'

Hugh turned to meet the vaguely familiar face of a male student: glasses, ponytail, piercings, strands of beard, busy important frown. Oh, yes: Craig, the Student Union's social secretary, recognisable from his campaign flyers a few months earlier. Hugh stepped aside. Craig took a few paces forward and stopped, leaning slightly forward from the waist.

'I'm sorry,' he said to the woman, 'but I'm going to have to ask you to stop singing.'

The woman shrugged. 'I have stopped,' she said. She had an accent that Hugh could only identify as English, and that sounded to him posh. The accent wasn't in the least like Voxy's, but the voice was. Her complexion and her eyes made him think of rowan and heather, of peat lochs under grey skies.

A few voices were raised in objection.

'Fuck off, Craig!'

'She's no using a mike!'

'Oi!'

Craig turned and glared, then spread his hands. 'Nothing to do with me, folks,' he said. 'It's the law, and you know it. If we allow singing or music in here, we'll lose our licence.'

'Aw, fuck, can you no turn a—'

'Same goes for swearing,' Craig added. 'Creating a hostile environment.'

'It's all right,' the woman said. She stood up and waved her forearms. 'Thanks for the support, everyone, but leave it.'

A few hands clapped, Hugh's included. The woman turned away and clicked open the snaps of a guitar case. The crowd dispersed, part of it following the social secretary in a still-protesting huddle. Hugh stayed where he was. The woman packed away her guitar. She seemed to be on her own.

'That was good,' said Hugh.

'Thank you.' She frowned. 'Do I know you?'

'No,' Hugh said. 'But ...'

He didn't know what to say.

'It's funny,' she said. 'I thought you looked vaguely familiar.'

'Maybe I just looked familiarly vague.' Hugh was at that time working on the theory that when you couldn't think what to say, you said the first thing that came into your head, however flippant or banal. It seemed to work for everyone else.

The woman gave a small, unimpressed laugh.

'Could I get you a drink?' Hugh said.

'Oh, would you?' She sounded surprised. 'Thanks awfully.'

'What are you having?'

'A vodka and lime, please. That's not too girlie, is it? You can say it's for yourself, can't you?' She grimaced. 'I don't have my cert updated, and anyway ... ' She shrugged one shoulder, then looked away.

'Yeah, I know,' said Hugh. This time he knew what to say, but didn't because the woman herself so plainly didn't want to speak about it: the humiliation and annoyance of having to show she wasn't pregnant before she could buy alcohol. Instead, he sighed sympathetically, then smiled complicitly. 'Mind my pint.'

He put the glass carefully on the nearest low table, and rejoined the queue. By the time he got back the beer was flat. He didn't much mind.

'Thanks, uh ... ?'

'Hugh Morrison.'

'Thanks, Hugh.' She sipped, regarding him.

'And your name is ... ?' he said.

'Hope Abendorf.' Another laugh, this time at herself. 'And I've heard all the jokes since kindergarten.'

29

'Jokes?'

'My nickname was Hope Abandon.'

With her slender English-posh vowels, that did sound a little like her name, the way Hugh heard it. *Hape Ebendon.*

'No jokes about that from me,' said Hugh.

'Good,' she said.

They went on talking, and didn't stop. There was one awkward moment, when she was telling him something about her course – art and business studies, which as she said was about right for minding some village gallery or craft shop in the Home Counties – and his attention wandered. A tall, long-haired, bearded guy in leathers and metal – could have been a biker, could have been a re-enactor – strolled past and suddenly turned and fixed Hugh with a blue-eyed glare and said, in a language Hugh didn't speak and had never heard but did understand, 'You be good to that one,' and strode straight on, through the wall as if it weren't there. Or as if *he* weren't, to be more rational about the matter. It had been ten years since Hugh had seen someone who wasn't there.

'Am I boring you?' Hope asked, her tone light but sharp.

'No. Sorry.' Hugh blinked, and shook his head. 'Something you said just reminded me of something, that's all.' He smiled. 'You have all my attention.'

The way he said it, slow and precise, it sounded like a promise. Which, as it turned out, he kept.

4

A Scar of Thought

Fiona Donnelly rang the doorbell at 10.15 the day after Hope's queries to her friends. She was about forty-five years old and she was a district nurse. She'd been alerted by Hope's monitor ring, which like all such devices logged its results with the local health centre and the national database. Her visit had popped up on Hope's diary when she'd fired up her glasses that morning, and Hope had nodded in agreement. Mrs Donnelly had been her visitor when she was pregnant with Nick.

Still, when Hope opened the door and saw Mrs Donnelly standing there in the little basement-flat front yard under a light dusting of snow, she felt a slight pang of dread, like she always did when she saw someone in uniform on her doorstep. It wasn't much of a uniform, just a hooded blue fleece over a blue tunic and trousers, with a few badges and discreet sensors – cameras, mikes, sniffers – pinned here and there over the chest, but there it was. Authority. Hope had had a slight nervousness about people in uniforms since she was a girl in Ealing, back when Ealing was still des res and she was about ten, and the men from Environment had come to take away the Aga.

'Hi, Mrs Donnelly,' she said. 'Come on in.'

'Fiona, please, Hope. It hasn't been that long. Let's not be strangers.'

'No, no,' said Hope.

Fiona took off her fleece, shook the ice particles off it, looked about for a peg and hung the garment on a handlebar. The two women walked crabwise past the bikes, and sat down at the kitchen table.

'Coffee? Tea?'

'Tea would be lovely, thanks. No milk or sugar.'

Hope put the kettle on and rustled up tea bags. Out of the corner of her eye she watched Fiona slip a computer out of her tunic pocket and wave it in front of her chest before setting it down on the table. The nurse peered and poked at it for a few seconds, then sat back, no doubt relieved that no molecules of dangerous substances had been detected in the air.

Over cups of tea Hope and Fiona did some catching up. After about ten minutes Fiona pushed away her empty cup, tapped the tabletop beside her computer and moved to business.

'Work OK?' she said. 'Not too stressful?'

'Oh, no,' said Hope. 'Not at all. It can run itself if it has to, and if it gets too stressful – can't imagine, but if – I can just let them know I need some time off. They're always happy to have me back after I've been away.'

'Fine, fine.' Fiona's finger twiddled on the tabletop, writing. 'Any general health problems? Anything that might not have shown up on the logs?'

Hope shook her head. 'I'm fine,' she said. She straightened her back and wiggled her shoulders. 'I should get a bit more exercise, and take a few more stand-up breaks, but with all this snow ...'

'Yeah, I know. Global warming. Well, so long as you keep that in mind. Get outside more than just the school walk and the shops, OK?'

'Oh, I do, I do, we go for walks at weekends ...'

'Fine, fine – like I say, keep it in mind, make a little extra effort. Anyway ... we'll book you in for a first check ... next month?'

Hope put her glasses on, invoked the diary, tapped the table and synchronised diaries with the nurse's computer.

'OK, the twelfth of April, fine. Twelve-thirty.'

Fiona looked down at the tablet, sighed, and looked up.

'Now,' she said. 'Sorry I've got to say this, but ... I've got to. You've thought about the fix?'

'I've thought about it.'

'And are you going for it this time?'

Hope compressed her lips and shook her head.

'Why not, if you don't mind me asking?'

'I do mind you asking,' Hope said, more lightly than she felt. 'But I just don't want to do it, and that's that.'

'Do you have any safety concerns about it?'

'No.'

'Faith issues?'

'No,' Hope said. 'I don't.'

'Shame,' said Fiona. 'Because I could have set your mind at rest about safety, and given you some tips about placing a faith objection.' She put a forefinger against the side of her nose, and tapped, gazing idly out of the window at the bare branches of the bush outside. 'You're absolutely sure you don't have a faith objection?'

'Yes, I'm sure,' said Hope. 'We – Hugh and I – have been over all this.'

'Much as it pains me as a not very good Catholic,' Fiona said, with a wry look, 'I have to tell you that there are non-religious faith objections, if you see what I mean. Off the top of my head, uh, Green Humanism for one . . .'

Hope burst out laughing.

'Green humanism? What's that? Humanism for little green men?'

'It's about leaving human nature alone, as I understand it,' said Fiona, a little stiffly. 'As well as the rest of nature. No mucking about with genomes. I gather they also object to the New Trees.'

'Well, there you are.'

'What?'

'I've got nothing against New Trees. And I could hardly pretend to, because Hugh works with new wood all the time. Well, half the time, but you know what I mean.' Hope propped her elbows and began waving her hands. 'Look, Fiona, Hugh and I have been through all this. It's not enough to claim you believe something, you have to show it in some way, and I'm just not prepared to do that if I don't actually believe in something, and the fact is, there's nothing out there for me to pretend to believe in, let alone actually believe in.'

'Well in that case, my dear, I'm afraid you're stuffed.'

'So to speak!' Hope acknowledged Fiona's joke. 'But isn't it enough that I just don't want it?'

'No,' said Fiona. 'It isn't enough.'

'Why not?'

'Well, if that was enough, if just saying no and not giving a reason was enough, where would we be? It would be just chaos.'

'It's enough now,' Hope said. 'Or was until a couple of days ago. And I don't see chaos.'

'Well . . .'

'And anyway,' Hope went on, 'the ruling is being appealed, so I'm not in any legal difficulty by not having the fix.'

'I'm sorry, Hope, but you are. The ruling stands, and unless it's overturned on appeal or the law is changed, we have to take it into account.'

'We?'

'The Health Service. We have to do our best to persuade.'

'Fair enough,' said Hope. 'But I can't actually be compelled. Not yet.'

'Uh, that's not strictly true, Hope. The local health centres have all changed their policy in line with the ruling. There's a provision already for court orders. We hope it won't come to that, obviously.'

Hope felt a cold jolt.

'But there must be thousands of mothers in my position! You can't take all of them to court!'

Fiona rubbed the back of her neck, between the collar of her tunic and the curve of her pinned-up hair.

'Well, no,' she said. 'But I'll be honest with you, the idea is that a few cases will be enough to make the rest fall into line. You just have to hope your number doesn't come up.'

'This is *so* fucking unethical,' said Hope.

'No, it's not,' said Fiona. 'Not on any ethics I was taught, at work or anywhere else.'

'What about my choice? Doesn't that count for anything?'

'Yes, it does. You do have a choice. That's what I'm trying to tell you.'

'It's no choice if it's hedged about with conditions I can't meet.'

'But the conscience exemption—'

'That goes against *my* conscience!'

'Look,' Fiona pleaded, 'the centre will give you every opportunity, they'll bend over backwards to accommodate everyone who has a genuine conscience-based objection, they'll hand out exemptions like Tesco vouchers. But what they can't accept is people just saying no for no reason.'

'I don't get it,' said Hope. 'If faith kids are allowed to be just the same as nature kids, the problem can't be that bad in the first place. I mean, you're not allowed to *beat* your child just because the Bible says you should. You're not allowed to rely on praying over a sick child, no matter what your beliefs are. If the child's sick enough, you'll still get hauled up for neglect if you don't call a doctor. So the fact that the nutters can get away with this one means the fix isn't all that important – it's regarded as a good thing to have, I'm sure, but not having it can't really be thought of as that bad. So why can't I just say I don't want it?'

'It's the principle,' Fiona said. 'When we had conscription, we allowed conscientious objection. But you had to convince a board that your objection was genuine conscience and not just cowardice, because otherwise every coward or anyone who just didn't want to be bothered could claim it was conscience. You can't have people dodging an obligation just because they don't feel like it.'

'That's not what I'm saying!'

'I'm sorry, Hope, but from where I'm sitting, it is.' Fiona shrugged. 'I sympathise, obviously, but all I can say is, I hope you're not one of those picked to be made an example of.'

The remark stung. Hope stared across the table at Fiona: friendly, businesslike, almost motherly. In the grey light from the window and the white light from the LED fixture, she sat in a halo in which she looked serene, concerned, informed, everything a visiting nurse should be. She'd sat across this table so many times, held Hope's hand, helped to bath Nick when he could be cradled in the crook of one arm. Hope knew she had her best interests at heart.

'Oh, thanks,' said Hope. She looked away. 'Well, the site can run itself but I don't earn any money that way ...'

'Of course, of course,' said Fiona. 'Thanks for the tea.'

'That's fine.'

Fiona gave a tight smile. She reached into her tunic pocket and took out a small yellow-and-white carton, about the size of an aspirin packet. Printed at the top of one side was *SynBio* in friendly, flowery pink font. She placed it on the table, carefully, but her hand shook a little and Hope heard a hollow, plasticky rattle.

'Just in case you change your mind,' Fiona said. 'One tablet, down with water. The sooner the better, obviously, but it can sort out quite a lot even after six months.'

Hope shifted her gaze from the packet to Fiona's face. She flexed one shoulder.

'Sorry,' she said.

Fiona made for the hall.

'You will think about it, won't you?' she said as she shrugged into her fleece.

'I'll think about it,' said Hope, opening the door.

Fiona gave her a tight smile and went out, into the now thicker snow. Hope got the door closed before she started crying. Fiona wasn't a villain. Fiona was just a person who represented an impersonal system closing in and grinding them down. That was how Hope saw her.

That morning, Hugh arrived at his work shortly after 9.30. He wasn't late: as far as he was concerned, the billed-for day began when he set off on his bicycle, and he'd set off at 8.00 prompt. The shower had ended as he reached Acton – or rather, he was out from under its cloud, which he could see behind him whenever he glanced over his shoulder. Which was often, given that many of the vehicles on the road were almost as quiet as his bike, and a lot faster and heavier, and the cyclists more dangerous than any of them. Unlike most of the heavier vehicles, bikes were steered by humans, and almost all by cyclists. Hugh rode a bike, but he didn't consider himself a cyclist.

As he whizzed through the traffic and raced across junctions and around roundabouts, Hugh found himself preoccupied – though not distracted, because the parts of his brain that dealt with cycling in traffic had long since laid down reflexes that operated below the level of his conscious thought – by the vision, indeed the full-sensory hallucination he'd had the previous evening. Sight, sound and smell; and to all appearances an awareness of Hugh's presence, though perhaps not that of anyone or anything else in the hall or in the house.

Hugh, for reasons that will later become painfully clear, was a confirmed scoffer about anything that smacked of the supernatural or even of the paranormal. He was less troubled by his visions than might be supposed. In his early teens he had read with delight the poem of Lucretius, in a tatty old paperback published by Sphere Books in 1969 with a Max Ernst picture on the cover. He'd found it in the attic of his parents' house, which had once been a Free Church manse, amid a stash of dusty old rationalist works, presumably from the minister's library. (Hugh had only made sense of this when he'd noticed that most of the books were critiques of the historical record of the Roman Catholic Church.) On the inside cover, the pencilled words were just legible:

Here rolls
The large verse of Lucretius, who raised
His index-finger and did strike the face
Of fleeting Time, leaving a scar of thought
The rain of ages shall not wash away.

No source for the quote was given. For years, Hugh had attributed the lines to the long-departed minister himself, inspired no doubt by the prevailing weather of his parish. It was an obscure thrill imparted by the lines that impelled him to turn over the pages of the book, and then to read it. He found a great deal in those pages that left imprints on his brain, but none more than the poet's explanation of how the existence of the gods was known: because they were seen and heard, in visions and in dreams. From their distant milieu between the worlds – in outer space, as Hugh read it – faint images were transmitted, which sometimes impinged on human senses, producing impressions of the gods: correct impressions, as far as they went. The existence of the gods was an entirely empirical matter.

From this Hugh had concluded, to his great relief, that when he saw and heard people that other people couldn't, he wasn't crazy. He was *seeing things* all right, but seeing things that really were *out there*, in a quite literal sense. At thirteen he'd heard and read enough about dark matter and exotic particles and quantum uncertainty and the possible infinity of possible universes to be convinced that the nature of things was as yet unfathomed. Perhaps he was seeing the same gods that the

Greek materialists had perforce admitted that they – like everyone else – saw. A few years later, further reading and online searching led him to speculate that the people he saw, in their barbaric attire, were perhaps real people from the past – not that he was seeing ghosts, but seeing into the past, reflected in some mirror of the face of fleeting Time – and that they, in seeing him (as he did not doubt they did), saw into the future. He even wondered, idly, what they made of him – a mage perhaps, able to conjure strange powers.

The Leosich had a name for the phenomenon, he'd learned on oblique enquiry. They called it the second sight. That sounded natural enough to satisfy the strictest materialist – and, indeed, the Leosich saw nothing supernatural in the phenomenon. It was simply a gift some people had, no more remarkable than any other talent. It even followed the rules of Mendellian inheritance for a recessive gene, which (Hugh thought) quite possibly explained its former incidence among the locals.

There was a reason why his enquiry had to be oblique.

At Ealing, Hugh turned off the Broadway and around a few corners into Bidwell Crescent, a long residential side street of Victorian-built semi-detached houses. It differed from his own street, Victoria Road, in that it was three times longer, the houses were built of red brick rather than sandstone, most of them didn't have basement flats, and about a third of them were empty: doors barred with nailed cross-planks, windows masked with charred and spray-bombed chipboard, front plots or patios choked with weeds that in turn were being choked out by the fast-growing saplings of New Trees whose branches' shapes – circular or rectangular, smooth or serrated, soft and pale or hard and dark – indicated to Hugh's practised carpenter's eye the type of product-plantation from which their seeds had (somehow, despite much small print and large promises) escaped.

He pulled in at number 37 and swung off his bike. He lifted the bike on to one shoulder and trotted up the steps to the door, which was already open. A buzzing in the sky made him glance up, though he knew what it was. He always looked back at police drones. This one, he watched out of sight, over the rooftops to the west. It was the drones you didn't see you had to worry about. These flew at fifty thousand feet and struck without warning. This one was no doubt just keeping an eye out for Naxal pop-ups in Southall.

Inside, the floorboards were gritty with cement spatters and soft with dust. The stairway had been torn out. Access to the first floor was by ladder. Hugh parked his bike behind a stack of paint tins, unfurled his overall and climbed into it, and set his dust mask on his forehead. The elastic tugged at his neck hairs, then settled. He followed the Radio One sound into the front room, waved at Ashid the plasterer, backed out and stepped into the kitchen. The kettle was not long boiled. Hugh brewed up an instant coffee in the unwashed mug he'd used the day before, and ambled into the dining room. There, he stood and sipped for five minutes, contemplating. The electrics were in place. Ashid had finished the plastering and painting. The floor was a tip. All that remained to be done was the woodwork. Its raw material was most of what made the floor a tip. Hugh's tools, trestles and workbench, and some rubble and splashes from Ashid's work, made the rest.

Cornices. Window frame. Door frame. The overmantel. Skirting boards. Their components had been grown to function, and now had to be cut to size and fixed in place. Hugh put his empty mug down on the raw windowsill and got to work. Through the morning the music from the radio trickled in whenever he paused. On the hour the news updates came: the war, the weather. The war was spreading from India and the weather was coming from Russia. Overshadowing both: the Warm War. No change.

Aberdeen. A city making a sharp turn, from oil rigs to windmills, with bits flying off – jobs, businesses, whole districts – from the centrifugal force of the swerve. A city of sharp edges, with a hole at its heart. You came out of the station and found yourself facing roadways, flyovers, walls; you had to walk half a kilometre and turn corners just to find shops. Apardion, the Vikings had called it, and Hugh liked that name. It called to mind a cold and barbaric past, like something out of the Conan stories, out of the Hyborean Age – itself named after the Greek word for the people of the far north, the Hyperboreans, the folk from beyond the north wind. The people in the sunshine beyond winter ...

The barbarian he'd seen last night, for instance – he could have been a Hyperborean. Aberdeen, when Hugh and Hope had been students there – that had been Hyperborean too. That summer. The last good summer. The last one when you could feel the Earth's warming in your bones. Ever since, you could see the warming on television and online, you could see the droughts and dustbowls and bergs, but you couldn't feel it. What you felt was cold and damp. Hugh remembered taking the bus with Hope from the campus into town on what now seemed like many long, warm evenings, talking non-stop through the ride, walking and then reeling between the remaining city centre pubs, and taking the bus back after midnight with the sky still bright to the north and a half-light gloaming at street level when the nightly hours-long power cut had extinguished all the street lamps.

How keen he'd been then to learn, to graduate, how eager he'd been to get to work, to get the wave and wind turbines turning! Green power to pick up the slack and fill the gap left by the black coal and the peak oil and the unbuilt dirty nukes. And then, *wham*, sudden as a mine closure, solar panels had started spreading across the Sahara like lily pads, powering half of Europe and the African Lion economies into the bargain, and syn bio tech had come on stream, springing full-grown from the bench like the Incredible Hulk bursting his lab coat, a great green monster that sucked carbon from the air and sprouted wood, pissed oil, and shat diamonds.

Hugh found his gaze wandering to some uninstalled window panes out in the lobby. Precisely sized to fit the frames – you couldn't cut the panes. There was nothing to cut them *with*. You could cut glass with diamond, but these panes *were* diamond. Laminated industrial sheet diamond. The very existence of such a thing still astonished Hugh. He'd read all kinds of excited speculation about its possible applications as a new structural material, but the diamond age was still a long way off. The stuff could still only be made in laminated sheets, or thin films like the surface layers of Hope's work glasses. Even as sheets, though, it was already being used in America for far more than windows: there, you could buy entire prefabricated houses as kits – walls and windows and roofs – and just glue the slabs together. This would come here, he knew, before too many years had passed. It would not be long before the whole of a house would be pre-shaped diamond and new wood, and its assembly a job that any clueless householder could do with an Allen key and a tube of superglue, like flat-pack furniture from IKEA. And then building-site work would be – what? Digging a hole and maybe laying foundations.

When Hugh had been a lad, back on the wind-power farm where his father was an engineer, he'd looked up to the labourers. The steady labourers, that is, not the natives like Murdo Helmand of the glass eye, who when he wasn't working simply drank. A lot of the Leosich were like that: they worked when they felt like it, and the rest of the time they drank. They got around the prohibitive alcohol taxes by distilling their own spirit, a harsh thrapple-burning usquebaugh they called peat-reek. Others – or sometimes the same people; the groups overlapped, or alternated, serially – frowned on the drink and went to church and sometimes under the preaching they got the *curach*, the concern about their souls, and after moping for a while found that God had their names in His book, and they changed their ways. They gave up the peat-reek and the ceilidh and the poaching. But they never shopped the location of the illicit stills and the smoky bothans, or the snares and shotguns. The English and Polish labourers were different: calm, deliberate men with steady hands and steady girlfriends, and when he was a wee lad they'd been Hugh's idea of a man. He'd always felt slightly awkward, slightly soft and posh and middle-class in their company, and in that of their kids – boys and girls alike, as it happened. He'd known he was going to be an engineer, he'd always known that, but he'd determined to be as tough as the roughest bricklayer on a site.

And now here he was, sawing new wood to size. Joinery. A posh, soft, middle-class job. That was just the way of it, all over the bloody world. When Ashid the plasterer knocked off for a break and came in with coffee, he – as nearly always – talked about his PhD in economics. He had a grudge that he deserved better.

At least you got as far as a fucking PhD, Hugh thought, wiping the back of his wrist across his mouth. What he said was: 'Things will pick up.'

Ashid laughed. 'This *is* things picking up.'

Hope left the carton containing the fix on the table all morning, ignoring it while she worked. Every so often she'd take off her glasses and look at it. When she stopped for lunch, she reached over, picked up the packet, and opened it. Inside were a folded leaflet and a plastic and foil card with a single bubble about a centimetre long. She turned it over in her hands. The bubble was transparent. The fix itself was a grey, almost metallic-looking capsule that tapered from the middle to two blunt ends. Like a fishing weight. A magic bullet. After a while she pushed the leaflet and the card with the fix back in the box.

She didn't want to leave this lying around, or even in the medicine cabinet. She wanted it out of her sight. She didn't want to leave it where Hugh might come across it. She walked through to the hall, stepped into the cupboard, stood on tip-toes, stretched, and placed the carton on the edge of the high shelf. Then she gave it a quick tap with her hand and sent it skittering to the back, against the wall.

5

The Railway Walk

On Friday the wind shifted and the clouds cleared away. Hope dropped off Nick and picked her way in her Mucks through slush over tapes of ice, along East West Road to Stroud Green Road to the Tesco, enjoying the sunshine and the clean cold air. When she paused, as she sometimes had to, to plot a route that wouldn't land her on her butt or her back, she looked up. The sky was a pale blue, and if she looked long enough she could see tiny dancing sparkles, particles of light. Orgone energy, she thought, grinning to herself at the fancy. She blinked, and when she looked down found herself dazzled by the sunlight off the remaining white snow on the pavements. By luck she had her work glasses with her – she'd snatched up the case and stuck it in her cagoule pocket in a moment of irritation when Nick's hand crept towards the forbidden gadget once too often – and she slipped them on.

Instantly the street changed. Everything was tagged: houses with their occupiers, floor by floor; vehicles with their drivers' names, shops with advertisements and reviews and supply chains, pedestrians with their IDs. Irritated, Hope blinked away the app. As she walked around Tesco similar tags kept popping up again. She was amused by the food miles and carbon counts – how on earth had these apps hung around? – but the relevant ones were no less annoying, nagging and wheedling, and in the end she just put the glasses away until she'd finished her shopping. At the checkout she put them back on to have a look at the news and mags. She selected *The Economist, Marie Claire* and *Psychologies,* and added the downloads to her tab as she bagged the groceries.

She lugged the bags home, and left the glasses firmly on the table until she'd made the beds and washed up the breakfast things. Then she made a coffee, cast off her apron and sat back, glasses on, for a half-hour of alternating self-indulgence and self-improvement. The former involved scoping out the spring fashions and wincing at their prices. The latter required skimming the serious articles. Something was wrong with bananas. Scientists at CERN had detected tachyon effects in a suspension of rhodopsin derivatives. The results were disputed. Brazil was hot. The Naxals had cooked up some kit that countered rust spray. There were ten good ways to have sex. The two women's mags had nothing about the nature kids issue, but *The Economist* did. Two columns of legal reasoning about the Kasrani case argued that the family court's decision was perverse, and should and most likely would be overturned on appeal. Hope found this so encouraging that she posted the link to ParentsNet before starting work.

The science bit, whose name was Geena – officially Evangelina – Fernandez (a name very useful to have on your ID card, as was the cross on the silver chain around her neck, if your skin was as dark and hair as black as hers, and especially useful when the cops were looking for Naxals, as they usually were when they stopped her in the street), read the same *Economist* article with her first coffee and paracetamol of the day. The article had been snagged by the Institute for Science Studies' overnight keyword trawl. The trawl was so undiscriminating that it had hooked her own piece in *Memo* a couple of days earlier, in among the haul from *Nature* and *PLoS* and the *TLS* and the *Journal of Synthetic Biology*. Under the *Economist* article was a list of links to it, close to the top of which – Geena was intrigued to see – was the root of a long thread on ParentsNet, posted by one Hope Morrison. Geena summoned databases to her glasses, and saw that Mrs Morrison was the mother of a nature kid, not registered as a conscience exemption, and pregnant again.

Interesting, Geena thought. The Kasrani couple, although their dispute had given her the hook for her own article, had struck her as unlikely to last long as a synecdoche for the issue. It was too entangled with other matters: family law, immigration, even Iran, a country whose militant secularism and indeed militant everything made relations with it awkward even for the US, let alone Britain. Whereas Morrison's case – if it ever became a case – had a test-tube simplicity. The variable was isolated, the question clear.

The question, as it self-assembled in Geena's brain, was not one about rights. Rights, to Geena as to those who had taught her, were an emergent phenomenon of social practices, which themselves arose out of certain material requirements, which ... but you know how it goes. No, the question was: is it in the interests of society (of all or most of the individuals in society, if you like) to permit a mother to risk the health of her future child and that of other children without giving any justification in terms of a strongly held belief?

It did not occur to Geena to question whether permitting someone to do such things *with* such a justification was in the interests of society. Society had already learned its lesson in that respect. Those with strongly held beliefs were best left to act them out, unless the consequences of that action were worse than those of the actions their commitment, if interfered with, was likely to make them commit. This was understood. The lesson had been driven into the flesh of the body politic like nails from a well-packed rucksack bomb. In social science, of course, that lesson could be questioned, could itself be interrogated. But – context was everything. One cannot run an experiment by changing every variable at once. In any case, that aspect of the question was outside Geena's field. Non-professionally, in her personal life, she had every reason to question it, and often did. Professionally, in her work, she put it to one side.

Ah yes, her work. Time to be getting on with that. The engineers were coming in. The guys, the lads. Keeping her glasses on as if reading, she glanced up and nodded and smiled at each, and surreptitiously made notes on their demeanour and time of arrival.

Brian Harvey arrived first, at 7.50. Appropriate, for the team leader. Late thirties, dark brush of hair, black stubble on his chin no matter what the time of day. He wore a suit whose jacket he shrugged off quickly, to expose the full eye-watering glare of the yellow and green diamond tile pattern on a woollen sleeveless jumper with two burnt holes near the midriff.

'Morning, Geena,' he said, rubbing his hands together. 'I'll get the coffee on. Oh, it is on. Thanks.'

He said that every morning, without fail. Ten minutes later, in came slender, smart-suited Michael Dombrowski, lank brown hair flopping across a wide brow. He hailed her and grabbed a coffee almost with the same sweep of the arm. Geena got on best with him, ever since they'd discovered a shared taste in filthy anti-clerical jokes. A few minutes after eight, Sanjay Gupta strolled in, flashing her a smile from his Bollywood good looks. Joseph Goonwardeene, the youngest, smaller even than Geena, almost as dark-skinned as she and probably twice as bright as any of them, sidled in after him. He was the only one who wasn't English-born and didn't have a west London accent. Still shy after all those months he'd worked here, he barely glanced at Geena, mumbled something to Brian and sat down as if in a hurry to log on.

'Hi, Joe,' Geena said, hoping to get him out of it.

His right shoulder twitched. Geena shrugged, swivelled her

seat and looked again at the trawl. Then she slowly spun the seat back around, still with her glasses on, sipped coffee and watched the first interactions of the day.

The SynBioTech Structural Product Research and Development Simulation Testing Environment Room Number 3, aka the dry lab, was not a big room. Its main attraction was that it had windows, overlooking the terraced cottages of Dawley Road and with a fine view of the railway line, Hayes and Harlington station, and the canal. Overhead lighting came from the undersides of broad, inch-deep suspended aquaria within which genetically modified bacteria turned cellulose into luminescence, an advertising tour de force for a product that had never cleared quite enough of the regulatory hurdles to ever need advertising. Beneath the windows a metre-deep Formica-topped shelf ran the length of the room, and the far corner of that made up Geena's workstation. The rest of the broad shelf supported the kettle, coffee jars, and mugs, as well as thrown jackets and coats, bits of electronic equipment in various stages of assembly or dismantlement, and stacks of paper.

The centre of the room, and indeed most of the floor space, was occupied by a Formica-topped rectangular table, about the size of a dinner table, around which perhaps six people could comfortably fit, and which gave barely enough elbow- and sprawl-room to the four engineers who sat around it. Geena had access to their shared workspace, and to all but their most personal comms. Management had access to everything, so nothing that Geena saw could make the guys self-conscious in that respect; and management had long since come to accept that what people like engineers did on the job was part of the job – within reason, and so long as it didn't include work on the side, gambling, accessing porn, talking to head-hunters, or building bombs. General idle surfing and chatting – which was usually work-relevant anyway – was accepted as necessary mental down time.

Seen through glasses, what looked like a metre-wide tangle of glistening, pulsing offal hung above the table like some obscene balloon: a realistic representation of cellular machinery on a scale where water molecules appeared as solid and pervasive as polystyrene packaging. Around this slowly writhing mass orbited phantom sheets of text and diagrams. Most of the work was done with calculations that rippled through the sheets. Now and again someone might reach in and click an atom into a different place. In response to these calculations or manual adjustments the molecular mess would squirm into a new shape.

Underneath the 3D diagram the men's hands moved between actual coffee mugs or pen-and-paper notes to flicking through the virtual pages of newspapers or (in Joe's case) Science Updates. At 8.25 Brian's *Daily Mail* disappeared and its place was taken by one of the worksheets; and one by one Mike, Sanjay and Joe joined in. They were modifying the gene expression for lignin in a new strain of new wood. The gene itself was already artificial, having been reverse-engineered and optimised from the original stretch of plant DNA, but the effects of further modification were by no means entirely predictable in advance. This meant repeated cycles of one-step changes and virtual testing: something altogether more crude and empirical than the high-level definition of synthetic biology seemed to imply, and that at other levels – certainly in comparison with the shotgun methods of early genetic engineering – it did indeed deliver.

Geena's research interest focused on the subtle changes in everyday practice and self-understanding this form of activity imposed on the engineers. In some respects the guys in this dry-lab team were becoming more like wet-lab scientists and field researchers; in others, more like programmers had been in the era – the glory days, as the old hands called that time, with a nostalgic backward glance to their youth in the nineties or earlier – when computers had become cheap and fast enough to make trial-and-error an efficient style of software development, and before structured programming and formal verification had become standard practice: before rigour had become de rigueur. The working title of her thesis was *Convergent agent-constitutive discursive practices in emergent technological networks: the case of a dry-lab synthetic biology team*, and the work fascinated her, though she could well see that it might not fascinate anyone else.

What it was all for – what interest, other than her own in getting a PhD, her research served – was for Geena a matter of idle and infrequent speculation. The Economic and Social Research Council was willing to sponsor it, and her tutor at Brunel, Dr Ahmed Estraguel, was willing to supervise it. That was enough to be going on with. The question of what institutional and economic and political interests actually benefited from social science research into science was itself a small but thriving area of social science research, and the question of who benefited from *that* research was a smaller area still. The one researcher who had taken the next logical step and investigated who benefited from research into research into research into research had concluded that the only beneficiary of his research was himself, a result so significant that its publication had ensured him a professorship at the University of Edinburgh.

Around 11.00 Geena got a message on her glasses from her friend Maya, who lived in Hayes and who worked out of an office in Station Road. As soon as she saw it, she had a bright idea, inspired by a morning's subconscious pondering over the predicament of Hope Morrison. She set up an al fresco lunch with Maya down by the canal for 12.30.

At 12.15 she pulled on her coat, nodded to the guys, and went out. Geena usually ate lunch alone in the employee restaurant – the engineers all took in packed lunches, and she needed only the occasional sample of their lunch time conversations to keep track of the discursive practices by which they constituted themselves. This time, she bought two insulated cups of take-out carrot soup and two baguette sandwiches. The bread roll for Maya was listed as 'vegan filled', which amused Geena as she left. Her smile broadened as she thought how good it would be to take advantage of the first blink of sun in a month by going for a walk.

She crossed Dawley Road at the cottages and headed down Blyth Road, then turned left into Trevor Road and Printing House Lane, a canyon of factories and office blocks, to where the road crossed the canal, and picked her way down crumbling concrete steps to the canal bank. As always, the chance association of the names set off an earworm of Betjeman's poem.

No phantom swimmers in this canal. Fringed by tall poplars, cruddy with litter and crusted with ice, the water's only visible life was a disconsolate duck and the monstrous ripples of the ten-metre-long flexible barges of biofuel that swam beneath the surface like lake monsters. Geena walked carefully along the uneven and ill-maintained towpath for a hundred metres until Maya appeared around a bend up ahead.

Maya waved. Geena waved back. They converged on an iron-mounted beam of greying wood that Geena assumed was something to do with the canal and that now served as a bench. It was just dry enough to sit on. Holding the hot soups out of the way at each side, Geena exchanged air-kisses with Maya and sat down beside her, lunches between.

'Thanks so much,' Maya said, pouncing on the vegan sandwich.

'You're welcome,' said Geena.

They popped the tops of the soup cups and inhaled the steam for a moment.

'Ah, bliss,' said Maya, and sipped.

Geena had met Maya when they were both studying sociology at Brunel, and they'd kept in touch in the two years since they'd graduated. Maya was a difficult person to get a handle on, and some of that difficulty showed in her appearance. From a distance she looked almost like a crusty, but close up you could see that her fair hair wasn't in dreads but in springy ringlets, freshly coloured and shampooed; her woollen-patch jacket smelled as if just out of the washing machine, her man-style shirt was cut for women and buttoned on the left, the T-shirt under it had a neat eyelet trim around the neck, her blue jeans had barely a crease and her boots shone. Even dressed for the office in neat blouse and skirt and a warm flared coat, Geena felt slightly dowdy and scruffy beside her.

Maya's look, Geena had discovered from some old photos she had shown her, was a cleaned-up version of that of her parents at the time they'd met, when they'd both been full-time climate campers, their lifestyle a permanent protest against other people's lifestyles. The couple had kept that up on a part-time basis, somewhat hampered by the string of part-time jobs they'd had to take to support Maya and her sibs, until Maya was about fourteen years old, at which time their entire preoccupation had been made redundant by syn bio tech. Without missing a beat they'd moved seamlessly into campaigning against *that*. Now, though, they did their campaigning in a mainstream manner, writing and lobbying rather than squatting in muddy greenfield sites, living up trees, or running onto runways.

'How's life in the Advice Centre?' Geena asked.

Maya sighed. 'Same as usual. It's like living in a fucking soap opera.'

She went on to talk about some of the problems the Centre's drop-in clients dropped in with. Most of them arose out of sublet living: inter- or intra-family disputes, rent arrears, repairs ... Hayes, like all the outer suburbs of London, was still recovering from a decade or so of battering from the tsunami-like surges of population movement that had begun when Peak Oil and Peak Debt had made suburban living unaffordable. Eastward from Hayes, in through Southall, Ealing and Acton, regentrification was taking place – which brought its own problems to high-street Advice Centres, as former squatters and renters were pushed out by new buyers. Outward – as in West Drayton and Uxbridge, where Brunel University was situated, and where Geena shared a couple of rooms with her boyfriend – the suburbs were still little more than redbrick shanty towns, every neat semi, bungalow and villa occupied by at least two households and every garden by its goat and chickens.

'You'd think,' Geena said, after Maya had finished outlining a particularly tedious tangle, 'that people could just sort these things out online.'

'That's the worst of it,' said Maya. 'They do go online. That's why the guy I was just telling you about got so stubborn. Turned out the advice he was taking was from a parser some law student had knocked up to read Home Office databases and cobble them into essay cribs that he sold to his mates, behind a law-firm front screen that everyone knew was a joke except this poor bastard who found it at the top of a search.'

'And other poor bastards too, no doubt.'

'Oh, I'll meet them, waving their glasses and standing on

their rights.' Maya wiped her mouth and scattered vegan crumbs to an investigating pigeon. 'Anything interesting going on in your place?'

'SynBioTech's shining towers? I wish.'

'Saw your piece in *Memo*.'

'Oh, Christ, that! Well, it was a bit more subtle when I wrote it, let's say.'

Maya gave an understanding laugh.

'Funnily enough,' Geena went on, 'it got picked up by the trawl, and ...'

She told Maya the story all the way to the bit about Hope Morrison.

'That's really, really interesting,' Maya said. Her eyes were bright. 'Somebody really should do something for her.'

'Oh, don't,' said Geena. 'Don't start all that again.'

'All what again?' Maya sounded hurt.

'Campaigning,' Geena sang, drawing out the word to draw the sting of what she'd just said. At Brunel, Maya had been heavily into campaigning. Her rebellion against her parents had taken the form of standing up for people who wanted to be left alone. To Geena it seemed to have exactly the same relationship to Maya's parents' passions as her clothes did to their fashions: a neater, cleaner, more bourgeois version of the same thing, cut from the same cloth.

'The rights of the individual and all that rubbish,' Geena added, emphatically.

Maya shook her bouncy shampooed ringlets that from a distance looked like dreads.

'Oh, don't worry,' she said. 'I just think it's so important that people in that position know they're not alone. That's all.'

'Well, if you're sure ...'

'Oh yes,' said Maya, smiling. She stood up and banged her arms around her chest. 'About time we got moving, no?'

'Yes,' said Geena. She crushed up their litter and bagged it, stood up and hugged Maya.

'See you again soon,' she said.

'Yes,' said Maya. 'I'll get the lunch next time.'

'No, no.' Geena knew she wouldn't, anyway.

'OK, thanks. Bye!'

'Bye. And remember,' Geena added, mock-stern. 'No campaigning.'

'No campaigning,' Maya said. 'Promise.'

Smile, wave, turn.

As she walked back along the canal bank, Geena thought: what have I done? What the fuck have I done?

She felt quite sorry for Hope Morrison.

Saturday morning began at seven, as most Saturday mornings did, with Nick bouncing up and down on the end of the bed. Hope yelped as a badly directed bounce ended on her foot, jolting her fully awake.

'Nick,' she pleaded, 'just go and play with Max.'

Nick walked on all fours up the bed and clambered in between Hope and Hugh. Hugh, his back to Hope, grunted and pulled the duvet over his head. Hope wrapped an arm around Nick, feeling the heat of his body through his pyjamas.

'Well, snuggle in and let's go back to sleep,' she said, nosing his hair.

Nick squirmed. 'Want breakfast.'

'Get it yourself,' Hugh said, from under the duvet and under his breath.

Nick heard. 'Can I, can I, can I?'

'No you cannot,' said Hope. 'Let's just snooze for a bit, OK?'

'I'm not sleepy,' Nick said. 'I'm hungry.'

'Oh for fuck's sake,' said Hugh.

'Hugh!' Hope chided.

'Yeah, yeah, sorry.'

'Fuck fuck fuck fuck,' said Nick, enjoying himself.

'And you stop saying that.'

'Daddy said it.'

'Yes, but he shouldn't have. Now go to sleep.'

Nick sat straight up, pulling the top of the duvet with him.

'Going to get breakfast,' he announced.

Hope sighed. This was how it always ended. Nick wasn't badly behaved most of the time, but Saturday mornings were far too exciting to spend in bed. Hope could understand that. Nick seemed to enjoy nursery (once he'd been prised off her leg each morning) but for him every new weekend was a fresh wonderland of freedom. Hope had a memory flash of how Saturday mornings had been before Nick was born. Oh well. Everything had an up side and a down side, and on balance she didn't regret it. She got up, winced at the cold, and pulled on her dressing gown and slippers in a hurry.

'Let's get breakfast,' she said.

'Yes!' said Nick. 'I'll get Max. He's hungry too.'

'Hugh, do you want a coffee and toast?'

But Hugh was already snoring again. Hope went through to the kitchen and made eggy soldiers for Nick and toast and honey for herself. As they ate, the garden brightened outside. The sky, visible by ducking down and looking up, was blue.

'Railway walk?' Hope asked.

'Yes!' said Nick. 'Railway walk, railway walk!'

So that was that. Saturday, sorted.

The railway walk was Parkland Walk. The nearest entrance was a kilometre or so along East West Road to the east of Victoria Road. Hope, Hugh, and Nick with Max on his shoulder set off about eleven. Hugh had the buggy folded up and concealed in a small rucksack, just in case. Parkland Walk followed the path of an old railway line, through a long cutting for most of its route. It was the first time they'd been there since the late autumn, and Hope felt a little down on seeing it still looked like winter. Mud, dead leaves, bare branches, a few buds, shopping trolleys, litter, frost in the shadows. But Nick ran ahead, breaking thin ice and splashing through puddles in his wellies and sending Max shinning up trees.

After a while she said to Hugh: 'We could just go on walking.'

'What?'

Hope waved a vague encompassing hand ahead.

'There are walks everywhere, they all connect up. Canal banks, cycle paths, that sort of thing. We could walk from here to anywhere in Britain and hardly go on the main roads.'

'We could,' said Hugh. 'If we didn't have to sleep or eat.'

'We could camp out,' said Hope, 'and live off the land.'

'The berries don't come out for months,' said Hugh. 'And the squirrels are skinny even when you can dig them out. Mind you, the roadkill keeps well at this time of year. Like a deep freeze, practically. And we could recharge the monkey at fuel stations, if we took the adaptor. Yeah, that sounds like a plan.'

'You're not taking me seriously.'

'That I'm not. And why would we want to walk to anywhere, anyway?'

'If we had to get away.'

'Jeez.' Hugh didn't sound amused. 'That's not how you do it. There's no *away*.'

'People talk about going off grid.'

'Yeah, they do. They talk about it. On the net. Nowhere's off grid any more.'

'There must be,' said Hope. 'There must be a place.'

Nick had stopped by the side of the path up ahead, and squatted down to gaze into the dark space underneath a huge holly bush. Max, programmed to occasionally ape its owner's actions, squatted beside him. As Hugh and Hope approached, they heard Nick talking, as if to someone under the bush. His elbows were propped on his knees, and he gestured with his hands and forearms, each motion mimicked by Max.

Hope turned to Hugh, smiling, and raised a finger to her lips. 'Cute,' she murmured.

Hugh nodded. But he waited only a few seconds, and then coughed, and scuffed the ground as he strode forward.

'Yes,' he said to Hope as he reached for Nick's hand and scooped Max to his shoulders. 'There is a place.'

He sounded happy.

6

The Bright Land

There was a place. Hugh was fairly sure it existed and wasn't one of his visions. The other lads, Malcolm and Donald, had seen it too. The reason he couldn't be entirely sure was that the lads were Leosich themselves, and they could have had the second sight too, for all he knew, and spoken of it no more than he did. But he was almost sure there was more to it than that, even to this day: that the glimpse his pals had shared, and denied, was of some far reality. Hugh's guesses as to the nature of its reality varied on a sliding scale of scepticism and self-mockery: an objective phenomenon, a space-time anomaly, a land under the hill, a fairy land, Tir Nan Og . . .

They'd all been about twelve years old at the time: old enough for big school, the Nicolson Institute in Stornoway. Old enough to look with a sort of affectionate pity at wee school, Valtos Primary, when they came back to Uig for the summer holidays. Seeing the parish again after a couple of terms in the town was unsettling. The black houses and the white, the sheep-fanks and bothans, the corrugated-iron sheds, the dry-stone walls another inch deeper in the grass, the ruins and the new build, the rusting cars and tractors in the middle of fields, all seemed primitive and petty, almost shameful to be associated with, something you'd outgrown like childhood toys. Only the windmills and the wooden houses looked modern.

The boys and girls whose parents were natives or settlers had work to do on the crofts or in the shops. The girl children of the wind-farmers had help to give their mothers around the house. The boys didn't (unlike the girls, who had home management in their curriculum). They mooched. They hung around the turbines and got in the way of the workers. Goggled and gloved, gaming, they squandered sunny days indoors until their mothers yearned to chase them out of the house with sticks.

Then a morning came when Hugh looked out of his bedroom window to see a sky whose blue was so deep and dark that he could have been looking at it through Polaroid sunglasses. He couldn't imagine staying inside. He pinged Malcolm the minister's son and Donald the rigger's boy. About half an hour later they met in the back yard of the house where Hugh lived. The house was a mile and a half away from the wee school that overlooked the bay. It stood on the slope of a hill, the highest house in a village that, like most villages in Lewis, consisted of a cluster of half a dozen old houses, a few new ones and sites for several more, all scattered around the landscape for hundreds of metres. The road ran below it, over a culvert where a stream from a small freshwater loch at one side of the hill flowed into the sea-loch around whose shore the village was spread. Minnows swam in that burn, preyed on by an eel, long and old and black, that lurked under the culvert.

The three boys scuffed pebbles in the yard and debated the shore or the loch or the glen farther up the road, but the deep blue of the sky turned their eyes to the hills above the village, and up to the hills they went. Within the old manse's glebe the ground was mossy and the grass long. Beyond the fence above it – the barbed wire was tufted with sheep's wool – the lads were wading through heather, tough and springy, that scratched at their ankles and tugged at their trousers. Old ash from past muir-burnings puffed up around their feet, making them cough, and blackening their trainers within minutes. Black-faced sheep and months-old lambs gave them the yellow slot-eyed stare, chewing impassively, or panicked for no clear reason and bounded away, then forgot why they were running and stopped to graze again.

The hill was not very high, but it was higher than it looked. As soon as the boys had toiled up one slope, another would loom ahead, usually with a bog to cross before they got there. The slopes themselves were strewn with erratic boulders, some big enough to have their own overhang and cave-like declivity beneath. After about twenty minutes of climbing, the boys reached the summit, a broad plateau of rocky outcrops crusted with lichens, some of them grey-green and others orange like splashes of earth-moving-machinery paint.

Hugh stood with the others and looked around. He knew that he was near the junction of two almost peninsular promontories of the long island: the one that stretched ahead of him across moor and lochs and hills to the distant headland of Aird, and the one behind and to his right, where the sea he could glimpse beyond the little long loch in the glen – the Atlantic that broke on the bay that the wee school overlooked, and whose sand was just visible from where he stood – was the same sea as lapped the village shore, via a few zigzag miles of beaches, cliffs and headlands hidden behind the hills immediately in view. Turning farther around to his left, his gaze swept that inlet and the hills and glens to the western horizon. From this height it was suddenly obvious that the land wasn't made of peat with rocks sticking out, but of rock with an uneven and broken overlay of peat like frayed hessian sacking over rubble. Clear too were the drove roads along the sides of the glens and across the moors, relict pathways along which cattle had once been driven and that now even sheep did not frequent. On almost every hilltop the blades of the great windmills spun like slow clockwork. The wind seldom ceased on Lewis, but today it was little more than a warm breeze.

'No a bad view,' said Malcolm.

'How about we go to the lochs?' said Donald, pointing ahead to where patches of water glittered in the middle distance.

Hugh felt a small thrill. Coming up this hill hadn't been forbidden when he'd been smaller, but going to the lochs definitely had been. He reckoned he'd now outgrown that injunction. Certainly it hadn't been repeated half an hour earlier when he'd told his mother where he was going. It hadn't been lifted, either, but he reckoned he was in the clear.

'Fine,' he said.

On they went. Like the summit, the lochs were more difficult to get to than they looked. As they walked across the rock, the surfaces planed by the glaciers of the ice ages turned out to be deeply scoured by the same process, with unexpected cracks and dips that the boys had to scramble down and up or leap across. Then the heather and peat and bog began again.

Another half-hour and the boys stood beside the first of the lochs. Less than a hundred metres at its widest, it lay still and black under the dark blue sky, banked by metre-high overhangs of heather-covered peat and here and there a tiny shingle beach.

The silence rang in Hugh's ears.

'Quiet,' he remarked, to break it.

'Wonder if there's a monster in it,' said Malcolm.

'I doubt there's a fish,' said Hugh.

'Or maybe a crashed plane,' said Donald.

Hugh and Malcolm triangulated him with scornful looks.

'That's what we thought when we were wee,' said Hugh. 'We used to have a crashed fighter jet in every lochan.'

Donald shrugged.

'Planes went down here,' he said, as if repeating a well-established historical fact rather than a rumour passed from cohort to cohort of primary-school kids.

'So why would they still be here?' Hugh asked. 'There would have been searches.'

'It was all secret,' said Donald. 'It was the Cold War.'

'Oh, the Cold War?' Hugh scoffed. 'It was the Second World War I was told. And that was about the wee loch above the school. There was supposed to be a Messerschmitt under the water. With the dead German pilot's skeleton still in it. When the sun was right, you could see the Iron Cross hanging in front of his collarbone. That's what Lachie MacIver told me, when he was ten and I was five.'

They all laughed, even Donald.

'It was the Cold War,' Donald repeated, in a stubborn tone. 'There was a MiG shot down over the sea that crashed in the hills around here. The RAF didn't want to let on. That's why there weren't any searches.'

'There must have been searches,' said Hugh. 'Or people might have found it by accident.'

'Och, if a plane crashed in a loch, the authorities didn't bother with that,' said Donald. 'They knew nobody would ever find it.'

Hugh stared at him. There was something baffling about his pal's insistence. He remembered how this sort of story wasn't the only one they'd all believed, in wee school. A few years ago he and his little sister had become convinced that there was some bogeyman – no, an actual flesh-and-blood man – living in the roof spaces behind the attic's thin partitions, and that he occasionally hid in the big shed at the back of the house. They had somehow believed that enough to terrify themselves now and again, yet most of the time didn't think or worry about this unseen presence at all. At no time had they ever given the practicalities of the matter a moment's thought.

Donald was thinking no more rationally than they had been. To ask him why and how the authorities could be so blithely sure that this scandalously, secretly shot-down MiG would not be discovered, let alone how the crash wouldn't have been noticed by any of the locals, would be as pointless as it would have been for someone to ask Hugh or his sister Shonagh how the man in the attic got his food or went to the toilet or got in and out of the house unobserved.

But thinking about this reminded Hugh of the people he'd seen who weren't there, and of Voxy. He didn't want to think about that. He could feel his face heat up, and he turned away abruptly.

'Let's get a move on,' he said.

They made their way around the side of the loch and were then lured by the glitter of the next, a few hundred yards of heather away. Again the lie of the ground was deceptive. About halfway to the next loch they found themselves standing on the lip of a small gully. It was about two metres deep and three across, its scree-covered floor rising on either hand to be lost amid the heather after a few metres each way. The far side of it looked like peat overhung with heather. They could easily have walked around it.

Hugh, with some impulse of bravado to compensate for his earlier moment of embarrassment, sat down at the edge, rolled, and dreeped. His feet landed with a thud on the scree and he took a step backwards.

Then another step, as he took in what he was seeing. The side of the gully right in front of him wasn't what he had expected. Just beneath the heather at the lip was a flat slab of rock, and under that slab was a dark opening about a metre wide and a metre and a half high. Two upended slabs of rock propped the sides, from the scree floor to the rock above. The rest of the bank was like the other side, hard black peat. Hugh had the impression that it was recently exposed, perhaps by a sudden slippage or even a flood.

He glanced up at Malcolm and Donald, who stood looking down at him.

'Hi, guys,' he said. 'I think I've found something.'

He could hear his own voice boom a little, echoing, he guessed, in the hollow. He took another step back, squatted, and skited a pebble into the dark hole. Far away, something rattled.

'There's a cave here,' he said.

The other two, for whatever reason – perhaps suspecting a prank on his part – didn't drop down the way he had, but went around to the end of the little gully and walked in, crunching and slithering down the slope of scree.

'Well, by Jove,' said Malcolm.

'That's not a cave,' said Donald. 'That's dug out. It's like yon Neolithic place in Orkney.'

'Dug out in peat?' Hugh said. 'Don't be daft.'

'Skara Brae wasn't dug out either,' said Malcolm. 'It was made of stone and got covered in sand.'

'Maybe this got buried in the peat, not dug out,' Hugh mused.

'How long would the peat take to build up six feet?' Malcolm wondered.

'Longer than your *bodach* thinks the world has existed,' said Hugh.

They scuffled for a moment.

'Quit it,' said Donald. 'Anybody got a torch?'

Hugh had: a nifty little high-power multi-LED one. He dug it out of his trouser pocket and flicked it on. Ducking down, he led the way into the opening. Even with the torch on, he couldn't see a thing.

'Turn it off,' Donald advised. 'Let our eyes adjust.'

They crouched for a minute or so in the entrance with their eyes shut. The air smelled of peat dust, dry bracken and ash.

'Right,' said Hugh, opening his eyes. He could now see dimly in the light from the entrance – what little of it got past their bodies. He switched the torch on again.

'Wow,' he said. 'It goes way back.' His voice echoed.

Donald and Malcolm crowded behind him, peering over his shoulders.

'Man,' said Donald.

Hugh flicked the beam around as he took a few steps forward. The ground – peat, with some ash, he guessed – felt springy underfoot. The bones of mice and rabbits lay here and there, fragile and brown. The walls were of close-fitting slabs, their bases sunk into the ground, supporting a ceiling of the same. He brushed his fingertips across a join above his head and could hardly feel a gap. Though the sides of the slabs weren't exactly straight, or evidently worked, they fitted almost to the millimetre. Without thinking, he ran his thumb across his fingertips, and felt grit.

'Just a mo,' he said.

He shone the torch on his fingers, and saw grey dust. He stooped closer to the side wall, and peered hard at it, angling the torch a little. The surface of the slab was grey, with a sand-grain sparkle. He rubbed his fingertips across it, and touched one with his tongue.

'Cement,' he said. 'Concrete.'

'So much for your thousands of years,' Malcolm jeered, after confirming the identification.

'The Romans had concrete,' Donald pointed out.

'And they never got here,' said Hugh. 'This is recent, all right.'

They huddled, looking down the cone of light. The passage went on at least another five or six metres, and the torch beam wasn't reaching the end of it.

'Go in a bit?' Hugh asked.

Glancing over his shoulder, he saw the others doing the same. The bright rectangle of daylight was a reassuring few steps behind them.

'OK,' said Malcolm.

'No so sure about that,' said Donald.

'Why not?' said Hugh.

'I think we should go back and tell . . .' His voice trailed off, as if he'd been about to say 'a grown-up' and had been too embarrassed.

'Nah,' Hugh said. 'What is there to tell them, anyway? We'll just go in a bit and have a look.'

With that he walked forward, leaving the others the choice of following or going back. They followed. After a few steps it became apparent that the passage had a slight downward slope and a curve to the right. About ten metres in, a backward glance revealed that the entrance was no longer visible. Hugh's neck and knees began to ache with the awkward, stooping walk. He felt chill air on his face, and smelled peat smoke. A moment later he saw a thin glimmer of light ahead.

'Light at the end of the tunnel,' said Donald, in the tone of having made a smart remark.

As they walked on, the glimmer took shape as a rectangle like the entrance. It was difficult to be certain what colour the light was, but it seemed to be the blue of a bright sky. The boys reached the end of the tunnel in a couple of minutes. The draught became stronger and colder as they moved forward. Hugh looked out, with Malcolm and Donald peering over his shoulders again. He blinked hard and shaded his eyes – the light was dazzling. The tunnel exit was evidently on the side of the hill, a steeper slope than the one they'd climbed. He saw the village and the sea-loch below, and the hills around, under the broad sky. But the houses looked different: darker, smaller and less regular in shape than the grey cement-block houses and slate roofs of the village he knew. The tide was far, far out, the sea-loch a distant glimmer. And the ground was covered in snow, of that he was certain.

He leaned forward, peering down the slope. A hundred metres below them, a tall figure was striding up the hill. A black shape against the white, with a gleam of eyes under a hood. Hugh recoiled. The other boys took his fright, and all of a sudden all three of them were scurrying back up the passage, the shadows of Donald and Malcolm weird and long in Hugh's wildly swaying torch-beam. Hugh could hear, above their own hurrying steps and rapid breaths, something or someone in the tunnel behind them.

Almost tumbling over each other, they hurtled out of the tunnel into the little gully and the blaze of sunlight, and scrambled up the far side, hitting the bank at a run and hauling themselves up on the heather. Only then did they glance back. No one else came out of the tunnel. They could hear nothing but their own breath and hammering heartbeats and the cry of a curlew.

They looked at each other and ran – around the end of the gully, with fearful sidelong glances, and across the moor, past the loch, across the bare rock and down the hill. They charged through heather and waded through bog and skipped and leapt over gaps in the outcrop and, on the way down the slope, hurdled erratic boulders. If any of them fell, they were up in a second, racing on.

At length they ducked through the fence of the glebe above Hugh's house and collapsed in the long grass, gasping, sides aching from the stitch, legs filthy to the knees, shirts ripped, heels of hands scratched, shins bruised.

None of them could have said why they felt safe on this side of the fence, but they did.

Hugh stood up, hands on knees, panting.

'Did you see it?' he asked.

'See what?' Malcolm asked. Donald, too out of breath to speak, scowled and shook his head.

'The village,' said Hugh. 'Down here, with the snow on it.'

'Snow?' Malcolm said, in a disbelieving tone. 'That wasn't snow. It was just the brightness.'

'Uh-huh,' Donald added, catching his breath. 'After the dark, it was so bright I could hardly make out anything.'

'And then,' Malcolm chipped in, 'you jumped back and nearly knocked us over and we thought something was wrong, so we ran.'

'You didn't see him?' Hugh asked.

'See who?'

'The man coming up the hill.'

'Now you're having us on,' said Donald, sounding uneasy.

Malcolm laughed. 'That's like the stories about crashes and dead pilots.'

Donald glowered. 'It is not!' he said. 'It's like the stories we believed when we were wee.' He raised his hands, fingers dangling and shoogling. 'Woo-oo-ooh!'

Malcolm clouted him. Donald kicked. They exchanged a few more blows. Hugh grabbed shoulders.

'Stop it!' he yelled.

They both pummelled him for a change, and then everyone backed off. No recriminations. They had outgrown telling on each other, but not outgrown hurting each other.

'Forget about the man,' Hugh said. 'But you saw it, you saw the land all bright at least.'

'So? It was the sun in my eyes,' said Donald.

Malcolm nodded along. 'Yes, that was it, the sun.'

Hugh knew they were lying. They'd seen what he'd seen.

78

'Och, that's what it was,' he said. 'And maybe I just saw a shadow, or a sheep.'

'We were fleeing from a sheep?' Malcolm asked, his voice squeaking with disbelief.

They all laughed, Hugh too.

'I've got a new game,' said Donald.

They ran down the last green slope to the back of the house and jumped on their bikes and raced away.

That evening, by way of explaining how he'd got his clothes, shoes and skin in such a state, Hugh told his father about how he'd been exploring a tunnel or cave or passageway up in the hills. He didn't say anything about what he'd seen.

'Show me your phone,' his father said.

Hugh handed it over and his father punched up the GPS tracker app. He slid the phone back across the table.

'See the place where you turn around?' he said.

Hugh looked down at the black squiggle of his route on the screen map.

'Uh-huh.'

'Now flick to . . . wait a minute.'

His father tapped at his own phone. The route line remained but the underlying map had changed, from a satellite pic with tags to a gridded white sheet with contour lines and little symbols. Right at the point where the route line doubled back was a row of tiny red arrowheads.

'Culvert,' his father said.

'What's it doing up there?' Hugh asked.

'The company was going to site a windmill there, a few years ago,' his father explained. 'Changed their minds, that's all, but not before they'd gone ahead and started building a culvert to draw off flash floods.' He frowned. 'Speaking of which. One rainstorm and that would have been you.'

'There was no chance of a rainstorm,' Hugh said, in a sulkier tone than he'd intended.

'Don't give me lip,' said his father. 'There's always a chance, you know that.'

'The water would just have washed out,' Hugh persisted.

'No, it wouldn't,' his father said. He stabbed a finger at Hugh's phone, magnifying the map. 'The culvert wasn't finished, see? It doesn't have a lower opening. It's probably flooded at the bottom already. So you stay out of culverts in future, got it?'

'OK, OK,' said Hugh.

'Promise.'

'Yes, Dad, all right.'

'Now help your mother with the washing and then go to your room.'

He didn't sound angry, or anxious, and Hugh left with some relief that he wasn't in as much trouble as he could have been.

He didn't go up that hill again.

7

Second Life

After Hugh had gone to work on Monday morning, Hope took her time over breakfast and found herself running late. She skipped the usual ten minutes of talking Nick into his clothes, and just picked him up and started inserting him in them. Underpants, warm vest, shirt, trousers ... at that point he kicked – not deliberately at her, but walking his legs in midair and landing an occasional random heel on her shins.

'Stop that!' Hope said.

'I'm not I'm not I'm not.'

He was drumming his heels on her now, squirming in the elbow she had around his waist.

'That bloody hurts,' she said. 'Stop it!'

Instead of doing what she instantly expected and gleefully repeating the bad word that had slipped out, Nick acquiesced in sudden sullen silence, stepping into his trouser legs one by one as she set him down and held them out in front of him. He even buttoned the waistband and buckled the belt, in a belated display of independence.

Then, as she held out his cagoule, he put his arms in one by one and said as he turned away to zip up the front: 'This is such cack.'

He said it in such a weary, resigned voice that Hope was more shocked by the tone than the content. His accent on the last word was like Hugh's, with a long vowel and a guttural: *caachck*. And he didn't say it in the defiant way he usually repeated naughty words, or as if said to provoke her. It was an aside, a remark.

So she didn't reprove him.

'What is cack, Nick?' she asked.

'It's what comes out of people's bottoms,' he said, without so much as a giggle, then added: 'You know – poo.'

'Yes, I know,' she said, getting into her own cagoule. 'But what is "such cack"?'

Nick pouted. 'The weather,' he said. 'Everything.'

'Surely not everything?' Hope said, holding out her hand.

'Not you and Max and Dad,' Nick allowed.

'Or nursery?'

'Nursery's all right,' he said.

They went out the door and into the rain.

'Well, I'm glad to hear that,' Hope said, locking the door. 'Off we go!'

Nick went up the steps. To him, they were high. His legs swung out to the sides as he clambered up.

They walked down Victoria Road, rain rattling on their hoods.

'Who did you hear saying that word?' Hope asked.

'What word?'

'You know,' Hope said.

'I don't know.'

'All right, "cack".'

'I meant I don't know who said it.'

'Was it your dad?' Hope asked, in an amused tone.

'Oh, no!' Nick looked up at her from under his hood.

'So who was it?'

'Don't know, don't care,' Nick sang.

That wasn't like him, either.

His hand tightened on hers as he swung over a puddle.

Oh well, Hope thought. Probably one of the kids at nursery. She'd have to have a word with Miss Petrie about language.

Miss Petrie, as it turned out, was outside the nursery gates when Hope and Nick arrived. She was standing talking to – or being talked to by – three mothers. One of them – Carolyn Smith, an Adventist faith-kid mum whom Hope knew well enough to nod to – saw their approach and pointed. Four heads turned. Miss Petrie looked worried, Carolyn a little embarrassed, the other two tight-lipped.

Hope marched up.

'Good morning, Miss Petrie,' she said. 'Hi, Carolyn.'

'Good morning, Miss Petrie,' Nick said.

Miss Petrie gave him a brief smile. 'Be a big boy and go in by yourself today, Nick,' she said.

She glanced at Hope, as if getting permission, then stooped and pushed the small of Nick's back with one hand while waving her phone at the gate with the other. The gate began to slide open. Nick seemed taken with the idea.

'Bye, Mummy,' he said.

But one of the two angry-looking mums blocked his path. He looked up at her, and then back at Hope and Miss Petrie. Finding no guidance there, he dodged to one side, lunch box swinging, and nipped past the woman's legs. She reached out and snatched at his shoulder.

'Oi!' Hope shouted.

The angry mum's fingers slipped on the wet cagoule and Nick darted away, through the gate. He'd disappeared and the gate had begun to swing shut behind him before Hope managed another word.

She stepped forward, getting in the woman's face. 'Don't you dare grab at my child like that!'

The other woman didn't back down.

'Your child's endangering my child,' she said.

'No, he is not,' Hope said. 'And that's not the point. Endangering is statistics. Grabbing is battery. I could report you to the police.'

'Now, Hope,' Miss Petrie interposed, 'that's not very helpful, is it?'

As Hope turned to reply, she saw that the other angry mum was holding up a phone, recording the confrontation. This made her more angry and more restrained at the same moment.

'Maybe it would be helpful if you could tell me what's going on.'

'Well,' Miss Petrie said, wiping rain from her eyebrows, 'Chloe and Sophie here were just raising their concerns about your little boy bringing in infections . . .'

'Look,' said Hope, gesturing in a vague way so it didn't look like pointing, 'there's Philippa Kaur going in with her kids, and they sure haven't had the fix. Why don't you have a go at her?'

Sophie, the one who was recording, clicked her tongue at this.

'What?' Hope said.

'Oh,' said Chloe, the one she'd just had words with, 'so you want us to single out the Kaurs, do you?'

'No!' Hope snapped, outraged at the unspoken imputation. 'I just don't see why you should single out me.'

'Because you're just doing it out of selfishness,' said Chloe. 'We're doing it and Philippa's doing it because of conscience.'

The penny dropped.

'Oh, your kids are faith kids too!'

'That's right,' said Chloe. 'So they're in danger of any infections your kid brings in.'

'Oh, Christ!' said Hope.

Sophie tutted again, and Carolyn, who'd been hanging back until now, assumed a pained look and said: 'Please.'

'OK, sorry,' said Hope. She took a step back, feeling crowded, and tried a different tack.

'Why can't we stick together on this? I know we all have different reasons for not wanting the fix, but let's be honest, our

85

kids give each other germs no matter what our reasons are, and they're not giving or getting germs from the rest. So it's only us and our kids this affects, right? Can't we, you know, live and let live about it?'

'You don't understand, Hope,' Carolyn said. 'It's our live and let live that you're putting in danger. You and people like you, all over England.'

'What d'you mean, people like me?'

'Oh, you know,' said Carolyn. 'Those Iranian atheists or whatever they are.'

'Nearly all atheists are absolutely up for the fix,' Hope said. 'Believe me, I checked. Anyway, I don't see how what I'm doing puts you in any danger. I'd have thought you'd, you know, sort of welcome it that we agreed on this point at least.'

'But we don't agree on it!' said Carolyn.

Hope blinked. 'If you say so. But leaving beliefs out of it ... why is it a problem for you if I do the same thing as you do? I mean, one more nature kid can't be that much of a risk, and it's a risk you're willing to take yourselves.'

Carolyn was frowning. 'You don't get it,' she said. 'You're missing the point. It's not the infections; it's that you're putting at risk the live-and-let-live thing. I mean, people put up with us because we have a good reason, and if you're doing it without a good reason and the Kasrani case becomes a precedent and all that, then they might well turn on us. They might say, well, if it's so important that we have to force it on a mum who doesn't want it, why should the faith mums be different? Because, see, the fix doesn't work for everything, and there's always the chance that one of our kids might catch something serious and pass it on to, you know, the other kids, so it's a balance, right? We've got our faith, well our faiths, OK, on our side of the balance, and people *respect* that, but you're just causing trouble.'

Chloe and Sophie nodded along. Miss Petrie looked from face to face helplessly. Hope took another step back.

'You're really telling me,' she said, 'that you'd rather I had the fix than not?'

Carolyn looked uncomfortable. 'Well, not exactly . . .'

'You don't actually care if other people have the fix, do you?' Hope accused. 'Just as long as you're left alone to stick to your, oh, your deeply held beliefs. You're as selfish as the anti-vaccers.'

'You're the one who's being selfish,' said Carolyn.

'You don't believe in nothing,' Sophie said. She'd just stopped recording, and now spoke up. 'I mean, what's it to you anyway? I have my guru, what do you have?'

'I have a job to go to,' said Hope.

She turned away.

Next day the weather was better: still chilly, overcast, but not actually raining or snowing. Miss Petrie's cagoule was open, over a buttoned-up green cardigan and flower-printed dress. The cagoule wafted behind her as she hurried about, talking to a dozen or so mothers and two fathers outside the nursery-school gate. As Hope walked up with Nick, the parents all lined up across the pavement in front of her. The three Hope had spoken to the day before – Carolyn, Chloe and Sophie – were in the middle of the row and slightly forward of the rest. Miss Petrie stood a little away from them, swithering for a moment, and then stepped forward.

'Can I take Nick for a little walk round the corner?' she said. 'Just for a few minutes, while you . . . ' She gestured vaguely behind her.

'No,' said Hope. 'You can't.'

Nick tugged at her hand. 'I want to!'

Hope looked down at his pleading face and tried to smile.

'Just hold on a moment, Nick,' she said. She turned to Miss Petrie. 'Not this again.'

'I'm sorry, Hope,' said Miss Petrie. 'All the faith kids' parents and some of the, uh, the other parents are concerned about—'

'Don't give me any more of that crap, Miss Petrie! I don't care what their concerns are. They're being ignorant, bigoted and unfair and that's all there is to it. Your job isn't to pander to them, or even argue with them. Your job's to ignore them, tell them to go somewhere else, and to get the . . . get out of our way before you call the police. They can arrange an appointment with Mrs Wilson if they want to discuss school policy. Now, will you tell them that, or will I?'

Miss Petrie's troubled face brightened.

'Well, that's a way of looking at it, Hope. I will raise the point about how this is out of my hands . . . '

Her voice trailed off and her gaze locked on something behind Hope's shoulder. Her mouth opened, and stayed open. Hope turned and looked around. Five or six young women, hands linked, were skipping along the pavement towards them. As they came within a few metres they started singing. The line split. Someone caught Hope's right hand, and someone else caught Nick's left hand, and in a moment the line had formed a ring, with Miss Petrie outside it. Hope felt an odd thrill as the stranger's fingers interlaced with hers, and an obscure sense that there was something missing, something not as obvious as a finger, about the hand, but before she had time to process either thought, she felt a tug to one side and to keep her balance had to sidestep, and then again, and then she and Nick were whirling around with the young women, who were all smiling and singing:

'Ring a ring a roses, a pocket full of posies . . . '

She heard Nick's voice joining in.

'Atishoo! Atishoo!'

She couldn't help joining in herself, on the last line, but the others didn't shout out what she did. They shouted:

'We all JUMP UP!'

And they did, giving Hope's shoulders a wrench as she tried to fall down as everyone else including Nick jumped up. She'd just sorted herself out from that when her arms were again tugged as the women and Nick all moved a few steps towards the school gate and then started again, side-skipping around in a ring. After a couple more rounds of this they were at the gate – Miss Petrie, and one of the fathers and two of the mothers who tried to intercept them, were brushed aside by the whirligig of bodies. The next time they stopped, Nick was standing right in front of the now open gate. Well done, Miss Petrie! Hope ducked and gave him a quick kiss on the top of the head, which got her an 'I'm-too-old-for-that' scowl.

'In you go!' she said.

Dizzy, and with a puzzled look, Nick ran in. He glanced back over his shoulder and gave a quick wave. Hope barely had time to wave back before her hands were snatched again and she was hauled into skipping along the pavement with the other women. She looked back, and saw Carolyn, Chloe, Sophie and the rest of the group of parents who'd tried to stop Nick going into nursery gazing after them with baffled looks. It had all taken about two minutes, though it had seemed longer. The line split and re-formed like molecules as it bypassed late-arriving parents and children and others on the pavement, and swung almost into the road as it swept around the nearest corner. Then they slewed to a halt, panting and laughing. Hope glanced around her unexpected rescuers. All six of them were women who looked a bit younger than she was. They were dressed for the weather and for running – jeans or short skirts with leggings, and trainers or Kickers. The rest of their clothing, in all its variety, had a craft-made or selective-vintage look: the sort of stuff, Hope thought with a brief pang, that she'd once imagined herself selling or making.

'Thanks for that,' she said. 'Who are you?'

'We just came together for this,' said the woman who'd held her hand. 'None of us know each other.' She grinned around at the group. 'Thanks, all. I'll take it from here.'

The rest nodded, smiled, and walked off, up or down or across the street. Hope stared at the one who remained, still grinning at her out of a sunburst of blond ringlets. The woman stuck out a hand.

'My name's Maya,' she said. 'I did this.'

Hope shook hands. 'Hope Morrison,' she said. 'You organised it?'

'Flash mob,' Maya explained, or rather, said as if it was an explanation.

'Hmm,' said Hope.

'They all live around here,' said Maya. 'Bet you didn't know you had so many interesting and supportive neighbours, huh?'

Hope felt patronised. 'How would you know that?'

Maya didn't seem fazed. 'If you did, you could have done something like this yourself.'

Hope couldn't think of a reply to that. Instead she asked, 'How do you know about me? How did you know I was ...'

'ParentsNet,' said Maya, looking away a little.

'Oh,' said Hope. 'Well. That's interesting. I start a thread and suddenly everybody knows my business.'

'You know how it is,' said Maya, sounding defensive for the first time. 'It's all out there. But the good thing about it is that you now have an army of flying monkeys.'

'I didn't *ask* for an army of flying monkeys!'

Maya looked abashed. 'Well, sorry, at least we did help you there, and ... Uh, do you have time for a coffee and a chat, maybe?'

Hope felt suddenly reckless. She deserved a bit of relaxation – not to mention explanation – more than she needed an hour's pay.

'Yes!' she said. 'Let's do that.'

She expected Maya to ask her to suggest somewhere to go, but instead Maya nodded and smiled and set off down the street. Hope fell in beside her. On reaching the next junction, Maya put on a set of glasses and looked around. As she did so, Hope noticed what it was about the woman's left hand that had struck her as odd a few minutes earlier. She wasn't wearing a monitor ring.

Hope hadn't seen a woman of childbearing age without a monitor ring since she didn't know how long. It wasn't compulsory, certainly not, but it was such a badge of adulthood – and indeed freedom, compared to the old system of monthly pregnancy tests and certification cards – that girls put them on long before they had the slightest intention or legal opportunity to drink alcohol, smoke or get pregnant. She'd seen ten-year-olds showing them off as if flashing engagement-ring rocks, though in these cases Hope rather suspected the rings were fake.

Maya led the way across the road, took a few confident steps onward, then stopped at the door of a small shop that didn't at all promise coffee. Its faded sign still said *Newspapers and Tobacco* and it sold sweets, convenience food and emergency groceries. Maya strode inside, nodded to the Sikh woman at the counter, and asked for two coffees.

'Real or instant?'

'Real, thanks.'

The shopkeeper opened an airtight jar and scooped some ground coffee into a paper bag.

'Milk?' she asked.

Maya looked at Hope.

'What kind would you like?' Maya asked.

'Uh, thanks, cappuccino, why not?'

'Ah,' said Maya. 'I think the choice here is with or without milk.'

Hope shook her head. 'OK, without, thanks.'

'Just one,' said Maya.

The shopkeeper measured a few mils of milk into a small plastic bottle, and popped a lid on it.

'Five pounds,' she said.

'What!' said Hope.

Maya grinned and raised a finger. 'Wait.'

She paid, and then led the way through a plastic tape curtain to the back. Hope fought down a momentary apprehension and followed, out through a door to a back green with cracked concrete paths. Just ahead, in the middle of the green, was an area covered by a shallow roof of two sloping sheet-diamond panes, visible only from the drizzle-drops that misted them, and held up by four stout wooden posts. In its shelter were half a dozen tables with benches, and a scatter of small round tables with plastic chairs. There was a good and noisy crowd of twenty-odd people at the tables, eating, drinking, some of them smoking. It had been years since Hope had seen so many people smoking, openly, in one place. At the back, a young Asian guy sat behind a table, keeping an eye on people pouring water from electric kettles as they made their way past with cafetières and mugs.

Hope stopped dead.

'I can't go in here,' she said. 'I'm pregnant.'

Maya, a step or two in front, looked over her shoulder.

'I know,' she said. 'You just take the ring off.'

'But it's dangerous,' Hope said.

'The smoke?' Maya flapped a hand in front of her face. 'Pffft!'

'Well, no, I mean taking the ring off. It'll get logged!'

'The Health Centres look for patterns,' said Maya. 'Not odd incidents. Relax.'

Not feeling at all relaxed, Hope turned the monitor ring to loosen it, slid it slowly off her finger and stuck it in the bottom of her jeans pocket. She looked at the pale indentation around her finger above the gold wedding ring, and felt naked.

They found a table. Maya took the packet of coffee and the bottle of milk to the queue. Hope sat down. She could smell coffee, tea, bacon – rolls bought somewhere else, she guessed – and cigarette smoke. The crowd looked like a mixture of art students and building workers. Quite a few of both types were wearing glasses and obviously into some virtual scene. While Maya waited for the boiling water, Hope put her own glasses on. The overlay snapped into view, showing, as she'd expected, people posing as their online avatars: two of the art students looked like dragons, others wore strange strappy costumes or had features like manga characters, all big eyes and chiselled cheekbones. Four lads stooped intently over a tabletop football match on a pitch the size of two chessboards. Hope was amused to see that they kept their mugs and plates off the virtual field. In a far corner, Indian Air Force jets made repeated bombing runs on a forested mountain slope, red and black blooms rising above the green.

Maya joined the queue and glanced back. Hope caught her features in the glasses, framed the face, and – guessing at the spelling of her name – tapped out a search. About a second later she was looking at a full-face photo of Maya, and all her occupational and educational details. Brunel MA (Hons.) in law and government, gap year in Nepal, front-line post in an Advice Centre, campaigns against refugee deportations, member of Liberty and Amnesty, assiduous writer of letters to the web . . . a troublemaker, without a doubt.

She took the glasses off, rather guiltily, when Maya returned with a full cafetière and two mugs.

'Isn't this illegal?' Hope asked. 'An outdoor smoking area?'

Maya shook her head. 'It's not open to the public and they're not serving the coffee or tea. The shop sells very expensive dry coffee and tea bags. What the customers do with it is their business. There just happens to be a place out the back where as a favour the customers can use the family's kettles.'

'And seats, and tables, and shelter.'

'Well, you know how it is with extended families,' said Maya, hand poised over the plunger. 'They need lots of room for get-togethers.'

'The inspectors will find some way to shut it down. Otherwise more people would be doing it.'

Maya smiled. 'More are. More than you'd think. Smoke-easies. Shebeens. Drinking sheds.' She tapped her glasses, in her shirt pocket. 'There's a black app for finding them.'

Hope was not interested in black apps. She felt disquieted that Maya actually had one on her glasses.

'No, I meant like cafés and so on.'

'That's not how it works,' Maya said. 'If you're running a café or a pub, the problem with a workaround like this is that it isn't covered by insurance. Suppose someone were to scald themselves with the kettle! Or trip and hurt themselves! Nightmare. You run into all kinds of legal minefields even before the health inspectors come down on you. And if they do, they can *close* a café. The most they can do with this is stop the shop owner from letting people use their back yard. Or someone else's back yard, for all I know. It's legally quite tricky. In fact what usually happens is the shop owner just stops for a bit, and a place just like it pops up somewhere nearby. Rinse and repeat.'

She pushed the plunger down, and poured. Hope breathed in fragrant steam, blew, and sipped.

'Why did you come here anyway?' she asked. 'Instead of to a café, I mean? You don't smoke, do you?'

'I'm a consenting and mildly addicted passive smoker,' said Maya, inhaling a passing wisp. 'I should explain. I work in an Advice Centre, out in Hayes. Lots of refugees and DPs, you know? Which means I work with people who – I'm not making this up – will list smoking under "outdoor activities".'

They laughed.

'But that's not why I picked here,' Maya went on. She leaned forward, elbows on the table, hand waving. 'It's sort of relevant to your problem, sort of an example . . . '

96

'Oh yes, my problem,' said Hope. She put the coffee mug down, hard. 'You have some explaining to do.'

Maya did some explaining.

Hope put her elbows on the table and her palms across her eyes.

'Oh *God*,' she said. 'I feel like I've been stalked or something.'

'I'm sorry,' said Maya. 'Really you haven't. It's just that, you know, you posted on ParentsNet, and then that other mum at your school uploaded yesterday's little contretemps, and—'

'Yes, I bloody know that!' Hope snapped. 'But that science woman, what did she have to poke her nose in for?'

'For God's sake!' said Maya. 'She hasn't done anything. She just told me about you, and I came up with an idea to help. To let you know you're not alone. And come on, I did help.'

'Yes,' said Hope. 'For today. But that doesn't do me much good, does it?'

'That's what I want to talk about,' said Maya, sounding both exasperated and embarrassed. 'About ways you can deal with the situation.'

Hope decided to give Maya a chance. 'OK,' she said.

Maya leaned back, as if making a conscious decision to get out of Hope's face, and waved expansively. 'The first way,' she said, 'is the kind of thing people do here.'

'Drink coffee and smoke?'

'No,' said Maya. 'Find workarounds. Look, I understand how you must feel, like everything's closing in on you. The health centre, the school, the insurance soon enough ... I know all about that sort of thing, because I deal with it every day. Laws and bureaucracy, God! But the point is, if you really want to, you can get around it.'

'Like?'

'Take the school, for example. All those mums who're giving you trouble – well, maybe you can shame them by going to school in a group with mums who support you.'

'I don't know any,' said Hope.

'OK, but have you looked? Asked? Anyway' – Maya waved a hand again – 'let's leave that for the moment. Sooner or later the insurance issue will come up – the school will be told it can't be insured against your little boy, or rather you can't be insured. Now, you have alternatives there: you could home-school ...'

'No way!'

' ... or join a parents' school group. I can help you find some.'

'No, again. I'm not taking Nick out of the nursery.'

'Well ... in that case, there are alternative sources of insurance cover you might consider. Mainly religious – Islamic, some kinds of Catholic, even, uh, Mennonite and so on, you know, *sects*. They'll all cover you and the school will have to accept that you're covered, because of various non-discrimination acts – you see how it works, you use one part of the law against others?'

Hope looked at the dregs of her coffee.

'Want another coffee?' she said.

Maya nodded. Hope used the five minutes it took to buy the powder and milk and queue for the water to think over why she objected so much to Maya's well-meant suggestions. By the time she got back, she thought she had it.

'I don't want to sneak around,' she said. 'That's what "workaround" means to me. I don't want to live in some hole-and-corner way, relying on the goodwill of sects and cults, thank you very much. I just want to live like everybody else.'

'OK, OK,' Maya said, again with the backing-off body language. 'All right, let's see how you can do it mainstream.' She gave an embarrassed smile. 'Have you thought of writing to your MP?'

Hope stared at her. 'What would be the point of that?'

'More than you'd think,' said Maya. 'They still take letters from constituents seriously. And come on, your MP is one of the better ones. Jack Crow.'

'He even lives around here,' Hope said. 'I've spoken to him, now I come to think of it. He knocked on our door at the last election.'

'An MP who canvasses?' said Maya. 'My, my. Did you vote for him?'

'None of your business,' Hope said.

Maya nodded. 'Fair enough.'

'But I did,' Hope added.

Maya looked surprised. 'I wouldn't have expected you to be—'

'Oh, no,' Hope said. 'I'm not. No, I don't believe in *all that*, but it's – well, it's two things. One is my job, you know? In China? So I'm all for that side of it, the war and so on; we really have to, you know, *defeat* those people. And the other is, uh, my husband. He's from the Highlands and he's half native, as he puts it, and I don't know if you know what the people up there are like, but I swear if he even thought I was going to vote any other way he'd walk out on me.'

'Really?'

Hope laughed. 'It's a slight exaggeration, but he takes it all very seriously.'

'Ah!' said Maya. 'So he might be quite pleased if you were to take it so seriously that you'd actually *join* the—'

'What! I couldn't!'

'Why not?'

'I mean, look at me!'

'I'm looking at a regular Islington mum.'

'Exactly! And my accent! Come on, I'm a Home Counties middle-class girl.'

Maya put a hand across her mouth and pinched her nostrils as if stifling a giggle.

'I think you'll find,' she said when she'd ostensibly recovered, 'that you'll fit right in.'

That evening, Hope wrote a letter to her MP, Jack Crow. She found no difficulty at all in composing it, but quite a bit in writing it. She hadn't hand-written an entire page since primary school. In the end she found an app on her glasses that sampled her handwriting and turned it into a font that looked like her handwriting would if it had been regular, and printed it off. There was even an app for the printer that indented the paper a little, and an ink that looked like ballpoint ink. She signed the letter in what she hoped was a sufficiently similar ink and script, and sealed the envelope. She looked up Jack Crow and was about to address the letter to him at the House of Commons, when she noticed that his own address was only a few streets away. The following morning, after dropping off Nick – no problems this time – she took the letter round and posted it through the letter box of the MP's house, a modest multi-household Victorian jerry-built tenement like her own but with, she was quite pleased to see, one floor fewer. It seemed appropriately modest, for one of the better MPs, one who lived in his constituency and actually canvassed.

As soon as she got home, Hope joined up. A few days later she got a package in the post enclosing: a plastic membership card with an offer of a Co-op Bank loan and a data chip containing more information about the Party, the movement, and parliamentary procedure than she could possibly live long enough to read; a welcome letter; and a plastic badge in the shape of a circle with a logo in fake enamel of a torch, a shovel and a quill pen. Around the border were the words LABOUR PARTY and across the middle was the word LIBERTY.

This looked promising. She pinned the badge to her coat collar at once. She knew that Hugh must have noticed it in the hallway when he came home, but he made no comment.

8

Subject Positions

That same evening, Geena walked home from Hayes to Uxbridge, thinking about Hope Morrison. Over another, slightly less chilly, lunch by the canal two days earlier, Maya had explained how she'd helped. Geena had been relieved by the moderation of the actions Maya had taken, and by the modesty of her proposals. But that wasn't why she was thinking about Hope. She was thinking about her because she didn't understand her.

It was a fine evening, the sun already set and the western sky before her lurid with greens and purples. Post-rush-hour traffic whispered past along Dawley Road, and then Hillingdon Road, leaving a faint waft of ethanol that set her monitor ring a-tingling. Heathland and golf course held up the horizon on her left. Lights came on in crowded suburban semis and went off in office and industrial blocks beyond them to her right. Geena strode along, boot-heels clicking, coat-tails snapping, head up, her glasses subtly enhancing the lower part of the visual field and flagging irregularities in the pavement so she didn't trip on any of them while she gazed straight ahead and took in the glorious sky and pondered the theoretical problem of Hope.

The problem, as Geena saw it, was this. Inside people's heads were brains, and these were increasingly well understood, or so Geena was given to understand. Her eyes had always glazed over at the details. But neurology subtends ideology, as Dr Ahmed Estraguel was fond of reminding his students; the object – the celebrated double handful of grey matter – subtends the subject. And the subject itself is no dumb internal essence, no spiritual spark jumping undetected across the synaptic gap. No. The subject speaks itself into being, and it speaks in – what else? – language. And language, from the first babble to the last sigh, articulates ideology. How could it not? Language arises spontaneously out of human interactions, and scientific knowledge of these interactions doesn't. Language is necessarily freighted with illusion.

So, in the first instance, human subjects constitute themselves out of ideology, even if – especially if – they call that ideology common sense. Common sense, Geena thought, would tell her that the sun had set. Scientific practice, as embodied in her glasses, showed her exactly where the sun was, a few degrees below the horizon.

She paused at the pedestrian crossing at a roundabout,

looking in several directions before stepping out, even though the little man was green. Her glasses showed her vehicles outside her line of sight, and reassured her that all was safe. On the other side of the road she paused again, to take in a rare sight revealed by her leftward glance: an airliner on approach to Heathrow. Seen, as now, head-on, with its landing lights and wing lights all in a row, it looked remarkably like a flying saucer. For seconds at a time it seemed to hang still in the air, lights shimmering a little in the haze and relative warmth rising from the ground. And then the angle changed, and the illusion – tenuous enough with the airliner's flight number tagged beside it by her glasses – was replaced by the unarguable, unmistakable cruciform of the craft.

Geena blinked and walked on. So much, then, for perception and common sense. What you see is not what you get. And what you think is not necessarily what you think. The internal monologue may seem like a pure subjective self, and it is, but that little voice in your head is speaking in a language, and language can only be social, which means it's ideological from the get-go. Your subjectivity is a *subject position*, a node in your real relations lived as an origin in your imaginary relations. It's not just that your thinking is ideological, but that your ideology thinks you. Your flights of fancy come with a flight-number tag.

The theoretical problem with Hope Morrison was that she refused, or was unable, to articulate her subject position. If she were to appeal to her rights, or ascribe her views to some belief or ideology that had inscribed itself on her mind, her subject position would be clear. Instead she persisted in her wordless objection.

An enigma.

Geena had now walked past the wide open space and into one of the streets off Hillingdon Road, part of her zigzag course towards where she lived in Uxbridge. As she passed one corner, she found herself glancing with idle curiosity toward a section of low garden wall that she'd noticed the previous evening. Quite unmarked to the naked eye, through her glasses (and, presumably, through those of anyone who passed with glasses on) it displayed a string of glowing letters, about half a metre high, that looked as if they'd been spray-painted in fluorescent ink.

The string spelled out the word 'NAXAL', with a swastika in the place of the 'X'. Geena smiled faintly to herself at the virtual graffiti. Put there – well, a tiny and almost undetectable transmitter dropped nearby, a speck amid the dirt at the foot of the wall – by some Indian old-line supporter, she guessed, maybe some kid whose family kept up a loyalty to one of the many parties of the Left on the subcontinent who opposed the Naxal insurrection and who often enough were the first in its line of fire.

Geena walked on, vaguely troubled. Something about the slogan rang false. It seemed to be making a simplistic equation: Naxal = Nazi. And that wasn't right. She half-smiled again, recalling the line from *The Big Lebowski*. Nazis, whatever else might be said about them, at least weren't nihilists.

You couldn't say that about the Naxals. In all she knew of history, Geena could think of only one parallel, and it terrified her. Way back in the thirteenth century BCE there had for many more centuries than thirteen been civilisation right across the Middle East. It had been brought down in the brief span of twenty-seven years, by people who had come out of nowhere and burned down every city in their known world. If, in any heap of ruins, enough survivors were left to begin rebuilding, the City Burners came back after a few years and sacked it again. With equal thoroughness they'd destroyed every record. The City Burners had come from the plains, the deserts, the mountains, the sea. They had completed their task, and then vanished from history. It wasn't even clear whether they were invaders from without or rebels from below. No history was written about them, because by the time they'd finished, there wasn't a person alive within a thousand miles who could write.

The Naxals were like that. They'd started out as some kind of Maoists, but their ideology had mutated into what seemed like sheer nihilism, fuelled by a hatred of industrial civilisation itself, with a strategy to bring it down. Her supervisor, Dr Ahmed Estraguel, whom she was vaguely planning to see tomorrow morning, had said that People's War resembled the Naxal strategy the way a protein resembled a prion. The movement was a pure self-replicator, recruiting new cadre out of the very devastation that their actions and the state's counteractions brought about. Decades of fighting across an ever-increasing range – far beyond the original 'Red Corridor' that they'd vaunted when it had merely extended the length of

India, and by now well to the north into central Asia and southern Russia and as far south as Indonesia – had turned them into an engine of destruction that would have made the Khmer Rouge shudder. (Say what you like about the tenets of the Angkar, dude . . .) They'd merged with and absorbed the defeated remnants of older, lesser movements – the Taliban, al-Qaeda, the rebels in Chechnya and Uzbekistan – and taken over what remained of their tattered, though still far-flung, networks. But the Naxals' longest reach was in inspiration and ideology, and in the virtual. They'd gone viral, inspiring pop-ups, usually but not always in communities of south Asian origin – including in Southall, a few kilometres away.

Which was why Geena had, in the two years she'd lived in Uxbridge, been stopped in the street five times and questioned by the police. Each time, a simple ID check and a few polite answers had seen her on her way. So when, half an hour after she'd seen the slogan, and just as she was a few streets away from where she lived, she turned a corner to find a police van parked at the wayside and three armoured cops blocking her path, she felt barely more than annoyed.

The street was otherwise deserted. Semis, bungalows, villas, New Trees. Smell of goats and chickens. Cars and bike racks. No kids running about. A policeman stepped forward, raising a Kevlar-gloved palm. The other two held back, hands lightly resting on holsters and batons at their belts. Geena stopped. She said nothing.

'Your ID, please.'

Geena handed over the card. The policeman held it in front

of the scanner on his helmet. Mirrored text scrolled on his visor. He asked her name, her address, her place of work, her ...

Wearily but promptly, she complied.

The policeman stepped back, still holding Geena's card, and with his other hand beckoned behind him. One of his colleagues took his place – a woman, Geena now saw, more slightly built and more heavily armoured than the others.

'Last night,' the policewoman said, 'you passed a piece of virtual graffiti, near the junction of Hillingdon Road and Huxley Drive. Could you describe it?'

'It was the word "Naxal" with a swastika in place of the "x".'

'Uh-huh.' A nod. 'And tonight you noticed it again?'

'Yes,' said Geena.

'About twenty minutes ago?'

'Yes,' said Geena, puzzled. 'I suppose so.'

'Plenty of time to report it, then.'

Geena felt baffled. 'Report it? Why?'

'It's a serious offence.'

'What? It's virtual graffiti!' Geena waved a hand around, indicating other samples of the art. 'I don't think there's even a law against it yet; you couldn't get them for anything apart from *littering*, and that's Council, that's—'

'The *content*,' the policewoman interrupted, her voice hardening. 'Glorifying terrorism. Written support of an illegal organisation. Aid and comfort to the enemy.'

'But ... but ...' Geena floundered, disoriented by the absurdity of the claim. 'It's *against* the Naxals! It's saying they're Nazis!'

'Ms Fernandez,' the policewoman said, with sarcastic patience, 'I do understand that you're from a Catholic background. But you must have celebrated Diwali at school, yes?'

'Yes,' said Geena, with a sudden lift-shaft feeling as she realised where this line of questioning was going.

'Then I take it you recognise the significance of the swastika in Hindu culture?'

'Yes, but—'

'So what this graffiti is really saying is something like "Hail the Naxals! Good luck to the Naxals!" Isn't that right?'

'Well, maybe,' said Geena, trying to keep a tremor out of her voice, and to sound like she was just thinking aloud. 'I suppose it could be read that way, but in a political context the significance of the symbol changes, and I'm sure most people would read it the way I did.'

'The way you *say* you did,' said the policewoman, also as if turning things over in her mind. She seemed to come to a decision. 'I'm afraid we're going to have to be a little more certain than that.' She waved towards the van. 'Would you step inside the van for a moment, please?'

'No!' Geena looked from side to side. Nobody around. Somewhere a dog barked. Blue flicker of plasma telly on curtains. Bleats and clucks. She wanted to run, even though she knew it was hopeless. Her legs wouldn't move. Her knees shook.

The policewoman took another step forward, hand reaching out, not yet touching her.

'No, please, no!' It came out as a wail.

Grabbed. The other two leapt forward, surrounding her. One of them wrenched away her bag. The other deftly pulled her glasses from her face. Her feet were off the ground. Bundled around the back of the van. In. Slam, muffled, like a bank vault.

The interior of the van had half a dozen seats with head and limb restraints. Geena thrashed like a child, and with as little effect. Before she had time to do anything, she was being held down, then fixed in. The restraints were syn bio stuff, soft on the skin, unyielding.

The policewoman lifted off her helmet, revealing a pleasant young face and a heap of tied-up hair. She held out a cupped hand. One of her colleagues, still visored, tossed her a small metal object that looked like a miniature grenade. She flipped the top off, pressed down a switch. An inch-long jet of flame shot up, blue and white. Geena couldn't take her eyes off it.

The policewoman reached for a seam in her jacket and pulled out a pin. She played the flame up and down it.

'This is to sterilise the pin,' she explained, kindly. The flame vanished with a click, and she passed the lighter back and leaned forward.

Geena clenched her fists on top of the armrests, straining against the clamps around her forearms. The policewoman prised up the middle finger of Geena's left hand, and pushed the pin under the fingernail.

There was no language. There were no words.

*

Sheet of paper. Small print; boxes to tick.

'Sign this.'

A smile. Another sheet of paper: smaller, folded in three, with coloured font.

'Take this.'

Geena looked down at it.

Trauma counselling. Helplines.

They returned her glasses and her bag. She stuck the leaflet in the outer pocket.

They opened the doors.

She went home.

9

Paper Tigers

The following morning Geena awoke sobbing. Her boyfriend, Liam, sat up and leaned over. His face interrupted her fixed gaze at the ceiling. Hair tousled, cheeks bristled, eyes bleary; breath garlicky from last night's chicken curry. She shut her eyes on his anxious gaze.

'What's the matter?' he asked, from far away.

'Nothing,' she said. 'Just a bad dream, that's all.'

'Aw . . .'

He laid a hand on her shoulder, pulling her towards him. She shrugged him away and rolled over, hauling the duvet.

'What's the matter?'

'Nothing,' she said, muffled. 'Just let me get back to sleep.'

She heard his breathing above her head for a minute, then a sigh as he turned away. He heaved himself under the covers, his back to her, and lay there until the alarm beeped. Then he got up. Geena heard him in the bathroom, in the shower, getting dressed, in the next room making his breakfast.

He came back into the room and kissed the top of her head.

'I've made you some coffee,' he said.

'Thanks,' she said, her face still to the pillow. 'Have a good day.'

He waited, then:

'You too. Bye.'

'Bye.'

As soon as the outside door closed, she jumped out of bed and hurried through to the front-room bay window just in time to see Liam go up the street. Tall and thin, he walked with his hands in his jacket pockets and his elbows out, shoulders moving in sync with his stride, as he always did. And as always, he turned at the corner, smiled and waved, though he probably couldn't see her. Geena waved back, slightly self-conscious at still being in her pyjamas.

When he'd gone, she sat down in one of the two old rug-thrown armchairs that faced each other across where a fireplace had once been. She held up her left hand. It shook a little. The dull pewter of the monitor ring on her wedding finger gleamed in the early sunlight. The blue sticking-plaster around her middle fingernail reflected more brightly, a jade satin ribbon of SynBioTech manufacture, its pad still dispensing antisepsis and analgesia in calibrated dosage. Adhesion, calculated too: when the plaster had done its job, it would drop off, like a scab.

The smell of coffee called her to her feet. She stepped barefoot across raffia to the corner with the table and the cooker and the sink, and pushed down the plunger of the one-shot cafetière. The monitor ring gave her its usual morning warning twinge about the caffeine. She ignored it, filled a mug, and sat down to sip, wrapping the injured hand around the hot china.

The obvious thing would be to call Maya. Geena flinched from the thought. She'd named Maya, she was sure of that. Fairly sure. She didn't remember all she'd said, blabbed, blubbered. Everything. Everyone. What a little sneak she had been. And it wasn't even as if she had suffered *real* torture. Just the clinical, sterile application of pain. Routine. Helping with enquiries. Nothing to write to Amnesty about. She must be weak, far weaker than she'd ever imagined.

Then, as her thoughts circled, like crows over roadkill, and her self-incriminations yelled accusations at her, she realised that this too was part of the ordeal. The aftershock was an intended result.

But they'd given her the trauma counselling leaflet! They must understand! They'd agreed she was innocent! They didn't intend her to feel like this. Or if they did, they'd provided a helpline. No doubt there was a call centre. Probably in China. Or, if the leaflet was personalised, Brazil. They spoke Portuguese there. A sympathetic shoulder, a familiar idiom, a friendly female voice and face on the phone. She could feel it now like a hug. It would be like calling her mother, whom she couldn't call because she didn't want to drag her into this, and because her mother would be ashamed.

No. This too. Trauma counselling was part of the process. Proactive prophylaxis against the possible disarticulation of the subject position. Or, to put it in plain English, they didn't want people just going to pieces. That wouldn't do at all. How many people, Geena wondered, had been through this and never spoken about it, except to a trauma counsellor? Nobody had ever told her about it. Not in so many words. So why had she panicked at the prospect of going into the van? A lifetime of glances, shaken parental fingers, averted looks, dropped hints, sick jokes in the playground. She had known, all right. She had known what went on in police vans. She had known more.

There had been that time, in Southall, when she'd carried a fragrant paper bag of coconut *barfi* out of a café, and stepped out on the pavement, and a man a few metres away had exploded in a red mist. Next thing she knew, she was sitting on the parapet of the bridge over the canal, by the pub, looking down at a paper bag butcher-shop-splattered on the outside and with a few yellow crumbs in the bottom corners, and all the front of her clothes sticking to her skin.

She should have had trauma counselling for that, Geena thought, as she drained the mug. Hah. She rinsed it in the sink and went to have a shower, ready to face the day. She knew who to talk to.

The Institute for Science Studies offices, all five of them, were in the Mechanical Engineering block, somewhat to the annoyance of the remaining Mech. Eng. lecturers, not one of whom didn't still think the taunt that *if you lot think science is ideology why don't you step off the roof?* was to the point. Geena spared a glance as always for the vast blue-painted cylindrical machine, a turbine she guessed, whose function she had never got around to enquiring about, that dominated the entrance hall, and hurried up the broad concrete stairs. Around and around, to the fourth floor. At each landing a helpful notice informed her how high a mountain a daily ascent to that level would represent over an academic year. This had never struck Geena as a sensible yardstick. Her Goan *great-grandmother* could climb Mount Snowdon if given three-hundred-odd days to do it, and look at her.

The door of Geena's supervisor's office was open. Geena leaned in and knocked sideways.

'Uh, Ahmed . . .'

'Ah, good morning, Geena! Come on in.'

Dr Ahmed Estraguel was a man in his mid-thirties, of short and agile build, with a walk like a dancer or a bantamweight boxer, and an alert, darting gaze. Black hair to the collar of his open denim shirt, pointed black beard, skin somewhat lighter than Geena's own. He stood for a moment, half-bowing to shake hands across the cluttered desk, and waved to the low-slung armchair in front of it. Geena settled, screwing up her eyes slightly against the sunlight slanting through the window over his left shoulder.

'How's things?' Ahmed asked. This meeting was one pencilled in, just a quick update on how her work was going, but it hadn't been definite, so he looked mildly surprised and pleased to see her.

'Things are fine,' said Geena. 'At SynBioTech.' She gestured a heap. 'Lots of notes. Good obs and some ... you know, the ideas are coming along.'

'Good, good. I've been following them on the doc space, and I agree it's coming along fine, but it's good to hear it from you.'

He shot her a quick, tight smile, as if to say she should drop in more often.

She acknowledged this with a glance down and a nod. Then she looked up.

'But apart from that ... uh, there's something I'd like to talk about. Privately.'

Ahmed's black eyebrows lifted. 'How privately?'

Geena looked over her shoulder at the door. 'Off the record. Personal logs only.'

His lips compressed and twitched sideways. 'Hmm. Very well. I'd better fix us some coffee. Usual?'

'Black, no sugar, thanks.'

Ahmed sidled past, and out into the corridor. As she waited for his return, Geena scanned from the low vantage of her chair the books on the shelves that lined the walls. Despite all advances in information technology – every title she could see was easily accessible on her glasses – most academics persisted in stockpiling hard copy, as if in anticipation of the day when some Naxal software worm or other global disaster brought down the Net. So Dr Estraguel had his own thesis (*Fictitious Capital and the Political Economy of Promise*) at floor level, then the sociology textbooks he'd read as an undergraduate – Giddens, Parsons, Habermas – and the theoretical works with which he'd supplemented them –

117

Foucault, Lacan, Derrida; Marx's *Capital* (three faded-brown-dust-jacketed hardback volumes in the antique Moscow edition, as well as the more familiar Penguin Classics in battered paperback), with commentaries thereon by Althusser, Dunayevskaya, Fine and Saad-Filho, Ticktin, Mandel and Rosdolsky; early science studies by Popper, Kuhn, Latour, Lakatos, Bloor, Baskhar; rows and rows of monographs and recent books, fiction and non-fiction; on higher shelves the current sociology textbooks, including the latest, to which he'd contributed a chapter himself. But upon them all, as far as Geena could see, dust was gathering. Like almost everyone else with shelved books, when Ahmed wanted to read one he'd glance at its title and summon it on his glasses rather than haul it down.

Coffee, though, you couldn't digitise that. Its smell and the warning twinge that went along with it. Ahmed came in with two plastic cups and pushed the door shut behind him.

'Now,' he said, back behind his desk, 'Geena, could you please ...'

He waved behind his right shoulder in the direction of the ceiling-corner camera.

'Oh, sure,' said Geena. 'Dr Estraguel, I'm requesting that you turn off the internal surveillance camera, and I'm affirming that I've read and understood the college regulations in this respect.'

'Fine, OK.' Ahmed slipped on his glasses and looked over his shoulder up into the corner, then snapped his fingers. 'Right.' He settled back and sipped. 'Fire away.'

Geena picked up her cup and put it back down at once, so as

not to spill it. She clasped her hands together on her lap. She told him what had happened.

'Oh, Geena!' Ahmed spread his arms. 'I would . . . '

'Thanks. I know you can't.' She sighed. 'I'm all right, really. It's just . . . I named you, you know, as someone I knew who was sort of radical . . . I didn't accuse you, didn't point a finger' – she caught her breath, tried to laugh – 'so to speak, as far as I can remember, but to be honest it's all a bit like white noise in my head, and I'm so sorry.'

Head in her hands, by this point. She sniffed hard. She heard a drawer open and close. Some light weight was scuffed across the desk.

'Tissues,' Ahmed said.

'Thanks.' She blew. 'Ugh.'

Steadier now, she took a sip of coffee. 'Like I said, I'm sorry, Ahmed.'

'You have nothing to apologise for,' he said. 'Anybody would do the same. It's expected.'

'I brought your name into—'

Ahmed waved a hand. 'Don't worry about me,' he said. 'Not for a second. They can't touch me on any of that nonsense.'

'You've written an article about the Naxals,' Geena said, as if he needed reminding. 'A few years ago now, but . . . '

'Ah, yes,' said Ahmed, with a fleeting smile. '"The Pure Theory of Primitive Military Accumulation". You've read it?'

'Yes, and . . . it could be interpreted as sympathetic, or at least – what do the cops call it?' She struggled to remember the phrase thrown in her face the previous night. '"Soft support".'

'Ah, fuck.' Ahmed exhaled the word on a long breath. 'Pardon my English, Geena.' He glanced over his shoulder, as if at the recording device that wasn't running. 'I trust that will be interpreted as an expletive and an intensifier. It's just that I'm a little taken aback that you might think that *they* might think that way.'

He touched his steepled, spread fingers to his mouth and nose, repeating this several times, his gaze abstract. Then he smiled, disarmingly.

'It's like ... you missed the memo. Missed a class, or something.' Again with the smile. 'I mean, don't take this personally, it's not a criticism of you, if anyone's failed it's me or one of my colleagues. Think methodology, Geena.'

Geena thought. 'Oh!' she said. 'You mean, a mathematical, materialist analysis of Naxal theory and practice can't be construed as even *soft support*, because it's *critique*, and critique has to assimilate the construction being deconstructed.'

Ahmed raked fingers backward through his hair.

'True enough, as far as it goes,' he said, sounding impatient. 'You didn't miss *that* class. But actually, what I was thinking of was more the question of *their* methodology. That of the repressive state apparatuses.'

He clasped his hands behind his head, tilted his swivel chair back, and rocked a few times.

'It's textbook stuff, to be honest,' he said. 'But maybe we don't spell it out clearly enough at the undergraduate level, and we sort of assume our graduate students will pick it up by some kind of tacit process, which ... is pretty naive and remiss of us, all things considered.' He brought the seat back to horizontal with a bump, and leaned forward, elbows on the desk, expounding. 'Sorry about that. Seriously. So ... here's the thing. Over on the, ah, *other side*, the smoky states, an article like mine – which was immediately put on the reading list of every staff college in the world, on both sides of the Warm Front – would have been enough to get me in serious hot water, and I don't mean metaphorically in some places. And even the Russians and the Indians are, well ... you know ... very much *hands-on* in dealing with dissent, which is I suppose understandable enough in that the Naxals, to say nothing of the underlying population, are a much more immediate threat *over there*. Over *here*, on the other hand, including in China, based on the long experience and political nous of stable ruling-class fractions, blah blah, you know the story – on *our* side, as I say, it's an absolute given that all revolutionaries are paper tigers. That Mao allusion isn't a joke, you know – China's where it all started. When you have a completely capitalist system run by completely conscious Marxist-Leninists, the relative autonomy of ideology becomes obvious to everyone whose opinion matters. I'm talking about the hegemonic class fractions, people who've been to Oxbridge and Harvard and Beijing, not your MBAs and politicians and journalists – not to mention the scientists you're working with, bless their *Daily Mail*-reading hearts, or their *Guardian*-reading hearts for that matter – or any other such-like foot-soldiers, but what the civil service used to call *first-class minds*. They all get a very good grounding in critical theory at university, that's part of what their parents are bloody paying for, even if they grumble in the comment columns about their little darlings coming out with all this subversive stuff that leftie lecturers have filled their heads with.'

'I know *that*,' said Geena, stung that he thought she didn't. 'We got that in Reflexivity 101 – the system *needs* critique and simultaneously recuperates it.'

'You understand *how*,' said Ahmed, resetting his glasses on the bridge of his nose, 'but you don't understand *why*.'

'No,' said Geena. 'I don't.'

'And because of that, you don't understand what happened to you last night.'

Geena nodded. 'Yes, but – I don't see the connection.'

She had her hands clasped in front of her, partly, as before, to stop the shakes and partly because she was so eager to know the truth that she felt she was almost praying.

'It's banal,' Ahmed said. '"Delay is the essence of the period", as Ticktin said.' He shrugged. 'Sorry. It's as simple as that.'

Geena shook her head. 'I don't get it.'

'The global system has reached the stage where the whole show can only be kept on the road consciously. And for that it needs all the critique it can get. On this side the critique has a left-wing coloration: Marxist, feminist, ecological, et cetera. On the other side it tends to be right-wing: free-market, libertarian, Hayek bloody Hayek. Either way, the critique holds each variant of the state-capitalist system to its own promises, and on both sides it is kept going, quite consciously, because the alternative is too disturbing to contemplate.'

'The Naxals? But you said they weren't—'

'"Any kind of alternative, but rather an extreme form of the destructive tendencies of the global system itself", yes, thank you, Geena, so I did.'

'What alternative, then?'

'The one that's implicit in the system itself.'

'Oh.' Geena felt disappointed. '*Socialism*. Like anybody would ever want *that*.'

'Well, indeed,' said Ahmed, in a wry tone. 'It would be so terrible that the most important task in politics has become preventing people from realising that they're already almost there. That train has left the station. We've already crossed the border. State-capitalism can flip over – or rather, can *be* flipped over, overturned – into socialism in the blink of an eye, the moment people become conscious of the possibility. The point is to *prevent* them becoming conscious. Both sides already *have* relative abundance, universal education, extensive planning, formal democracy. Imagine the horror if people got it into their heads to put all these together for the purposes of, let's say, liberty, equality, fraternity!'

Geena couldn't imagine it, but she laughed to show she'd got the joke.

'Oh, the horror!'

'I'm not being ironic,' Ahmed said. 'The economy and the environment are in such a precarious balance, it's like we're riding a unicycle on a tightrope over a flaming abyss while juggling chainsaws. The last thing you want in that situation is some clown bounding along behind you and contesting the saddle. So . . . the question becomes one of maintaining control

123

over the underlying population. Here's where what they did to you and what they didn't do to me comes in. *Over there*, well, I've told you what they'd have done to me. What the cops would have done to you – a student fleetingly suspected of not being fully on-side – would have been to beat you black and blue, taking care not to mark your face or break bones or cause internal injuries, and either arrest you or send you on your way, lesson learned. And you come crying into the office of your supervisor, and she, or he for that matter, gives you a hug, and a coffee or something stronger, maybe even offers a cigarette, and a spiel that would be nothing like as direct as the one I've given you. If you were to read a transcript of such a conversation in Moscow University, you wouldn't know what they were talking about. But they would.

'Whereas *here*, it's a sterile pin, a sticking-plaster, a helpline to prolong your feeling of being a victim, and no hug from me. Contrary to received wisdom that control over there is physical and over here it's ideological – hegemony, false consciousness and all that Critical Theory 101 guff – it's almost exactly the other way round. Ordinary, non-political, everyday life is far more regulated here than it is in Russia or India. Why else do you think we maintain the low-carbon regulations, the holiday-flights ban for instance, and all the preventive health measures, when syn bio has cracked the carbon problem and fixed cancer and heart disease?'

'That sounds kind of ... Foucauldian,' said Geena, trying to keep her mind on an academic track. 'Like, it's all about control over bodies? Biopower? But isn't that already part of the critique?'

Ahmed laughed. 'Exactly! Bloody Foucault's where they got the idea from!'

'There's just one problem with what you're saying,' Geena said, leaning forward. 'The unicycle thing, yes? It seems to me there are *two* unicycles on this rope, and they're heading towards each other.'

'Yes,' said Ahmed. 'Hence the overwhelming importance of delay. They might just slow down and meet in the middle, instead of colliding. And then we have a chance of, maybe, heading in a common direction, *off* the rope.'

'But meanwhile, the flames from the abyss are reaching the rope, and the Naxals are busy trying to saw through it.'

'Yes,' said Ahmed. 'Speaking of which.' He jumped up, looking unexpectedly cheerful. He took his glasses off and slipped them in a shirt pocket, behind the obligatory row of pens. 'Here, let me show you something. Could you give me your specs for a moment?'

She dug the glasses out of her bag and passed them over. Ahmed synched them with his desk screen, rotated the screen so that they could both see it.

'Nothing private when you last wore them?'

Geena shook her head. Ahmed began rattling his fingers on the desk.

'OK,' he said. Scenes blurred past on the screen as he spoke: Dawley Road, Hillingdon Road, the aircraft . . . 'I've skipped back to yesterday evening, about teatime, scrolling forward, slow down – ah! Here we are! That little bit of graffiti. The source of all your woe. Now . . . let's just open that up, see the projection raw.'

A sudden flourish of the fingertips, *fortissimo*. The corner-of-the-eye glimpse of wall and lettering gave way to a screenful of letters and numbers that seemed to Geena pure gibberish. Ahmed scrolled.

'See that string?' he said, pointing and highlighting. 'It's an IP address, which . . .'

Another flourish, another screen.

' . . . just happens to be the IP address of your glasses. The graffiti could be seen by you and nobody else.'

'Shit!' said Geena, heedless of speech codes. 'The cops planted it! For me!'

Another rapid-fire rattle, and the screen went blank.

'Uh-huh,' said Ahmed, handing back the glasses.

'Why?'

Ahmed shrugged. 'Fishing.'

'It's that specific?'

'It's that specific. Let no one say the state is not concerned about the individual.'

Geena smacked a fist in her palm. 'We've got them!'

'What do you mean?'

Geena stared at him. 'I mean, we've got a legal case. Entrapment, provocation, whatever, it can't be legal, can it? I was going to ask . . . a friend about all this, get some advice, but . . . I couldn't because . . . well, I named her and . . . anyway. So I came here to ask you, and you've . . . This is brilliant! Thanks, Ahmed! I knew you'd help me.'

'This never happened,' Ahmed said.

'What?'

'I've wiped the record of our little investigation. You won't find a trace of it on your glasses, or on mine, or on my desk.'

'Why?' Geena asked, dismayed.

'It's better not to talk about these things. Better for you. Just ignore it, say nothing, and, believe me, it'll be like it never happened.'

'It won't be to me!'

'No, and I'm sorry about that, but it will be to the police and all the rest of them. They've made their point. As long as you don't take it further, they'll leave it at that. But if you do ... well, that's ... I was going to say rocking the boat, but what I should say is, *shaking the rope*.'

'In other words,' said Geena, 'all that you said, all that sharp criticism, it doesn't *mean* anything.'

'It means everything,' said Ahmed. 'That's what I've been trying to explain, dammit! It's *all* conscious. Including, you know, this.'

'This ... what?'

'This conversation. This moment. Everything I've said. It's *all understood*. It's understood because I and people like me have explained it to them, in the same terms as I've explained it to you. With footnotes, references, bibliography ...'

'Oh,' said Geena, in a dull, flat voice, feeling that she too had understood, at last. 'They got to you, too!'

'They got to me a long time ago,' said Ahmed, in a tone of mild regret. Half-smiling, he drew his glasses from his pocket and put them back on. He waved into the corner to the right and above, and snapped his fingers. 'Surveillance on.'

He walked around her to open the door, returned to his desk and sat down, then leaned forward, elbows on the desk, and smiled brightly.

'Right, that's the personal matter out of the way. Hope our little chat's been helpful. Any time, my door's always open. Now, about your thesis ...'

Around mid-morning, Geena walked off campus, up long paths among green meadows, feeling quite cheerful. Spring was definitely in the air. At the edge of the campus she swithered about walking to Hayes, and came down on the side of catching the bus from Kingston Lane. As she waited at the bus stop, she mused over why she felt so much better, despite the anger that seethed inside her. Birdsong and blue sky had a lot to do with it, she decided, but underneath all that was a solid foundation of understanding, of acceptance. The world was what it was. Critique had always left her with a vague sense of obligation to find fault with the world. Now she understood it as *part* of the world, a spinning flywheel that helped keep it upright and rolling along. It was all right to enjoy the world. She always had, but she'd always had the nagging suspicion that intellectually it was hard to justify uncritical enjoyment. Now that suspicion was gone. Everything was as it had to be. *Amor fati* and *carpe diem*, that was the ticket.

And what she was enjoying right now was her rage. She accepted it. She let it flow through her. She observed her hands shaking. She noted with interest their spontaneous self-positioning into strangulation mode: open, mirroring each other, fingers and thumbs curled. She could very easily imagine them around Ahmed Estraguel's neck. Deliberately she let them relax, and stuck them in her pockets.

It was the betrayal that did it, she thought, the blatant way in which a man she'd have expected to be outraged at what had happened to her had been merely sympathetic. And the way in which all the techniques of critique she had so painstakingly learned had turned out to be an instrument of the very systems of domination they anatomised. It was as if she had been naive. Ahmed had explained it as something that should have been obvious all along. There was no going back from that, she realised. From now on she was inextricably in a different subject position. She understood.

She also understood Hope Morrison, no longer an enigma, and she knew what she could do – the only thing she could do, and the thing only she could do – to help.

Back at the lab, Geena made her usual discreet notes on the behaviours of Brian, Sanjay, Michael and Joe, added a page's worth of text to her thesis draft, and then turned to doing a little research of her own.

As an accredited postgrad at Brunel, she had management-level access to public-health databases. And as a participant observer at SynBioTech, she had the same kind of access as the research teams: to data for specific individuals. It was taken for granted that she wouldn't combine these permissions on her own behalf. She had them solely to observe the work of the researchers. To use them for research of her own would be considered unprofessional. But that restriction was entirely in her head – or, to put it more scientifically, in her socialisation into the subject position of a social science researcher.

Well, fuck that. They'd pissed away twenty-three years of socialisation in the second it had taken them to shove the pin under her fingernail.

She called up the genetic profiles of Hope, Hugh and Nick Morrison, and began poking around.

10

May Day

Hope stood in a side street in Finsbury Park clutching one pole of the North Islington Constituency Labour Party banner and ducking into a flurry of apple blossom and snowflakes. With her free hand she held on to the crown of her broad-brimmed straw hat. Her long blue serge skirt kept her legs warm, but her pin-tucked muslin white blouse felt far too thin for the wind, even with a wide green-and-purple satin sash across it. The look for the day was suffragette. Hope had pinned the sash into place with the new retro repro Party badge that had been enclosed in her welcome pack, and criss-crossed it with the strap of her shoulder bag. The red banner, gold-fringed and heroically embroidered, flapped and strained like a sail in the chill breeze. Bloody global warming, Hope thought, wishing she'd complemented the look with gloves.

There were scientists who claimed to have evidence that the

climate was changing under the impact of human activity. They were called deniers. They argued that the New Trees and other engineered organisms were removing carbon dioxide from the atmosphere far too fast, and that this – along with the increasing use of non-fossil-fuel energy sources – risked tipping the planet into a new ice age. Their work appeared only in the unregulated wilds of the internet, beyond the firewalls and filters that kept most discussion relatively sane. But even that was hardly necessary – it was generally taken for granted that the deniers were beholden to the polluting industries of the smokestack states, Russia and India, where denial was policy.

Hope was only sporadically aware of the deniers' existence. In her mind, as in the online world, they inhabited the same spaces as people who posted bomb-making instructions, Naxal agitprop, and child-violation videos. But some days, such as this first day in May, she had the fleeting thought that they might have a point.

The street was one of the narrow residential streets like her own, ribs to the spine of Stroud Green Road, in which tall apple and cherry trees vied with New Trees to half-hide the pinched, overgrown front gardens and the frontages of three- and four-storey houses in which two or three families lived on top of each other. For about a hundred metres the carriageway was crowded by rank upon rank of May Day marchers. Although, now she thought about it, 'marchers' didn't seem too apt a word for the few hundred people here, diversely clustered under union branch, community group and peace campaign and Woodcraft Folk as well as Party banners. The mood, as far as Hope could judge it, was more festive than militant.

Not that militancy had anything to do with the Party. Hope had been to two branch meetings – the date of the first had come up a few days after she'd joined – and had found them somewhat dispiriting affairs. The meetings were held in one of the junior classrooms of the primary school at the other end of East West Road, the very one Nick was due to start attending next September. Hope had found it difficult to take seriously a two-hour-long, procedure-dominated agenda earnestly discussed and minuted by people sitting on bright-painted wooden chairs designed for five-year-olds. It hadn't helped that the third item discussed had been about the importance and urgency of getting the Council to close down the very same open-air back-yard smoking café where she'd talked with Maya. Hope had sat on her hands and kept her mouth shut through that one, and the following morning, after dropping Nick off – as always now, without any trouble – at the nursery, had nipped straight round to warn the shopkeepers of the exact time of the likely visit from Environmental Health.

Apart from that, and Hope's total, gut-level disagreement with assumptions that everyone in the branch seemed to take for granted, Maya had been correct about her fitting right in. The North Islington branch of the Party was run almost entirely by Islington mothers and grandmothers. The only opposition came from the daughters, one of whom was – much to Hope's surprise – one of the young women who'd joined in Maya's flash mob. Her name was Louise and she betrayed no sign of recognising Hope. Her dissent was articulated as a grumble that the Government and the Council were 'doing all right on the green issues, but not so well on the red issues', a comment that Hope felt not at all inclined to ask her to elaborate.

The other person Hope had recognised, to her even greater surprise, and who had recognised her and welcomed her to the room, the branch, the Party and the whole great global movement in one rush and gush, was Deirdre, one of the friends whose unhelpful response to her initial panicked email about the nature-kids thing had been so disheartening. Deirdre was a tall, slim woman with slightly forward-placed teeth, a feature she evidently disliked but which – when she forgot it enough to let her lips open – gave her a bright, pleasant grin, and an enigmatic, questioning look when she smiled with her lips closed. She managed a café – smoke-free of course, but also sugar-free, fat-free, caffeine-free and salt-free – in Seven Sisters Road, just opposite Finsbury Park Station. Her two children, both New Kids and thriving with it, attended the school where the meetings were held. Her husband dropped the kids off and picked them up, made their breakfasts and their dinners, and minded the house with more or less competence, in between co-ordinating from the front room a vast, unending camera-drone operation over Peru, allegedly for some coalition of development and human rights NGOs but (Hope had long suspected) actually wirelessed in to the ongoing counter-insurgency: fingering militants to death squads, targeting air strikes on peasant villages. In short, an ideal Labour family.

At the second meeting, one soggy Wednesday evening in

mid-April just after Hope's first pre-natal check-up, Deirdre had introduced the item on the preparations for May Day, and gone on to explain the issue that the branch and the whole CLP and indeed all of London's Party wanted to highlight, and the importance of the issue itself and the relevance of the suffragette theme, and had wound up by enthusing about how all the women in the branch had pitched into dressing up for it, a detail that had apparently been decided months ago and which had led on Hope's part to an hour of indignant wardrobe rummaging for old maxi skirts and even older fancy blouses, followed by annoyed dusting and repairing and decorating of a much-despised straw sunhat that her mother had bought her on their last shared holiday, in her mid-teens, back when there were holiday flights.

And here came Deirdre now, carrying a 'SAFE WORK FOR WOMEN' placard that was, like all the rest that bobbed above the crowd ('PROTECT WOMEN AND CHILDREN', 'SAFER WORKPLACES FOR ALL'), neatly printed to look as if hand-lettered with a marker pen.

'Great, isn't it?' she said, glancing over her shoulder at the assembling marchers and doing her relaxed grin. 'It's so inspiring.'

'Yes,' said Hope, uninspired.

Deirdre did the closed-lips enigmatic smile.

'Are you warm enough?' she asked. She'd had the sense to wear a jacket, a neatly fitted long-sleeved and short-waisted velvet number in a dark blue that pointed up the white lace jabot at her throat. The whole look suited her a lot better than it did Hope, who felt dumpy in an old skirt that had fitted fine when she was a student but whose waistband opening was now secured by a well-concealed safety-pin halfway down the zip.

'I'll be fine when we start walking,' said Hope.

Deirdre took glasses from her handbag and slipped them on, checking incoming messages. 'Just a few minutes,' she said. 'See you in a bit.'

And with that she bustled off, up towards the front. *Literally* bustled, Hope noticed, as Deirdre trailed her hem up the street. She seemed to be taking the stunt far too seriously. Hope's partner on the other pole of the banner, a stocky red-haired man in his sixties called Fingal, grinned across at her as she turned away from watching Deirdre.

'Very committed, our Deirdre,' he said.

'Yes,' said Hope. 'Just what I was thinking.'

'She can be a bit overbearing sometimes,' Fingal said, out of the side of his mouth. 'But still, can't hold it against her. I remember when the branch could hardly muster enough warm bodies to hold both poles of the banner.'

Hope laughed, just enough not to show too much interest. She didn't know Fingal very well, even for someone she'd seen only twice, sitting at the back of the meetings, precariously tilting his plastic chair, letting one or both of his straggly eyebrows rise as he listened to some point being made. She had a suspicion that at the slightest prompt he would want to talk about old times or, worse, inveigle her into internal branch or Party politics. He had the air of someone on the lookout for kindred spirits.

She was saved from having to answer further by the sound of the brass band at the front striking up.

'Speaking of which . . . ' she said.

Fingal nodded. He and Hope leaned further into the wind and started walking forward.

Hope had never been on a demonstration before, and she'd found the prospect daunting. Hugh had been happy enough to look after Nick for the day – it was a public holiday, after all, and he'd intended to take it as a day off rather than a day's overtime – but had worried about Hope getting into trouble.

'Especially with you . . . ' he'd added, looking pointedly at her belly, which was showing the beginnings of a bump.

'Oh come on,' Hope had said. 'It's not like one of those demonstrations. The Party's the *Government*, for heaven's sake! We're not going to get attacked by the police, now are we?'

Hugh had given her that sullen, doubtful, cynical look that Hope privately thought of as his Lewis face. She'd known exactly how his next sentence would begin.

'As my father always said,' said Hugh, blithely confirming her silent prediction, 'you should never go on a march unless you're ready for a fight.'

'Piffle,' said Hope. 'Leosach whinge.'

'My father's not a Leosach,' said Hugh, in a slow, deliberate way.

'No, but the iron got into his soul. And the rain rusted it!'

Hugh laughed. 'Spoken like a Leosach yourself,' he said. 'All right. But it wasn't from Lewis he got that about the marching. It was from London, when he was young and marched against the war.'

'The war?' Hope asked. 'It hadn't even started then.'

'The war before this one,' Hugh explained.

'Oh!' said Hope. 'Ancient history. Anyway, it's not *that* kind of march. It's May Day. It's a celebration.'

'Hands across the sea,' said Hugh, again with the Lewis face. He scratched the balding patch towards the back of his head. 'Oh well. Take care.'

'Of course I'll take care.'

But he'd left her worried. Her first morning sickness, the following day, hadn't helped.

Now, however, out on the street and into the swing of it, Hope felt quite different. The brisk walk soon warmed her. The flurries of snow ceased. The brass band up at the front was blaring out something martial but bouncy, and a few dozen rows behind her a Jamaican steel band on a truck was playing a different tune and different music altogether, whose rhythm snaked around and intertwined with that of the band.

The local contingent swung around the corner into Stroud Green Road, past helpful police in no riot gear whatsoever, and slotted into a gap in the main march coming down over Crouch Hill. Now they were part of a column of thousands. Hope glanced over her shoulder, and along to the far front of the march, entranced.

'Wow!' she said, impressed despite her doubts. 'There's so *many* of us.'

'That's nothing,' said Fingal. 'Try your glasses.'

Hope opened her shoulder bag awkwardly, one-handed, as the banner pole tilted and recovered, and put the glasses on. Something local and eager pulsed in a corner of the sky. She blinked it up. The shopfronts and shoppers and trees of Stroud Green Road were rendered as a faint, pencil-sketch overlay, through which to her right she could see nothing but crowds all the way to the horizon, with red banners and balloons and long dragon puppets bobbing above their heads: Beijing, earlier in the day. Elsewhere, more or less in front of her, a similarly huge demonstration filled Tehran's Revolution Square. From Mumbai and Calcutta came more recent images, of streets a mass of red flags, a sea whose every shore was pebbled with the black helmets of the police, and fringed with long black sticks beating down relentlessly and rhythmically on every head they could reach. Way off to the left, and almost in real time, a smaller march in Moscow was holding out against the traditional baton charges and tear-gas rounds, red and grey smoke intermingling merrily above the skewed flags and hurled placards. By late afternoon the view would no doubt include the gigantic May Day parades in Washington, Chicago, NYC and LA, but for now the Americans were mostly still abed.

It got dizzying, and Hope took the glasses off and put them away. Despite herself, despite her lack of interest in politics ('but politics is interested in you', some earnest lad at university had once told her, a remark she now recalled with a belated shiver, instead of the dismissive laugh she'd given it at the time) and in what she'd called, to Maya, *all that*, meaning all that justice and equality and progress stuff that the Prime Minister banged on about – despite all that, Hope found herself uplifted and enthused by the feeling, no, the *perception* of being part of something huge, worldwide, hands across not just the sea but across the stormy fronts of the Warm War. Her eyes, too, could sting to the tear gas in Russia; her shoulders could flinch and her feet stumble under the *lathi* slashes in India; and likewise, her feet could skip and dance along with all those enjoying the day in the parts of the world where they were free to celebrate it in peace.

America, Britain, Germany, Iran, China ... she could see, she could literally see why they called the New Society countries the Free World.

On they went, down past the station and around the corner into Seven Sisters Road, and then into the broad open green space of Finsbury Park. Past the small enclosed patch of sand and swings and shelters where the One O'Clock Club had given her such a respite and Nick such fun when he was too young for nursery. Out on to a wide, sloping green, already dotted with stalls and fronted by a stage and sound system. As she and Fingal stopped, two women from the branch who'd walked behind them offered to take the poles.

'Thanks,' said Hope, letting her shoulders slump and arms hang loose. Her biceps ached. She looked at Fingal.

'Well done,' he said. He might have winked. 'Be seeing you.'

He wandered away, but after a few steps into the crowd

struck off in a purposeful stride. Hope looked around. The march, which had filled a main thoroughfare more or less from side to side and from end to end, now looked a small huddle in the wide-open space. Around its edges stood a scatter of stalls, some selling political literature and merch, others snacks and soft drinks. Faint smells of candy floss and veggie burgers drifted and mingled. Stray balloons floated up through the steady drift of apple and cherry petals and soared and sped through the silver sky like UFOs. The park was busy with its predictable public-holiday crowds, couples and kids and families and picnic parties braving the stiff breeze, and few of them paid any attention to the compact mass of the march. The latest hit of some local trash band that had made it big and daringly called itself Urban Heat Island thudded from the sound system. Police and park attendants – it was hard to tell which was which – patrolled the edges of the gathering and now and then, in an apparently random but (Hope did not doubt) algorithmically choreographed pattern, elbowed their way through it, sniffers and other sensors prominently deployed.

Hope headed for the front of the crowd, wending her way between clusters of people around various banners, avoiding eye contact with anyone who offered her leaflet, journal or chip. She arrived just a few rows away from the front of the low stage as the music stopped. The band filed off to loud applause and the dignitaries filed on, to lesser applause. The Mayor and her wife, the chair of Islington Council, a couple of other councillors, a trade union speaker, Deirdre, and Jack Crow, MP. Crow was a wiry man in his thirties who wore a leather peaked cap, a denim jacket, corduroy trousers, black yellow-laced Docs and a pointed ginger beard. He was greeted with louder applause than the band. He waved his thanks and sat down on one of the folding stools on the platform. Hope had a bit of grudge with Jack Crow. He hadn't answered her letter. She ignored him and smiled up at Deirdre, who nodded and smiled back.

The Mayor took the mike, thanked everyone, and hastened to assure them that the speeches would be short. By her standards they probably were, but not by Hope's; after twenty minutes she had resorted to putting her glasses on and catching up with her mail. Nick and Hugh had sent her pictures from Hampstead Heath, where they were flying a kite that Hugh had somehow magicked up from scrap plastic and an old fishing line. Hope found herself shame-facedly jealous and idly curious as to when Hugh had ever been fishing ... he couldn't have been more than, what, fifteen, when the sport was banned?

Deirdre's voice cut across Hope's reverie. She let her attention snap back, and put the glasses away.

'Now, we've all heard what Louella, our sister here from Unite, has been saying,' Deirdre announced, with a sisterly backward wave to the previous speaker, 'and I find it hard really to add anything to what she's so eloquently told us, so I just want to reiterate and emphasise how important this Safe Work for Women campaign is for all of us. More and more women are finding it difficult to work outside the home because of health hazards in the workplace. So we need to ensure that workplaces are safe for women – and that means safe for men, too, as well as safe for children. And if they're safe for children, we could even have workplace crèches! And why not? Our mother's generation had crèches –in a borough like ours, at least. We should build on that and take it forward again.

'But really, the main thing I want to say is that Safe Work for Women won't get passed without legislative action, and no amount of pressure is going to work unless we have MPs who are on our side, and I'm proud to introduce someone who of course needs no introduction, an MP who is and always has been on our side, Jack Crow.'

Everyone clapped, even Hope.

'Thank you, Deirdre,' Crow murmured, then went on in a raised, booming, platform voice: 'Madam Mayor, councillors, brothers and sisters, it's a tremendous privilege for me to speak to this splendid rally, which as you know if you've been checking the news is part of a magnificent mobilisation of tens of millions, all around the world.'

Yeah, yeah, thought Hope. Get on with it.

Get on with it he did. He outlined the Government's and the Council's achievements. He pointed out where the Government had back-slided from election promises, and proclaimed his intent to hold them to their commitments, if not in this parliament, then in the next, where he was sure the Party would have an even stronger majority. (Applause.) Then he leaned forward, clutching the mike and speaking quietly, so that people strained a little, listening.

'But, brothers and sisters, comrades, this is no time for

143

complacency. No time for smug triumphalism. No time for sitting back with our thumbs in our lapels and our feet on the table. The New Society, the free and social market, is under attack as never before. Not a military attack. Not a physical attack. Personally, as you all know, I have never aligned myself with those, even within our movement, whose first and last answer to any international problem is military action. Yes. The Russian imperialists, the Indian chauvinists, the Naxal nihilists – yes, these are all threats, and we all know about them. And we know how our brothers and sisters from Delhi to St Petersburg have been bludgeoned on the streets today, for exercising exactly the same rights as we are now, for celebrating the same May Day as we do here.

'We stand with them. Shoulder to shoulder. But what they need from us is not military threats to their governments. It's our solidarity itself. It's what we're doing here. Standing together. All of us, young and old. Peacefully and freely.

'And in doing that, we are also dealing with the real threat, the serious threat, to all we've fought for. The insidious threat, the threat from within. The Conservative and Liberal Party ...'

Crow paused. The expected roar of laughter came. He waited.

'The Conservative and Liberal Party,' he went on, smiling, 'is not that threat. It merely gives a voice to it. That threat, my friends, is the stupidity, the short-sightedness, the greed of the business class, big and small. Let's hear no nonsense about class conflict. No governments in history have done as much for free enterprise and honest profit as the governments of the United Kingdom and the United States – and, let me say, perhaps controversially, but in all fairness, the People's Republic of China – over the past ten years. We have underwritten risky ventures with trillions in public money. And these ventures have paid off – in clean air, in a safe environment, in abundant energy, in vast, exciting new fields of endeavour, and – I need hardly say – in very healthy profits indeed. All we have asked from business in return is that they pay their taxes and co-operate with the government in its social policies.

'Have they done anything of the sort? No! They've responded to tax reform by working through shell companies in India and Russia. And they fight tooth and nail against every tiny step forward on health and safety and regulation. The sort of opposition that Safe Work for Women faces from these quarters is astonishing, and frankly disappointing. I've even been lobbied myself, by the usual suspects claiming that it'll put people out of work, like the same usual suspects have said about every piece of progressive legislation since the Factories Act and the Ten Hours Bill.

'I need to be able to stand up in the House of Commons and show how this lobbying is outweighed by a deluge of support, and I know I can count on you to deliver that deluge of support, just as you know you can count on me. Thank you.'

Applause. Crow acknowledged it with a smile and a wave, and stepped back. Deirdre said a few closing words. Music, this time recorded, started thumping out. The speakers chatted to each other and began to leave the platform.

Hope made her way to the side of the stage to intercept Jack Crow as he came off the steps.

'Uh, Brother Crow? Could I have a word?'

Crow stopped and moved aside, out of the way of others stepping down, and gave her a friendly but wary smile.

'Yes?'

'Interesting speech,' she said. 'Inspiring.'

'Thanks.' He still looked slightly puzzled. Hope imagined that she must cut a strange figure. She'd meant to ask Crow why he hadn't replied to her letter, but when it came to it, she hesitated. She wasn't sure how quickly MPs were expected to answer letters, and as she was hoping to get some help from him, she was wary of starting off on the wrong foot. Instead she found herself saying the first thing that came into her head – something that had genuinely puzzled her for weeks.

'I've only recently joined the Party,' she said, 'and I'm not too clear on everything, how the ideas fit together, you know?'

Crow laughed. 'Me neither!' he said. 'Don't worry about it. The Party's, you know, a broad church, as the cliché goes. What do you want to know?'

He had his head cocked to one side, beard clasped between thumb and forefinger, elbow clutched in the other hand. A slight frown, barely more than a crinkle around the eyes, made him look like a teacher waiting to hear a question from a precocious child.

'I was just wondering,' Hope said, 'how the Safe Work for Women campaign sort of fits into the "free and social market" you talked about?'

'Ah!' Crow's expression cleared, and brightened. 'That's pretty straightforward. Glad you asked. The free and social market is one of our most successful and useful ideas, one I think the Government has got right. The economics are quite technical, there's stacks of literature debating it – you know what academic economists are like, and if you don't, ha-ha, count yourself lucky – but the basic idea is very simple, really. The neoclassical . . . uh, the standard model of a truly free market assumes that everyone in the market has perfect information. They must know what choices they're making, otherwise it isn't a free and rational choice, right?' He raised a didactic finger, half-smiling in acknowledgement that he was about to forestall a sensible but predictable objection. 'Now *obviously*,' he went on, 'this doesn't *actually* obtain in the real world. Nobody really has perfect information. In fact, even if we make it a bit more realistic, they don't have all or even most of the *relevant* information. So for the market to be really free, it has to work *as if* everyone involved had perfect information, or at least as if they had all the relevant information. This is where the social side comes from – the state, of course along with civil society, the unions and campaigns and so on, steps in to allow people to make the choices *they would have made* if they'd had that information. Because these are the really free choices.'

'Not the ones they actually chose, then?'

'Exactly!' said Crow. 'Because they're not the choices they would have made if they'd known all the facts, which would have been the rational choices, so society helps them to make *those* choices. And that's your free and social market, right?'

'But it doesn't *feel* very free,' Hope said, 'having other people make your choices for you.'

'It feels a lot freer than making the wrong choices,' said Crow. He pinched his lower lip for a moment, thinking. 'Suppose you were a mother, right?'

'Well, I am actually,' said Hope.

'Oh! Great!' He gave her an up-and-down look, and met her eyes again with a wry glance. 'And ... if you don't mind me saying ... with another one on the way, yeah?'

'That's right,' said Hope.

'Congratulations!' Crow beamed. 'Perfect examples, then. When you buy a toy for your little ...'

'Boy,' said Hope.

'... you wouldn't feel you'd made a very free choice if it turned out to be painted with lead paint that could be chewed off, or its head, say, was stuck on with a sharp spike that could injure the child if he pulled it off. Which they do, don't they? Pull the heads off. Mine always did. Or if you were buying milk powder for the baby and it turned out to be contaminated with poison. These things did happen, and not so long ago. Tragic stories. The reason they don't happen any more – well, hardly at all, because something will always slip through – is because the state – here, in China, and so on – makes regulations and employs inspectors to enforce them, and locks up and fines and even expropriates people who break them. Now, you wouldn't feel very free if you had to do all that checking yourself, would you? Or if you couldn't do that because it wasn't practical, and just had to trust to luck, and you could never be sure, you'd

148

always have a nagging doubt, and the effort of putting that doubt out of your mind. Whereas now, you can buy toys and milk and clothes and so on for the kids and feel free from all that worry. Not to mention free from the regret over making the wrong choice.'

Hope felt baffled. 'But lead paint on toys and contamination in food is . . . something like fraud, isn't it? It seems a long way from that to saying that everything needs to be controlled that way. And a long way from saying the government has to make choices for women about where they work.'

'It's the same principle,' said Crow. By now he was beginning to look a little impatient. 'The government isn't making choices for anyone. Like I said, it's *enabling* people to make the choices they would make for themselves if they knew all the consequences of those choices.'

'But . . .'

'I mean, would you want pregnant women to have the "choice"' – he waggle-fingered the quotes – 'to work down coal mines?'

'Well, no,' Hope conceded. 'But working in offices where people once smoked thirty years ago doesn't seem quite so risky.'

'Oh, it isn't,' said Crow. 'But it's still risky. That foul stuff leaks out of the walls and floors for *decades*.'

'Only in tiny amounts,' said Hope.

'Yes!' said Crow. 'That means it's actually riskier than smoking itself, because the amounts are so tiny. I mean, we're talking about *femtograms* per cubic metre. You know how small that is?

It's smaller than a subatomic particle! When you had actual smoke particles in the air, you could at least cough, you had some natural protection – not enough, of course, but some – whereas these nano- and femto-particles can slip right between the molecules and into your lungs and bloodstream. Not to mention your foetus's lungs and bloodstream.'

'Yes, well I do understand that,' said Hope. 'But what I don't get is, this just excludes women from more workplaces.'

'No, it doesn't,' said Crow. 'The law will mandate that employers of women between the ages of blah-blah, et cetera, will have to strip out or cover with sheet diamond any surfaces that—'

'But I work from home,' said Hope. 'Our house is over a hundred years old, and I'm pretty sure somebody must have once smoked in it. Does that mean we're going to have to—'

'Ah!' Enlightenment dawned on Crow's face. '*That*'s what you're worried about. I'm so sorry, I was beginning to wonder if you were some kind of Tory infiltrator!' He laughed. 'No, you needn't worry about that at all. Applying this law to home working would be *going too far*. It's specifically excluded from the draft bill. Here, let me show you . . .'

He reached inside his jacket and pulled out glasses.

'Honestly,' he said, half to himself, 'you'd think the branch would have made a better fist of explaining all this to our own members.'

He slipped the glasses on. Hope could see his eyes blink rapidly. A surprised look came over his face.

'Oh!' he said. '*You're* Hope Morrison!'

'Yes,' said Hope. 'Pleased to meet you, too.'

'Why didn't you say so in the first place?' Crow gave a rueful laugh. 'Mind you, if I'd known . . . you've no idea of the trouble you've caused me. Nearly got yourself into, too.'

'How?' asked Hope, taken aback.

Crow passed a hand across his eyebrows. 'That letter you hand-delivered.'

'What?' Hope had that sick feeling of having done something she hadn't known was wrong, and feeling guilty about it.

'*Nobody* hand-delivers letters. Look, you could have written to me at the Commons, written to my office, heck, you could have posted the letter to the house. If you'd looked me up, you would have seen how to book an appointment – there's even my personal phone number.' He tapped the earpiece of his glasses. 'You'd have got a message, but I'd have got back to you. But hand-delivering a letter without a stamp . . . we have to treat that as a terrorist attempt. Like the anthrax letters, way back before you or I were born. Standing regulation – I had to call the police, and they had to scan it and analyse it. Wasted a good couple of hours.'

'Surely a bit of common sense . . .'

'Out of my hands,' said Crow. 'It's the rules. It's the law, come to that. I admit it's a nuisance, but still . . .'

'It makes you feel free, does it?' Hope asked, tartly.

Crow grimaced. 'Well, again . . . freer than being blown up or poisoned. Anyway . . . I have to admit I was a bit annoyed. I'm afraid that's why I haven't got around to replying.'

'Don't worry about that,' Hope said. 'But now that we're here, maybe you could tell me what you think.'

'About your problem?'

'Yes.'

'Well ...' Crow took a deep breath, then let his shoulders slump. 'I don't agree with your stance, as I understand it, but I can certainly help you with practical matters – finding legal advice, dealing with the Health Centre, that sort of thing.'

'I'd be very grateful for that,' said Hope. 'But I was kind of hoping you could, I don't know, raise the matter in the House, or something? Because all it would take would be a tiny little tweak to the law, just to make a conscientious objection something that doesn't need to be justified in terms of belief.'

'Can't help you there, I'm afraid,' Crow said. 'Personally, I think the exemptions go far too far as it is. And we can't be seen to pass a law just to get around a judge's ruling; it'd be interpreted as interference with the independence of the judiciary and the family courts. It would take a complete redraft of the relevant section of the Act, and to be honest, there's not the slightest chance of any parliamentary time being allotted for that.'

'You could put down an Early Day Motion,' Hope persisted. 'It wouldn't have to be a law or anything, just ... an expression of the sense of the House, isn't that what it's called?'

Crow took a step back, frowning. 'You seem to have this worked out.'

'I've been reading up on parliamentary procedure.'

'Admirable,' said Crow, still frowning. 'So I'm sure you understand the practicalities. There's no chance of anything getting through before – to be blunt – the matter becomes moot as far as you're concerned, and in any case, quite frankly, as I said I don't agree with your objection, and I have a great deal on my plate as it is. So, practical help, as your MP, yes, of course, but otherwise, sorry, no.'

'Why don't you agree with it?' Hope demanded. She rapped a thumbnail on her badge. 'Doesn't "Liberty" on that mean anything?'

'Yes, it does,' said Crow. 'As I've been trying to explain. *Genuine* liberty, based on informed choice.'

'What about *my* choice?'

'If you want *that* sort of choice,' said Crow, sounding as if he'd lost patience, 'you can go to Russia.'

Hope stared at him, open-mouthed. 'That's totally uncalled for!'

'I'm not sure it is,' said Crow, frowning again and blinking rapidly. 'If you look at the sources of a lot of this sort of so-called libertarian rhetoric, you'll often find a stack of Russian money behind it. Not to mention Naxal ideological diversionary operations.'

'Naxal?' Hope cried, in such a dismayed tone that nearby heads turned.

Crow nodded, then took his glasses off and put them away, with a sudden self-satisfied smile. 'In any case, I have to go. Do please contact my office for any help we can give you.'

Then, taking her by surprise, he shook her hand, smiled artificially, nodded vigorously, and turned away. He'd disappeared into the crowd, nodding and chatting and glad-handing, before she could gather her wits.

So much for that. Unexpectedly hungry for a snack, Hope wandered over to the stalls. She bought a sugar-free spun-sugar-like confection and chomped into it as she drifted down the line. At one stall she found Fingal, the guy she'd carried the banner with, in earnest conversation with Louise, the young woman who'd joined the flash mob to support her.

'This is completely *insane*,' Louise was saying. 'There's no way the unions have enough power to pressurise employers to take on women rather than just declare their workplaces unsafe, so all we're doing is just pushing women further back into the home or into small-business employment, where they don't have any union representation at all!'

'It's a question of the balance of forces, innit?' Fingal explained.

Yeah, thought Hope, you could say that.

Louise leaned forward to reply. Hope couldn't catch her words, but from her tone it was clear she was giving Fingal a piece of her mind, giving as good as she got. Hope hadn't the heart to get involved in the discussion. The candy floss suddenly tasted like paper. She tossed it in a bin, sucked her fingers and licked around her lips, careless of how unladylike this looked, and stomped off home.

11

Another Light

On the second of May, Geena walked to Hayes for the first time since her interrogation. For weeks now she'd been taking the bus, to and from work. She hadn't been able to face walking the same roads. But today the weather had cleared and she was feeling better for the day off, though she wasn't entirely sure why. She hadn't spent it well.

Her boyfriend Liam had worked the Bank Holiday, leaving Geena in bed. She'd dutifully trudged to the window, waved, and then retreated under the duvet. She huddled there for half the morning, dozing, until she'd really had to pee, and that was what had finally propelled her out of bed. In the bathroom she'd been overcome with weeping, and showered away most of the evidence, applying make-up to the rest. She'd then spent the best part of the day moping around the flat and shutter-shopping in Uxbridge High Street, feeling like a zombie drawn inexorably and inexplicably to a closed mall in an old movie.

It began as another routine day in the dry lab, except that Brian made them all laugh by reading out what the *Daily Mail* thought of the previous day's demos: the huge loss to the economy, the waste of police time, the outrageous misuse of public money and resources for party-political propaganda, and the shocking demagogy of what some MPs and even ministers had proclaimed from shaky platforms.

Geena duly added this to her notes – it was one of the few scraps of directly political comment she'd observed here – wrote a little more of her thesis draft, and turned to her slow, painstaking investigation of the Morrison family's genomes. There was plenty of software for running comparisons, but all of it assumed you knew what was significant, and Geena didn't. Apart from some of the more common disease-linked loci, she had to look up everything as she went along. Right now she was looking at the RHO gene on chromosome 3, where Hugh Morrison and his son Nick shared a small mutation, and she had no idea of its significance. Her searches weren't turning up anything: evidently it hadn't been investigated or documented. This was in itself odd, in that rhodopsin mutations were associated with a number of well-known pathologies of the retina.

The medical records for the man and his son showed no problems with vision. Geena felt a small surge of excitement. This might be something new, or at least unusual. Maybe now would be the time to ask one of the guys to run her a predictive sim of the gene's functioning. The easiest to approach, and the one least likely to ask questions, would be Joe Goonwardeene, the shy Sri Lankan. He was working on his own at the moment, not elbow-deep in the VR rig at the table.

At that point Geena's eyes brimmed with tears. She turned away into the corner, dabbing with a tissue. She felt desperately guilty about Joe. Nearly as guilty as she felt about Maya, and she was going to have to face that soon. She should have faced it ages ago, the very first day, just as she had with Ahmed. But it was different with Ahmed. He was a man of the world. A made man. Ahmed could take it. He had resources. He had connections. He had nothing to worry about.

She took a deep breath, saved her work, stood up, grabbed her jacket and walked over to Joe. She cleared her throat. Joe lowered his glasses, flexed his hands and peered at her over the top rims.

'Yes?'

'Uh, Joe, could you possibly . . . take a break for a few minutes? There's something I'd like to ask you about and I don't want to disturb the others.'

Joe glanced at Brian, who hadn't been too absorbed to notice. Brian nodded to him, and gave Geena a sly, questioning glance.

'Just some background stuff,' Geena said. She shrugged one shoulder. 'Maybe a bit personal. We can go outside.'

Brian waved. 'Go, go.'

Outside, on Dawley Road, Geena struck out to the right, towards the bridge over the railway. The usual traffic mumbled past. The pavement was dusty as usual, scuffed, and, most importantly, deserted. Apart from the old man sitting in a deckchair in the tiny front garden of one of the row of houses, who glared across the road at them as if their footsteps disturbed his peace. Geena had seen him do this before. He wasn't sunbathing. He was waiting for the aliens. So the rumour went.

'Well, Geena,' said Joe after a silence of fifty yards, 'what is it?'

Geena glanced at him sideways. Eye to eye, a rare thing for her.

'Uh, Joe,' she said, 'I have a confession to make. A few weeks ago I was stopped by the police and, uh, questioned.'

Joe looked straight ahead. 'You named me.'

'I'm afraid I did,' Geena admitted.

'What did you say?'

'The first thing that came into my head, of course. You can guess.'

'Tamil Tigers?'

'That's the one,' Geena said.

Joe's light laughter pealed.

'You have no imagination, Geena. Neither have I.'

'What do you mean?'

'I have confessed the same myself,' said Joe. 'Several times. It seems to satisfy them.'

They walked up the curving slope to the bridge over the railway and looked down for a while at the tracks.

'Hmm,' said Geena. 'Well, I wanted to say I'm sorry, that's all.'

'Think nothing of it,' said Joe. Another sideways glance.

'Was there something else? I notice you seem to be doing some ... technical work.'

'Well, yes actually,' said Geena. 'I would like you to run a predictive sim on a gene. Unofficially, of course.'

'Tomorrow morning,' said Joe. 'About six – would that suit you?'

It wouldn't suit Geena at all, but she supposed she'd better agree.

'Perfect!' she said. 'Brilliant! Thank you so much!'

They walked back to the works entrance. At the gate, Geena hesitated.

'Tell the guys I'm taking the rest of the day off,' she said. 'Library work, you know?'

'Very good,' said Joe. 'Study is vital!' He said it so enthusiastically that she half-expected him to repeat it as a shout, with his fist clenched to the sky.

'Thanks,' she said, with a wan smile. 'See you tomorrow, then.'

'Six sharp,' said Joe.

'I'll be there,' said Geena. 'See you then.'

She turned around and walked quickly away, down the long canyon of Blyth Road to the high street.

'You've left this a bit *late*,' said Maya, when Geena had finished.

'I know, I know!' Geena cried, almost sobbing. 'I'm so sorry, Maya.'

Maya, on the other side of her desk in a tiny office in the

159

Advice Centre that smelled faintly and (to Geena) foully of illicit smokes, looked at her with sympathetic puzzlement.

'But it's all right,' she said. 'It's not *too* late. We're not talking statute of limitations here. You turned down the trauma counselling, OK, not good, and you signed the chit, but we can wangle a way round that. Lemme think about this for a minute ...'

She gazed off into the distance and drummed her fingers on the desk, as if typing – which, for all Geena knew, she was.

'What?' said Geena.

Maya gave her a look. 'You want me to put in a complaint, yes?'

'Oh no!' said Geena. 'No, no. I don't want any fuss.'

Maya's smooth brow creased. 'So why are you telling me all this?'

'You're not upset?'

'I'm upset for you, all right,' said Maya. 'Good grief, it sounds horrible.'

'No, I meant upset with me.'

'What for?'

'Maya, I *betrayed* you. I'm so, so sorry.'

Maya's expression changed. She jumped up, came around the desk and hugged Geena.

'Oh, you silly girl,' she said.

She stepped back and sat on the edge of the desk.

'Look, Geena,' she said. 'These guys you rushed past in the waiting room, yeah? The ones skulking around the side of the building for a smoke, too? Half the fuckers have shopped me for something. Terrorist sympathies? Hah! They've fingered me for a lot worse than that. Drug dealing. Corruption. Running prostitution rings. Molesting their children. *Plausible* stuff, you know? Then they come crying to me. "Oooh, Miss Maya, I do terrible thing, how can you for*give* me?"'

Maya's derisive mimicry shocked Geena almost as much as what she was saying.

'Half?' she said, struggling to keep up.

Maya waved a languid hand, like a classic film actress trailing a digitally deleted cigarette.

'I exaggerate, dahling. Call it ten per cent.' Her shoulders slumped. 'Fuck. I'm sorry. I shouldn't make fun of it. I'm *not* making fun of it. It's just ... oh, fuck.'

And then she was sliding down and forward, and it was Geena's shoulder being cried on.

'So what happens to you?' Geena asked, after Maya had shaken herself away and blown her nose and sat back down.

'Oh, nothing,' said Maya. She looked at the damp tissue clutched in her hand, threw it in a bin, rolled her wrist under her nose, and sniffed. 'Of course the police don't take all these accusations seriously. They aren't even admissible as a basis for starting an investigation, unless something else corroborates them, let alone for pressing charges.'

'So why ...?' Geena took a deep breath. 'Forget that, I already know why they do it. They don't care what you confess, they don't care what you think, they want you to *know* they can *make* you confess. So ... what happens when you put in complaints?'

Maya shrugged. 'Most of my clients don't want me to. Sad but true. And not much comes of it when they do. An apology and token compensation. Well, it's token for the authorities; to some of these guys a few hundred quid can be life-changing, which is why I always urge them to do it. But most of them are too ashamed and too worried about making more trouble for themselves.'

'But we shouldn't be putting up with this!' Geena said. 'I mean, I had no idea. If it's as common as all that, good God, it shouldn't be just a matter of putting in complaints. There should be some kind of political campaign against it.'

'There is,' Maya pointed out. 'Several, in fact. Amnesty, Liberty, there's even groups inside both parties against torture. Nobody cares. It's like the war. It's one of those things everyone understands you can do nothing about. Come to think of it, it's part of the war. Security. Like computer security, you know? It just runs in the background.'

Geena laughed at the analogy, then frowned.

'I'm not so sure security's part of the war,' she said. 'I'm beginning to suspect the war is part of *it*. That's how my supervisor sees it, anyway.'

'Oh, yeah, Dr Estraguel. Heard him going on about it in lectures at Brunel. Imperialism and reaction and all that. Bloody Marxist rubbish.'

Geena hesitated. 'It's a bit more complicated than that,' she said at l: st. 'Uh, actually it's got me thinking about how we can help Hope Morrison.'

162

'We?' Maya teased. 'Well I'm not sure I have helped her much, but I'm glad you think there's something we can—'

She was interrupted by a hesitant knock on the door.

'Five minutes!' she yelled. She turned back to Geena. 'Well, better make it quick.'

'I got the idea that there might be something in their genes that the fix would change but might actually be, you know, quite good to have. I mean, I know most mutations are deleterious, but there's always a chance, and I've found one that looks sort of interesting and I was wondering if that might be a good reason she could give not to have the fix. Is there something like that in the law?'

Maya sucked in her lower lip and slowly rolled it out again. 'Hmm,' she said. 'Very naughty of you. But very interesting. I hadn't thought of that. Because in the original legislation, it wasn't supposed to be compulsory, so it wouldn't be framed as an exemption, any more than all the conscience-clause stuff was. All of that was ostensibly put in as cover for doctors, so they couldn't get sued later if the parent had refused the fix for such-and-such a reason. It would be put in as a good medical reason not to prescribe.' She reached behind her and retrieved her glasses from the desk. 'Let me just check.'

She waved her arms as if pulling down a rope.

'Ah!' she said, after a few minutes. 'I think I've found just the thing.'

The sky was brightening in the east as Geena set off from Uxbridge, leaving Liam for once to sleep later than her, and the sun was well up over the factories and office towers of the blocky Hayes horizon and melting the overnight frost when she arrived at SynBioTech just before six. No one was about. Her glasses – on for the code, off for the retinal scan – got her into the building, the lift and the lab. Joe arrived just as she had the coffee going.

'Good morning, Geena.' He looked around, grinning. 'It feels funny having the place to ourselves, eh?'

'Yes,' she said. 'Coffee?'

'Oh, very welcome indeed,' said Joe. He took his mug to the central table. 'Now, what was it you wanted to check?'

Geena put on her glasses and sat down beside him.

'A mutation in RHO. Undocumented, but no apparent dele-terious effects in, uh, the phenotypes.'

He shot her a look under his black brows.

'I won't ask how you know about the phenotypes.'

'Wise move,' said Geena. 'Better you don't know.'

Joe laughed. 'We both know that doesn't matter ... Very well, patch it across.'

Geena waved hands and waggled fingers and blinked. The seaweed tangle of the virtual gene popped into existence above the table. Joe reached forward and rolled it around, this way and that.

'OK,' he said. 'That's the mutation locus. Now let's see what protein it codes for.'

Molecules of RNA did their thing, and the cascade began. Geena had seen this many times, but she was still struck by how mechanical it all was, at least in this representation, a matter of this fitting into that and bumping off the other. The protein formed.

'Now the predictive sim,' said Joe.

The scale changed, from molecular to structural. A sheet of crystalline opsin rippled into view, snapped into stability. Virtual wave-packets flashed down to it like sprites. Electrons – not to scale – spun off and squirmed through the molecules. A number array, incomprehensible to Geena, built up like a spreadsheet.

Joe leaned back and looked at it for a long time.

'What?' said Geena.

'Interesting,' said Joe. 'It's responsive to wavelengths outside the visible spectrum. It's like ... No!' He laughed to himself. 'It's too silly.'

'What?' Geena said again.

'Last year we worked on UV sensors. Built them up from insect visual-pigment analogues.' He turned to her, with an upraised finger and intent frown. 'Did you know, Geena, that there are species of insect whose eyes are most responsive to wavelengths that are not present in the spectrum of the Sun? It's like they are adapted to life under another star.'

12

Ticking Boxes

Two weeks into May, three months into her pregnancy, Hope had her second pre-natal check-up. The appointment was at 10.30. She worked the hour after dropping Nick off – still without problems at the gate – and left the flat at ten. Though still chilly, the weather had improved since the beginning of May. No more flurries of snow. A bit of sun. She walked briskly up Stroud Green Road. The clinic was a two-storey redbrick building in a side street off Crouch Hill, overlooking the railway line. Hope went through the biometric scan at the door and into a reception area with the obligatory decor of plastic stackable chairs, beige walls tacked with children's drawings and plaintive advice posters designed to look like children's drawings, and a faint pine-and-lemon smell of disinfectant. She checked in at the desk and sat down by a table stacked with tattered glossy hard copy, which she turned over and flipped through one by one. She'd read more recent issues of all the magazines that interested her on her glasses, but it appeared to be the expected thing to do, and doing the expected thing seemed important in her situation. She wondered how many of the six other women waiting were doing it for the same reason. A big poster on the wall forbade, for privacy reasons, the use of glasses or hand-helds in the waiting room.

Her previous check-up had passed without incident, other than the doctor's pointed, pained look at the gap in her monitor-ring record where she'd taken it off in the open-air café. Dr Sheila Garnett had scanned and sampled and nodded and smiled and encouraged. No doubt she was aware of the sex of the foetus, but Hope knew better than to ask: that information was embargoed until it would be too late to have a legal abortion. But everything else Dr Garnett was happy to share. The foetus was normal and the pregnancy was going fine. The only mention of the fix had been that now might be a good time to take it.

'Mrs Morrison to see Dr Garnett.'

Hope looked up, flashed a quick smile at the other mums-to-be and headed off down the corridor. Dr Garnett's office was small, with just about enough room for a desk, a couple of office chairs, the scanning equipment and the examination bed. And for Dr Garnett herself, a tall woman with ginger hair and a Canadian accent. She unfolded herself from her chair, loomed, and shook hands.

'Hi, Hope. Good to see you. Feeling OK?'

'Fine, thanks.' Hope shrugged. 'The morning sickness seems to be a bit less frequent.'

Garnett smiled complicitly and sat down.

'Your monitor ring, please.'

Hope slid it off and passed it over. Garnett placed it on her hand-held and scrolled the readout, which gave a more detailed account than the automatic log the device transmitted.

'All looks fine,' she said. 'And you've been keeping it on all the time.' She handed back the ring, with a half-smile and raised eyebrows. 'Let's keep that up, shall we?'

Hope nodded.

'No need for a scan this time,' Garnett said. She tapped at the screen a few times, ticking boxes. 'Just one more thing, Hope.'

'Yes?' Hope knew what was coming.

'I see you haven't taken the fix yet. Time's getting on, you know.'

'If you look at Fiona's – Mrs Donnelly, the health visitor's – report, you'll see what I have to say about that.'

'I have looked, of course,' Garnett said, frowning down at her screen. 'It's all here.' She looked up. 'I was rather hoping you'd changed your mind.'

Hope shook her head.

'Well,' said Garnett, 'that puts me in rather an awkward position, I'm afraid. If I sign off this visit without an agreement with you about the fix – just an agreement in principle, just ticking the box *saying* you've agreed; you don't have to do it right away – the report gets copied to Social Services, automatically.

168

And just as automatically, you become a *case*. Now, I know you're willing to take that consequence, and I see that Fiona's gone through everything with you, all those options you've refused to take. I won't go through it all again. But ... '

She leaned forward and reached out open hands, pleading. 'This time I'm asking you for my sake, I'll be quite honest about it. If this goes through as it stands, without that one little tick, my insurance premiums go up because of the added risk to the foetus, and I can say goodbye to my quarterly bonus. Apart from this, you know, my record's perfect. Would you really want to spoil that for me?'

'Why should your premiums go up,' Hope demanded, cutting across the appeal, 'when your own scans and so on show the baby – the foetus – is completely healthy anyway?'

'Come now,' said Garnett, 'you know that's not how insurance works. It's all about probabilities. And then there's the absolute certainty of legal issues arising – that all goes on my insurance too. This principle of yours, whatever it is, is really going to cost me, Hope. I'm asking you to consider that. Please.'

Hope suddenly felt utterly weary about the whole thing. She couldn't articulate her objection even to herself, let alone anyone else. Hugh supported her but didn't agree with her. Her MP had nothing to offer but sympathy mingled with suspicion. The Labour Party certainly wasn't going to help her. The argument was dying down on ParentsNet. The only victory she'd had was the ending of the school-gate harassment, with the help of Maya's flash mob. That would be no help with the problem inside the gate, once the insurance issues kicked in.

'All right,' she said. 'All right. Put me down as agreeing. Tick your box and be done with it.'

'Thanks so much, Hope,' said Garnett.

In the moments when Hope had considered giving up, she'd imagined that at least this moment would be one of relief. She didn't feel relieved at all.

Back at the flat, Hope tied on an apron, made herself a coffee and sat down at the kitchen table to think. She still felt defeated and down. Her choices, given that she wanted to continue the pregnancy – and she did, oh how she did! – remained what they'd always been: to take the fix; to feign some faith position that would give her a conscience exemption; or to continue to refuse. The last of these would mean escalating pressure, all the way up to having some court order slapped on her and being finally, physically, forced to take the fix. The second was beneath her dignity, and if she tried it Hugh would throw a fit.

That left the first. The fix. It wasn't so bad. If the foetus was as healthy as all the evidence showed, the fix wouldn't even *do* very much. It would, on the other hand, do a lot for her. Just swallow one little tablet, and her troubles would be over. She winced at that way of putting it to herself. She was still thinking of it like a suicide. And so it would be; it would be killing something of herself. But what? Was it even an admirable part? She had no colours nailed to her mast, no principle to betray. Just this wordless objection. What if it was just spite? Just stubbornness? That was certainly what everyone else thought. Probably Hugh, too, loyal though he was. And Nick wouldn't thank her for the disruptions in all their lives if she fought this thing to a finish – a finish that would, in any case, be just the same as if she hadn't fought it all.

Ah, the hell with it, she thought.

She jumped up, suddenly decisive, and strode through the kitchen door to the hallway. She opened the cupboard, switched on the dim energy-saving bulb, kicked aside boots and toys and gloves on the floor, stood on tiptoe and reached up to the shelf. Her groping fingers connected with nothing. Damn. The carton containing the fix was still right at the back, where she'd flicked it. What a surprise. She sighed, fetched a chair from the kitchen, and set it down carefully in the cupboard. After giving the chair a preliminary shake to make sure it didn't wobble, she stepped up. Now she could see the top of the shelf. The little yellow-and-white carton was indeed at the back. Right next to it was a frayed brown cardboard box, a bit bigger than a shoebox, whose top she couldn't see over. She reached for the smaller carton, blew dust off it, and stuck it in her apron pocket.

She wondered what was in the other box. She didn't remember leaving it there, but that didn't mean she hadn't. Probably an empty box that some gadget or toy had come in and that she'd tossed up there with the vague idea that it might come in handy to return or pack whatever the object had been. She hooked a finger over its rim and gave it a tentative, experimental tug. The box barely moved. Inside it, something clinked against something else.

Not empty, then. What could she have left up there? It annoyed her that she'd forgotten. That wasn't something she usually did. Well aware that she was indulging in displacement activity to delay the inevitable, irreversible moment of swallowing the fix, she grasped the cardboard more firmly and pulled. The box slid across the shelf, with more rattling and clinking, and a friction suggesting a weight of two or three kilograms. She drew it off the shelf, on to an upturned palm, and stepped backward off the chair. Now on secure ground, she lowered the box with both hands and looked inside.

A 70cl bottle of Glenmorangie, the lid's seal unbroken. A battered cardboard box a few centimetres square. And a large metallic-looking automatic pistol.

She almost dropped the box. Hands shaking a little, she laid it down on the seat of the chair and stared at its contents. She closed her eyes for a moment and shook her head. When she opened her eyes, the gun was still there. She'd never been this close to a gun. Apart from on the hips of police and other officials, and in the hands of soldiers, she'd never seen a firearm in real life at all. She picked up the small cardboard box and prised open its furred and ragged flip-lid. Inside were lots of small lead pellets, rounded at one end, flared at the other. Air-pistol ammo. That was a small relief. Technically the pistol wasn't a firearm, but by legal definition it was. Its relative lack of lethality didn't make it any less illegal, or any less of a shock to find in her house.

Hugh had never shown the smallest interest in guns, other

than the odd passing mention of how common shotguns and rifles were on the long island, where – for anyone other than a licensed game warden – they were just as illegal as here. But it must have been Hugh who'd hidden away the box. For a moment Hope considered another explanation: that it had been left by the flat's previous owner. But – quite apart from the likelihood of its being discovered in the process of moving out and moving in – whoever had left the gun had also left the whisky, and that didn't ring true at all. The single malt had probably cost a hundred pounds. Nobody would willingly abandon, or easily forget, something like that. And Glenmorangie was Hugh's favourite whisky, though he could seldom afford the indulgence. It had taken him about a year to get through one bottle, before Hope had become pregnant with Nick. She wasn't bothered that he had another bottle stashed away. He might even be keeping it to wet the baby's head.

But what *the hell* did Hugh think he was doing stashing an illegal weapon in the house? Hope found herself looking over her shoulder. From where she stood, just inside the cupboard, she couldn't see any cameras. She leaned backwards and looked up and down the hallway. She could see one lens above the front door and one at the opposite end, above the doorway to the kitchen. None at the sides.

She replaced the ammunition box and picked up the pistol. It was heavier than she'd expected. Though she knew rationally that it couldn't explode, she handled it as if it were a ticking bomb. Angling it so that she could see the muzzle without pointing it at herself – she knew that much – she saw that the actual small air-pistol muzzle was set a centimetre or so back inside the barrel, presumably to make the replica more convincing. She placed the pistol back in the box, took the whisky bottle out and placed it on the floor, then climbed up and put the box back where she'd found it.

She took the whisky bottle through to the kitchen and set it on the table beside her glasses. After gazing at it for some time, she picked it up, shoved it to the back of a kitchen cupboard, put on her glasses and got back to work. It was only when she took her apron off at 3.20 to go and pick Nick up that she noticed again the yellow-and-white carton in the pocket, and realised that she'd put it completely out of her mind. She couldn't understand quite why, but this made her feel happy. She stuck it in her jeans pocket and went out.

About nine that evening, after Nick had finally fallen asleep, Hope sat beside Hugh on the sofa in the living room and turned over the pages of one of her art books. Hugh was watching the television – like her, he preferred the implied sharing of the screen to glasses, even if they weren't both watching, and even if, as now, the sound was going to the ears of only one of them. A BBC Horizon programme: the latest pictures of the latest Earth-like extrasolar planet to be imaged, the fourth with visible signs of life. For Hope the fascination of this had worn off since the global excitement over the first, though every so often she'd find herself pulled up short by the thought of life lit by the rays of another star. The strangeness of it, the sense of plurality, of possibility, of decentring . . . she imagined that this was how it must have felt for the first generation after Copernicus. Of course by now the clamour was for signs of *intelligent* life. There was even, in the tones of some of the regular news anchors and commentators and columnists, and for that matter people in the queue at Tesco, a feeling that the astronomers had somehow let everyone down by not having spotted the lights of cities and the jets of starships: they promised us little green men, and all they have to show us is little green patches!

Hope had no longing to meet aliens. She had a dark suspicion that it would not be a welcome encounter. But now and then, when the thought drifted through her mind like the clouds did in scenes from the space telescopes, she found an odd consolation in the now-certain knowledge that, altogether elsewhere, life, of whatever kind, went on.

She closed the book and walked quietly into the kitchen. She returned bearing a tray with the bottle of Glenmorangie, a small jug of tap water, and two heavy glasses. She set the tray down on the long low table in front of the sofa, and sat back, looking at the screen. White whorls swirled above jigsaw-piece shapes, some blue and some of other colours, pixels of vermilion and verdigris. A Chinese woman in a white coat talked. An American man with white hair gesticulated. A classroom full of black-haired students nodded and made a note. Back to the planet, this time a view of the night side, sharper in focus but more enigmatic in interpretation. The saccade of Hugh's gaze suddenly snagged on the bottle. He sat upright and flicked at his ears, turning the sound off.

'What's that for?' he said.

'That's what I was going to ask you,' Hope said.

She reached for the whisky bottle and picked with her thumbnail at the notch in the dotted double line of the seal. Slowly she peeled the strip of soft heavy metal away, and then pulled off the entire seal.

'Nasty stuff,' she said, looking at the shard of painted alloy. 'You could cut yourself. Surely it's not made of lead?' She folded it into a tiny parcel and dropped it on the tray. 'You know, like bullets? Or airgun pellets?'

Hugh's face reddened.

'Speaking of bullets,' Hope went on, 'I've always thought this looked like one.'

She set the bottle back on the tray and tugged from her side pocket the carton containing the fix, opened it and tapped out the plastic and foil bubble. She turned it this way and that, letting the dull glint catch Hugh's eye. 'The fix. A magic bullet.'

She tossed it and the flowery-lettered carton on to the tray, then wiggled her monitor ring off her finger and dropped it there too. It bounced and rang to a stop. She picked up the bottle again and twisted the cork, easing it out.

'Something to wash it down,' she said. She placed the open bottle and the cork on the table.

'Now wait a minute,' said Hugh.

Hope sat back. 'I'm waiting,' she said. 'You know where I

found that bottle, and what I found it with. I'm waiting for an explanation.'

'Oh fuck,' said Hugh. He shifted on the sofa, leaning back into the corner. 'I didn't mean for you to find that.'

'I appreciate that,' said Hope. 'In both senses of the word, you know?'

Hugh gave her an aw-shucks grin and open-handed shrug. 'I feel very protective towards you and Nick,' he said.

'That's not why,' she said. 'Or it would be in a more convenient place. Like under the bed.'

'It has to be somewhere the boy can't reach.'

'You still haven't said why.'

Hugh licked his lips. 'My father gave it to me, when I was thirteen or so.'

'You could have left it with him,' she said. 'Come on.'

'Well, you know how it is.'

'No, I fucking don't know how it is!' She put her hand across her mouth, with the vague idea that no one who looked at the camera recording could use it to lip-read. 'It's illegal! You could get us both arrested!'

Hugh shifted again on the couch. He sighed and stretched out a hand to the whisky bottle, and looked at her.

'Do you mind?' he said.

'Go right ahead,' said Hope, with a flourish of her hand like a waiter showing someone to a table. 'I was thinking of having a dram myself.'

His hand jerked back. 'No, sorry.'

'Only joking,' said Hope. 'Have a dram. I don't mind.'

Hugh poured himself a costly measure and added a splash of water. He leaned forward, hand wrapped around the glass. He took a sip and closed his eyes, inhaling.

'Ah, that's good,' he said.

'Don't rub it in,' said Hope.

Hugh scratched the back of his head. 'All right. Think of it as medicinal. Or as a truth drug.'

'OK,' said Hope, leaning back with her arms folded. 'Talk.'

'All right,' said Hugh. 'Um, why. Well.' He took a longer sip. 'I thought I might need it, some day, if ...' He twisted his lower lip against the edges of his upper teeth. Sniffed. 'There's something I have to tell you.'

Oh fuck, thought Hope, fearing the worst and unable to imagine what it could be.

When he finally got it out, and when she finally understood what he was getting at, it was such a relief that she had trouble not laughing.

'You thought ... you might find yourself ... in the *past?*'

'Yes,' said Hugh, nodding vigorously. 'Or that someone might come for me, out of the past, and ... you know, I might need some ...'

His voice trailed off, as if he found what he was saying ridiculous.

Hope closed her eyes. 'Oh, Jesus.' She opened them again. 'But you said yourself, it's just sight.'

'No,' said Hugh, his voice heavy. 'Some of it is, the people.

But no – it's smell too. And that land I saw, I felt I could have climbed through to it. I felt the wind on my face. I could smell the smoke. And I heard the footsteps behind me.'

Hope felt the tiny hairs on her cheeks and the back of her neck prickle.

'Smells and sounds can be hallucinations too,' she pointed out.

'I know that! Don't I know that! But I'm telling you, that was what made it seem more real. I was terrified. I had nightmares. That's why I asked my dad for the . . . for the thing.'

'And you're telling me you *still* have that fear you had then?'

'Not exactly,' said Hugh. 'It's just that . . . it's like superstition. Like you might come to think of something as lucky, because it seemed to work once or twice, and, you know, better safe than sorry. So I keep it like a . . . a talisman. And anyway, like I said, I still see them sometimes. The barbarians. And hear and smell them, for that matter.'

'But they've never threatened you at all?'

'Just that one in the culvert. He . . . I suppose it was he . . . really did seem to be coming after me.'

'But apart from that?'

Hugh shook his head. 'No, no, never.' He smiled, as if clouds had broken for a moment. 'And the first was Voxy, and she seemed to grow into you.'

'Yes, you told me that, thank you,' Hope said, with some asperity. She hadn't felt exactly flattered by his account of how he'd fallen for her. It was as if she had fitted a previous fantasy image. As quickly as the thought recurred, a more reassuring interpretation occurred to her, and it cheered her up immensely. All of a sudden things made sense again.

'But I think I understand,' she went on. 'Let's leave aside your second-sight theory, OK? I don't know anything about that, and it doesn't seem likely to me. Look at what we get if we assume it's all psychological, it's all in your head.' Hugh looked poised to interrupt. She raised a hand. 'No, wait, hear me out. Lots of people, far more people than ever admit it, see people who aren't there. It's quite common in kids. Take your case. You start off with an imaginary friend, OK? And then you become embarrassed by her, and she disappears. As you get older, you see others, but just when you're at or near puberty and feeling all sorts of stresses you don't understand and can't process, you have a really quite disturbing and scary vision, hallucination, whatever. You start having nightmares. So you ask your dad for something that reassures you, that you feel keeps the bad thing at bay. And it does. After that ... right up to now, right up to your most recent encounter, sort of thing, the visions become much more benign. The one you saw when you met me, it was a kind of blessing on us, wasn't it? It was saying I was the ideal girl for you, an ideal you'd begun to form when you were quite small – just becoming aware of the difference between boys and girls, and how that had something to do with how your parents loved each other, and at the same time you were just a little bit ashamed of the warm and tender feelings you had towards these, yuck, *girls* – and that grew with you. You see?'

'I'm not sure I do,' said Hugh.

'These visions you have aren't something bad. They aren't

something to be ashamed of. They're one part of your brain telling you things about yourself. Mostly good things, apart from that one scary episode. You're all right, Hugh. You're all right. That's what I'm trying to tell you.'

'Thanks,' said Hugh, with a wry smile.

'And you don't need that thing in the box any more.'

Hugh looked dubious, almost stubborn.

'Maybe not, but I don't want to risk it. I don't mean risk what I thought might happen when I was thirteen. I mean risk doing something to what's keeping me stable, right? Even if what you say is how it is, and I hope so, maybe the thing in the box is important to me psychologically. Like a symbol, you know? If it's all in my subconscious – well, the subconscious has a thing about symbols. I don't want to disturb that.'

'You're a grown man now,' Hope said. 'You don't need a security blanket.'

For a moment Hugh's expression didn't look very grown-up at all.

'I might find I needed more of the drink, instead.' He poured himself another generous slug. 'It's funny. My private name for the box was "the suicide box".'

'You weren't feeling *suicidal*?' she asked, shocked.

'No, no,' said Hugh. 'Not for one second. It was just a wee private joke to myself. You know, about the old ruling-class tradition of what to give someone when they've really fucked up and need to make a graceful retirement from the scene? Doesn't mean anything more than that.'

'OK, OK,' said Hope.

There was an uncomfortable silence. On the screen, strange organisms were extrapolated from faint exoplanetary atmospheric traces of organic molecules that hinted at a different genetic code.

'Are you sure you were just joking,' said Hugh, awkwardly, 'about having a dram yourself?'

'Not entirely.'

His cheek twitched. He rubbed his chin just under the mouth. 'Were you really considering taking the fix?'

'Damn right I was,' said Hope. 'I'd decided. The only reason I didn't was that I'd hidden this box' – she flicked it with a fingernail – 'beside yours.'

'Why?'

'Fiona – the health visitor – gave me it, and I didn't want to think about it, so I put it somewhere—'

'I meant, why did you change your mind about the fix?'

She told him. By the time she had finished, she was crying in his arms.

'Oh, Hope,' he said, stroking the back of her head.

And nothing more. After a while her shoulder and her neck hurt. She sniffed, blinked, pulled away and sat back at the other side of the sofa, legs curled up. A slug-trail of snot glistened on Hugh's shoulder. Hope tugged out a tissue and dabbed it off, then settled back again.

'Nothing to say?' she said.

Hugh sipped his whisky and looked at her. 'I don't know what to say,' he said.

'Oh, damn it!' Hope felt all the more irritated with him and with herself for having picked up Hugh's Leosach genteel swearing. She reached for the bottle and poured a small dram into the empty glass, and a larger volume of water. Even so, the first sip felt like fire in her mouth. She waited for the sensation to subside to a spreading glow. Along with it came the realisation that she'd crossed a line, trivial though the transgression was. Hugh watched without comment, then raised his glass.

'*Slainte*,' he said, in an ironic tone.

'*Skol*. Now, talk, for crying out loud.'

Hugh took a deep breath. 'All right,' he said. 'You know I'd prefer you to take it. I've said so often and often. I've never understood your objection. In fact I think it's irrational, to be honest. But I'd rather you didn't take it at all than take it because you feel defeated. That isn't you, Hope.'

'Well, I do feel defeated,' Hope said. 'Because I am. Or I will be. Like I said, it makes no difference in the long run what I do. It all ends up in the same place, with me swallowing that thing. Hah! Might as well wash it down with whisky right now, and get it over with.'

She actually reached for the tablet. Hugh's hand shot forward and grabbed her wrist.

'Not like that,' he said.

She relented, not that she'd really intended to do it. She'd got the reaction she'd wanted. Well, maybe. She sipped the whisky, regarding him. After more than three months without alcohol, even this small amount was making her feel a little light-headed, a little loquacious and pugnacious.

'So, like what?' she demanded.

'Like, somewhere where you're not pressured all the time, where you're not being got at. Where you can make your own mind up. We could just go.'

'Go where?' Hope demanded. 'I'm not going to the other side, and everywhere on this side is just like here, and everywhere outside them both is a shit-hole and either a failed state or a tyranny where the fix is bloody compulsory.'

'Just because Jack Crow told you to go to Russia,' said Hugh, teasing, 'there's no reason to rule out the other side. I mean, there's work in Russia.'

'There's work, all right,' Hope said. 'Work or starve. And there's always a lower depth for that, all the way down to scavenging the rubbish dumps. No thanks.'

'Anyway,' said Hugh, 'I wasn't thinking of Russia. I was thinking of Lewis.'

'Lewis?' Hope wasn't sure whether to take him seriously. 'From what you've told me, Lewis is even more infested with social workers than London.'

'Yes, it is,' said Hugh. He took a long swallow of whisky. 'Thing about social workers in Lewis, though. You can see them coming from a long way off.'

Hope laughed. He had that dry, disillusioned, defiant note in his voice that was the up side of the Leosach gloom, and a wry gleam in his eye. This was the Hugh she knew. Not the strange man who stashed a powerful air pistol and a bottle of single malt and who saw people from the past walking through walls. But they were the same man, that was what she would have to get used to.

'Besides,' he said, 'it's a different country. Different laws, different health and social services and everything. They still don't have all the databases joined up. Not by a long chalk.'

'Yeah, but come on,' she said. 'It's hardly practical for us to move to Lewis.'

'I'm not talking about moving,' Hugh said. 'More like a long holiday, and if we have to stay longer, well, we can both work. You can work from anywhere, and there's plenty on Lewis that I can do.'

'I don't see much demand for fancy joinery on the long island.'

'No, but – they've started dismantling the wind turbines, my dad's been lured back to the farm from the croft by the wages they're holding out to him. Plenty of on-site work there for me too – even theoretical knowledge must be worth something, it must come in handy.'

He didn't sound like he was convincing himself.

'And what about your work right now?' she asked.

'The Ealing jobs? Each of them just takes a few days, so I can leave at short notice if I have to. The whole lot finishes in a couple of weeks. Beginning of June at the latest. By then it's just a matter of taking Nick out of the nursery a month before the summer holidays start anyway.'

'A month ...' The reminder troubled her. 'You know, my next check-up's a month from now. If I haven't taken the fix by then, they'll know I lied to Dr Garnett, and then they'll really start turning the screws. So all that leaves me is two weeks in June to decide about the fix. Two weeks of this no-pressure situation in Lewis? Huh.'

Hugh looked a bit hurt.

'OK, it's not much, but it's better than staying here. Isn't it?'

Hope shrugged, and gazed moodily into her glass. She swirled the dilute whisky around, and breathed the fumes.

'It isn't just a matter of time,' she said. 'It's a matter of knowing there's something I can do if I do decide not to take it. I mean, it's a big step. It would mean going on the run, basically. And Lewis has never struck me as a good place to start running.'

'No,' said Hugh. 'It's a place to *stop* running. I have lots of friends and relations on Lewis. All we have to do is keep moving around for six months. Social services up there aren't so efficient or well-resourced that they can go on chasing us. They go after easy targets, because they measure success by targets, so to speak. No doubt they'll want to make an example of someone, but if we make that enough hassle for them, it doesn't have to be you.'

'That's a bit selfish,' said Hope

'Yes. And?' Again with the wry smile.

'It would just set up somebody else,' Hope said.

Hugh looked her straight in the eye.

'Oh!' Hope said. 'That's . . . You think that's what it's all about, for me. That I don't care what happens to any of the other mums in this situation, so long as it doesn't happen to me.'

'"Do it to Julia",' Hugh said, in a heavy voice, so she could hear the quotes.

'Who's Julia?'

'In *Nineteen Eighty-Four*, remember?'

Hope had only scrappy memories of the book, which had been compulsory reading in Year Two English in high school. There had been something horrible about rats, which she had tried to put out of her mind. And the teacher had explained how it was really all about how the West and China had always been allies against Russia, from the Cold War all the way through to the Warm War. That had troubled her a bit, because she was sure she remembered being scared of China when she was a small child. But she hadn't said anything, because China was definitely friendly now, and Russia definitely wasn't. In Russia the government watched people all the time, with cameras everywhere, and everyone was afraid to say what they really thought. Whereas here we had transparency and accountability. Everything was transparent and people were accountable. Or everything was accountable and people were transparent. One or the other.

'Oh, nothing like that!' Hope said. 'Look, I've tried and tried. Argued online. Argued with the faith mums to their faces. Come on, I even joined the *Labour Party*.'

'Quite a sacrifice,' said Hugh. She couldn't tell if he was being ironic. He sounded aggressive. 'Done your civic duty. Gone through the proper channels.'

It was the whisky talking, she thought. Disinhibition. He'd been off alcohol for three months too, and he'd just drunk about three times more than she had. She was feeling a bit disinhibited herself. She drained the glass and put it on the table, then moved forward along the sofa on her knees.

'Come here,' she said, and wrapped her arms around him and pulled him down to the couch.

13

Genetic Information

'There's a girl at the door asking for you,' said Ashid, smirk on his face, head poking up through the floor from behind the top of the ladder. This house was even more of a wreck than number 37 had been.

'Is she selling something?' Hugh asked, putting down a diamond-bladed saw.

'I don't think so,' said Ashid. 'Indian. Christian. Very black.'

'Oh, great,' said Hugh, following Ashid down the ladder. 'Probably saving my soul.'

The suspicion that the young woman was peddling religion hardened as Hugh caught sight of the tiny silver cross on a chain around her neck. The sight also explained how Ashid had known what religion she professed. Standing in the open doorway in puffa jacket, slate skirt, and flat shoes, her arms down and hands locked in front of her, she looked prim enough to be a missionary. The mission to building workers. Sorely needed. The Meddling Little Sisters of St Joseph the Worker. Early twenties, he guessed. A few years younger than him. But somehow more assured. Confident.

'Hello?' said Hugh. 'Can I help you?'

'Hi,' the young woman said. 'Hugh Morrison?'

'Yes?'

His tone was, what's it to you?

'My name is Evangelina Fernandez.'

Knew it, thought Hugh.

She paused, as if expecting him to recognise the name. Or, perhaps, confused by the way he'd looked for a moment as if he had.

'But you can call me Geena,' she went on, evidently giving up on the recognition thing. She stuck out a hand. 'I'm a sociology researcher.'

Marketing, was how Hugh interpreted that. So, wrong wrong wrong, Ashid. She *was* selling something.

He shook her hand solemnly. 'Pleased to meet you. I'm a carpenter.'

'I know,' she said. 'I looked you up, and found your location tag.' She glanced past his shoulder. 'Could I come in for a moment, please?'

'Oh, sure, come on. Mind your step.'

Hugh guided her into the big front room, finished but bare. It smelled of plaster and paint and new wood.

'I'll give that stool a wipe,' he said, looking for a cloth clean enough.

'It's fine,' said Geena. She scuffed a hand across the back of her skirt, a gesture that suddenly made her seem a lot less prim. 'Dirt-repellent fabric.'

She perched on the stool and looked at him as if confirming something in her head.

'Uh ... tea?' he asked. 'It's about time for ...'

It was about eleven.

Geena nodded. 'Milk, no sugar, thanks.'

Hugh went to the kitchen, brewed up a pot, called to Ashid, then carried two mugs through to the front room. He dragged up a trestle and another stool, and sat down.

'Thanks.'

They sipped for a moment.

'So ... what's this about?'

'Um,' said Geena. She looked around, as if for inspiration, or as if she was checking for cameras. There weren't any. Hugh felt uneasy. He hadn't been alone with a woman or child in an unsurveilled, unrecorded room since ... Lewis, he guessed. At least Ashid was in earshot. Well, probably not, the sound of the radio almost certainly drowned their conversation out, but it was the principle. Ashid was in earshot of a scream, at least.

'It's funny,' she said. 'I've thought and thought about this, and now I'm here I feel, uh ...'

'Unprepared?' Hugh prompted.

Geena laughed, some tension dissipating. 'Yes!'

She put the mug down on the trestle and placed her hands on her knees.

'Tell me, Mr Morrison, is there anything *unusual* about your vision?'

'Twenty-twenty, last time I got it checked,' said Hugh.

What was this about? Glasses? Laser eye surgery?

'I don't necessarily mean your acuity,' she said, with unnerving precision. 'I mean ... have you ever noticed that you see things a little differently from other people?'

Hugh warmed his hands around the mug. He felt cold all of a sudden. This wasn't about marketing.

'If you've looked me up,' he said carefully, 'you'll know I went to university. I did a year of philosophy, and if I remember right, that's one of the classic hard questions. Qualia, isn't that it?'

'Yes, but that wasn't my question.'

'Perhaps you should start again,' said Hugh.

'Yes, indeed,' said Geena. She took a deep breath. 'Has your wife ever mentioned a woman called Maya?'

Hugh blinked. 'She may have done.'

Some minor incident at the nursery gate, he recollected. Hope had laughed it off, telling him very little, but he'd noticed that she'd got the bee in her bonnet about the Labour Party shortly afterwards. He'd worried, but he hadn't pried.

'Oh, good. Maya's a friend of mine. She thought she could help, uh, Hope, and I think she did, for a bit, but I've come up with something that can help you in a big way.'

'What makes you think we need any help? What's this about? Are you trying to sell us something?'

'What?' She sounded baffled.

'Sociology research. Sure you don't mean market research?'

'No, no, I really am ... I'm a postgrad at Brunel, you know, in Uxbridge? And I'm doing research at SynBioTech, in Hayes.'

'I thought you said sociology.'

'STS ... sorry, science and technology studies. I sit in on a lab and observe the engineers.'

'Oh,' said Hugh, 'I know about all that. Like they're a strange tribe.'

'Like they're a strange tribe,' she said, in the tone of someone who'd heard it before.

'And you pretend you don't know if science works or not, yeah?'

'Please don't tell me the one about jumping out of a window,' Geena said.

Hugh had been about to. He felt abashed.

'I suppose it's like having an unusual name,' he said.

'Yes,' she said. 'Like Hope Abendorf.'

Hugh spluttered tea. He wiped the back of his hand across his mouth.

'Pardon me,' he said. 'OK. One more time: can you please tell me what all this is about?'

She told him how she'd come across Hope's name and predicament, and how her friend Maya had tried to help. He listened, with an uneasy feeling of having been watched from behind.

And then she looked away and looked back and said:

'One thing about the fix that I know and most people don't, Mr Morrison ... there is a basis for exemption apart from the conscience clause.'

'What!'

'It's buried in the miscellaneous administrative provisions, not in the primary legislation. Even the recent rulings don't change it, they can't because, well' – she smiled here – 'it's unexpressed, so to speak. I mean, the legislation was drafted with one eye on the possibility – which the government was publicly denying at the time – that some day it might become compulsory. That's why they built in exemptions in the first place. The main way the fix works is by correcting the expression of deleterious genes, right? It turns genes on or off, depending. Sometimes it repairs a stretch of code. It doesn't really add or take away anything. That's one reason why it's acceptable even to the bloody Catholics.'

His eyebrow twitched at that, and his gaze flickered to the cross on her neck, but he just nodded.

'So,' Geena went on, 'this usually involves changing a mutant allele back to the wild type. But there are complications. You know about sickle-cell anaemia?'

'Sure, that's the one that's bad for you in some ways but protects you from malaria. Does the fix leave that one in, then?'

'Good grief, no! It's a very painful condition, and it doesn't have any advantages now even in Africa. But some young hotshot in the Lords who was on the committee that drafted all the amendments had had a smattering of biology education, and he was quite exercised on this point. A little knowledge is a dangerous thing, and all that. So he got a line or two stuck in that stated that a good medical reason for not taking – or more to the point, because it wasn't compulsory then, not prescribing – the fix would be if you could show that your genome had a *beneficial* mutation.'

'But how could you show that? How could you know?'

'Well, exactly. In practice it would be vanishingly rare anyway. So after a bit of to-and-fro, their Lordships decided to let him have his way, assuming no doubt that this was' – she smiled again – 'the legislative equivalent of non-coding DNA. It's certainly never been publicised, probably because they don't want people coming up with nonsense claims about their beneficial mutations. Of course, people who would do that are the same people who'd in any case be exempt on the grounds of some wacky religion, so it all comes out in the wash.'

She cocked her head to one side and smiled at him, as if waiting for applause.

'But *you* know this,' he said, 'because you learned it in sociology of science, or something?'

'No, Mr Morrison. I actually found this out a couple of weeks ago, when I asked Maya to look for something like it in the Act and the administrative provisions. I just *knew* there had to be an allowance for rare but beneficial mutations. Well, I didn't know, but I guessed. And the reason I was looking is' – she flung out an arm, ta-da – 'I found that you and your son have a possibly beneficial mutation.'

'How did you find out?'

Geena looked uneasy. 'Um, I ran some scanning programs on your genome sequences.'

'I could figure that out for myself. You're not supposed to do that, are you?'

'Uh, no, but . . .'

'What I mean is, how do you know it's beneficial?'

Geena put her empty mug down on the trestle and began waving her arms around. 'Well, the way syn bio works is they run sims of how a gene translates into a protein; you can actually see the exact cascade, and you can predict the properties of that protein.'

'I know that, too,' said Hugh. He did some hand-waving of his own, at the cornices. 'New wood. I work with it. I read the specs.'

'Of course. I should have known. Anyway. The mutation I found – there were lots, of course, everybody has some, but they were nearly all neutral, and anyway they were already well documented, but this one wasn't in any of the databases. It's in the genes for the retina. Specifically, the one for rhodopsin, that's one of the rod-and-cone components. This gene results in a rhodopsin variant that has greater sensitivity to light, including outside the visible spectrum. So – how's your night vision, Mr Morrison?'

Hugh shrugged. 'Good, I suppose. Can't say I've ever noticed any difference from other people's, though.'

Geena smiled. 'Like you said, it's a hard problem. But there must be ways of objectively testing for that, and for other sensitivities – I suspect you may be able to see a bit into the ultraviolet, for example. In any case, you have a perfect get-out card to give your wife. She doesn't have to take the fix, and she doesn't need to plead conscience.'

'But she doesn't have the mutation.'

'No, but you do, and your son does. Who's to say the next baby won't?'

'Well, there's one problem right there,' said Hugh. 'The chances are fifty-fifty the baby won't have it, and I don't see any way of proving it one way or the other without some kind of intrusive sampling, which I don't think Hope would go for. In fact, you can take it from me, she wouldn't. I think it's her squick about that sort of thing that's behind this whole objection she has to the fix.'

'That doesn't matter,' said Geena. 'The wording of the provision is quite clear. It just has to be one of the parents, and therefore a possibility in the offspring.'

Hugh took a couple of steps back and rubbed his eyebrows, eyes closed tight behind his hand. Patches of false colour swirled and exploded like fireworks, behind a fading after-image of the big bay window. He wondered how much, if anything, to admit. It was only a week since he'd told it all to Hope. He didn't feel like going through it all again with a total stranger. Come to think of it, he hadn't told Hope everything . . . Maybe he should have. He felt guilty about that.

Then another point struck him with such force that he blurted it out.

'Wait a minute!' he said. 'The gene's recessive!'

'What?' Geena shook her head. 'I didn't say that. It must be a dominant allele, if it's not in one parent but still shows up in the child.' She frowned. 'Do you know about this gene already?'

Hugh felt like kicking himself. He covered his confusion with a sheepish grin.

'Sorry, just a conclusion I jumped to. I was thinking about sight, and – ah, forget it.'

'No, no,' Geena insisted, leaning forward on the stool. 'What?'

'It's . . . kind of embarrassing.'

Geena made a show of peering around, hand cupped behind her ear. 'Nobody's listening, Mr Morrison. Except me, and I'm a scientist.'

'That's just it,' said Hugh. 'That's why it's embarrassing. It's about a . . . superstition. Well, a traditional belief.'

'I can cope with hearing about *traditional beliefs*, Mr Morrison.'

'Well . . . where I come from, in the Highlands, there's a traditional belief in second sight. It covers what the old parapsychologists used to call remote viewing and precognition. Except it's pretty much involuntary. Maybe other things too, like, uh, seeing ghosts or . . . or the like.' Hugh grimaced. 'Runs in families, but in odd patterns. Skips generations, that sort of thing. When I was a callow lad, I sort of figured that the patterns were like those for a recessive gene. That's all.'

'Are you telling me *you* have this second sight?' Geena sounded excited.

'Not exactly, no.' He shrugged. 'Just . . . a speculation, is all.'

Geena slid off the stool and stepped towards him. Eyes bright, the short black hair that framed her face all aquiver.

'Have you had any experiences that this might help explain?'

Hugh backed away, towards the door. 'No!'

He could hear the lie himself, in the vehemence of his denial.

'Why don't you want to talk about it?'

'Well, you know, it's all hearsay. Old wives' tales. Village rumours. Playground tittle-tattle. And it can be very damaging.'

'Damaging? How?'

This was the bit he hadn't even told to Hope. He nerved himself to spit it out.

'It can lead to accusations of witchcraft.'

'Witchcraft?' Geena laughed in his face.

His forearms came up and his hands clawed, as if to grab her shoulders and shake her.

'This is no laughing matter, dammit!'

He was almost shouting. He stepped back at the same moment as she recoiled from him. He took a deep breath and let his arms hang down. She looked scared.

'Sorry,' he said. 'Sorry.'

'No, I'm sorry,' said Geena. 'I had no idea you were so serious about it. Is it something to do with the churches up there ... what do they call them, the Wee Frees or something?'

'Not exactly,' said Hugh. 'It's a bit of that and something else. The population of Lewis – that's the island I'm from – has more or less doubled this century, after declining for a very long time. Mostly because of the wind farms and immigration, but that in itself helps to retain the native population, with jobs and opportunities and so on. And just when this turnaround was beginning – way before the wind farms, towards the end of the last century – a lot of the incomers were kind of New Age types, people who wanted to get away from the cities and open a wee craft business or start an organic farm or whatever. Some of them were hippies, pagans, that kind of thing. Big families, kids running wild, all that. One consequence was a child abuse scandal that got fuelled by local suspicions on the part of those Wee Frees you mentioned about anyone who wasn't a good Christian, let alone people who openly called *themselves* pagans and witches. Whatever the details of the original case – it may have been open-and-shut for all I know, it was many years ago – that kind of thing can rankle for generations. Some people in the generation *after* those pagans and witches found a way of hitting back, and a very nasty, underhand way it was too. They kept an ear to the ground for rumours of the second sight, and passed anonymous tip-offs to social services about anyone who was said to have it. On the grounds, you see, that this was an occult practice and therefore a risk indicator for satanic child abuse. They witch-hunted the locals *right back*. And of course in wee close-knit communities like that, just getting investigated is a disgrace, even if there's nothing in it.'

Geena was shaking her head slowly in amazement. 'That's appalling!'

'Aye, it's appalling. Now this was before my time, the last case like that was before I was born, but people have long memories in small communities. So when I first got curious about the second sight – I found the term in an old book on Highland folklore that was lying around in our house – I asked my pals at high school, and they sort of tapped their noses and talked behind their hands about certain folks in the locality, and next time I was home I asked my dad about it, like, "Dad, is it true that old Mrs Macdonald has the second sight?" I guess I was about, uh, thirteen or so, not a little kid, and for the first time in my life my dad takes me out the back, literally behind the woodshed – well, the peat shed – and gives me a clip on the back of the head. Not hard, not to hurt, but like a glancing blow, you know?'

Geena nodded. 'Uh-huh. I've had a few myself.'

'Right. It was enough of a shock to me, I can tell you. So now he'd got my attention, so to speak, he told me what I've just told you about what had gone on, the investigations and that. He said never to mention the subject again. And I didn't. Until now.'

Hugh felt a pang as he said that. He hadn't even told it to Hope.

Geena was giving him a very quizzical look.

'Why did you get interested in the second sight in the first place?'

'I was a curious lad,' Hugh said.

Geena considered this.

'Well,' she said, 'none of this really matters any more. The point is your wife now has a good case for not taking the fix, and maybe identifying this gene will clear up all the superstition about the second sight.'

Hugh glared at her. 'You don't understand,' he said. 'There's just no way I'm going to open that can of worms. No fucking way. I'll tell Hope about it, and it'll be her choice, but I'm sure she'll agree.'

'You think?'

'Yes. I know my wife better than you do.'

'Fair enough,' said Geena. 'But I'm betting otherwise.'

'Like it's any of your business.'

'I just wanted to help,' said Geena, sounding upset.

'I know, I know. I appreciate that.' Hugh frowned. 'Why did you want to help us, anyway? Why take these risks? Is it because you're a Christian, or what?'

Geena snorted a laugh. 'I'm not a Christian! What makes you think that?'

Hugh pointed. 'That cross around your neck.'

Geena looked away, then back. 'It's a cross I have to bear,' she said.

'Family pressures?' Hugh guessed, with some sympathy.

'Good God, no! My parents are as godless as I am. It's a ... cultural thing. I'm from a Catholic community – Goan, you know?'

Her voice had taken on a higher pitch: light, over-casual.

'Oh, I get it,' said Hugh. 'Same reason as my colleague Ashid' – he jerked a thumb over his shoulder – 'wears the round cap, even though he isn't a Muslim. Community identity, loyalty to—'

Ashid's voice suddenly boomed from the hallway, through which, in one of those bloody-typical moments, he happened to be lugging a bucket of rubble.

'You're a bloody fool, Hugh!'

Hugh turned, embarrassed, into the full beam of Ashid's grin. The plasterer's gaze basked in Hugh's discomfiture for a second or two, then switched to Geena. He patted the top of his head and tapped his chest.

'You and me for the same reason, eh? To show the cops we're not bloody Hindus! Every time they stop me they check me over and I tell them I'm a good Muslim and then they send me on my way with the same joke: they miss the jihadists, hah-hah! Like their fathers missed the IRA!' Ashid mimicked a posh English accent, very badly, to add: 'Sporting chaps the IRA were, at least they didn't blow *themselves* up!'

Geena giggled. 'Yes, that's it!'

Ashid waved and went on. When Hugh turned back to Geena she was blinking rapidly and sniffing.

'What's the matter?'

Geena turned away and blew her nose, then turned back. 'Sorry, nothing. It just upsets me sometimes. The stops. You'd think with all the information they have on us they'd not bother, but they do.'

'You get hassled by cops?'

Geena gave him a *what planet are you on?* look. 'Yes. And so does your friend, by the sound of it.'

'He's never mentioned it.'

'People don't,' said Geena, in a bitter tone.

'Ah, I'm sorry about that, I didn't realise. Still,' he went on, trying to lighten the mood, 'I know what it's like not mentioning things.'

Geena gave him a pitying look this time. 'No, Mr Morrison. You don't.'

After half a minute of silence, she spoke again: 'I think we're about finished here.'

'Thanks for trying to help,' Hugh said, ushering her to the door.

'You're welcome,' said Geena.

That evening, after the ten o'clock news, Hugh waved a hand in front of Hope to ask her to disengage from her glasses, on which she was surfing. She took them off.

'Yes?'

'I've got a confession. Today a very pretty girl came to see me at work.'

'How nice for you.'

Her tone was light but wary.

'Ah, that's not really the confession.'

'I didn't think it was, somehow.'

Hope put aside her glasses and leaned back. Hugh leaned forward and began talking.

When he finished, her eyes narrowed, as they had when he was going through the bit about the witchcraft accusations.

'That's all?' she said. 'That's everything? You don't have any more secrets you'd like to get off your chest?'

Hugh thought about it. 'No.'

'Good.' She sounded miffed, as well she might.

However, to Hugh's surprise, she took the rest of his account of the morning's events in her stride. She insisted that the new information didn't change anything. The gene was probably for nothing more than a susceptibility to hallucinations. She certainly didn't want to make it the basis for any appeal.

'I couldn't bear it,' she said. 'For Nick.'

'The publicity?' Hugh asked.

'The being made to feel different.'

'They make him feel different already,' said Hugh, with some bitterness.

'That's just prejudice,' said Hope. 'I'd hate for it to be science.'

Something was bugging her about the science, but she couldn't put her finger on what it was.

14

Joining Dots

The following morning Hope finished the nursery walk and the breakfast dishes and the beds before 9.30, then sat down at the table and fired up her glasses, stared at the endless scroll of language-mangled queries and thought: fuck this.

Let Searle handle the questions for today. She couldn't concentrate. She hadn't slept well. Hugh's late-evening belated confession had shaken her even more than the one last week, the one that had started with her confrontation with him over the gun. That Hugh, in their apparently open, weepy, letting-it-all-come-out-at-last conversation, hadn't actually told her what was evidently one of his biggest bugbears about his hallucinations, and one of the main reasons why he'd kept it bottled up so long – that really, really pissed her off. Especially given that this aspect of his story was directly connected with the matter of social services and child protection, not to mention making Lewis seem an even less attractive place in which to get away from all this for a while.

She loved him, but, aagh.

Hope jumped up from the table and stalked over to the sink, where she'd earlier noticed that the regularly recurring pinkish algal slime on the dish drainer was back. She dried the almost-dry plates and mugs racked there and put them away, then pulled on an apron and rubber gloves and filled the sink with hot water and started scrubbing the empty drier. When that was clean, she noticed that the sides of the sink were grubby, and scrubbed them.

That bit of displacement activity out of the way, she ambled around the flat, tidying up. Nick put away his toys every evening, or at least stacked them against the living-room wall, but it was amazing how many he could scatter around in the hour between getting up and going to nursery. She dusted the bookshelves and took books down and opened them and turned over pages of heavy, glossy exhibition catalogues of artists, photographers and designers, and thin, dense-printed textbooks of economics and business administration and management studies, each little more than a taster for the DVD or CD in a plastic envelope attached to the inside back cover, and therefore almost completely useless. Somewhere in the flat there had to be a DVD player, but she couldn't think where. As if searching for a scientific answer to that question, she moved on to Hugh's battered old engineering manuals and science references, some of them handed down from his father like a family Bible and likewise unchanging and full of small type, with constants and formulae defined for all time in bold black font barbed with serifs, a King James Version of truth. Then her browse took her to cookery books – again, the most used handed down, this one from Hope's grandmother – and as she flipped through recipes whose results were appetisingly and artfully photographed in an advertising style her arts-trained eye could recognise at a glance as early 1980s, she lit upon a faded glossy pic of a beef casserole. She could almost smell the steam, and a sudden craving told her exactly what they'd be having for dinner this evening.

She went out into bright sunshine to Tesco. The New Trees had reached forty feet and their broad, overlapping leaves cast an almost unbroken shade. On East West Road Hope blinked in the glare and hastily put her glasses on, waving a hand to flip them to polarising mode. One or two people in the street gesticulated or waggled their fingers as they walked, but without glasses. Contacts, the very latest thing. The thought niggled, somehow.

In the store she bought a kilo of beef and some root vegetables – it wasn't the weather for a casserole or anything heavy, but she was the one who was pregnant and if her body or the baby's said it needed iron or whatever she wasn't going to argue, and anyway Hugh would eat anything after a day's work – and as she bagged them under the checkout scan and gazed abstractedly at the floating virtual display of the magazine downloads on offer, the niggle returned to her mind. She paused to focus on the niggle, and it vanished beneath the surface of her mind like a minnow into a deep pool as a shadow falls. Hope frowned, and deliberately turned her mind away. She knew it would come back if she didn't concentrate; it was like letting a search run in the background, sooner or later up it would come.

Back at the flat, she tied on an old blue-and-white-striped butcher's apron, turned the slow cooker on to high, and got to work, peeling potatoes, slicing garlic and onion, chopping carrots and a turnip, dicing meat, searing and simmering amid increasingly savoury smells. Every so often she wiped her hands on the apron, leaving smears of blood or flour or stock-cube crumbs. Just as she'd turned the cooker down to simmer and put the Pyrex lid on the pot and picked up the big knife to place it in the sink, the missing thought rose to the top of her mind's stack and pinged for attention.

Rhodopsin, it reminded her, and *tachyons*.

That was it, that was what had been bugging her ever since Hugh had mentioned the word last night. Rhodopsin was the visual protein for whose gene he and Nick had a mutation, and she knew she'd come across the word before, in another context. Three months ago she'd read in *The Economist* that scientists at CERN had detected possible tachyon effects in a suspension of rhodopsin derivatives.

Hope put down the knife, wiped her hands again, and scanned the shelf of Hugh's old reference books. She pulled down an encyclopedic dictionary of physics, searched, and found.

Tachyons. Hypothetical particles that moved faster than light, and, therefore, backward in time. From the future into the past.

She went over to the table and picked up her glasses carefully by the edges, nudging the earpieces open with her wrists. She ran a semantic search on the topic, and found little beyond the initial *Nature* paper, a small flurry of letters in *New Scientist*, and the same *Economist* article. No follow-up, no further research reported. It looked like one of those discoveries that flared for a moment then faded. But still . . .

It got her thinking. If something derived from rhodopsin detected particles moving backward in time, and Hugh had a mutant version of rhodopsin . . . was it possible that the visions he saw were caused by tachyons? Not directly, surely – no tachyon flux could behave like light, and she doubted that the particles could be focused on the retina – but stimulating the brain to form an image nonetheless. Hope knew from her art training that the visual field was mostly an internal construction anyway, a vast canvas corrected and updated piecemeal by the pencil torch of the optic nerve's input, whose bit-rate was far too low for it to produce the whole panorama at once. So some visual reconstruction cued by odd fleeting particles didn't strike her as impossible.

In which case, the barbarians Hugh saw weren't from the past. They were from the future.

Which – if you followed through the logic of the wild speculation – raised the awkward question of how they saw him (and indeed, in one instance, her), as Hugh had insisted they did. Because in that case, they would be seeing into the past. Was there such a thing as an anti-tachyon? Not part of the Standard Model, that was for sure! So then, she'd have to fall back on the hypothesis that these interactions were hallucinations, construction of Hugh's brain, in which case ... why even go down the physics route; why not admit the whole thing was a hallucination? And yet, and yet – Hugh had claimed his boyhood pals had seen something real, under the hill above the house ... Did these lads have the same mutant gene, or was there a quite different phenomenon involved?

She was still pondering this when, quite unexpectedly, the doorbell rang.

Hope checked on her glasses who was outside, and saw the avatar of Fiona Donnelly, the health visitor. She jumped up, took off her glasses, cast off the grubby apron and, without thinking, hastily wrapped and tied herself into the big ruffle-bordered floral-patterned pinafore. Now why had she done *that*? she wondered for a moment. She glanced in the mirror, tucked back a stray strand of hair, felt the slick of sweat on her brow, saw the flushed look of busy domesticity – harried, married – realised it was exactly the image she wanted to present to her visitor, then went to open the door.

Fiona Donnelly stood in sunshine amid catkins with bees crawling on them.

'Hello, Hope. Mind if I drop by?'

'Come in, come in,' said Hope. She waved at the outside before she shut the door. 'Quite a change since the last time you were here!'

'Yes, isn't it?' said Fiona, heading through to the kitchen without further invitation. Hope followed, perplexed.

'Have a seat,' she said, but Fiona had already sat down, her back to the window, just as she'd done in March. She looked around and inhaled appreciatively. 'Mmm, something smells good.'

'Tonight's dinner.'

'Oh, well done.' Then she just sat there.

'Cup of tea?' Hope asked.

'Yes, thanks, I'm parched.'

Hope busied herself.

'Everything all right?' she asked, sitting down.

'Not really, I'm afraid,' said Fiona.

'Oh,' said Hope. 'What's the problem?'

'You told Dr Garnett last week that you were going to take the fix, and you still haven't,' said Fiona.

'How would you know that?' Hope demanded.

'Oh come on, Hope, it would show up on your monitor-ring log.'

'Have you been *checking* that?' Hope asked.

'Why shouldn't I? I'm concerned. I'm even more concerned that you drank alcohol last week. You tried to conceal it by taking your ring off, but there were still traces in the morning.'

'It was only a few sips.' Hope essayed a smile. 'Half a dram.'

'That's not the point, and you know it. But what's really concerning me, Hope, and believe me this is for your own good, is how it impacts what's been happening recently to your personal profile. It's coming dangerously close to affecting your parental suitability.'

Hope felt a cold clutch of dismay.

'What?' she said. She couldn't think of anything other than that one lapse to make her feel guilty, but feel guilty she did, mentally flailing for anything she might have done wrong.

'It's all small things,' said Fiona, in a reassuring tone, 'but you know how these small things add up when they're not taken in isolation but are brought together in the database and begin to form a picture.'

'What picture?' Hope's tone had shifted register, from shock to anger. 'What database?'

'*You* know,' Fiona said, with an impatient frown. 'Your personal profile is automatically updated all the time, from surveillance and from your interactions – purchases, interpersonal connections, interactions with official bodies, social services, health, police ...' She waved a hand and repeated, '*You* know.'

'Yes, I know!' Hope said. 'But I haven't done anything wrong.'

'Look, Hope,' said Fiona, 'like I say, it's all automatic, and it hasn't rung any warning bells yet, but I've been concerned about you, so I've been having a look. Which I'm perfectly entitled to do, by the way. And I have to say that it's getting very close to the tipping point where social services and child protection would be required to take an interest.'

'That's ridiculous!'

'Would you think it was so ridiculous if I told you that a lot of the negative situations being flagged up come from the police?'

'The police?' Hope heard her voice rise incredulously. 'I haven't *had* any encounters with the police.'

'Oh yes you have, Hope. That letter you dropped into Jack Crow's house, that brought you to police attention, even if it only wasted a lot of police time. Then you confronted him three weeks ago, at the May Day rally in the park. He was obliged to report that.'

'Obliged?' cried Hope, by now outraged. 'To report *me?*'

Fiona nodded. 'Yes, obliged. He uploaded the part of your conversation that took place while he had his glasses on. The word "Naxal" came up, I understand, but let's leave that aside. He found your whole line of argument disturbing. As if you hadn't joined the Party for any kind of sincere reason. As if you had an ulterior motive.'

'Damn right I had an ulterior motive,' said Hope. 'I was hoping he would help me with this compulsory-fix business. What's wrong with that? People join parties to advance their interests, including their bloody *business* interests if North Islington CLP is anything to go by.'

'Yes, yes, Hope, I can quite see that. But you have to consider what happens when the police intelligence gets hold of something like that. It raises a little flag, you know? And then the intelligence has to cast its net wider, it has to start looking for other traces of you, using face recognition and tags and so on. And then it starts making connections. Joining dots.'

She slipped her computer out of her breast pocket and laid it on the table. 'Here, let me show you some of the dots they joined. Just put your glasses on.'

Hope did. The devices linked. She saw a dark background spidered with red lines linking her with Maya, with a woman she didn't know, with Hugh, Nick, Jack Crow, various sites: ParentsNet, SynBioTech, the health centre; phone and street-camera photos of all these people and locations and more . . . it just went on and on, the viewpoint zooming and swooping through the web, while Fiona's murmured voice-over kept up a running commentary.

'You see, it starts with that disturbance outside the nursery, and all of a sudden you're part of a flash mob initiated by that woman Maya, who has lots of warning flags against her, nothing actionable but still, not good . . . You go skipping off with her to a dodgy little place, an unlicensed café no less, where you take off your monitor ring, and later it shows cotinine traces, very bad sign, Hope, as you should know. That links up with the alcohol incident, it adds up, you see. Then there's the two incidents with your MP, both with some vague terrorism connection, questions raised, nothing more, and then it gets really interesting. This woman here, Geena Fernandez, is picked up and questioned about a terrorism-related offence. She's already connected to you because she's shown an interest in your case, she works at SynBioTech, the company that makes the fix, she's a close friend of Maya's, and – she visited your husband at work yesterday! So . . . '

Fiona disconnected Hope's access to her personal profile. The network swirled away, to be replaced by the normal view through the glasses. Hope found the overlay distracting – right now, still tuned to Fiona's avatar, it was telling her about all the accomplishments on the health visitor's CV – so she took them off.

'... that's it, that's what the police and social services databases are quietly thinking about you right now. Nothing strong enough yet to alert a human operative, but definitely moving in that direction. I'm sure there are perfectly innocent explanations for every one of these links and nodes, but ...'

Fiona let the word hang, like a virtual link.

'But nothing!' Hope said. 'It's just ridiculous. Terrorism? Come on.' She fluttered her hands towards herself. 'Look at me, sitting here in my pinny! A terrorist in a frilly apron!'

'I think the correct term for that is "domestic extremist".' Fiona paused, for a laugh that didn't come. 'Nobody's going to say you're a *terrorist*, Hope. No need to be all dramatic about it. No, the point is that it's all building up to a profile that doesn't look like someone capable of providing a safe environment for a child.'

Hope had a flash of fury. She had to press her hands firmly to the table, so as not to slap Fiona across the face. She took a few deep breaths, then sipped now-tepid coffee from the mug, clutching her hands around it. She had to relax her hands a little, so that the mug didn't shatter.

'All right,' she said. 'I know how these automatic systems work, they're as mindless as the one that's doing my job for me today while I get on with the housework. No doubt I'll have to make some corrections and allowances for it tomorrow. And that's how it is, you see? All that needs to happen about the profile thing is for someone with a bit of sense, someone who knows me, someone professional, to squash all that nonsense and *say* I'm a good mother.'

Fiona nodded soberly. 'Yes, that would certainly weigh in the balance. But you see, once the system raises the problem to the level where it alerts the services, there are procedures in place. Wheels are set in motion. Guidelines are followed. Matters would be quite out of my hands, I'm afraid.'

Hope felt cold all over. 'You're saying ... they could take Nick away from me?'

'I'm sorry, Hope, but yes. Best practice might indicate intervention first, investigation later. On a precautionary basis, of course, with no aspersion cast or intended, certainly not by me. I know you're a good mother.'

'Well,' said Hope, trying to keep the exasperation from putting too much steel in her voice, 'why the heck can't you say so now, and smack that stupid system back down where it belongs?'

'There's the problem,' said Fiona, sounding genuinely sympathetic. 'There are no *procedures in place* for that. All I can do is log my own reports, which are of course part of the profile. The trouble is, they're part of your profile already. And as you've just seen, they haven't been enough.'

'Oh God,' Hope groaned. 'This is just ... oh God.'

She closed her eyes and rested her forehead on her hands. Tears trickled on to her wrists. After a moment she felt Fiona's hand on her shoulder.

'There, there, Hope,' she said. 'It's not that bad. It's not at the danger level yet. I'm just telling you all this because I'm on your side, really I am. And, well ... you know the one thing you could do that would clear all that nonsense away, without so much as a word from me. You know what to do, Hope.'

Hope didn't look up. 'I know, I know.'

She stood up and blundered towards the work surface by the sink, groped for the roll of paper towels, tore one off and blew her nose and wiped her eyes.

'I'm thinking about it, all right?' She knew she sounded defiant and petulant, like a teenager just before conceding a point.

'Good,' said Fiona. 'Do please think about it, seriously.' She stood up. 'Thanks for the tea, Hope. Enjoy your dinner tonight! It's all right, I'll see myself out.'

Hope nodded, unable to say anything more. She was angry enough to smirk at the sounds of Fiona Donnelly bumping into a handlebar, and then closing the door behind her so firmly it was almost a slam.

The casserole was, indeed, good, though Nick was very picky about it, leaving a ring of carrot slices around the edge of his plate and insisting that Hope tease apart the beef chunks into strands and mash them in with the potatoes before he deigned to eat them. After dinner he wanted to play outside, and Hugh, though tired as well as replete, loyally went out with him to kick a ball about on the back grass.

By the time they came back in – Hugh with a stitch, Nick all grubby – Hope had finished washing the plates and the pan and the big heavy crock-pot and was lying feet up on the sofa, reading on her glasses. Hugh took this as a hint, and busied himself getting Nick to tidy away his toys and get ready for bed. By the time Nick came through in his pyjamas for his good-night kiss, Hope had fallen asleep herself. She woke to the boy's voice and to text scrolling across her vision like a fragment of dream. She swung her feet to the floor and sat up, taking her glasses off.

'Good night, Nick.'

'Good night, Mummy.'

She hugged him a little harder than usual, breathing in the smell of his just-washed skin. Off he went, Max trailing him, both waving from the doorway.

'Night night,' she said, waving back.

Hugh came back about ten minutes later and joined her on the sofa.

'Ach,' he said. 'I'm tempted to pour a dram. But I won't.'

He waved towards the screen. Hope leaned forward and chopped her hand down, turning the television back off.

' 'Scuse me,' she said. 'Something we've got to talk about.'

She told him about Fiona's visit. He listened in silence until she'd finished.

'We have to go,' he said. 'Tomorrow night.'

Nick was having none of it.

'Grandpa's chin is scratchy and his house smells.'

'But he's very kind to you,' Hope said, cutting toast for eggy soldiers. 'And Grandma Island is lovely. She's so fond of you, and she's such fun.'

'Not as much fun as Granny Abendorf.'

Hope wasn't sure if this was Nick being stubborn or loyal. She decided to make light of it.

'Well, Granny Abendorf is fun, yes, but she doesn't live in a big sprawly house on a hill with the sea down below and lots of sheep and cows around and eagles and seagulls in the sky, does she?'

'It rains all the time and the house is smelly.'

For answer, Hope flicked up the weather forecast on the big screen in the living room, and pointed Nick to it through the knock-through. 'That's Lewis up at the top, see? And it's sunny today.'

They sat down at the kitchen table. Hope munched her cereal and Nick dunked his eggy soldiers. Then:

'It's still smelly.'

'Oh, for – look, Nick, it's just cooking. And peat smoke.'

Nick wrinkled his nose. 'And fish.' He pushed away the remainder of his breakfast. 'And wet things.'

'All right, fish and washing. But you soon don't notice smells, and it's nice in other ways.'

'I'll miss my friends.'

Lower-lip tremble. Time to move fast.

'It's only for a little while, and you can talk to them any time, and you'll have lots of exciting things to tell them when you come back, and you'll make new friends while you're up there.'

'Can I take Max?'

'Of course you can. Now let's get you ready for nursery.'

Nick slid off the chair and ran to the hallway for his jacket, apparently cheered up. He got it on after several attempts, proud of his new accomplishment, while Hope packed his lunch.

'I'll tell all my friends we're going to Lewis,' he announced, as they headed out the door.

Uh-oh. That could be awkward. She couldn't tell him to keep it a secret – like all kids at nursery and in primary school, Nick had been solemnly warned against any adult at all telling him to keep secrets. Nothing was more certain to get social services on the case than a whisper of secrets.

'I've had an idea,' said Hope, climbing up the steps. 'Let's not tell them until we're there, and it'll be a nice surprise.'

15

The Stornoway Run

Hugh cycled to work as usual, in a cheerful mood. Last night the hot rush of his anger and protectiveness had turned Hope on, and she'd dragged him off to bed almost before he was ready, and they'd had hotter sex than they'd had for a while. Every so often his mind went back to it with a reminiscent smile.

The weather was sunny and not too warm. The leaves and grass along his route had a gloss to their green. As he whizzed along Camden's back streets and canal banks and along the edge of Regent's Park he sometimes glimpsed the whole scene as a vast, broken woodland, the forest of London. It was like when as a lad he'd seen from the hilltop how the landscape of Lewis wasn't moor and field and bog with outcrops of rock, but a gnarly mass of rock with a thin overlay of peaty soil. The vision of the city as a forest uplifted him. It was almost utopian, and within it he felt the bike's smooth engineered wooden frame and handlebars as an extension of himself.

On top of that elation, he was cheerful because the Ealing job was about to finish. The timing had worked out well, right to the half-day – he only had a morning's work left. Ashid still had work to do, and Hugh had a waiting list of clients for renovation work, so he could easily have stuck around, just up the street. But at noon today he'd get his cash in hand, and tell Ashid he was taking a short holiday.

He also felt cheerful about leaving London for Lewis. The reason was one he could have done without. But if you looked at it the right way, it appeared positive. He didn't care what Hope decided. He just wanted her to make her own decision, without social services and the Health Centre breathing down her neck. He'd never understood her objection to the fix. It annoyed him sometimes. That, he now realised, was one reason why he felt so cheerful. One way or another the matter was going to be resolved.

'You see the future,' Hope had told him, in a mutually exhausted moment last night. Then she'd explained. Tachyons and rhodopsin, good grief. Just as well she hadn't brought that up in her latest confrontation with Fiona Donnelly! A gene for hallucinations – now *that* would have convinced Donnelly to back off! Aye, right. Even if there was anything to it, there was no way he was seeing the future. What sort of future had barbarians in it? If he was seeing anything real, it was people from the Dark Ages. Far more likely he was . . . maybe not *seeing things* – meaning, seeing *not* things but figments – he was convinced there was something objective behind it, though not necessarily what he saw. Which, to any outside observer, meant hallucinations. He was glad Hope had more sense than that science girl, Geena. Strange woman. There had been something odd about her intensity. Something she wasn't letting on. She hadn't told him why she was so interested. That query had been diverted by the stuff about police stops, at the end. More emotional than you'd expect.

Hugh made the connection with what Hope had told him about what Fiona had said so abruptly that he almost lost control of the bike. Geena had recently been questioned about *Naxals*. Of course, of course! And it hadn't been one of the usual stops, the ones that she and Ashid had shared a nervous laugh about. She'd probably been hauled into the back of a van. She might even have been tortured. No wonder she was upset!

No wonder, also, that she had such a strong interest in their case. It went beyond the kind of curiosity that made sense for someone in her academic field – well beyond. Hugh thought he could understand why. For her it would be a kind of revenge on the state. A revenge of the weak, underhand and indirect, and therefore all the more dangerous and unpredictable.

That meant he had to be wary. For one thing, Geena might be *using* him, though he couldn't see how. She might have been radicalised by her experience, and actually become a Naxal sympathiser herself. It wouldn't be the first time such a thing had happened, not by a long chalk. For another, the state's surveillance system might be even more sensitised to her than Fiona Donnelly's demonstration had suggested.

Hugh already had a travel plan. It had come to him the moment he'd decided they had to leave. Now he had to complicate it a little.

At noon Hugh pocketed a few thousand pounds from the house developer, said goodbye to Ashid and wheeled his bike up the road towards Ealing Broadway. He selected a quiet alley between two boarded-up houses, took out his phone and called his father.

'Oh, hello, Usdean,' his father said. He sounded as if he was chewing something, then swallowing. Probably caught having his lunch. He was obviously outdoors. Hugh could hear the wind past the mike. 'How's things?'

'Oh, fine, fine,' said Hugh. 'You and Mam?'

'Bearing up, bearing up. What brings you to break radio silence?'

'Och, Dad, it's only been two weeks since—'

'Yeah, yeah, just winding you up.'

'Anyway, seeing as you ask, me and Hope and the boy were thinking of popping up to stay for a bit, if that's OK.'

'OK? It's brilliant! When can we expect you?'

'Maybe tomorrow or the day after? Thing is, we decided at the last minute, kind of, and just to save a wee bit of dosh on a non-advance fare we thought we'd hook a lift on a—'

'Oh, sure, the Stornoway run. Give me a minute òr ten, and I'll tab you a code then fix a pick-up. Mid-evening suit you?'

'Anything after, uh, eight or so.'

'Aye, fine, no bother at all. Most of the overnight rigs pull out at ten, so you've got plenty of time.'

'Ah, thanks, Dad.'

'Just give us a bell when you're on your way.'

'Will do. See you soon.'

'If we're spared.'

And with a dark chuckle at that dour caveat he rang off.

Hugh stuck the phone in his pocket, mounted his bike, rode to the junction and turned left into Ealing Broadway. He rode west, through Hanwell, where he had to dodge goats, children, and driver-controlled motor vehicles, and into Southall, a welcome relief of neatness, colour and neon, its streets purring with bikes and autopilot electrics. The pavements bustled with men in suits or drab cotton salwar kameez, women in bright silk salwar kameez or saris. The only jarring note was the police presence. Hugh could see two foot patrols along the high street at a glance, and he could imagine the drone patrols he couldn't see overhead. The borough hadn't suffered the tidal wash of population, in and out, that its neighbours had over the past decades. It had remained a solid, respectable place, its only problem being that most of its population had Indian roots and continuing connections – business, political and personal. This made them doubly suspect: linked with the other side in the Warm War, and at high risk (as the phrase went) of recruitment or radicalisation by the enemy of both sides, the Naxals. The feeling of being watched from above tensed the back of Hugh's neck.

A flicker of shadow passed over him. He glanced up, and saw a hang-glider about sixty metres overhead, its flight path along the line of the street. It seemed far too low, an emergency landing or a collision with a rooftop inevitable. Hugh glanced in his mirror, stuck out his left arm and pulled in to the side of the road, putting one foot down on the pavement. The hang-glider, now about a hundred metres further on and five metres lower down, wheeled, soared as if on a thermal updraught, and flew back towards him. Nobody else – not even the pair of cops a block away and almost beneath its path – took any notice of it. As it approached, Hugh clearly saw its frame of struts, like the finger bones of a bat, and the pilot's blue face and fur waistcoat and boots. The eyes were goggled, but Hugh felt their gaze meet his for a split second as the glider passed above him. His head whipped around. The glider banked, vanishing over the rooftops.

Hugh looked around again. No one had noticed, though one or two people on the pavement were giving him puzzled glances. As he checked over his shoulder for traffic before pulling out into the road again, he saw out of the corner of his eye another flying object, this time moving across his line of sight. His gaze locked on to it and he felt his mouth open. Moving through the air, not far above the rooftops, from one side of the street to the other, was a contraption so weird that it was as if his brain was telling him that both it and the hang-glider were definitely hallucinations. It was a small airship, its glistening balloon distended in odd places like some enormous inflated pig's bladder. The gondola slung beneath it was quite clearly a longboat made from cured animal skins stretched over a wooden frame. Three men, in hooded robes like those of monks, sat one behind the other in it, laboriously propelling it across the sky with long sweeps of what looked like elongated fans mounted on poles, which they moved like oars.

Hugh watched it out of sight, shook his head as if to clear it, blinked, then cycled on until he spotted an electronics shop. He pulled over, locked the bike to a lamp post and went in. A bright, cluttered cave, most of whose customers at this time of day were smartly uniformed schoolchildren on their lunch hour. Hugh bought the cheapest and most break-able (in every sense) computer he could find, and made a point of paying by cash. Ten minutes later he sat down in a café with a tall glass of *lassi* and a bowl of *saag paneer*, for which he paid by cash, and used the new computer to check out flights east. After a good quarter-hour of poking around, he made a provisional booking for three seats on a flight the following morning from Gatwick to Prague, putting down a non-returnable deposit of two hundred pounds from his bank account.

As he stood up and shifted the empty glass and bowl on to a tray, the edge of the tray nudged the computer off the table. When he picked it up, the screen was cracked, the resolution clouded.

He muttered under his breath, laid the broken device on the tray, and returned the tray to the counter.

'I'm sorry,' he said, as he handed it across, with an indicative

227

downward glance. 'Could you dispose of the computer for me? Piece of junk.'

'No problem,' said the guy behind the counter. He took the computer off the tray, placed it under the counter, and put the tray with the dishes on the rack behind him. 'I'll recycle it later. Have a nice day!'

'You too. And thanks. Good afternoon,' said Hugh, and left.

He unlocked the bike, wheeled it across the street, mounted and set off for home. As he rode, he wondered if he'd done enough. If he was under heavy surveillance – no. But otherwise, if it was all still being neural-networked by the bots, one travel plan would be flagged as real, and one as a laughably obvious diversion. The trouble was, he had no idea which.

It was a summer evening like one of those Auden had imagined for after the revolution, with light traffic and loud sound systems standing in for the bicycle races and exploding poets. Hope walked along East West Road with her guitar in its case slung from her shoulder. A big backpack, with smaller bags stacked perilously on top, was strapped to a collapsible two-wheeled trolley, which she trundled in front of her. Hugh, with a frame rucksack on his back, led the way. Nick, with Max on his shoulders and carrying a token knapsack, scampered alongside him.

The lowering sun was getting in her eyes a bit, so she had her glasses on. Local situation reports, summarised from police radio chatter, social and mass media, and radio-station call-ins, scrolled in the bottom left-hand corner of her shaded vision. Nothing much was happening: a traffic snarl-up at Highbury Fields, a street scuffle out in Muswell Hill. In the bottom right corner a black app, patched from Hugh's phone, traced the slow progress of the truck on which Hugh had hooked a lift. Right now, it was negotiating the one-way system at King's Cross. With Holloway Road about ten minutes' walk away, they were in good time to meet it.

The trolley wheels juddered and bumped on the uneven pavement, each jolt giving Hope a split-second advance warning of where to place her heel, and each lurch making her grab for one of the upper bags. It didn't seem right that at this time in history, cracked and tilted flagstones should be a nuisance, but icy winters and rainy summers did their work regardless: freezing and erosion, two of the implacable processes that James Hutton had, with a wild surmise that had led him to search for and find the rocks that demonstrated it, held to account for the whole history of the Earth. No vestige of a beginning, no prospect of an end . . .

A bag slithered. Hope caught it and stopped to sling it and another two awkwardly on her shoulders, and pressed on with a surer step. She must, she thought, look a bit oppressed, trudging along like this behind the men of the house. In this instance she preferred walking behind, because it let her keep an eye on them.

Minute yellow flowers drifted down from a tree she passed under, around which a peculiar smell, like honeysuckle but with a sharper, almost aniseed note, hung like a vapour. The flowers, or perhaps floating seeds, looked like tiny cogwheels. It bothered her that she didn't know enough to identify them as natural or synthetic. If for any reason she never returned from this flight, or holiday, or adventure, she would always regret not having done more with the back garden. She'd planted a few rose bushes and a clump of sunflowers, but most of her effort in the garden had been a holding action against its return to the Thames Basin's local version of the climax community, slightly contaminated by stray syn bio weeds.

Her mind returned to what Hutton saw, the slow cycle of erosion and uplift, and she found herself wondering about whether it might be possible to tell if Hugh's visions showed the past or the future, according to whether or not synthetic biology plants featured in what he saw. It needn't even be in the landscape, in the visible biota. It could be some scrap or trace in a garment, a tool or a jewel. A whole new discipline rose in Hope's imagination: psychochronobotany.

She laughed, and hurried on forward to where Nick and Hugh stood at the corner of Holloway Road, waiting to cross, silhouetted against the sunset sky.

The lorry came up Holloway Road, quiet on big fat tyres, a cab up front and a long container trailer behind. When it was about a hundred metres away, Hope watched its icon on her glasses brighten and begin to flash. Hugh stepped forward, waving his phone like a hitch-hiker. The truck slowed, indicated, and pulled in as close to the side of the road as it could get, the cab just beside the waiting family.

Hugh's thumb twitched on his phone, and the side door of the cab swung open. He scrambled up the ladder, hauling his backpack, then turned around and reached out for Nick as Hope handed him up. Hope passed up her guitar and bags, folded the trolley, and climbed into the cab. Hugh was in the driver's seat, Nick in the middle, both strapped in. She reached to slam the door, but it swung slowly shut by itself, closing with a muffled thump and a firm snick, like a bank vault.

'Buckle up, Mum,' said Nick, as if trying to sound grown-up. His voice piped a little. It wasn't often he'd even been in a vehicle, other than a bus. Hope tousled his hair and fixed her lap-and-diagonal strap, settled in, and gave the thumbs-up. Hugh grinned, tapped on his phone, and sat back. The indicator light on the dash flashed, the gear changed from neutral to first, the engine rumbled, and the brakes relaxed with a loud hiss. The lorry pulled out and joined the stream of traffic, up the incline and under the bridge.

Hugh sat back, hands clasped behind his head, obviously tempted to put his feet on the dash. Nick's gaze switched back and forth from the buildings and traffic to the movements of the gear stick and steering wheel.

'It's like there's an invisible man driving,' he said.

'Oh, that's good,' said Hope. 'It's called the automatic driver, or drone driver, and it kind of is like an invisible man, but it's a program in the lorry's computer.'

'I know *that*,' said Nick, scornfully. He patted the toy monkey on his lap. 'I was just explaining to Max. I don't think Max understands AIs.'

'Oh, I'm sure he does,' said Hugh. 'You just have to explain it to him in very simple terms.'

Which, for the next five kilometres or so, Nick did.

Hope woke from a doze. Black road, white lines, blue signs. Bioluminescent trees lined the motorway, the light they cast easily visible because the lorry's headlights weren't on – they didn't need to be, except when behind a human-driven vehicle, and there were none such in the two lanes reserved for vehicles on autopilot.

'Where are we?' she asked, stretching her legs and wiggling her shoulders.

'Halfway up the M1,' said Hugh.

'Nick should be—'

'He is,' said Hugh. 'There's a wee bunk in the back. He's even in his PJs.'

'Good for you. What have you been doing?'

'Reading. Staring out the window.'

'Are we going to pull off any time soon? I need a pee.'

'There's a perfectly good toilet in the back,' Hugh pointed out.

When she returned, she took her boots off and tilted her seat back.

'There's a coffee machine and everything, a regular wee

galley. It's sort of mad, all the comforts for a driver who nine times out of ten won't be there.'

Hugh rubbed his eyebrows, yawned. 'Economies of scale. You couldn't drive like this in Turkey.'

'Uh-huh.'

Hope gazed out of the window again. The truck sometimes overtook other vehicles – buses, usually, with a bored driver, there only as reassurance, dozing or reading in the front seat – or was overtaken itself. Looking into the empty cabs as they drew level was a little unnerving, and those which, like theirs, contained people dozing or chatting even more so. There didn't seem to be any pattern to the overtaking, the slowing and accelerating, but there was a rhythm. The drone-driven vehicles had no speed limit, and generally moved at over a hundred miles an hour, but she always had the feeling there was a safe distance between them – shorter than the human safe distance, because of the machines' reaction time. At one point they passed through a heavy shower of rain, and the windscreen wipers didn't come on until Hugh, with an irritated gesture, flicked the lever. Hope found some reassurance in the steady whump.

She dozed. After a while, a shift in the engine's note and a sway to the side woke her up, as the lorry pulled off for a service area. It rolled, with perfect timing, into a vacant slot by a row of fuel pumps. The moment the engine stopped, she heard clangs and bumps from behind, followed by the throb of the pump and the sound of flowing liquid. The same process was being carried out on the trucks in front, the hoses and nozzles moving like hand-puppet snakes.

As the lorry pulled out and before it headed for the exit ramp, Hugh waved his phone.

'Want to stop for a bit, stretch your legs?'

Hope grimaced. 'Kind of, but I'd rather not disturb Nick. Besides, I just wouldn't feel safe, I'd be nervous of the lorry going off without us.'

'Couldn't happen,' said Hugh.

'You know how it is.'

'Yeah.'

Back on the motorway, Hope put her glasses on and, feeling like she was being just a bit obsessive-compulsive, checked in to the house wifi. Everything seemed to be in order: burglar alarm armed, the deadbolts in place, blinds down for the night, cameras all showing empty rooms. The bathroom light went on, then off, which startled her for a moment but made sense as part of the programme to make the flat look occupied. Her vision flitted from camera to camera like a ghost. The tap in the kitchen sink was dripping. She could see each drop gather, glistening in a stray street-light gleam past the edge of the front blinds, and after a second or two plop into the sink, then the next would begin to form. Drip, drip, drip.

She blinked hard and shook her head at that. She could hear the drips. Now that she noticed, she could hear sounds from all over the house and outside – boards creaking, cars passing, a dog barking. All very faint in the earpieces, and she might not have noticed them above the motorway noise and the truck's engine note, if it hadn't been for that drip.

Hugh was gazing out of the window, watching the traffic and the road as intently as if he were actually driving. Hope found herself hesitating to break his concentration, then shook off the illusion.

'Hugh?'

'Yes?' He didn't look bothered at all. Maybe he'd just been bored.

'Do the house cameras record sound?'

'What? I'm not sure. Never bothered to check, actually.'

'Well, they do.'

'Oh,' said Hugh. 'How did you find out?'

She told him. He fired up his own phone, put in an earpiece and looked at the screen. She could see the dark rooms flick by, one by one.

'So they do. Hang on.' He frowned, and poked about on his screen. 'Oh yes. Here it is. Homebase catalogue.' Flick, flick, flick of his thumbs. 'Home security products. Cameras. Got it. Oh yeah, there it is. "Also records sound with piezoelectric module in shaft." Talk about small print.'

'Oh well,' said Hope. 'So much for putting my hand over my mouth that night.'

'So that's why you were doing it? I did wonder.' He laughed. 'That wasn't the only sounds they must have picked up, eh?'

Hope smiled. 'What can I say?'

'Look,' said Hugh, in that irritating male tone of patient explanation, 'the whole *point* of having cameras in the house – apart from making burglars wear masks, I guess – is to have a record if you ever get accused of some kind of domestic violence or . . . you know. Nobody but us can see them without a warrant. If it comes to the cops checking our cameras we're in the shit anyway. And we're not.'

'That's reassuring.'

Hugh seemed to take this literally. He nodded and went back to gazing at the road.

Hope now felt a bit paranoid. She ran a search for any references to herself. None were current. The argument about the implications of the Kasrani case that had started the whole trouble had dropped far down the list of threads on ParentsNet, and only cropped up here and there on legal sites whose jargon she found impenetrable. She wished she had access to her own personal profile. Fiona, as a relevant professional, could look at any time at Hope's ever-evolving profile, but Hope, as its subject, couldn't. For sure it would be evolving now: unconventional though their mode of transport was, it wasn't quite illegal, although no doubt Hugh's father had cut a few corners setting it up. They hadn't made any attempt at concealment – for people like themselves, as opposed to professional criminals, spies and the like, such attempts were foredoomed to be worse than useless – so the cameras and face-recognition software and all the rest of the surveillance systems were right now aware, at some level, of their location and destination. Her glasses, and Hugh's phone, were in themselves quite enough to pinpoint their location to the nearest metre. The only precaution they'd taken was to block calls from Maya or from Geena, to prevent at least these dots being joined to them again. The outstanding question was whether the priority algorithms thought Hope and Hugh's actions significant enough to call for human attention, and intervention.

Probably not, Hope thought, though she kept a wary eye on police vehicles in the fast lanes until she fell asleep, to dream of shining lines connecting dots.

She woke to dawn, and Scotland. Hugh was in the back. He came through with two paper cups of coffee.

'Mmm,' said Hope. 'Thanks.'

She stared out, bleary-eyed, feeling stiff and sticky. They were just past Berwick-upon-Tweed. Low, rolling hills to the left looked rugged and high after most of England. To the right, she caught glimpses of cliffs and the North Sea. Hugh sipped, while thumbing rapidly on his phone.

'Done,' he said.

'What?'

'Cancelled our flight to Prague.'

'What?'

'More than twelve hours' notice, so I've kept the penalty down to the deposit.'

He looked pleased with himself.

'What flight?'

He hadn't told her. He did now.

'I'm not sure how clever that was,' Hope said. 'It looks exactly like an attempt at a diversion.'

'Well, it worked, didn't it?' Hugh waved an arm. 'We're in Scotland!'

'Maybe you could ask Nick to repeat that explanation he gave Max last night. About how artificial intelligence works. Because you bloody need it!'

Hugh shrugged. 'Aw, come on.'

'How much was the deposit, anyway?'

'Two hundred quid. Think of it as the fare for this journey, and it's a saving on the bus or the train.'

'Think of it any other way, and it's a waste.'

'Peace of mind, then. Insurance.'

'Hmph!'

Hugh leaned over. 'Come on. Good-morning kiss?'

She had to smile. 'All right.'

Nick emerged from the back of the cab and climbed on Hope's lap.

'I'm hungry, and Max needs recharging.'

'Good morning to you, too.'

Something between a shrug and a squirm.

'Ah, come on, let's sort you out.'

Hope went into the back of the cab and got Nick washed – or wiped, anyway – and into his clothes. While he went into the front to sit in her seat, Hope washed her own face and changed her underwear and pulled on a fresh shirt. Back in the front, sitting in the middle, she even found a way to recharge Max, from a socket marked mysteriously with a symbol for a lit cigarette. After a while, the Firth of Forth swung into view, then disappeared and appeared again, then vanished entirely as they hit the city bypass. Hugh tapped on his phone so that they pulled off just south of the Forth Road Bridge, and rolled into the lorry park of a McDonald's.

Hugh looked over at Hope.

'Now ... sure you're not nervous about leaving the cab?'

'Yes, I am, but I'm a bit more willing to risk it in daylight. It's not like we're in the middle of the night and the middle of the motorway. Anyway, hunger rules right now.'

'Don't it just.'

They stretched their legs, had McBreakfast, bought drinks and snacks for the rest of the journey, and piled back into the cab, hands overloaded, laughing.

As they crossed the Road Bridge, the biotech towers of Grangemouth glittered to the left, and the Forth Rail Bridge and the vast array of tall windmills decommissioned but not yet dismantled on the horizon beyond it loomed to the right. Nick couldn't decide what to look at, and compromised by surging from one side of the cab to the other.

'And what's that thing out there?' he asked, pointing across Hugh, to the right, at a derelict platform in the middle of the Firth just beyond the Rail Bridge.

'It's a place where they used to fill up the oil tankers,' said Hugh.

'What's oil tankers?'

That explanation kept Nick occupied most of the way to Perth. A junction ahead offered one route to the north, the other to the west. Just before the choice had to be made, Hugh's hands hesitated over the steering wheel; then he shrugged and sat back. So the vehicle stayed on automatic, all the way up the M90 to Inverness. It took about an hour and a half. A long, slow ascent, it felt like, then a descent so fast it made your ears pop, like in an aeroplane. Along the way, Hope felt almost oppressed by the sheer density of New Trees and other plantations that pressed close to the sides of the motorway, for most of the time masking all the scenery except the windmills. Beyond Pitlochry they were in the Cairngorms National Park, from which synthetic organisms were excluded. Here, the view opened out, and natural trees and heather did losing battle with flash-flood erosion. Snow patches shone on summits and lurked in shadowed corries.

'I've heard it said,' Hugh told her, looking straight ahead at the road, 'that up near one of these summits there's a wee stretch of burn that stays frozen all through the year.'

'A tiny glacier!'

'Exactly. And it gets a bit less tiny every year.'

'That would be big news, if it's true. So why haven't I heard?'

Hugh shrugged. 'It's a rumour. And the rest of the rumour – wouldn't you just know it? – is that it's kept secret. The place is supposed to be in an area of the park that's strictly off limits, to keep nesting eagles undisturbed or something like that.'

'That just raises the question of how anyone knows about it at all.'

Hugh tapped the side of his nose. 'Some park ranger who had a dram too many in a bothan. So the story goes.'

'And where did you hear it?'

'Ach, years ago in Aberdeen, drinking with some climbers.'

'It's taken you all this time to mention it?'

'You have a point there,' said Hugh. 'To tell you the truth, it was one of those memories you file and forget, if you see what I mean.'

Hope didn't, but she decided to let the matter drop before Nick got curious.

The motorway gave out on the approach to Inverness, and with it the automation. Normally the lorry would turn off to the Business Park and pick up a new driver at this point, but the codes on Hugh's phone overrode that. He took the wheel, to Hope's silent disquietude and Nick's noisy admiration, as the lorry approached the Kessock Bridge, and another splendidly distracting view on both sides.

Hope relaxed as Hugh drove on, with every appearance of confidence, across the Tore roundabout, turned left outside Dingwall, left again at Garve ... She supposed the skill of lorry-driving was like cycling: once learned, never lost. The long road west was four-lane all the way, a smooth ride that Hugh kept below sixty. For some reason he didn't explain – it could have been arbitrary, a mental coin-toss, or else the outcome of some intuitive summing of the likelihood of any security inspection – he had chosen to head for the Uig, Skye-to-Tarbert, Harris ferry rather than the more obvious Ullapool-to-Stornoway, a shorter drive but a longer voyage. Hope kept Nick entertained by pointing out eagles and buzzards, camera drones and jet fighters, deer herds and wolf packs, through a monotonous succession of glens and moors. After they'd turned left at Strathcarron, the scenery itself held his gaze: the long stretch of the sea-loch above whose southern shore they climbed and descended on switchback braes; the precipitous view over Strome; the bleak moor of Durinish. Then the swoop back to another wide four-lane highway, and the scary climb up and over the Skye Bridge. Across Skye, Nick was kept variously occupied by crisps, the Cuillin and the Quiraing.

On the ferry to Tarbert there was no problem keeping him amused for the hour and a half it took, or afterwards in the slow progress through the huddled port. The boredom and fractiousness only kicked in after the steep ascent to the island's plateau, a glacier-scored surface reminiscent, as Hugh put it, of space-probe photos of Callisto, but less lively. Nick cheered up as they crossed into the strange synthetic woodlands of Lewis, and on to Stornoway, and the grandparents.

16

The New Woods

'Who would have thought it?' said Nigel, watching the container lorry roll away from the pier towards the unloading dock. 'Cars from Africa, and in boxes like toys!'

'Plastic models, scale one to one?' said Hugh.

'That's it!' Nigel laughed, and clapped him on the back. 'Well, let's get you all into ours, wicked petrol-burning steel contraption that it is.'

Nigel had for years cultivated an air of ironic grievance that his car, a decades-old Nissan 4x4, was not allowed off the island.

Hugh picked up his own pack, Nigel hefted Hope's, and they set off towards the car park, with Hope and Mairi, Hugh's mother, walking ahead with Nick between them, capering along and swinging from their hands. It was late afternoon, about six, but the sun was higher than it would be at the same time in London, so it felt earlier. Every time he came back, Hugh had the same slight disorientation. Stornoway was disorienting in another way, too. Strung around a natural harbour, under a wide sky, the town almost made you turn in a circle to take it in as soon as you arrived. It could make you dizzy. Ever since he'd started at the Nicolson Institute, the big school after wee school, Hugh had experienced Stornoway as a textbook example of uneven development, the sort of place you'd see in television documentaries about African Lion countries where at some point the presenter, as if by contractual obligation, would let slip the phrase 'land of contrasts'. He'd written a poem for second-year English composition that began:

> Colour washes, council schemes,
> seagull cries and jump-jet screams.
> Ocean air and petrol stink,
> Free Church elders, too much drink . . .

And so on. Typical teenage verse: moralistic, observant of the obvious. But all the things he'd mentioned were – to be fair to his earlier stuck-up self – still very much in evidence, apart from the 'too much drink', alcohol consumption having been driven out of sight and out of mind here as everywhere else. Fighter jets and choppers still came and went from RAF Stornoway, the gulls were noisy and arrogant as ever, the vehicles to this day were more polluting than those you'd find on the mainland, and on top of all that, yet more contrasting features had been stacked: the windmills, the tower-block developments like fence-posts around the older part of town, the USS *Donald Rumsfeld* bristling in the bay, the shrimp boats and inshore trawlers slipping past it like canoes under the bowsprit of Cook's *Endeavour*. The stiff breeze still came off the Atlantic, strong and fresh.

As for Free Church elders, well . . . the closest to that in the vicinity, by appearance at least, was Hugh's father, in his usual get-up for a visit to the big city: Homburg hat over the bald pate that lay in Hugh's probable future, close-cropped salt-and-pepper hair underneath the black brim at the sides and back, black natural-wool coat over a serge suit and blue cotton shirt and silk navy tie, polished brown brogues spattered with droplets of mud from the puddles of a recent shower. Hugh glanced away to hide his half-smile, his almost smirk. His father tried to dress the part, but he'd never quite get it right.

Fourteen years ago, half Hugh's life ago, Nigel had without warning gone native in a big way: learning Gaelic, keeping the Sabbath, minding his speech, and regularly attending the local Free Church. He never publicly or privately professed its doctrines, but he never contradicted them either, and in Hugh's university days had sometimes enjoyed baiting him with arguments against the mainstream understanding of biology and geology, with which sciences he shared with his son a purely pop-scientific acquaintance, and a certain disdain arising from their common study of electrical engineering. In all of these – the Gaelic, the Wee Free adherence, the Young Earth Creationism – Nigel was placing himself in an eccentric minority even for Lewis. Within that minority he was himself a minority of one, as a non-native Gaelic speaker, a non-native churchgoer, and a man whose first name was so unusual for Lewis that he didn't need a nickname. (With only one Nigel in the parish, if not on the island, there was no need for a disambiguating 'Nigel Turbine' or 'Nigel Sassenach'.) His surname was Leosach all right, traceable to an ancestor who'd been cleared off the land near Mangersta some time in the nineteenth century, and who, after many wanderings, had settled in Hendon. Hugh had never understood why his father had adopted his ancestral religion and way of life, like some black-faced sheep let loose upon the heather, but he occasionally surmised that it was some perverse revenge on the forces and interests that had driven that earlier Morrison from his croft and his wife from her spinning wheel and creel. Certainly Nigel had made no attempt to convince or convert Hugh, Hugh's sister Shonagh, or Mairi, who, as a hereditary and incorrigible but entirely nominal adherent of the Church of Scotland, had taken it all with a detached, tolerant bemusement.

Hugh, of course, had reacted with all the self-righteous moral indignation and disappointment appropriate for a fourteen-year-old. Even today, he couldn't recall the scene he'd made without an inward groan and an outward blush.

*

246

'It's those damned books you've been reading! You've been filling your mind with rubbish!'

'I think you'll find,' his father said mildly, 'if you care to look into them yourself, that they were written by men of some intellect, of parts and learning, to say nothing of shrewd psychological insight and worldly wisdom.'

'There are better books in the house, and all the great literature of the world out there on the net, right at your fingertips. Wouldn't it be a better use of your time to read them?'

'Novels?' said Nigel. 'At my age you lose the taste for fiction. Read novels and plays and the classics yourself, while you can still enjoy them and you're young enough to learn something from them about human nature.'

'You could still read science, history, philosophy . . . '

'Well I do,' said his father. 'As avidly as ever. Just not on a – not on the Lord's Day.'

'A day you waste completely!'

'Waste it? I take a well-earned rest, one whole day in seven. One day when I not only don't work, I don't even think about work, or watch or listen to the news. And your mother appreciates not having to cook or clean that day. It stands us both in good stead for the other six, I can tell you that!'

'Sitting about reading old books, and three hours listening to sermons and singing psalms? Call that a rest? Wouldn't a walk do you more good?'

'I can take a stroll up the glen, if it's a fine afternoon, for a bit of quiet meditation. Not even the minister has a word to say against that. It's not like the old days, though you might find the old folk raising their eyebrows.' A sly smile lit his sombre face for a moment.

'But – it's the hypocrisy of it all! How can you pretend to believe . . . all that . . . and put up with and conform to a load of stupid rules that don't have any justification but—'

'You will not tell me, *boy*,' said Nigel, shaking his forefinger at Hugh with an odd flash in his eye, a mixture of anger and irony, 'what I do or do not *believe*. And I do not *pretend* to believe anything.'

'That must make it difficult, when you hang out with Wee Frees!'

'Look, Hugh, I already know the men of the congregation, from the sites and the locality. Most of them make no more claim to be godly than I do. The few that do, the communicant members, the elect, are not a problem. They don't exactly proselytise, you know! When spiritual matters come up in conversation, I keep my own counsel.'

'Silence is consent!'

'Not around here, it isn't. As for the rules – well!' Nigel spread his hands. 'What am I losing? Sunday television? Give me a break! To put it exactly! And the rest? Swearing is vulgar, and offensive in mixed company. Theft and murder are wicked by the light of nature, likewise dishonouring your parents. Drinking and dancing? There are no pubs except in town, and the Stornoway pubs are not my scene at all, at all. I was never much of a one for the shebeen, the bothan or the ceilidh, and all your Hielan' fiddle-de-dee music can set my foot tapping but it doesn't move me more than that, never

248

has. I'm free to drink in moderation and within my means, which I do, to smoke if I want to, which I don't aside from the occasional pipe, and the thought of adultery has never crossed my mind.'

'You're still upholding a morality that's oppressive to women and gay people and young people.'

'*Young* people!' Nigel laughed. 'When have they ever given a thought to morality in these matters? Women? Ask your mother or your sister, or the lassies on the site. That's the women I have to do with – and you too, come to think of it. If you're concerned about the oppression of women, you might consider getting off your lazy arse around the house when you're at home, and being a bit less of a lout and a boor when you're away, at school and in town.'

'Hey, come on,' said Hugh. 'That's a bit—'

'Personal? Unfair? I hope so! And as for *gay* people ...' Nigel's face clouded for a moment, then cleared. 'Do you know any?'

'There's Ms Merton, the geography teacher, she's a lezzie. And—'

'Personally, I mean. Of your own age, or thereabouts.'

Hugh shook his head. 'That's not the point.'

'Ah, but it is,' said Nigel. 'You see, you do know some.' He leaned back in his chair, folded his arms, and looked quizzically at Hugh. 'Statistically, it's close to a certainty. Have you ever wondered *why* you don't know *who* they are?'

Hugh scratched the back of his head. 'Not exactly. I never thought of it that way.'

'Well, you go off and think about it. That would be some-thing ... worth thinking about. You might even say it would be Christian.'

Hugh didn't know where to look.

Hugh and Nigel slung the baggage in the back of the Nissan and they all piled in, after an awkward round of mutual assured deferring for the front passenger seat that ended with Mairi and Hope sitting in the back, Hugh between them, and Nick up front with Nigel. Nigel had brought a booster seat for Nick, so he had a view as well as being safe. Hugh couldn't see nearly as much from where he sat, an arrangement that suited both him and Nick. Nick was fascinated by the peculiar local variant of New Trees, whereas Hugh was somewhat depressed. What would become part of Nick's childhood memories was a wrenching dislocation of Hugh's. He missed the moors, not so much for what they were as for the views they had afforded, of the hills to the west and south.

On what had been open moorland of bog and peat, that thin post-glacial deposit over the pre-Cambrian gneiss, a covering tattered with innumerable lochs – some little more than pud-dles, others wide and deep enough to sustain their own lake monster or crashed aeroplane – and outcrops, there now grew dense plantations of modified pine. The trees grew like weeds until they reached a height of ten metres, whereupon an enzyme was activated to weaken the trunk about half a metre above the ground. Any force greater than a puff of wind on that fracture line and they'd topple, silently felled, leaving a neat stump. If the fallen tree wasn't harvested within about a week, further phased activation of enzymes changed its colour to a muddy yellow and started a rapid disintegration into a crumbly woodchip, which could itself be harvested for its fibres or left to consolidate, with unnatural rapidity like the unrealistic processes fancied by Flood Geology, into peat. The trees' propagation was limited by sensitivities to sand in the soil and salt in the air. That to sand kept them off reclaimed land and off the fertile machair predominant on the east coast; that to salt stunted their growth in the west. These intrinsic safeguards were themselves fine-tuned by brute-force genetic overrides that kept the trees out of sites of special scientific interest and out of the island's scenic areas: in the west, on the Ness peninsula and around Stornoway.

But the trees had the formerly bald central patch of the island to themselves, and to the communities that had likewise sprung up out of nowhere to process them. A network of new roads, noded with villages, spread through the synthetic forest. Every so often a log-laden truck would emerge from one of these side roads to trundle along toward Stornoway. Less often, other trucks of about the same size rumbled by with long cylindrical loads made up of spindled reels of cable, or with windmill blades as big as the wing of a small airliner, or with girders from their towers. Hugh recalled how when he'd been growing up he'd seen many trucks with the same loads, going the other way, from Stornoway to the moors and hills, and to assemble rather than dismantle. Even on the main road Nigel would, from habit rather than strict necessity, give each truck a wide berth as it passed, along with a wave to the driver.

He did this, Hugh noticed, even when the truck had no human driver. Perhaps his father was in his heart as much a mechanist as he was himself.

An hour after they'd left Stornoway, the car went around a bend and the village came into view, on the other side of a tongue of the sea-loch. There on the hillside opposite stood the house, the former manse, grey-walled and tile-roofed, sprawling, no trees New or old near it but a couple of tall pines in its sloping glebe and a cluster of smaller trees nearby. Amid the scores of houses and other buildings clustered around the shore and up the other hillsides it looked isolated, set apart, as if it were still a manse.

The car swung around another bend, revealing the narrow, dark glen, then across a bridge and back towards the village, past the craft shops, B&Bs and small restaurants and the two remaining churches. Nigel asked Nick, as if for a great favour, to hop out and open the gate, then close it again behind them. After Nick had proudly climbed back in, the palms of his hands reddened with rust, Nigel drove up the wee brae on the crunching gravel of the drive, to park between the peat stack and the shed.

'Well,' he said, 'here we are.'

'Home,' said Hugh.

Hope gave him a look as they got out.

17

There Are Many Rooms in My Father's House

Nick had been right: the house did smell, every room different. As they trooped through the back door into the short hallway, and then on through the house to drop off the baggage, freshen up and reconvene for dinner, Hope paused for a moment on the threshold of each room and passage to inhale its distinctive odour, familiar from her past visits, redolent of the place. The big difference from her own flat and from most of the others she knew was the number of rooms, the sheer volume of available space.

The hallway had the curious feature of a frosted-glass window in the ceiling, a relay for the skylight in the room immediately above. Its smell was of coats, anoraks, overalls and waxed jackets, all of which had many times been hung there wet and left to dry. The scullery on to which it opened smelled of laundry detergent and washing-up liquid. The adjacent kitchen-living-room, in which armchairs, other chairs, a dresser and a folding table huddled around an ancient stove, smelled at this moment of roast lamb, and generally of baking and boiling, of peat smoke and of peat ash. Through that room and out in the house's main hall, the smells of old wood and recent floor polish took over. At the end of that corridor, the downstairs bedroom that had been assigned as before to Nick – its door faced that of Nigel and Mairi's, he'd always slept soundly in it, and it was only a few steps and no stairs from the bathroom – had a warmer and more inviting smell of wool blankets and duvet fluff.

Hope left Nick there to bounce on the bed, open and shut the wardrobe door, climb into the window's deep internal sill, rediscover the stacks of two generations' worth of children's books and toys, and generally settle in. She went back down the corridor and up the narrow staircase by the kitchen door to the attic, a big, dimly lit, cluttered space off which three doors opened: to a bedroom at each end, and to the room at the side that Nigel and Mairi used as an office and workroom, and which the house's previous occupant, the minister, had used as a study. At the moment its door stood open, letting in daylight from the same big window that indirectly illuminated the hall-way downstairs. The daylight was partly blocked by Hugh, standing in the doorway looking into the room.

Hope dropped her bags in the first bedroom beside Hugh's and padded to the study door.

'What are you looking at?' she asked.

Hugh turned and smiled. 'Something that isn't there.'

Hope looked past his shoulder.

'Cameras?'

'There are no cameras in this house, but it's something else, something you couldn't see isn't there.'

'What's that?'

'The paper snowdrift.'

He stepped aside and waved her into the room, a bright but cramped space, half of whose ceiling sloped in parallel with the house roof, and a quarter of whose floor was fenced off by an oblong box of chicken wire over the horizontal window that relayed light from the big skylight set into the sloping ceiling. Under the window were a sewing machine and a bright red cardboard box of drawers, all partly open and overfilled with fabrics and sewing equipment. To the right of the door was a desk with a screen and keyboard, the adjoining corner and walls lined with bookshelves.

'When I was a kid,' Hugh went on, sweeping his hands at waist level, 'this was all piled with the old minister's secular books. When he retired he took his volumes of theology and sermons and Bible commentaries with him, you see, but he left all his non-religious books behind. Some of them anti-religious, even.'

Hope felt puzzled. 'Why would a minister have anti-religious books?'

Hugh shrugged, with a forced downturn of the mouth. 'Know your enemy, I suppose. And dropping in the odd allusion to the awful things the godless say must lend a bit of credibility and spice to a sermon. Besides, quite a lot of them were attacks on the Catholic Church.' He smiled. 'I remember finding one that listed the degrees of punishment for clergy who engaged in illicit intercourse, starting with, you know, a monk with a quadruped . . . '

'Quite eye-opening, I should imagine.'

'Yeah. I had great fun in that heap.'

Hope peered at the thick spines of the books on the shelves, many of which were illustrated with small grey photographs of churches or stern, bearded men.

'Looks like Nigel has made up for the loss of the minister's books . . . What happened to the others?'

'Oh, they're still around somewhere, as far as I know.' He jerked a thumb over his shoulder. 'Probably stacked in a dusty corner of the attic.'

Hope sidled past him to stand under the window, turning over the patterns and pads on top of the cardboard cabinet – ooh, sketchbooks! – and gazing out at the hill behind the house and at the sky behind it, still bright with the sun high in the west at eight o'clock.

'You should dig them out,' she said.

'Hmm,' said Hugh. 'Don't know if the old man would be too pleased. Anyway . . . time to go downstairs.'

Mairi didn't do pinnies. She wore an embroidered denim shirt loose over denim jeans, and walked with quick clicks of cowboy-boot heels. Her brown hair had not a strand of grey, but the shade looked natural. Hope guessed that, unlike Nigel, Mairi wasn't too proud or too conservative to swallow the gene-tampering tabs that kept the colour flowing from the follicles. She kept a small shop down by the shore, selling local craft-made tourist tat, some of it her own, and local delicacies: oatcakes, black puddings, smoked gannet chicks, barrel-salted meat so salty that just thinking about it made Hope's mouth water, even though she didn't like the stuff. Mairi dished up a late dinner with an impressive economy of effort and means: for the adults, slow-roasted mutton that had been in the bottom of the oven all afternoon, for Nick, a fast-baked tray of crumbed processed-meat shapes from the top of the oven; boiled potatoes and carrots on the side. As the plates steamed beneath their noses, Nigel said a slow-spoken but brief grace that concluded: 'We ask this in the name of the Son. Amen.'

Or was it, Hope wondered, 'in the name of the Sun'?

She'd never asked Nigel what he really believed, but Hugh had told her about the adolescent arguments he'd had with his father, and what came through these accounts and everything she'd seen and heard of the man was a studied ambiguity, an outward conformity to usage that gave nothing away of what went on behind his bright, sharp eyes. Above the armchair in the corner was a framed tapestry, in silver thread on a collage of black velvet and blue-black silk, that Mairi must have worked over many a winter evening. Its lower quarter displayed a chain-stitched Bible quote: *In My Father's house are many mansions . . . If it were not so, I would have told you.* The word of God, verbatim from King James, unexceptionable to the most orthodox visitor, to elder or minister of the Kirk. But the picture above it was of a brilliant light in a starry sky above a blocky line of rooftops. It could have been the Star of Bethlehem. It could as well have been a UFO over a capital, or an airliner on approach over a low-build industrial estate in west London. The picture was as unexceptional as the text, and as haunting. There were mystics, obsessives and New Agers who took these words of Jesus as a hint that he had other worlds in mind, and indeed in his care. Was Mairi, in the ambiguity of that needlework, alluding to such speculations?

Eating, and soon conversation, drove the question from her mind. Nigel was witty, Mairi warm, Hugh taciturn, and Nick just this side of insufferable: overexcited and tired at the same time, splashing his plate and the tablecloth around it with ketchup, talking too much, interrupting, leaving the table to consult the roaming Max. From where Hope sat, she could see out of the window, across the grassy shoulder of the hill on which the house was built and over to the higher hill beyond, a steep heathery mound with a rocky outcrop at the summit, above which even at this distance she could make out, as black specks, the pair of eagles who made that rock their roost. Their presence had spared the horizon a windmill, and for that Hope gave silent thanks to something – to division, to contradiction, to ambiguity perhaps.

A god of small mercies.

'The wee fella's doing all right,' said Nigel.

Hope had just got Nick settled, despite his insistence that it was still daytime, and had joined the others in the big front parlour, a chillier and more formal room than the kitchen, with a wide bay window overlooking the village and a corner of the loch. Its distinctive smell was of furniture polish and a faint aroma of pipe smoke, which made Hope's monitor ring tingle. Hugh had already produced the slightly depleted bottle of Glenmorangie (which made her wonder whether he'd also brought along his air pistol) and placed it on the coffee table amid four small glasses and alongside a teapot and four cups.

'Yes, he's doing fine,' said Hope, taking a seat.

'Lively enough,' Nigel went on. 'Bright.'

'Oh yes.'

'No problems from you not taking the fix, then?'

'No,' said Hope, a little taken aback. She waved a flat, open hand, fingers spread. 'A few childhood illnesses, nothing serious.'

'Uh huh,' said Nigel, leaning forward and pouring tea for everyone. 'I understand you're in a wee bit of trouble over it.'

'Well, yes,' said Hope, accepting tea and a drop of milk. 'That's part of the reason why we're here. Apart from, you know ...'

'How wonderful we are?' said Mairi. 'Don't worry, we understand.'

'But what are you expecting to get out of staying here?' Nigel asked, settling back in his deep armchair, propping cup and saucer on the arm. 'You're welcome, of course, as long as you like, but this is hardly a refuge from the big, bad world.'

'No, no,' said Hope. 'We just want – I just want a bit of space to make up my own mind.'

'That's all right, then,' said Nigel. He shot her a sly glance. 'I was a wee bit concerned that you might be thinking that an association with the Kirk I attend would give you the conscience let-out.'

'Good Lord, no! Sorry, that just slipped out. But anyway, no, it never crossed my mind. I take it your church is against the fix?'

Nigel shook his head. 'Not at all. It's a blessing. "The fourth commandment requireth all lawful endeavours to preserve our own lives, and the lives of others", as the Shorter Catechism has it, and the fix most definitely counts as a lawful endeavour. As do all the other advances – come on now, it's an age of miracles we live in! The blind see and the lame walk. Why should we reject that?' He raised a hand, as if to forestall an objection. 'But of course, the Church also takes a stand for liberty, lawful liberty that is, and I wouldn't dream of prying into your reasons for such a personal decision. I think the pressure being put on you and others is not a good thing at all, at all.'

'Well, I'm glad to hear it,' said Hope, a little stiffly.

Mairi stretched across and squeezed Hope's hand. 'Don't you worry,' she said. 'We'll stand by you, whatever you decide. Nigel's just a bit formal in his way of putting it.' She turned to her husband. 'Isn't that so?'

'It is indeed,' said Nigel, just as gravely as before, then he relaxed and grinned. He put the cup and saucer back on the table, and reached for the whisky bottle.

'I have a wee hankering for a dram and a pipe. It's a fine evening. Why don't we step outside?'

The lip of the bottle hovered over each glass in turn. Hugh and Mairi nodded, Hope shook her head.

'I'll take a cup of tea out with me,' she said.

Rather to her surprise, it was the back yard and not the concrete veranda at the front they went out into. In the crook of the L-shape of the house, it was fenced and pebbled, the side facing the house a dry-stone wall at the foot of the green bank where the hill had decades ago been dug out. Mairi brought out a brace of stools, on which she and Hope sat while Hugh and Nigel used the wall as a bar.

Overhead the pale sky darkened, pricked by the first stars. A match flared as Nigel lit his pipe, carefully downwind of Hope; she didn't feel a thing.

'I remember seeing the Northern Lights from here,' said Hugh, looking upward.

'We used to call them the Merry Dancers,' said Mairi.

'That's lovely,' said Hope.

Nigel pointed with his pipe stem to the hills in the west, black against the red sunset.

'Remember the windmills? The ones along there are gone, we took them down this past month. I have a longer drive in the morning.'

'I was thinking of going along with you,' said Hugh.

'Were you indeed? Now that's not a bad idea at all. But not tomorrow, or the day after for that matter, and then it's the weekend. I'll put the word out on the site, see if there's anything going. You have the car and take Hope and the boy to the beach or the hills. Make a wee holiday of it.'

'Won't you be needing the car?'

'Ach, I'll grab a lift on a lorry,' said Nigel, thumbing his pad. He finished the message and winked. 'I'm good at that.'

Hope drove. She could see Hugh was a little surprised by which door she went for, and said to him over the top of the Nissan: 'Hey, I'm a west London girl! Think I can't drive a Chelsea tractor?'

Hugh laughed and got in the back, after sending Nick down to open the gate.

But in truth it was a long time since she'd driven anything, and she was grateful she had the gravel brae, short though it was, to get the hang of the gears and pedals. Nick closed the gate behind them, standing on it as it swung towards the post, after a quick glance over his shoulder to make sure their backs were turned, and not realising they were watching him in the mirrors. He slid the bolt to, clambered in and settled on the booster seat in the front, proudly fixing the seat belt himself.

'Which way?' Hope asked.

'Left,' said Hugh. 'Then left again at the junction.'

This took them out of the village and along the side of the little loch beyond the shoulder of the hill on which the house stood. The day was warm and overcast, the air still. Perfect fishing weather, of which someone in waders was already taking advantage, casting a fly far down the loch. Ahead the view opened to a machair and a beach.

'The beach!' said Nick.

'In a minute,' said Hugh, leaning forward from the back. 'I just want to show you something first.'

Hope drove on past the end of the loch, past the machair and the crofts around it and up the sloping road along the side of the hill that overlooked the bay. As she approached a small cluster of buildings to the right, Hugh asked her to pull over on to a side road that passed directly in front of it.

'Come on,' he said, jumping out.

Hope looked up. It was a small school building. On the hill above it stood the last legs of a windmill, around which a few vehicles were parked and people in overalls and hard hats worked. A generator thumped, beside some kind of winch.

Hugh led them around the side wall, overlooking a patch of asphalt playground, a shelter, and some adjacent sheds. It was still termtime, but not playtime. The children were in the classrooms.

'You can see right in!' said Nick.

'Never thought of that,' said Hugh.

'It feels wrong, seeing a primary school without a screen,' said Hope. 'I don't mean *wrong* wrong, just . . . odd. Unexpected.'

'Uh-huh,' said Hugh.

He walked on up a rutted, unpaved road on the hill behind the school, past the place where the tower was being dismantled, until he'd reached a point where he could look down at the site.

'I saw that being built,' he said.

'Why are they taking it down?' Nick asked. He sounded uneasy as much as curious.

'We don't need the wind towers any more,' said Hugh. 'We get all the electricity we need from the sun fields in the Sahara, and from wave-power stations, like that one you can see way out in the sea.'

'But still,' Nick persisted. 'We might need *more* electric. Like Max.'

'Very clever,' said Hugh. He glanced across at Hope. She laughed.

'I don't have the answer to that either!'

'Oh, I know the answer,' said Hugh. He squatted down to look Nick in the eye, man to man. 'Yes, we could leave the towers up and we'd have more electricity, but the thing is, the turbines and blades and so on wear out, and people have to work to make new bits for them or to fix the old bits. And when you add it all up, it turns out to be more work than the electricity is doing for us. It's like pouring water into the bath when the plug's out. It never fills up. We'd be better off if these people did other work instead of fixing the wind turbines all the time.'

Hope wasn't sure if Nick was quite able to grasp the concept of opportunity cost, but then neither were most adults. But he nodded, looking serious.

'What's the big wheel thing?'

'It's called a winch. They're using it to haul the cable that used to carry the electricity out of the ground, where it was in a sort of pipe. Because it turns out there's lots of other uses for that cable, maybe in India or China or Africa. And they're winding it on to these big reels that are stacked up there, and when enough are stacked up, a lorry will come to take them away, like the lorries we saw on the road.'

Nick suddenly pressed his face against Hugh's shoulder.

'Don't like it,' he said. 'Don't *like* it.'

'Why not?' asked Hugh.

'Scary,' said Nick. 'Dark.'

'It's all right, Nick,' Hugh said, with forced cheer. 'It won't leave us in the dark.'

Nick faced away, up the hill.

Hugh straightened. 'Let's go up there,' he said. 'I've got something to show you at the top.'

Nick raced ahead as they toiled up the heathery slope.

'What was all that about?' Hope asked.

'No idea,' said Hugh. 'You know how kids are. One day they'll be scared of a colour, or a shape, because it reminds them of a bad dream or something that troubled them on television.'

'I suppose.'

'You know,' Hugh confided, in a low voice, 'I got a funny feeling there myself.' He glanced over his shoulder, back at the site. 'Not scared but ... like there was something wrong with what I was seeing. Like ... you know those puzzles in comics, "What's Wrong With This Picture?". Some detail out of place?'

'Uh-huh.'

'It was like there's some hazard down there that everyone's overlooked.'

'Elf 'n' safety?' Hope sing-songed.

'Something like that,' Hugh said. 'Oh well. Maybe I just picked up some nervousness from Nick.'

'He's an odd little chap!'

They both laughed, clearing the air.

Nick waited for them at the skyline.

'What are you going to show me?'

'Over there,' said Hugh, a few steps below, pointing ahead, 'there's a big dark loch, and ...'

Hope and Hugh cleared the rise and looked down. Ahead of them was a hollow between low hills, and in the bottom of that hollow, a few paces away, was a shallow loch you could throw a stone across.

'Oh,' said Hugh. 'Not quite how I remember it.'

'Has it got smaller?'

'I think maybe I've got bigger,' said Hugh.

But Nick was pleased enough to go to the water's edge and be shown how to skip stones. Hope joined in, laughing at Hugh's surprise as she demonstrated her own mastery of the knack.

'Want to go down to the beach?' Hugh asked, just before Nick got bored.

'Yes yes yes!'

They turned and went down the hill. As they passed the site, Hope noticed, Nick kept his eyes averted. She didn't say anything, but reached down and held his hand.

At the car, she hesitated. 'Do you want to drive round and down, or ...?'

'Run down!' said Nick.

They crossed the two roads, looking carefully to left and right though there was no traffic within sight or sound, and

Nick scampered off ahead of them down the marram-covered dunes.

Hugh stopped for a moment, looking out towards the horizon.

'I once wrote a poem about this place,' he said. 'Want to hear it?'

Hope nodded.

Hugh grinned self-consciously and declaimed:

> 'The waves roll like logs into the bay
> and splinter, hissing, up the beach.
> Violent, even on the calmest day.
> God does not know how long they took
> to grind these cliffs exceeding small
> to a thousand million tons of sand.
>
> 'The new cemetery on the headland fills
> with headstones like hilts in a stabbed back.
> The minister stands on slowly shifting hills
> and does it by the book: "Their souls are immortal,
> their bodies
> rest till the resurrection."
>
> 'Their souls are electrochemical
> tracks in others' brains. Their bodies
> under the sharp, salt-water grass
> are earthed.
> The Atlantic ignores the land.'

Hope mimed a startled recoil of the head. 'You wrote that?'

'When I was in school, like. I mean, I was fifteen.'

He sounded defensive.

'No, no, it's not bad, I just never thought . . .'

'I had any poetry in me? Not now I don't. But we had to do it for English.'

'No, I meant . . . it's kind of harsh. What brought that on?'

'Ach,' said Hugh. 'I had not long discovered materialism, and my father had just discovered Presbyterianism.'

Hope considered him gravely. 'I think that excuses it,' she said.

'Race you to the beach,' he said.

'Not in my condition.'

'Oh. I forgot.'

She clouted his shoulder.

They raced each other down to the sand.

18

Not Even God

That Sunday morning, Hugh retrieved an old suit, shirt and tie of his from a wardrobe. They fitted well enough, though he kept running his finger under his collar. He borrowed a Bible, left his phone on the bedside table, and after breakfast walked with his father to the church. Hope and Mairi had plans to take Nick for a drive to the nearest beach – in the last couple of days he'd taken in a big way to playing in breaking waves, and Mairi had bought him a drysuit at one of the village shops. Mairi's own shop was closed for the day, in her only deference (other than not doing any housework) to Nigel's Sabbath-keeping. The previous evening, Nigel had pitched in with Mairi and Hope in preparing as much as possible of today's meals in advance: peeling the potatoes and carrots, boiling a chicken in the pressure cooker, even setting the table for breakfast. The irony that all this work was being done on the actual, original, Biblical Sabbath didn't seem to bother him at all, and Hugh had long since given up baiting him on the subject.

The rest of the village had long since given up on keeping the Sabbath. Most of the shops were open. The tide was out and the seaweed smelled like bad breath. Tourists and visitors strolled about in the sunshine, buying tat and hiring cars, bikes and boats. Among them, carefully ignoring them, little trickles and rivulets of more soberly clad people – men in dark suits and Homburgs, women in skirts below the knee and wearing often elaborate hats, children in smaller versions of the same outmoded outfits – walked from a few houses and from the car park to the church down by the shore, and, as if to their own surprise, converged as a congregation of three score or more.

After they'd gone to bed on the Saturday night, happily tired after a day walking in the hills and running on a beach, Hope had suggested to Hugh that she accompany Nigel to the church.

'No,' Hugh had said, without hesitation.

'Why not?'

'You'd find it strange.'

'That's the point. I'm curious.'

'Maybe another time. When you know Nigel better. Trust me, you'd find it boring and alienating.'

'You mean you'd find it embarrassing.'

'Yes,' he'd conceded.

He didn't find it embarrassing himself. In his teens he'd gone along a few times, he knew what to expect. Other than the fine woodwork of pew and pulpit, the church was harsh in its simplicity: whitewashed walls, windows of frosted rather than stained glass, no choir or musical instruments to accompany the singing. So too was the service. Psalms dolefully sung sitting down, prayers nasally intoned standing up, a sermon expounding an Old Testament verse and offering the gospel in a take-it-or-leave-it manner, with a heavy hint that most of those present, despite hearing such sermons at least twice a week all their lives, would leave it, and be left themselves to the outer darkness, where there would be wailing and gnashing of teeth. The burden of the sermon was an explication of the imprecations against Babylon in one of the psalms, the Authorised Version of which the minister had read as his text and the Scottish metrical version of which the congregation had sung. The sermon seemed to be making some contemporary reference, but it was so coded in metaphor and allusion that Hugh wasn't sure whether Babylon represented Moscow, Beijing, Washington, London, Brussels, the Vatican, or some hydra-headed multi-tentacled hallucinatory manipulatory illuminati behind all of them. His voice joined those of the congregation in the psalm's uplifting cadence:

> *O daughter thou of Babylon,*
> *near to destruction!*
> *Blest shall he be who thee rewards*
> *as thou to us hast done!*

Yea, happy surely shall he be
thy tender little ones
who shall lay hold upon, and them
shall dash against the stones.

Afterwards, as the congregation crowded out, warm smiles and handshakes all round, a little confidential and not always spiritual chat, and then dispersal to houses or cars.

Hugh and Nigel walked back home in silence. The others were still out.

'Better not boil the veg just yet,' said Nigel. 'But I can warm a wee pan of soup.'

He took the cold chicken from the fridge and cut a few slices, which he and Hugh ate with bread and bowls of chicken soup thick with carrots and rice. When they'd finished, Nigel stood up and took off his tie, then his fine leather shoes.

'Shame to waste such a fine afternoon,' he said, pulling on walking boots. 'Fancy a stroll up the glen?'

Hugh did. He too left his tie, and beside it a note, saying where they'd gone. Just in case they worried. He was halfway down the drive when he remembered he'd left his phone behind, on the bedside table. The thought of walking up the glen without his phone made him a little nervous, not just because he'd be beyond emergency contact but because he'd be without GPS. His parents had dinned into him the rule about not going into the hills without his phone. It was like brushing your teeth and washing your hands.

*

They followed the road west, out of the village, past the bridge and up the glen. It seemed smaller than the glen that figured in Hugh's childhood memories and haunted his dreams, but it was still impressive, steep-sided, almost a canyon. A little dark burn burbled along beside the road, its white noise only adding to the quiet. Now and again a car passed, or a sheep called, or a curlew cried, but after each interruption the feeling of silence came back. After a few hundred metres of silent strolling along the bottom of the glen, Hugh noticed a familiar gully by the side of the road. He tracked it by eye up the cliff.

'Wow,' he said. 'You can still climb up there.'

Nigel looked upward. 'You've climbed that?'

'Yes, often, when I was wee.'

Nigel chuckled. 'As well your mother and I didn't know that.'

'Aye.'

'Care to try it again?'

'Yes,' said Hugh, surprised. 'You don't mind?'

'"Bodily exercise profiteth little",' said Nigel, in an ironic tone. 'But a little is better than nothing. Lead the way.'

Some of it was a scramble, but most of the ascent was like a rugged staircase. Hugh even remembered the steps. About forty metres up he found again a semicircular shelf, thick with heather and bracken, in which he had occasionally sat and surveyed the scene.

'This is where I climbed to,' he said. He squatted, shaking lightly clenched hands in front of him, miming firing a machine-gun. 'Guarded the approach roads.'

273

'Ah,' said Nigel. He sat on the heather, legs hanging over the edge of the shelf. 'Quite a view.'

They looked out over the glen and the loch for a while.

'Sometimes,' Hugh said, 'on a quiet, hot afternoon like this, climbing in the glen, I used to feel in the silence and the sunlight a sort of ... a sense of presence. You know, like in an empty room when you feel someone's there?'

'I know the feeling,' said Nigel.

'Could that be what people mean by God's presence?'

'Nope,' said Nigel, with a brusque head shake. 'It's your brain's agency-detection module resonating. Like the noise you hear in silence, or the colours you see in the dark or with your eyes closed. The nerve keeps on firing, you see.'

Hugh laughed. 'Very materialist!'

'You could say that,' said Nigel. 'Or you could say scientific. I've looked up the neurology of it myself, and it seems conclusive enough to me. And I've listened closely to what people say about feeling the presence of God, and I can't say it's anything I've experienced myself, though I've experienced the feeling you mention often enough.'

He took his pipe and pouch out of his jacket pocket and slowly filled the one from the other.

'What I take from that feeling is absence, because I know what causes it. The only presence is the rock, the sheer non-human immensity around us. I believe it was once called the sublime. It is not to be mistaken for a spiritual experience.'

'Now you're sounding like the minister.'

274

'There's that,' Nigel said. 'They are very careful to distinguish odd feelings from the marks of grace.'

He lit the pipe with a match, took a few puffs, then blew out a long stream of smoke, which the breeze caught and wafted instantly away. Then he turned to Hugh with a dry smile. 'I have none of the marks of grace.'

'Well,' said Hugh, uncomfortable, wishing he hadn't said a word about God, 'I never thought ...'

'We can speak freely here.' Nigel flourished the pipe stem at the horizon. 'We have no phones with us. We are off the radar, so to speak. No doubt we are visible to satellites and drones, but I doubt they have capacity to spare for the likes of us.'

Still sitting, he pushed himself backwards and leaned against the rock face, careless of the back of his suit jacket. 'I want to say some things to you. I was going to arrange it at some point, but you've given me the opportunity to talk in a place where no one else can hear what's said.'

'Not even God?' said Hugh, unable to resist the prod of the old imp.

'Not even God,' said Nigel, in a firm but complacent tone. 'In this world we are almost certainly beyond the reach of God, if indeed he exists at all.'

'Never heard you say that before!'

'Never had occasion to say it.'

Hugh shook his head. 'How could we be beyond the reach of God, *even if* he exists?'

'Och,' said Nigel, 'this is something I've thought for a long time. Every world that is logically possible feels just like a real world if you're inside it. Now, not even God can make a logical possibility not a logical possibility. Not even God can make two plus two not four. Not even God can make a triangle with four sides. Not even God can make a valid conclusion not follow from a premise. So even if God were to intervene from outside, as it were, into a world, and change events, the most he could do would be to spin off a new world. The logically necessary original world would continue on its merry way, implication after implication' – he made chopping motions with his hands – 'ca-chung ca-chung ca-chung, you see?'

'Mathematical universe theory,' said Hugh. 'I've come across it. At university, I think.'

'Did you now? Well, I worked it out for myself, looking at Maxwell's equations late one night long ago, and pondering how it could be that they so unreasonably matched the world. And then, you might say, the light dawned. I had no idea there was a name for it. Anyway, that is what I think.'

'So why,' Hugh asked, 'do you go to church, and behave accordingly? I've never understood that.'

'No, you haven't,' said Nigel. 'It is not all pretence, you know. Like I said to you at the time. And like Spinoza said a few centuries earlier.'

'You read Spinoza?'

Hugh had tried, once.

'Yes,' said Nigel. 'I rummaged the minister's discarded books long before you did. And what I took from Spinoza was a consequence of the way I already saw the world. Religion is philosophy for beginners, you might say. At its best, it teaches you to live at peace with your neighbours and to reconcile your own will with what can't be changed, whether you call that the will of God or the course of Nature, which according to Spinoza are two ways of saying the same thing. These are no small matters to accomplish. And besides – there was another reason, a more pressing reason, for my outward conformity.' He tapped out his pipe on a stone, then looked up at Hugh. 'I did it for you, and . . .'

'What? For me?' Hugh shook his head. 'I don't get it.'

'. . . and to protect myself,' Nigel went on. He stared straight ahead, at the cliffs on the other side of the glen. 'You see things, don't you? And the boy does, I know that, I noticed it when he was two years old.'

Hugh said nothing. Involuntarily, the tip of his tongue moistened his lips.

Nigel sighed. 'I see things too.'

'Oh,' said Hugh. He laughed. 'I didn't see that one coming.'

Nigel laughed too, but by way of showing he'd got the joke.

'Och, whatever the old folks used to say about the sight, it's not a great deal of use. The day before your grandfather died, I saw him dressed in a suit and laid on the ground out the back of the house. And you know what my first thought was? "The old man never wears a suit except for weddings and funerals." And then I came to myself, and blinked, and it was gone. I called him straight away, and he was pottering about on his allotment, hale as ever. I didn't say a word about my premonition. Next day, bang, heart attack, down he goes, felled like a tree. Maybe if I'd warned him . . . told him to see a GP right away . . . or maybe the surprise of that would have struck him down then and there.' Nigel sighed, drew on his pipe and blew out smoke. 'Who knows? Not me, for sure. And other times . . . now and again over the years . . . I've seen events that came to pass, but . . . I don't think it ever shows you something you can change. Which it couldn't do, I suppose, if it really showed the future. The future can't be changed, no more than can the past in my view. It's not always even personal. There are times when I see the glens full of life, not like now with tourists and wind farms and the like, but as it was in the days when our ancestors built the brochs and the drove roads, smoke coming up from the wee bothies, folk in the fields and boats on the sea, and the lowing of cattle. Now – would that be the past or the future I'm seeing, eh? Answer me that if you can!'

'I can't,' said Hugh. He looked away for a moment. 'I've seen the like myself. Uh . . . how did you know about me?'

'I've known since I overheard you talking to yourself, as it seemed, when you were five or so, and I put it out of my mind, until that day years later you asked about it. That was when I got alarmed, you see, that you might be interested, that you might talk, and that word might get around, and . . . you know. And now . . .'

Nigel got to his feet. He gazed down at Hugh with a curious intensity.

'That is what this is about, isn't it? The business with Hope not taking the fix? She wants to keep the gene for the second sight.'

Hugh shook his head. 'She was against it long before I ever told her.'

'I bet that was an interesting conversation.'

278

'It was that,' said Hugh.

'Hmm,' said Nigel. 'But why did she object to it in the first place?'

'She never says why. That's half the trouble.'

Nigel shot him an understanding smile. 'And no wonder she doesn't know. If she has the gene herself, it's recessive. It's not expressed, so she can't express it, so to speak. But she feels it in her bones.'

'I doubt that's how it works,' said Hugh.

Nigel shrugged. '"We walk by faith, and not by sight", as the man said.' He stepped carefully to the edge of the shelf. 'Let's go down.'

As they picked their way back down the gully to the road, Hugh realised that he hadn't asked his father to say more about what it was he saw, though he was burning with curiosity. He recalled that Nigel hadn't asked him to elaborate on the little he'd said himself. Maybe it was a subject like one's sex life, about which you could volunteer information, but to enquire of it would be indelicate, a breach of tact.

And yet it had all been unspoken. Out of such moments, such hesitations and reserves, might there not come habits, then manners, then customs, then traditions, then a way of life?

They reached the road and walked back towards the village. They'd just come in sight of the house when two jet fighter-bombers flashed into view around the shoulder of the hill on which it stood, screamed overhead, banked just behind them, the starboard wingtips almost scraping the road, and hurtled away between the narrow walls of the glen.

'Training exercise,' Nigel explained, as Hugh's ears rang from the sonic boom. 'I don't know what they're training for, but if they ever have to bomb Lewis, it's a fine job they'll make of it.'

Hope and Mairi and Nick had returned, hungry and sandy. The vegetables were simmering. Nick's drysuit was in the sink, getting wet. Hugh went upstairs to recover his phone. He switched it on, stepped out of the bedroom and, on impulse, into the office. He stared out of the window at the hill.

Up there ...

He took his phone out and went back through its memory, passed on like a gene from chip to chip through generations of technology. There it was: the map of his and his pals' route up to the culvert.

He stood there thinking about GPS, and tracking. Then he pointed his phone at the printer on the side of the desk. The device whirred. He picked up the sheet of A4, folded it twice, and stuck it in his shirt pocket. He was about to go downstairs when it struck him that a map wasn't much use without a compass. He went into the bedroom and rummaged in the bedside cabinet. All sorts of boyhood junk fell out, among it a small transistor radio and a Silva compass. He opened the back of the radio, and found to his relief that no battery had been left inside to corrode it. He stuck the radio in his pocket, hung the compass by its lanyard on the dressing-table mirror, and went downstairs.

19

Workaround

Geena sat on her stool in the corner of the lab and gazed list-lessly out of the window at the bright blue June sky and the fluffy white clouds above the skyline of Hayes. She felt depressed, and there seemed no rational reason for it. The flash-backs had stopped, and she now had a nightmare only about once a week. She no longer flinched visibly at the sight of a police vehicle or uniform, and the sound of a siren no longer made her jump, though it made the hairs on her back and the nape of her neck stand up as if cold water had been poured down her spine. On the whole, she was quite glad that she hadn't opted for trauma counselling. According to her cursory online research on clinical outcomes, she was recovering better by herself than she would have done if she'd sought professional help.

Her notes were all written up and her field observations were almost complete. She really had more than enough data now to work with, and she already had reams of outline written on the theoretical questions she had posed to herself when she'd set out on the thesis. All that remained was to integrate them, to match her observations with (or pit them against) the various contending-but-compatible theoretical frameworks – she could already see, to take an obvious example, that the all-male composition of this particular dry-lab team raised interesting questions about the extent to which the self-understanding emerging from their practices was gendered. The developing crash-and-burn, trial-and-error style of work was, you could say playfully, penetrated by masculinities, undoubtedly macho. And the precise location of value production within the intellectual process would be fascinating to pinpoint. A critical-ecological and non-anthropocentric approach to the animal and plant products (aha!) that provided what was so revealingly called the raw material for genetic manipulation, even in the case of pure synthetic biology, promised to yield some fruitful (so to speak) lines of investigation.

Lots to be getting on with.

And yet, and yet ... she couldn't, now, revisit the texts or her own preliminary theoretical notes and queries without seeing, like barbed wire woven through a flowery, fecund trellis, the actual functioning of those theories and texts, as explained to her by the estimable Dr Estraguel, as well as the point that had been brought sharply to her attention by the ministrations of the police. She had lost the taste for theory; in fact, thinking about it nauseated her, quite literally: it gave her

282

actual physical nausea. Rereading the notes she'd written when the project had been all shiny and new and exciting, on the other hand, merely made her want to cry.

The cause that she'd taken up in dogged retaliation for her enhanced interrogation and in expiation of her earlier un-witting and recent coerced complicity in the whole system of ideological and physical repressive apparatuses – her support for Hope Morrison – that too had lost its savour. It had run into the sand last week, when Hugh Morrison had dismissed her suggestion for how to get his wife off the hook. She'd tried calling him, but his phone had given her an even more un-ceremonious brush-off. She was thinking of somehow getting around that, of appealing to Hope directly, over her husband's head or if necessary behind his back, just in case he was stand-ing in the way of or distorting the truth about what Hope might herself seize on as the exact solution she was looking for, her get-out-of-jail free card, and would jump for joy and weep with gratitude on Geena's shoulder for its delivering.

Geena indulged this rescue fantasy for the minute or so it took her to recognise it as a rescue fantasy, then dismissed it. She took a certain grim satisfaction in her own lucidity and self-awareness, and then went back to wondering why she was depressed. She went through again all the possible grounds she might have for feeling down.

No. No rational reason whatsoever. She really should get a grip on herself.

On top of everything else, there was now a diffuse pain in her midriff, which had been growing for half an hour and was now becoming difficult to ignore. Perhaps she was going down with something, and that was why she felt so unaccountably depressed and listless and why her stomach hurt. She was about to bestir herself to look up summer-flu symptoms when she heard behind her an apologetic cough.

She turned, almost falling off her stool, and saw Joe standing a few paces away, clutching a pad and looking at her with sympathy and concern. The lab was otherwise empty, the work table littered with sandwich containers and cardboard cups lipped with drying soup.

'Are you all right?' Joe asked.

'Yes, I'm fine, thanks,' Geena said.

'You don't look fine.'

'Oh!' Geena gave a shaky laugh. 'I missed lunchtime, because I was so wrapped up in ... my thoughts, and I'm hungry – that's what's the matter with me.'

'Oh,' said Joe. 'In that case, would it not be a good idea to go to the canteen? Everyone else has had their lunch and gone out to catch the sun.'

'Why didn't they invite me?'

Now she was feeling paranoid, as well as depressed and (now that the pain had been identified, thankfully) absolutely starving.

'You seemed preoccupied, and the guys thought it best—'

'They discussed this?'

'Yes,' said Joe.

'Jeez.' Geena stood up. 'I must have been, as you say, preoccupied. Let's go.'

The canteen was still busy, clattering with cutlery and abuzz with talk. Geena chose a sandwich and soup, Joe a slice of meat with two veg. He noticed her puzzled look.

'Synthetic,' he said.

Glancing at the plate, she saw that the slice had a most unnatural pattern, an intricate imbrication of different colours and textures, like a cross-section through a vertebrate thorax.

'Hmm,' said Geena. She knew vegans – Maya for one – who wouldn't eat synthetic meat, because ... well, there was an animal cell somewhere in its ancestry, and anyway it was cheating. Evidently Joe's (presumed) Buddhism drew different lines.

'I have a question,' he said, after they'd found a vacant table and sat down facing each other. 'Have you had any results with ... the phenotype of that interesting gene?'

Geena shook her head, munching. She swallowed and said: 'Well, kind of. He was aggressively uninterested. Insisted he didn't have anything unusual about his vision. Then he blurted out that the gene must be recessive.'

Joe carefully cut a square inch of synthetic meat and slid it around in gravy.

'How would he know that?'

'He seemed to assume it was connected with a superstition some people in the north of this country have about, well, a hereditary capacity for, uh, precognition and other so-called psychic powers.'

Geena felt a little embarrassed even talking about it.

'That's interesting,' said Joe. 'I have something to show you. Perhaps after we have eaten.'

To her surprise, he didn't take her back to the lab to show her. Instead, over coffee, he took out his pad and doodled with a fingertip.

'Take a look.'

She put on her glasses and made the connection. It was the same sim as he'd run before, but this time, instead of showing a response to photons, a different sequence took place. A shimmering wave propagated up through the opsin sheet, and in turn sparked an expanding shower of photons. Almost but not quite at the same moment, a massive particle slammed through the display, in a downward direction.

'What's going on here?' Geena asked.

'A few months ago,' said Joe, 'there was a piece about tachyon detection in a rhodopsin suspension. Some contested results at CERN ...'

'I remember,' said Geena. 'In *The Economist*, wasn't it? I caught it in the trawl.'

'Uh-huh,' said Joe. 'After our discussion last week I ran some searches on any recent work on rhodopsin, and came across the same thing. Dug up the original paper – it has to do with cosmic rays – you know, high-velocity particles, from—'

Geena nodded. 'I know what cosmic rays are.'

Joe smiled. 'The tachyons scatter *before* the charged particle that causes them arrives ... well, that's one way of looking at it. Anyway, I ran a sim on the same event, but using the actual functioning rhodopsin in the retina, and ... that's the result. You only get it, though, with your mutant rhodopsin.'

'So how did they get it at CERN? Were they using mutant rhodopsin?'

Joe shook his head. 'No, they were using a suspension of normal rhodopsin. I guess it must be the physical arrangement that makes the difference – the molecules of normal rhodopsin would be much farther apart.'

He leaned back and sipped coffee. 'The trouble is, of course, that the results are contested, haven't been replicated, there's a serious doubt that they detected tachyons in the first place . . . you know how it is.'

Geena grinned mischievously. 'You mean, the science hasn't been socially constructed?'

'That is one way of putting it,' said Joe. 'Not the way I would.'

'It's all right, I'm just teasing. What's the connection with what we've been talking about?'

'Tachyons,' said Joe, 'move faster than light. Which means they move backwards in time.'

He said this with the sort of self-satisfied expression Geena was all too used to seeing from the guys when they thought they'd given her an explanation.

'Yes? And?'

'It could be a physical basis for precognition.'

Geena looked away, looked around. The canteen was empty-ing. Its big windows showed the strip of green grass in the sunlight outside, and the wall, and the blue sky above it. The whole conversation seemed utterly unreal.

'Precognition?'

'You mentioned it.'

'So I did.' Geena sighed. 'The guy I spoke to said it was involuntary.'

Joe laughed, spluttering coffee. He wiped the back of his hand across his mouth.

'Sorry,' he said, and dabbed his lips and the table with a napkin. 'If it's the result of cosmic rays, I should bloody well think it's involuntary!'

'How seriously do you take this?' Geena asked.

'Quite seriously,' said Joe, frowning. 'I would not have put in a weekend to do the research and create that sim if I did not.'

'Oh,' said Geena, somewhat abashed. 'I see. I'll ... I'll have to think about this. But thank you.'

'You're welcome,' said Joe. He stacked his cup and saucer on top of the empty lunch plate on a tray. 'Oh well. Back to work.'

Geena did think about it. She thought about it so much that she had to call Maya. They agreed to meet after work in a café on Hayes High Street. Maya tabbed her the location. When Geena arrived at five thirty, she found the place a dingy hangout for people who looked like Maya's clients: war-zone and climate-change refugees. The walls were papered with news screens in a babel of languages and hung with black-framed portraits of bearded men, from Osama and Che to more recent martyrs who had achieved less notoriety. Somebody was smoking, out the back.

Feeling slightly dizzy from the swaying, swooping scenes and talking heads, Geena tuned her glasses away from the views and her earpieces away from the voices, found Maya, and sat down. The coffee was vile. Geena recounted what Joe had shown her, between sips and grimaces.

'This is wonderful!' Maya cried.

'Well,' said Geena, 'it's also pretty speculative.'

'That doesn't matter,' said Maya. 'The point is, there's a very sound basis for, um, our friend to make an appeal. I mean, even the possibility that there might be something in it would have scientists and medical people absolutely falling over themselves to check it out. They'd practically *forbid* her to have the fix.'

'Um . . .' said Geena. 'Not quite what she would want.'

Maya waved a hand. 'Figure of speech. And as well as the scientists, all the woo-woo pedlars would be jumping up and down about it, that's another constituency of support.'

'Well, again . . .'

'You're being too literal,' Maya told her. 'Look, I'm making political calculations here. None of this actually has to happen. It just has to be understood as something that could happen, and social services and councils and all the rest of officialdom have to take it into account.'

'*If* it goes public,' Geena pointed out. 'Or, OK, if there's the possibility it could go public. Sure. But the next step from that could just as easily be to make sure it *doesn't* go public.'

She drew a finger across her throat, a rather reckless gesture in this particular venue.

Maya snorted. 'They don't do things like that.'

'Now *you're* being literal. I mean, they could suppress the story, even disappear ... the subject.'

'But why?' Maya demanded. 'Look, despite what some people say, I'm not a conspiracy theorist, or even a dangerous radical. I don't think the authorities are evil.' She held up a hand. 'I know, I know. But they don't do these things for fun. They do them for what seem to them good reasons, pressing reasons, often even from wanting to do good. After all, the business of making the fix compulsory isn't some evil plot to control the evolution of the human race, or whatever. It grew out of increasing the pressure to get the fix taken up, and then finding there was a tiny minority who were beyond rational persuasion.'

'Who then have to be coerced for their own good? Isn't that against everything you believe in? I seem to remember John Stuart Mill himself made that the central distinction in—'

'Yeah, yeah, don't try to ... Hell, Geena, you know I don't give an inch on that. But they have a way round the good old argument in *On Liberty*. They're not coercing the recalcitrant for *their own* good. They're doing it to protect the recalcitrant's unborn children, who have nobody but the state to stand up for them.'

'So it's *for the children?*' Geena sneered.

Maya bristled. 'I don't buy that either, as an argument. But I'm willing to accept it as a motivation. And that motivation sure doesn't allow for snuffing out something that is at worst harmless and at best could be ... heck, a real psychic superpower!'

She was smiling as she finished, knuckles at her forehead, forefingers waggling like antennae. Geena smiled back, thinking: *you are so fucking naive.* She guessed that Maya's passionate commitments to liberty and human rights were her way of articulating her subject position – of course they were, it was her bloody job! She had to believe all this, including the fundamentally good even if misguided intentions of the human components of the repressive state apparatuses, to do her job at all, which was to ease some of the frictions resulting from population movements and spatial reconcentrations and dispersals of capital. A tiny proportion of the rent skimmed off from these impersonal, inhuman movements of human beings and alienated labour and all the rest was, for the system that generated them, a small price to pay, certainly compared to riots and crime and detention centres.

A grease-monkey! An apprentice with an oil-can! That's what you are, Maya, in the great scheme of things!

Geena said none of this. Instead she said: 'Well, why don't you give her a call?'

Maya nodded. 'Good idea. Might as well do it now.'

She fished out her phone, thumbed to the number.

'Shit!'

'What?'

'She's screened me out.'

'Same thing happened to me,' said Geena. 'With her husband. Let me try her.'

Same result.

They sat looking at each other for a moment.

'Now if only,' Maya mused aloud, 'there was someone who understands what all this is about and how important it is to get through to our friends here, and who isn't known to them and whose phone isn't blocked by theirs . . .'

'I'm not dragging Joe into this,' said Geena.

'I'm just saying,' said Maya.

20

Conversations

Hope sat by the patio doors in the back room of Mairi's shop, overlooking the shore. Through the glass panels she could keep an eye on Nick, firmly injuncted to stay within sight and at the moment beachcombing amid the stinking seaweed with every appearance of absorption and enjoyment. The rest of her attention she divided between her work in China and sorting out some spreadsheets for Mairi. It was mid-morning on the Wednesday after they'd arrived, and Hope was beginning to think about coffee and biscuits.

Mairi was in the front of the shop, minding the counter, chatting to the occasional customer, and knitting ruffled scarves at an astonishing speed from native wool. The heathery perfumes of soaps and unguents pervaded the whole shop, as did background music of generic Celtic sound, on endless shuffle.

For the first time in months, Hope felt relaxed and at peace with herself and the world. Hugh had just the previous day started work on the same site as Nigel, way up in the hills above the synthetic woodlands, partly doing basic stuff like removing bolts with a powered spanner, and partly the more complicated and delicate job of disconnecting and dismantling the turbines. He'd come back tired that evening, but with an outdoor glow, and in a cheerful mood.

The phone rang. Hope tapped her ear lobe. 'Yes?'

'Hello? Am I speaking to Hope Morrison?'

The speaker sounded Indian.

'Yes,' Hope said warily.

'Very good, Mrs Morrison. My name is Joe, and I wish to speak with you urgently on a matter of considerable import—'

Hope rang off. Jeez. Hadn't had one of these for years. Thought they'd all been call-screened to extinction. Now she'd have to update her phone-spam blocker, if she could ever find it on the menu.

The phone rang again. Same number.

'If you don't—' Hope began.

'Excuse me,' said a new voice, female, London-accented. 'Sorry about that. We're not a call centre. Joe really is called Joe – he just has his own form of courtesy, and it's easily mistaken for the usual spam intro. My name is Geena Fernandez. I spoke to your husband last week, and—'

'Oh,' said Hope. 'You. I've blocked you from calling me.'

'I know, Mrs Morrison, that's why I asked Joe to call you on his phone. Please let me explain, it won't take long.'

Hope stood up and stepped to the window, checking on Nick. He was squatting beside a tidal pool, arm in to the elbow. The sun shone on the water, making the pool as bright and bottomless as the loch.

'All right,' she said. 'What is it now?'

'Mrs Morrison, do you know about tachyons?'

'*Of course* I know about tachyons,' Hope snapped, using the irritation in her voice to cover her surprise. '*And* I know about rhodopsin, thank you very much.'

There was a pause of about two seconds. Hope smirked to herself.

'So you know about the connection between them?' Geena asked.

'I read. I've made my own speculations.'

'Ah!' Geena sounded relieved. 'Well, now it's more than speculation. Let me put Joe on for a moment.'

The male voice came back. Hope listened as Joe outlined his professional background and described his experiment, as he called it. She tried to overcome the prejudice, acquired in childhood and early teens, that anyone on the phone with an Indian or similar accent, describing something complicated, was trying to scam you.

'It's a simulation!' she objected, when he'd finished.

'Mrs Morrison,' he said, in a tired tone, 'yes, it is a simulation, but it's a very accurate one, using the same methods as are used all the time to make new products, day in and day out.'

'All right. Put your friend back on.'

Hope slid open the double-glazed doors and stepped out and

closed them behind her. The seaweed smell assailed her, then retreated as her nasal receptors became saturated, leaving nothing to smell but the clean fresh breeze off the sea. The tide was coming in, covering the live seaweed, which smelled quite inoffensive, but it wouldn't reach the rotting seaweed at the top of the shore except in a spring tide and a storm; and that would no doubt leave more dead seaweed heaped up, to rot down in its turn. No vestige of a beginning, no prospect of an end.

'Me again,' said Geena, in a bright tone.

'Right, Ms, uh, Fernandez. Now, listen to me. I'm sure you mean well, and your friend has put in a lot of work, but you haven't told me anything I hadn't already figured out for myself. I know what you said to Hugh, and I have a pretty good idea what he said to you. Let me tell you myself, straight out: neither of us has any interest at all in us or our child becoming an object of scientific attention. Not to mention media attention. Do you understand?'

'Yes, yes, of course, Mrs Morrison, but what I'm not sure you understand is that this gives you a perfect legal ground for not—'

'Oh God,' Hope groaned. 'I am so fucking bored with hearing this. I'm not scrabbling around for any kind of get-out, you know. I just want to be left alone to make up my own mind, and for my decision to be respected just because it is *my own fucking decision*, OK?'

'OK,' said Geena, sounding surprised and relieved. 'That's fine, that's all right. I just wanted to make sure.'

'Thank you,' said Hope. 'Goodbye.'

She caught the sound of Geena saying 'Bye!' just before she rang off. She blinked up the number of the phone that had been used to call her, and blocked it.

As soon as she had put the block in place, however, she regretted it and at the same time realised its futility. There was an unlimited number of other phones, after all, which any of these three people – Maya, Geena and Joe – could use to contact her. She could restrict incoming calls to her known contacts, but that risked missing important calls, or friends whose number had changed. That was the futility. On the other hand, blocking these particular phones would at least show she wasn't in regular communication with the supposed terrorist suspect Geena, and the libertarian loose cannon Maya, and this Asian guy who was evidently a friend of Geena's.

The regret came from something else. She might be missing out on something wonderful, as well as spurning a genuine offer of help. Well, she was definitely doing the latter, though how significant that was depended on the former. The more she thought about it, the more uncertain she felt. Was it really so awful, being an object of scientific attention? Even for the kid? There was no question of anything physically intrusive – their genetic samples, after all, were already taken. Blood spots on the Guthrie cards, genome sequence in the solid-state storage of computers. For her and for Hugh and Nick, no more would be involved, surely, than a few parapsychology experiments, whose inconclusive and disputable character was almost spookily predictable. Academic ethics would ensure the anonymity of the subjects. Nick needn't even know what it was all about. Better that he didn't, actually, what with the double-blind protocol and all that.

And wouldn't it be wonderful, in a way, to find that you or your child had a wild talent?

Well, yes, but Hope knew that this sort of thing was evasive, anecdotal, it slipped through your fingers like water. Most likely because there was nothing there in the first place. It was all nonsense.

She slid the patio doors open a fraction, stuck her head through and called to Mairi that she was taking a short walk. An indistinct but positive-sounding reply floated back, as if carried on the shop's soapy smell. She made her way across the mossy strip of lawn behind the shop, stepped over a token fence and then took a larger step across the strand-line seaweed and on to the stony beach. The shop was near the end of the village, just past the church and before the bridge where the road turned off to Stornoway or continued up the glen. Nick had moved a little farther along towards the bridge and the old pier.

He stood close to the edge of the sea, on a boulder, gazing intently down at the encroaching margin of incoming tide, now about a metre away. Hope placed her feet carefully on stone after stone amid the shingle, approaching him as stealthily as the tide. As she came within a couple of metres of him, she heard him talking.

'It's like watching the big hand of a clock, if you look at it long enough you can see it moving, but it's faster than that.'

He paused, and after a moment went on: 'A clock is round and has two hands, except they're not really hands, they're more like thin sticks, coming out of the middle, and the little hand moves round two times in a day and the big hand moves around one time in an hour, and that way you can tell the time any time of the day.'

'But you can't always see the sun.'

'Oh, right!'

It was like listening to someone talking on the phone. No, not quite, Hope thought. It was like hearing only one side of a conversation. She stopped and stood still, balanced precariously on two round slippery stones, one foot on each.

'O . . . K . . . ' Nick said, looking up and around. 'If that's how you do it . . . I think it's about an hour before noon. And that means it's time I went and found my mummy and asked her for tea and a chocolate digestive.'

He cocked his head slightly, as if listening, then laughed and turned round.

One of Hope's feet slipped off its stone and she stumbled, flailing her arms, then regained her balance. She crunched across pebbles to Nick.

'Hello, Mummy.' He didn't look surprised to see her, or offended that she'd snuck up on him.

'Time to get off that rock, I think,' she said. 'The tide's nearly around you.'

Nick looked down, then held out his arms towards her. She lifted him off the boulder and swung him around and set him down on the shingle.

'Did I hear something about tea and a biscuit?' she said.

'Oh yes please,' said Nick.

They set off towards the back of the shop.

'But I don't think he understands about tea,' Nick said.

'Who doesn't?'

'Max.'

Hope looked down. 'But Max isn't with you.'

'Oh no, wait,' said Nick. He turned around and called out: 'Max! Max!'

The toy monkey popped its head up from behind a boulder a few metres away, then bounded from stone to stone and jumped into Nick's arms.

'He's with me *now*,' he said, in a voice that meant he thought he'd got away with something on a clever technicality.

'You can tell him it's like getting your battery charged up,' Hope said.

'What's like?'

Hope leaned down and tickled Nick's tummy. 'Tea and biscuits.'

Nick giggled.

'I don't think he understands . . .'

His voice trailed off.

'Batteries?' Hope said. 'Surely Max understands batteries?'

'Oh yes, of course he does,' said Nick.

But he didn't try to explain biscuits as batteries to Max; in fact he said nothing at all as they walked back to the shop to recharge.

*

They sat around the table in the back room of the shop. Mairi had her back to the window, keeping half an eye on the front of the shop, and sharing a pot of tea with Nick. Hope sipped instant coffee. Mairi chatted to Nick, telling him about the village, and about the local sealife, the seals and trout and the herring and mackerel out in the ocean, and the gannets that dived from the cliffs.

'Was the sea always here?' Nick asked.

Mairi glanced at Hope, half amused, half querying.

'The sea has not always existed,' she said.

'Where did it come from?'

Hope, rather unfairly, expected Mairi to start talking about the six days of creation. Now, which day was the sea created?

'The water came from space,' Mairi said, 'billions of years ago.'

'Oh, I know that,' said Nick. 'I saw it on the telly. Comets! Whoosh! Splash!'

'Careful you don't splash your tea.'

'All right, Granny. But that's not what I meant. I meant the sea out the back there.'

'Oh, that,' said Mairi, glancing over her shoulder. 'No, Nick, that loch wasn't always there. Thousands of years ago, in the last ice age, the sea was much farther out. The islands like Pabay Mòr and Pabay Beag that you saw the other day, across from Valtos with the beach, and the big islands to the south like Berneray and Taransay and Scalpay and even Uist, they were all hills of the same Long Island back then.'

'So you could walk out there? To the wee island?'

'Oh yes,' said Mairi. 'You could walk out there too. That would all have been a glen, you see, and the island would have been a hill.'

'So where was the water?'

'It was all in the ice, piled up above the hills.'

Nick thought about this.

'But all that ice must have pushed the land down, so the sea—'

'Wasn't as far down as it might have been!' Mairi cried. She clapped her hands together. 'Clever boy! Yes, and today the land is still coming up with the weight of the ice off it, and the sea is still rising too with the ice melting into it. So it's complicated.'

'But,' said Nick, frowning, 'long ago there was ice on the top of the hills and the sea was way out, like if the tide had gone out a really really *really* long way, and stayed out for years and years and *years*, so there was grass and trees and things where the loch is, and there were animals and people and villages and smoke and everything.'

Mairi shrugged. 'I suppose so. I don't know about the villages, but all the rest, yes. It would have been a bonny glen.'

'And they had boats made out of bent branches and skins.'

'They did that,' said Mairi. 'They're called coracles. That's how the Gospel came to Scotland, when Columba paddled across the sea from Ireland in a coracle.'

'And they had gliders made out of skins and bent sticks too.' Nick planed his hand above his head. 'Flying over the glen!'

Mairi shook her head. 'No, dear, there's no evidence – they didn't have gliders, the people in the ice age and after.'

'They did so!' Nick sounded indignant. 'I saw them!'

'Where did you see them?'

He looked down into his cup. 'Pictures,' he said, quietly.

Mairi ruffled his hair. 'Of course. It must have been a story, or on the telly.'

'It was pictures,' Nick insisted.

'Yes, dear,' said Mairi. 'It was pictures, that's all.'

She stood up. 'Well, I'd better get back to the counter, and I'm sure you'd like to get back out in the sun. Enjoy it while it's here, eh?'

After they'd both gone, Mairi to the shop and Nick to the shore, Hope sat with her glasses on but seeing nothing.

When Nick had been a year younger, he'd been troubled by vivid dreams just before falling asleep. He'd called them pictures.

No way, she thought, was he going to be an object of scientific investigation. Not by her doing.

21

Tunnel Vision

Hugh's phone was ringing. The trouble was, the phone was in the back pocket of his jeans, underneath his one-piece waterproof overall, and he was lying on his back in a safety frame underneath a turbine, spanner in hand and a brace of screwdrivers in his mouth. Normally in that circumstance he'd have let the phone ring out and go to voicemail – yesterday morning the same thing had happened and the message, when he'd finally taken it, was some Asian-sounding guy claiming the implausible name of Joe, probably a cold-caller – but this time the ringing wasn't normal. It was a peculiar harsh bray that he hadn't heard before, at least not since he'd set the phone up a couple of years ago. He wasn't quite sure what the ringtone meant, but he was sure it was nothing good.

He elbowed the concrete and rolled the frame out from under, put down the screwdrivers and spanner, and stood up carefully in the low-ceilinged turbine chamber beneath the half-dismantled tower. He unzipped his overall and reached in awkwardly to the back pocket. The phone was still ringing when he took it out, and the screen was flashing bright red letters that told him exactly what the ringing meant:

The burglar alarm in the Islington flat was reporting a break-in in progress.

Shit shit shit. Hugh punched through to the house wifi to find out what was going on. The camera in the hall, facing the door, showed the wood around the locks splitting. Thud followed thud. There was no sound of the alarm: it was a silent alarm, which right at this moment would be alerting the nearest police station. For a moment Hugh felt a grim satisfaction at the thought.

The door jamb gave way, splinters flying. The door banged wide against the wall, and the police burst in. Hugh stared in disbelief. He hadn't expected this at all. The first officer through wore a visored helmet and a flak jacket. He arrived at a slowing run, carried by the momentum of the final swing of the battering ram, and stopped just short of colliding with the bikes. The rest, the squad of six or so who crowded in after him, were in standard police uniform. They looked alert but not anxious as they edged past the bikes, loomed into the view of the camera for a moment, then dispersed to the various rooms.

Hugh, hands shaking, flipped the view to the other cameras, splitting the screen sixfold to accommodate as many of them as he could. The uniformed figures gave cursory glances around, and here and there some peered into cupboards and under beds, but the one thing they all did was look for the cameras. One by one, quite eerily, a glance would alight, a face would appear close-up in goldfish-bowl distortion, and then a hand would come up holding a multi-tool open as pliers. The view would sway, swoop, and go dark, presumably from within a pocket or bag, though a confusing babble of sound still came through, including that of the cameras clinking together.

All this took place – Hugh found when he jolted himself out of his trance of shocked fascination – within about two minutes of the door being burst open. Nothing useful was coming from the phone, just darkness and noises. He stared at it for a few seconds nonetheless, as if hoping that something would make sense, or make a different sense. He knew that the moment he reacted would change his life for ever.

He moved. He called Hope. She'd be down at the shop, not long started this damp Thursday morning.

'Hope?'

'Yes? What's wrong?'

'The police have just broken into our flat. They're ripping out the cameras.'

Silence for a moment. She must be feeling the same sensation he had, like standing in the doorway of an aeroplane before a parachute jump.

'What do we do?' she said.

'Is Nick with you?'

'Yes, he's right here. It's a bit wet out.'

'Fine. Just go back up to the house, grab some water and food, couple of torches, and wait for me. I'll be along in, uh, half an hour or so.'

'What do I tell Mairi?'

'Just say you have to go back to the house. Act casual.'

Hope made an inarticulate noise, breath going out as a snort, going in as a sob, and rang off.

Hugh scrambled up the ladder and out of the hatch. The site was, aptly enough, windswept, a hilltop overlooking the synthetic forests to the east and in the other direction the hills and moorland to the west. Drizzle drifted in swathes. The cloud cover was not far overhead. He could see right to the coast, and through the rain he could almost make out the village, about thirty minutes' fast drive away. He glanced around, and spotted his father talking with one of the dozen or so other workers on the site. He hurried over.

'Excuse me, Nigel.'

Nigel gave him a worried look.

'Something wrong?'

So his expression must be as much a giveaway as his voice.

'Maybe. I need to get back to the house.'

'Is everyone all right?'

'Oh, yes, nothing like that. It's just . . . a bit of an emergency.'

Nigel handed over the car keys.

'Will you be all right?'

'Yes, sure, Donald can give me a lift back. Want me to put in a word with the foreman?'

'Yes please,' Hugh said, though he didn't think keeping the

307

job was top of his list of worries at the moment. 'Thanks, Dad. See you.'

Nigel wiped droplets of water from his eyebrows, caught Hugh's elbow and turned him aside.

'Is this it?' he asked in a low voice, not looking at Hugh.

'Could be,' said Hugh. 'Police have broken into our flat.'

Nigel swung around, facing him.

'What could that be about? Not Hope, surely?'

'I don't know. Nothing wrong we've done, anyway.'

Nigel's eyes and lips narrowed.

'I'll come with you.'

Hugh shook his head. 'No. I need you to . . . be around, and not to know where I've gone.'

Nigel considered this for a second, then nodded.

'Don't do anything foolish,' he said, as if Hugh were still a teenager, setting off for a night in Stornoway.

Hugh clapped his father's shoulder and ran to the Nissan. He strapped in, backed out of the awkward space in which it was parked, and bumped down the unpaved track to the road. He turned on the headlights and drove as fast as he dared, swinging around bends, hurtling along straights. Across the moor and into the glen and along to the village. It took him twenty-five minutes. He left the car outside the front gate and sprinted up the drive and around the back of the house.

Hope and Nick stood in the open doorway, wearing wet-weather jackets, boots and hats, and each clutching a small backpack, as if they were going for a walk in the rain. Hugh skidded to a halt, brushed Hope's cheek with a kiss and Nick's head with a pat, then sidled past them and into the house. He stepped out of his boots, stripped off his overall and hard hat and slung them in a corner of the scullery, and ran upstairs to the bedroom. It looked untidy, with the dress that Hope must have thrown off to pull on her trousers crumpled on the bed. Hugh took from the dusty top of the wardrobe the air pistol and pellet box he'd left there as soon as he'd arrived. He fingered inside his shirt pocket to make sure he still had the printed-off map, then picked up from the dressing table the old Silva compass he'd left hanging by its lanyard on the mirror. The little radio was still in his trouser pocket, with a new AA battery in it, along with one spare.

His booted feet thundered down the narrow staircase. He rushed through the living room and into the hallway and pulled on his jacket and boots. He stuck the air pistol in the jacket pocket. He jammed on Nigel's waterproof hat.

Hope and Nick watched him from the doorway.

'Why are we in a hurry?' Nick asked.

'Something interesting to see,' said Hugh.

'Then we'll need binoculars,' Nick pointed out.

Hugh tied his bootlaces, stood up, and grabbed the smallest pair of binoculars hanging in the clump of instruments on the coat hooks. He zipped up his jacket, closed the door behind them all and went out into the thin rain.

'Where do we go?'

Hope's upturned, enquiring face was beaded with water. She looked a lot less agitated, and more trusting, than he'd expected. This was more than he deserved. He had expected calls and emails from social services, maybe a visit, perhaps some legal pressure, the sort of thing that could be evaded for long enough by a simple change of address. He'd already sounded out an aunt in Tolsta and a cousin in Garynahine. But at another level, he had contemplated the escape he now had in mind. Why else had he made the map, and brought the pistol? The plan had had the quality of a daydream. Now it seemed the only way out. It also seemed delusional.

He thought, for a moment, about the car at the foot of the drive, and then dismissed it. The vehicle was relevant to the social-services scenario, not to this. If the police were looking for him and Hope, there was nowhere to drive to. Four roads led out of the village. Two were dead ends, on different sides of the same small peninsula. The other two – the Stornoway road over the bridge, and the Timsgarry road up the glen – offered more possibilities but for the same reason would be the first to be blocked. And the car would in any case be tracked automatically.

His mind was made up.

'We're going for a walk up the hill,' he said. 'Let's turn off our phones. Nick, do you want to see how people could find their way, before GPS?'

'Yes,' said Nick, doubtfully.

Hugh switched off his phone. Hope took out her glasses, looked at them almost helplessly for a moment, then dashed back into the house and came out without them.

'Let's go,' she said, clutching Nick's hand.

Hugh led them around the back of the house and up the

slope to the fence. He lifted Nick over, pushed the top wire down for Hope, then vaulted the fence himself. He looked at the roads, saw no police cars, and set off up the steep, rocky, heather-covered slope. At this point he didn't need the map; he remembered the route just fine, partly because it was the only sensible way to go. He watched Nick go a few steps ahead, and let Hope set the pace as she walked beside him.

'Do you have a plan?' Hope asked.

He had, but he wasn't telling her.

'To hide out in the hills. Shelter in that tunnel I told you about. At least until we know what's going on.'

'Hours? Days?'

'Not days,' Hugh said. 'Maybe overnight.'

'We won't find out what's going on without you turning your phone on. And then we'll be located in minutes.'

Hugh slapped his hip. 'I have a radio. If the police are looking for us, it'll be on the local news.'

'Why did they raid our flat? I mean, they must know we're here anyway.'

'Looking for evidence.'

'Evidence of what?'

'That terrorism nonsense.'

'Oh, I know. I'm not kidding myself. I've been so worried about that. Ever since that call yesterday.'

'What call yesterday?'

'It was that woman who spoke to you before. Geena. She was using a friend's phone, to get around the block. Same old thing about the magic gene. Her friend claimed he'd run a sim that showed you could see tachyons, or something. I just told her the same answer as I gave you. Not interested.'

'Why didn't you tell me?' Hugh tried not to sound as surprised and indignant as he felt.

'I didn't think it was worth bothering you about,' Hope said. 'But now . . .'

'Oh yes, but now!' said Hugh. 'Fuck!'

He didn't need to spell it out. Something about that call had tipped Hope's personal profile over the edge into something of active interest. The raid on their flat would be only one part of the response: the police in Stornoway would no doubt have been alerted before the raid even took place, and were almost certainly already on their way.

'Sorry,' said Hope.

'Can't be helped.' He smiled sidelong at her, put an arm around her shoulders. For a moment she leaned against him, then they walked on.

How long would it be, Hugh wondered, before she realised that hiding in the hills would be impossible for more than a few hours, that running away was not going to help their case at all, that the plan he'd told her made no sense whatsoever and that his secret plan would sound delusional even to him, were he to speak it aloud?

He looked back again. Still no sign of pursuit.

They reached the top of the hill after about half an hour's climbing. The smirr of drizzle had drifted inland. Out to the north and west, the sky had cleared. Hugh didn't welcome the blue.

They all paused, taking a breath. Hugh took out the binoculars and scanned the roads. Nothing, nothing . . . wait. There. A police car came around the shoulder of the far hill, on the Stornoway road. No flashing light, no siren. No rush. No need, Hugh thought bitterly. He nudged Hope, and pointed. She suppressed a gasp.

Hugh stepped back from the skyline and walked a few yards on to the plateau.

'Now,' he said to Nick, 'let me show you how we find our way with just a compass and a map.'

He didn't really need the map, nor the waste of the minute or two spent taking the compass bearing and explaining the process to Nick. He could see the lochs, way ahead across the wilderness of boulder and outcrop, bog and bracken, heather and moss. But somehow it had seemed important to include the boy in it, to show him at least the rudiments of a skill that he might not otherwise come to know about, one small element of independence from the satellite-surveillance world. And more urgently, to make him feel part of this, involved and not just dragged along.

Hope passed Nick a water bottle, then a chocolate bar. She offered one to Hugh. He shook his head. On they went. Hugh took to swinging Nick across dips and holes in the peat and clefts in the rock. The sun was out now, the shadows short. Hugh opened his jacket, and took his hat off, then put it back on again.

From above, he heard a faint, persistent buzz. He looked up, and back. The drone was climbing in an ascending, widening spiral above the village and its surrounding hills. Its next turn would take it almost overhead. There was nothing to be done about it. Nick looked delighted at the sight.

'What are they looking for?' he asked.

'Oh, I don't know,' said Hugh. 'Maybe someone's got lost on the hills.'

Now Nick looked worried.

'Or maybe they're just practising,' said Hope.

They reached the loch. Hugh stopped, checked the map and the compass, confirming his memory.

'That way,' he said.

They hurried around the shore of the small loch, and on across the rough, rocky ground.

The buzz of the drone became louder. They all looked back. The drone swooped towards them like some predatory ptero-dactyl. Nick cried out, his arm shielding his face. The drone passed a few metres overhead, a small unmanned microlight about a metre and a half in wingspan, then soared to circle high above.

'Are they looking for us?' Nick asked.

'We're not lost,' said Hope. 'So they must be practising.'

Hugh looked behind him again, and saw five figures just reaching the top of the hill, skylined. They weren't even run-ning. They were that confident. Hope saw them too.

'This is useless,' she said. Nick was as usual a few paces ahead, unaware of the pursuit, out of earshot of her low voice. 'We can't hide.'

'We can,' said Hugh. 'There is a place.'

'I knew this,' said Hope. 'I knew that's where you're taking us. Your bright land.'

'You do realise,' he said, 'that this is completely insane?'

'No, I don't,' she told him, fiercely. 'I believe you more than you believe yourself.'

Hugh grinned at her. Together they ran a few steps forward, to where Nick hesitated at a hollow in the heather, and caught a hand on each side and swung and jumped at the same time.

'Nearly there,' said Hugh.

'Nearly there,' Hope echoed.

She didn't believe him at all, Hugh thought. It would have alarmed him if she had. He wouldn't have wanted her caught up in it, turning his forlorn hope – hah! – into a *folie à deux*. She was coming along, she was going along with this, because she needed to know, to see for herself whatever it was that had so shaped his life, and indirectly her own.

She couldn't, surely, expect to escape, into that past or future or parallel world from which his visions came? At some level he, he knew, didn't expect to either. He just wanted to give them a run for it.

He looked behind. Five police officers, now about half a kilometre away.

Up ahead, Nick stopped and looked back, and then pointed. 'Dad! Mum! There's policemen behind us!'

Hope and Hugh hurried up.

'It's all right,' said Hope. 'They must be looking for someone. Maybe we can help them.'

Hugh looked down. Nick had stopped because he'd reached the edge of a hollow far too wide for him to jump over, and almost two metres deep.

It was the place.

22

The Light at the End of the Tunnel

'It's a game,' Hugh said. 'The police are practising finding people on the moor. And here's how we can help them. We'll hide, and make it more interesting.'

'Where can we hide?' Nick asked.

'Right here,' said Hugh. 'I'll show you.'

He sat down on the edge, then pushed himself off, landing with a lurch. He turned and lifted Nick down, then caught Hope under the shoulders as she slithered over the bank. To the pursuers they must have simply disappeared into the ground. Even the drone was, at that moment, below their skyline. Hugh looked quickly to left and right. The dark rectangular opening was still there.

'Let's hide in here.'

Hope and Nick followed him as he ducked into the culvert's entrance. Nick hung back, just inside.

'Don't like it,' he said. 'Dark.'

'It's all right,' Hugh said. 'I came here when I was a boy, and it's all right. There's something really exciting inside. Have you got your torch?'

Nick reached into a coat pocket and pulled out a yellow plastic torch and switched it on. Hugh turned away, blinking at the after-image, and switched on his own torch. Hope's beam joined it, wavering around the floor and walls.

The floor was damp, and the smells were stronger than he remembered. Old concrete, mould, rotted vegetation, droppings that had dried and then got wet again. He had to bend almost double to walk forward. He looked behind, at Hope and Nick huddled together. Hope looked excited, surprised, Nick a little scared.

'I'll go in front,' he said. 'Nick behind me, OK?'

'Yes,' said Hope, easing Nick forward.

They'd taken only a step or two when the drone's buzz came out of nowhere behind them, loud in the tunnel, a waft of air disturbing the floor litter. Hugh could imagine the drone banking to angle its camera, skimming the lip of the gully, and the cops running. He hastened forward, torch beam probing ahead. The downward slope and rightward curve were just as he recalled, his progress more uncomfortable with his adult height, but quicker.

He saw the light ahead, and stopped, switching off his torch. Nick bumped against the back of his legs.

'Do you see it?' Hugh said, looking back. 'The light.'

'Yes,' said Nick.

Hope was peering forward, over Nick's head, and had just opened her mouth to say something when a much brighter light shone behind her. An amplified voice boomed down the tunnel, echoing against the sides, distorted but plain enough:

'Armed police! Come out at once! Throw out your weapon!'

'*What* bloody weapon?' said Hope.

Hugh gave her a feral grin, and slapped his jacket pocket.

'Oh God,' said Hope. 'What use is that?'

'It's not for them,' Hugh said. 'Come on!'

And with that he lowered his head and shoulders and almost ran, knees partly bent, in an ape-like shamble. The light ahead became brighter than the light behind. He felt the fresh air on his face again. He guessed Hope felt it too; he heard her gasp.

Another shout echoed down the tunnel.

Hugh ignored it. The light was now plainly a rectangular opening a few metres ahead.

'Hugh,' Hope said, 'they're coming after us!'

He looked backward. Were those shadows, moving, on the sides of the tunnel, not far behind?

'Nearly there!' he said.

He flashed an encouraging grin at Nick. The boy didn't look back at him. His gaze was fixed on the light ahead. Behind Nick, Hope was stumbling along, in the same half-crouch, torch swaying in front of her, head down. Hugh couldn't see her face.

He looked ahead and found himself a step or two from the door in the hill. He reached back, catching Nick's hand, and drew forward, squeezing to one side so that Nick could press in alongside him and look too. Side by side they took the final few steps, and gazed out.

Hugh saw the same landscape as he'd seen before, but this time in summer, the steep hillside covered not with snow but with heather and gorse and patches of grass speckled with daisies and buttercups. Woodsmoke drifted above the small houses and huts in the middle distance, and some way beyond them, the sea-loch shone blue.

For a moment, woodsmoke apart, it could have been static scenery. Then the bat-like shape of a hang-glider rushed into the view, as if it had just been launched from a little farther uphill on the slope behind and above their heads. Hugh saw the pilot's legs swing to the side as the glider banked and passed out of view.

'Wow!' said Nick. 'It's real!' He shaded his eyes, leaning forward, peering out.

Hope had come to a halt right behind. She reached forward and gripped Nick's shoulders.

'Hugh!' she groaned. 'Please! Don't *do* this to us!'

Her voice didn't echo. The heavy footsteps not far behind her did. Over his shoulder, over her shoulder, Hugh saw the swaying lights, the shadowed figures moving slowly forward. As he looked back, they came to a halt. They might have been twenty metres away.

'Don't do what?' Hugh asked.

'Don't wade into that pool.'

'Pool? There's no pool.' He turned back to the light, waving a hand at the opening. 'It's – it's what I told you I saw long ago. It's open! We can go through!'

'There's *nothing there*, Hugh.' She was still clutching Nick's shoulders, but she looked as if she wanted to grab Hugh's and shake him. 'It's just *water*, and the torchlight shining off it. It's deep, it must be, the slope goes sharp down and the roof comes down to the top of the water. You'll drown, and you'll drown Nick.'

'No, Mummy!' Nick cried. 'It's real! It's not a picture! It's a nice place! Why can't you see it?'

'I can't see it because it's *not real*,' Hope said, to Hugh rather than to Nick.

Hugh looked from her beseeching, angry, tearful face to the hills and the blue sky outside. He felt dismayed and defeated.

From behind him a voice boomed:

'Throw down your weapon! Raise your hands and turn around!'

'Oh, fuck this!' Hugh snarled. He reached into his pocket, pushing his hand down hard in the squeeze between him and Nick, and pulled out the air pistol. He passed it to his other hand and groped for the ammo box. It might have seemed to Hope he was trying to turn around, to bring the futile weapon to bear.

'No!' Hope cried. 'Hugh, no!'

She let go of one of Nick's shoulders and lunged to grab Hugh's wrist. He evaded her, and threw pistol and carton as far away as he could in front of him. He thought he heard a clink as the pistol hit the ground outside; a skitter of metal on rock. Then he lifted both hands above his head, stepped forward and turned around, blocking Nick between him and Hope. The

321

light from the torches shone straight in his face. He couldn't see who was holding them.

'It's all right!' he shouted. 'We're not armed! We're coming out!'

'Stay where you are! Throw your bags and torches forward!'

'It's *my* torch,' Nick protested, as Hope took it from him.

'It's all right,' Hope whispered. 'We'll get them back.'

She slipped the small rucksack from Nick's shoulders, and unslung her own.

'We're doing that now,' she called out, and tossed the bags forward, then the torches, still shining. Some kind of pole or probe waved above the bags, poked them, then withdrew.

'Walk forward slowly with your hands in front of you and away from your sides.'

Then:

'The child first.'

'No, Mummy.'

'He's afraid,' Hope shouted back.

'All right,' the voice boomed.

They walked forward, Nick upright and straight with his hands up, as if playing soldiers; Hugh and Hope knock-kneed, bowed, arms outspread as wide as the cramped space would permit. In front of them, the shadowed figures and the lights backed away. Hugh took a last look over his shoulder. The light was still there, the door to the bright land.

He turned his head away from it and walked forward, into the different light, the light at the far end of the tunnel.

23

Hope Abandon

Hope emerged from the culvert into the gully, daylight, sunlight, and arrest. Her arms were grabbed the moment she stepped out, and the two policemen rushed her up the gravel slope to the end of the gully in seconds. They cuffed her hands behind her back and ran a scanner up and down her body. She was just able to turn her head enough to see Nick being scooped up by a policewoman and carried, yelling, thrashing and lashing out with all four limbs, to the other end of the gully. Good boy, she thought. Get in a bite while you're at it. A moment later, Hugh stumbled out and was grabbed too.

Then, to her utter surprise and indignation, she was shoved down on to her knees.

'Hope Morrison,' said one of the cops, 'I am arresting you on suspicion of offences under the Children and Young Persons Protection (Scotland) Act.'

'What?' Hope yelped.

'You do not have to say anything, but anything you do say will be taken down and recorded and may be used in evidence . . .'

He was a big man with a Lewis accent and the correlated ruddy, freckled features and sandy hair, and looked slightly embarrassed as he recited the formula. Hope turned her head around and looked up at him.

'Look, this is about the fix! I know it is! I'll take the bloody fix! It's in my pocket! Just give me it and some water, you can put it in my mouth yourself if you like.'

At that moment, she meant it; she meant it as firmly as she'd ever meant any promise in her life.

'Do you understand what you have just been told, Mrs Morrison?'

'Yes, I understand. Don't take the boy! He has nothing to do with this. Just take him to the house down the hill, or Mairi's shop, she's his grandmother.'

'Well, Mrs Morrison, that's—'

Another voice and accent interrupted. 'That's not for us to decide, Constable.'

Anything Hope might have said next was drowned out by the sound of a helicopter, approaching and then landing behind her. She felt its downdraught through her clothes, whipping her hair. As the rotors' throb slowed to a steady whump, earmuffs were placed on her, and she couldn't hear anything. Two men in flying suits hurried past, carrying between them some heavy apparatus and a coil of cable, towards the gully. Her elbows were grabbed; she was hauled to her feet and propelled towards the helicopter. It was a big yellow Sea King. Her shins banged on the steps. Inside, she was pushed into a bucket seat, facing the rear of the cabin, her arms around the seat back, and was strapped in using the fitted safety belts. Her ankles were zip-tied to the seat's supports.

The two officers who'd grabbed her then moved towards the front of the cabin. She turned her head around just in time to see Hugh likewise bundled on board. He had a hood over his head and face, with earmuffs on top of it. He was pushed out of her sight. Then the door was closed.

'Where's Nick?' Hope yelled, struggling against the straps. Her voice sounded strange. 'Where's our son?'

The Leosach constable came around and stood in front of her. He gestured with his finger across his lips, and mouthed, 'Shut up!'

'Where's our son?' Hope shouted again.

From an inside pocket the policeman took a paper sachet and ripped it open, then slapped an adhesive tape, like a sticking-plaster without a pad, across Hope's lips. Then he went away.

She tried to open her mouth but the tape hurt too much when it pulled on the skin. The engine's vibration changed, the noise became loud even through the ear protection, and the floor lurched and tipped. Acceleration and inertia swayed her, this way and that. After a minute or two the aircraft levelled off into forward flight. Hope slumped in the seat, her mind lurching as uncontrollably as her body had during the take-off. One moment she would be frantic at the thought of Nick alone among the strange people who had taken her from him; the next she would reassure herself with images of him being taken to Mairi's place by a kindly police-woman. Then she would think of him falling into the care system, taken away, fostered – no! They couldn't do that!

But she had just been arrested under the child-protection laws . . . which meant they *could* do that . . . and that thought would segue into relief that at least she hadn't been arrested under the terrorism laws, which she'd half expected. Under the child-protection laws she could fight, she could get legal support, she wouldn't just disappear into the global archipel-ago of interrogation cells and black sites and ghost prisons, about which the authorities were reticent but rumour was eloquent.

But Hugh had been hooded, and that wasn't something they did for child-protection arrests, except for abusers, and it couldn't be that, so maybe he was being arrested under the ter-rorism laws . . .

At this point she realised that she was inflicting on herself the kind of undermining and disorientation that the arrest and interrogation process was designed to induce, and to which she would no doubt be subjected in the coming hours and maybe days, and that she might as well leave it to the professionals, who at least knew when to stop, or so they claimed, though maybe . . .

Stop.

She stopped, and turned her head to the side, not so far as to be uncomfortable, but far enough to let her see the patch of sunlight on the floor. She concentrated on that, and on imagining the land below.

The helicopter landed. The two policemen reappeared in front of her, and released Hope from the seat straps and leg restraints. She stood up, and stuck her chin forward. The policeman who'd put the tape across her mouth shook his head. He and his colleague took her by the upper arms and escorted her to the doorway, and then one of them went in front to guard and guide her down the steps on to a runway. A police car was waiting just beyond the rotors' circuit.

She had a moment to look around and see the sea and green machair, a control tower, a jump jet and two naval helicopters parked in the middle distance, before she was rushed to the police car. She ended up sitting in the back, hands still cuffed behind her, between the Leosach constable who'd arrested her and a policewoman already in the car. The policewoman fixed the seat belt across her. As she was doing this, Hope saw, through the car's open doorway, Hugh, still hooded, being frogmarched across tarmac in the direction of one of the airfield's buildings.

The driver looked in the rear-view, got nods from the two officers in the back, and drove off the airstrip and on to a perimeter road, then out through the main gate. Hope saw a sign just outside the gate, and her diagonal glimpse left her with the impression 'RAF Stornoway'. The drive was short – across open moorland, then through the streets of Stornoway – and ended outside a small and quite ordinary police station.

The policewoman leaned over and ripped the tape from across Hope's mouth. She expected it to sting, but it didn't, and she guessed it was some new material designed expressly for the purpose. She was allowed to get out, very awkwardly, in her own time, and then escorted into the station. It was a poky place, smelling of vomit and disinfectant. At a counter at the end of the reception room, Hope's handcuffs were taken off, her pockets emptied and the contents bagged, along with her jacket, watch, boots and belt, the rings from her fingers, and her own rucksack and Nick's. Seeing Nick's rucksack made her cry for a moment, but she sniffed and wiped her eyes and nose with the back of her wrist and signed for everything.

She was then taken to a cell whose walls, floor, ceiling and the seating along one side were all tiled white, and left there. She looked around for the camera. There it was, in a corner of the ceiling. She settled herself in the opposite corner, on the cell's built-in bench, leaning against the two walls, and watched the camera right back.

After an hour or so of this, the cell door opened, and the policewoman who'd been in the car escorted Hope down a short corridor to an interview room. It had a table and three chairs. A young man with a suit, a beard and a pad was waiting inside. As the policewoman closed the door behind her, he shook hands with Hope and introduced himself.

'Hamish McKinnon,' he said. 'From McKinnon and Warski, solicitors, Stornoway. I've been appointed by the sheriff as your legal representative. You're of course entitled to choose your own lawyer. Do you wish to do so?'

Hope shook her head.

'So you're happy to have me represent you?'

'Yes,' said Hope.

He motioned her to the seat at the back of the table, and sat down at the side. The policewoman sat down opposite Hope, and turned on some very visible and clunky recording devices. She introduced herself as Police Sergeant Dolina Macdonald, gave the date and time for the recording, and got down to business.

'Are you Hope Morrison?'

Hope glanced at the lawyer.

'You have a right to remain silent,' he said, 'but I don't advise it. If there are any questions I think you shouldn't answer, I'll tell you at once.'

'Yes,' she said.

'Is that in answer to my question?' said Macdonald.

'Yes,' said Hope.

'Are you married to Hugh Morrison, of 13 Victoria Road, Finsbury Park, London?'

'Yes.'

'And are you the mother of Nicholas Morrison, of the same address?'

'Yes,' said Hope. 'And I want to know where he is now.'

'I'm sorry, I can't tell you that.'

'Can't, or won't?'

'I can't,' said the policewoman, 'because I don't know. And if

I did know, I would not be allowed to tell you at this stage of the inquiry. I assure you he is in safe hands.'

'I'm sure he is. I'm sure he's also very distressed.'

'Every effort will be made to comfort and reassure him. As I said, I'm certain he is in safe hands, and between ourselves I'm certain he's more than safe.'

'I hope for your sake he is.'

'Really, he is,' said Macdonald. 'Now, Hope, let me explain the situation to you. You have been arrested on suspicion, but you have not yet been charged. Your rights have been explained to you, so you are being interviewed under caution. Do you have any complaints about your treatment up to this point?'

'Yes, I have,' said Hope. 'I was roughly handled, and restrained unnecessarily and uncomfortably, despite the fact that I had made no resistance. I was gagged, merely for asking after my son.'

Macdonald looked impatient. 'These are very minor complaints.'

'I'll take them up later,' McKinnon said.

'Very well,' said Hope. 'I'm making them for the record. Particularly given that I'm, uh, four months pregnant.'

'I'm sure the recordings from the arresting officers' lapel cameras will show that you were treated properly.'

'I'm sure they will,' said Hope. 'I have a different recollection, and I'll say so.'

'That is your right,' said the policewoman. 'Now, do you know why you've been arrested?'

'No, I don't,' said Hope. 'I haven't done anything wrong.'

'So why did you flee from the police?'

'Flee?' said Hope. 'We were walking in the hills. We saw the police behind us, and the drone above us, but didn't run from them. They didn't pursue us, or call out or challenge us in any way. For all we knew, they were on a search-and-rescue exercise.'

'Mrs Morrison,' Macdonald said, with affected weariness, 'you were found hiding in a disused culvert.'

'We weren't hiding,' said Hope. 'We were exploring. We entered the culvert – well, we entered the gully that it led off from – in full view of the police and I guess of the drone.'

'Exploring,' said Macdonald. 'Exploring. Your husband walked off a job he had just started, without giving explanation or asking permission, and drove at speed to meet you. You had also just walked off a job, in a comfortable office, taking your child to the house in pouring rain. You met your husband and immediately set off up the hill, leaving behind or switching off any devices on your persons that might have been used to track you. Can you explain any of this?'

'You don't have to explain anything now,' McKinnon interjected.

'No, it's all right,' said Hope. 'I can explain. My child was bored and fractious. I was unable to concentrate on my work, and he was annoying his grandmother, too, in the shop. When my husband called to ask how I was getting on – it was the first wet day we'd had here, the first day the boy was pretty much stuck indoors – I'm afraid I was so fed up that I begged him to skive off. He had the idea of teaching Nick orienteering, which is why he switched off his phone – to demonstrate to the child that we can navigate without GPS.'

'Mrs Morrison, your husband was carrying an illegal firearm.'

'I didn't know that,' said Hope.

'The weapon was clearly shown on the drone's imaging equipment. Your husband was also seen and recorded apparently discarding the weapon in the tunnel, in the course of some altercation with you.'

Hope shrugged. 'I'd like to see the evidence for that.'

'Oh, you will, Hope, you will. Do you deny that it happened?'

Hope said nothing.

'You needn't say anything at this stage,' said the lawyer. He turned to Sergeant Macdonald. 'You said "apparently discarding". Why "apparently"?'

'You're in an interview room, not a courtroom,' Macdonald told him.

'I'm well aware of that,' said McKinnon. 'Nevertheless, my client and I are entitled to know what evidence you have against her.'

'Not at this stage in the proceedings you aren't!'

'I'm only raising the point,' said McKinnon, 'because your choice of words suggests to me that you have *no physical evidence* of this firearm.'

Macdonald glared at him, then looked away. McKinnon sat back, looking smug, and tapped a note on his pad.

'Mrs Morrison,' Macdonald went on, 'you most certainly

fled from the police while you were in the culvert. You, your husband and child ran away down the culvert when they called on you to come out. You were warned that they were armed. You do know that running away after a warning from armed police can have very serious consequences? Even fatal consequences?'

'Yes, I'm well aware of that,' said Hope. 'And you must be aware that amplified sound in such a confined space can be very distorted, as well as alarming. It certainly alarmed our child, who took off as fast as his legs could carry him. Naturally we ran after him, if you could call that running.'

'According to the police video evidence, Mrs Morrison, your husband was in front, then the boy, and you brought up the rear.'

Hope shrugged. 'Maybe so. It was dark, lots of shadows, very confusing. My husband may even have had the impression that Nick was ahead of him.'

'I find that very unlikely. You ran from the police. That's not the reaction of innocent people.'

McKinnon leaned forward again. 'Perhaps, Sergeant, it's the reaction of innocent people who think that they are being threatened and pursued by whoever the police were searching *for?*'

'You're not here to suggest lines of argument to your client, Mr McKinnon.'

'When we entered the culvert,' Hope said, gratefully grabbing the lifeline, 'the police were hundreds of metres away, and not obviously pursuing us. Then the drone buzzed the gully, and we heard shouts and loud noises behind us. It was a moment of panic. I can't even say what I thought I was running from.'

'I bet you can't,' said Macdonald. 'But not because you didn't know you were fleeing from the police.'

'Fleeing where?' Hope asked. 'We were in a dead end.'

'Oh,' said Macdonald, 'and how did you know that? Before you reached it, I mean.'

'Oh, I can explain that,' said Hope. 'My husband grew up in that very village, in the house just down the hill, as you know. He found the culvert when he was ... in his early teens, I think, with some pals. No doubt they can verify that; they shouldn't be hard to trace. Anyway, Hugh remembered it as quite an adventure, and thought it would be exciting for Nick to see it too.'

Macdonald was about to respond, with irritation judging by the look on her face, when McKinnon raised a finger.

'One moment,' he said. 'I notice that you asked my client if she knew why she had been arrested. She said she didn't. And you haven't yet told her. Nor have you alleged any breaches of the Children and Young Persons Protection Act.'

'Yes I have,' said Dolina Macdonald. 'The child was, with the full knowledge and consent of your client, in the presence and in fact jointly in the care of a person carrying an illegal firearm.'

'For which, it seems, there's no physical evidence, and no evidence at all other than some no doubt ambiguous images on a drone camera.'

'I've seen these images,' said Macdonald, 'and I assure you, Hamish, there's nothing ambiguous about them. The drone carries a military-grade sub-millimetre radar-imaging device, widely used in all conflict theatres. In a combat zone, an image like that would be more than enough to justify calling down a drone strike.'

'We're not in a combat zone, Dolina, for which we must be thankful.'

'Legally we are,' Macdonald pointed out. 'Near enough.'

'I'm familiar with the emergency provisions for the North Atlantic defence perimeter, thank you very much, Dolina. But even if that image on its own could convince a jury, and not some military kangaroo court, which I doubt, it's no evidence at all about my client's full knowledge and consent, which is what you have to establish.'

'We can establish that, right enough,' said Macdonald. 'The Metropolitan Police were this morning issued a search warrant for the Morrisons' flat, and a seizure order for the interior cameras. A police semantic AI is trawling the sounds and images as we speak. We have every reason to think that this will within an hour or two provide incontrovertible evidence on the point of your client's knowledge and consent.'

'Excuse me!' cried McKinnon, almost jumping up. 'Their flat in London was searched? On what possible basis? And what evidence – seeing you admit you don't have any from the search – sent the Stornoway police supposedly chasing after this family in the first place?'

'I'm afraid I can't tell you that, Mr McKinnon.'

'If you can't even give me prima facie evidence to justify the arrest . . .'

'I already have, Mr McKinnon. The image of the gun, and the recording of the altercation in the tunnel.'

'If indeed there was an altercation between my client and Mr Morrison about this alleged weapon,' said McKinnon, 'that would tend to suggest that she did not know or approve of his carrying it. Would it not also suggest, that she was shocked and surprised to see it? Or perhaps to see something which – in the dark and confusion and panic she has described – she might have mistaken for a weapon?'

'Such as what?' asked Macdonald.

McKinnon spread his hands. 'Any number of things. A torch, perhaps awkwardly held? A tool of his trade – you said he had walked off a job in a hurry. I saw from my first glance at the preliminary documents' – he looked down and poked at his pad – 'that Mr Morrison is a carpenter. A carpenter's square, or a power tool with a pistol grip, could easily have been in his pocket, forgotten. What if he realised at the last moment what all the shouting was about, and removed that tool from his pocket?'

'Some fine speculation, Hamish, but none of that alters the prima facie basis of the arrest, which is the drone image. And that was no power drill, or any such thing.'

'That doesn't explain what the investigation was all about in the first place.'

'Och, Hamish,' Macdonald said, 'if you had done more than "glance" at the preliminary documents, you would know fine well—'

'Don't you "och, Hamish" me, Dolina!' snapped McKinnon.

Macdonald's face froze. 'Let's try and keep this professional.'

'Indeed,' said McKinnon. 'Sorry.' He cast Hope an embarrassed glance. 'Stornoway is a small place, Mrs Morrison, and everybody knows everybody else, and as it happens Sergeant Macdonald and I have known each other, off and on, since we were at primary school.'

'Hence the lapses into talking as if you still were?' Hope asked, tartly.

The lawyer and the copper looked equally abashed.

'Let's take the apologies as mutual and move on,' said Macdonald. 'As I was saying, Mr McKinnon, the initial basis for the investigation is given in the preliminary documents.'

'A moment ago you said you couldn't tell me that. Now you say it's in the documents.'

'I can't tell you everything,' said Macdonald, 'because it might jeopardise another line of inquiry, currently under active and urgent investigation. But it's also true that there's enough in the preliminary documents to justify this investigation, and the urgency of today's search for the Morrison parents.'

McKinnon looked down at his pad and twiddled a theatrical finger on its surface.

'Sergeant Macdonald, I assure you' – he glanced at Hope – 'and you, Mrs Morrison, that I have read every line of these documents, quickly but carefully. What I see here are some social-service background reports, on a quite irrelevant matter of private conscience, which is for the present a live issue only in England and Wales, and some records of phone calls between Mrs Morrison, Mr Morrison, and two people who have separately confessed to terrorism offences under circumstances of severe duress, which you know as well as I do is enough to have them thrown out by magistrates and sheriffs, let alone by the courts. Not even the Met have the brass neck to take such stuff to a magistrate, in most cases.' He turned to Hope. 'This is what you meant, was it not, when you said at the moment of arrest that this was all about the fix?'

'Yes,' said Hope. 'The social services and the Health Centre back home have been putting me under a lot of pressure to take the fix, and I came here in the hope of getting away from all that for a bit. Some chance! They've obviously decided quite arbitrarily to make an example of me, and that's why they've put this trumped-up nonsense about terrorism to the police. It's all just a ploy to make me out to be an unfit mother.'

'As I thought,' said McKinnon. He held up his pad, between thumb and forefinger. 'This is pish.'

He let the pad drop, to clatter on the table, and sat back, folding his arms. Hope looked over at him with gratitude and admiration. For the first time she saw the law as Maya had once explained it to her, not as an impersonal and ever more complicated system to crush you, but as a system whose very complexity and impersonality could shield you; and in that moment she saw McKinnon as a knight holding that shield in front of her.

'You may well think so, Mr McKinnon,' said Macdonald. 'But the magistrate in Islington did not, and the sheriff in Stornoway did not, and you will soon find out why. In the meantime, you have no grounds for questioning the prima facie case for arrest in the circumstances of earlier today, regardless of how these circumstances came about.'

McKinnon scowled. 'This is getting us nowhere. I suggest we wait until you can produce some evidence, rather than holding it over my client as a threat or inducement, and in the meantime that you provide her with some refreshment.'

'I'm happy to take up that suggestion,' said Macdonald. She consulted her own pad. 'Interview adjourned. Expect to resume within two hours.'

'In the meantime,' said the lawyer, 'I wish to talk to my client in private.'

'Denied,' said Macdonald. 'You can't do that until she's charged, and we don't have to charge her for sixty-four days.' She smiled maliciously. 'Minus three and a half hours.'

The interview resumed. Hope felt somewhat the better for having had two cups of tea, a beaker of orange juice and a pizza, especially as the policeman who came to her cell – the Leosach who'd arrested her – had allowed her to order from a takeaway menu, and had smiled understandingly and glanced at her bump when she'd specified anchovies and pineapple. And now there were cups of water on the table. But as she took her seat again, her heart sank at the expressions of Macdonald and McKinnon: the policewoman chipper, the lawyer glum.

'Mrs Morrison,' Macdonald said, after getting the formalities out of the way, 'I would like now to bring to your attention some new developments and productions.'

'Productions?'

'Items of evidence,' McKinnon explained.

'With regard to productions,' Macdonald went on. 'The forensic semantic AI trawl of your home cameras has been completed, and in accordance with privacy legislation only those sections directly relevant to the case or cases have been made available by the AI to the investigation.' She looked up at Hope, with a thin smile. 'Just in case you were worried about coppers sniggering over your personal life. Isn't allowed, doesn't happen. All right?'

'I'll take your word for it,' said Hope.

'Very well. Further sections may be made available on a new search warrant. I have here' – Macdonald nodded down at her pad – 'a recording of you moving off camera, verifiably into a cupboard in your home, then coming back into view in a . . . distracted condition. From the evening of the same day, a conversation with your husband, Mr Hugh Morrison, obliquely but clearly alluding to the presence of an illegal firearm, very probably a pistol, in a box or similar unsecured container in that cupboard. Mr McKinnon here has viewed the recording and can confirm its contents. Do you wish to view the recording yourself?'

'Not at the moment,' said Hope.

'OK. Now, as to new developments. Mrs Morrison, your husband has been formally charged with offences under the Terrorism Act, the Children and Young Persons Protection Acts of both jurisdictions, the Firearms Act and the Firearms (Scotland) Act.'

'What?' Hope tried to sound disbelieving and outraged, although she'd expected something like this. 'That's ridiculous!'

'I insist,' said McKinnon, 'that my client be told the details of the charges against her husband.'

'I was coming to that,' said Macdonald. 'They are very much relevant to the charges she faces, and others that she may yet face.' She thumbed her pad and read out:

'You, Hugh Morrison, of 13 Victoria Road, London, et cetera, are hereby charged with the following offences, to wit, that you did have in your possession at the above premises an illegally held firearm, further that you stored it on said premises in an insecure manner contrary to the provisions of the Firearms Act and of the Children and Young Persons Protection Act, that in violation of the Firearms (Scotland) Act you transported said firearm to Scotland, concealed it likewise illegally and insecurely on the premises of The Old Manse, Uig, Eilean Siar, in further violations of the same Acts as applied to Scotland, et cetera, that you carried it illegally from said premises on this day, and that furthermore on challenge by the constabulary you failed to surrender the weapon as ordered and instead deposited it in a place of concealment and refused to disclose the location of said place of concealment, said place being within the North Atlantic Forward Defence Area, a region covered by the emergency provisions, thus violating such-and-such provisions of the Terrorism Act, as amended et cetera et cetera.'

Macdonald looked up. 'I've paraphrased to skip all the sections and dates referred to, but that's the substance. Do you wish to read it yourself?'

'Not at this moment.'

'Mr McKinnon, have you read the indictment?'

'Yes.'

'Is it correctly and legally formulated, and have I given your client a correct impression of its substance?'

McKinnon hesitated. 'On an initial reading, and without prejudice to any objections that might be or might already have been lodged by Mr Morrison's own solicitor, I would have to agree, yes.'

Hope saw the room begin to fade to monochrome. She felt dizzy and sick. She closed her eyes, took a deep breath and held it, then opened her eyes and breathed out and took a sip of water. She tried not to think about what Hugh must be going through. At least nothing had been said about a confession. She was not sure whether or not that was something to be thankful for. It might mean they hadn't worked him over, or it might mean they were still working him over. Or had just started working him over.

Stop. She sighed again, and took a gulp of water, and looked Macdonald straight in the eye.

'So what all this adds up to,' she said, 'is that the police still haven't found this supposed firearm, and they're using this absence of evidence as evidence that Hugh has hidden it so cleverly that they can't find it!'

'My client has put the matter very well,' said McKinnon, visibly brightening. 'I suggest you explain the relevance of these ridiculous charges to her own position.'

'Indeed,' said Macdonald. She leaned forward, elbows on the

table, and fixed Hope with the sort of concerned, helpful gaze that Hope had come to expect from Fiona Donnelly, the health visitor.

'Look, Hope,' she said, interlacing her fingers and then spreading her hands, a couplet of gestures she repeated apparently at random as she went on, 'I'm asking you, with your best interests and the best interests of your wee boy very much in mind, to reconsider your position. You've been denying all knowledge of the firearm in your husband's possession. I've just drawn attention to evidence that you were well aware of its presence in your house, and that you failed to urge him to turn it in or to report it yourself, thus making you an accessory to his crime as well as liable to the charges under suspicion of which you've been arrested. If you continue to deny the obvious truth, you will be charged. And just to anticipate Mr McKinnon, that charge need not refer to the events of this particular day. It could just as well refer to the even more serious charge arising out of your knowing about the illegal gun in your own house, where a child was present – in breach of both the Firearms Act and the Child Protection Act. These charges would of course be brought by the London Metropolitan Police, quite separately from the similar charges that could be brought against you by us. Do you understand that?'

'Yes.'

'Now as you know, Hope, even having that charge brought against you, regardless of the outcome of the case, is quite enough for the social services, in this country as well as in England, to apply for a court order to the effect that you are unable to provide a safe environment for your child, and to have the child taken into care. Do you understand that?'

'Yes, I do,' said Hope, fighting down dismay with anger. 'And it's outrageous. Even if I'm found innocent, I'm still guilty.'

'I'm afraid that isn't how it works, Hope. You see, that would be a matter for the family court, and it would be quite free and indeed obliged to take into account all the relevant evidence, including evidence that might not be admissible in a criminal trial, or that might not be enough to convince a jury beyond a reasonable doubt. Mr McKinnon will confirm that point of law.'

McKinnon nodded, unhappily. 'That's true, yes.'

'It's in this context,' Macdonald went on, 'that the matter that Mr McKinnon alluded to earlier, the matter of private conscience as he put it, is not as he said irrelevant to the present case but very relevant indeed. Because the developing legal position in England and no doubt very soon in Scotland is that refusal to take pre-natal genetic medication without good cause is tantamount to child neglect, and itself grounds for declaring you an unfit mother.'

'Oh Jesus,' said Hope, her head in her hands. 'I *knew* this was about the fix.'

'No, Hope, it isn't. That's just part of it, which I'm reminding you of in your own best interests. And it's only a small part, because now that serious charges have been laid against your husband, you – look up, Hope! Look at me! – you too are open to having serious charges laid against you.'

Hope looked up. Macdonald's face blurred. The policewoman passed her a tissue. Hope wiped her eyes and blew her nose.

'Go on,' she said.

'Hope, your husband has been charged with terrorist offences. Because of the detail of these offences, and the specific events of this morning and early afternoon, you could now be charged as an accessory to these same offences. All that I've said before about the charges you were arrested on suspicion of applies many times over to the much more serious charge of being an accessory or indeed an accomplice to an act of terrorism. Now, you may think this is trumped up or overblown, but believe you me, Hope, deliberately concealing a firearm in a secret location in an area covered by the emergency provisions, which given its front-line location the Isle of Lewis most definitely is, is beyond any quibble an act of terrorism in its own right, regardless of any further connections or conspiracies that may be alleged or discovered. If you continue to stonewall this investigation, there may be no alternative but to charge you as an accomplice to that terrorist act. And don't kid yourself for a moment that your guilt or innocence of this charge depends on your *husband's* guilt or innocence.'

'What?' Hope cried. McKinnon jolted upright in his seat.

'Yes,' Macdonald went on, with a smug glance at the lawyer, 'the charge against you depends on your *having good reason* to believe that such an act was committed, and the evidence you have been confronted with is *in and of itself* good and indeed compelling reason, in the eyes of the law, for you to believe that. Regardless of whether that evidence leads to a conviction,

345

you would still be deemed knowingly complicit in the alleged act.'

Hope glared at Macdonald and turned to McKinnon. 'Is that so?' she asked.

'Yes,' said McKinnon. 'I'm afraid it is. Lots of precedents over recent years, in Scotland and in England.'

'But that's just another . . . ' Hope's mouth was dry. She took a swallow of water. 'Another case of being guilty even if you're innocent.'

'Be that as it may,' said Macdonald, 'the fact remains that it's the law, and under the law, if you're found guilty on this charge you could be put away for life, and if you're innocent you could still lose all access to your child. And, Hope, I hate to bring this up, but that applies also to the child you're expecting.'

Hope sagged forward in the chair. 'No!'

'Yes,' said Macdonald, 'I'm sorry, but that's the case. Another point I'm reluctant to bring up, but which I'm obliged to in your own interests, is that once you've been charged with or even suspected of terrorism, you become liable to enhanced interrogation to uncover any further possible lines of inquiry. Oh, Hope, don't look away, don't hide from the truth! Save yourself, for heaven's sake! You have no idea what else your husband could be charged with – treason, even.'

'Treason?' Hope had thought she was now beyond surprise, but no.

'He booked a flight to Prague last week, and spoke of emigrating to Russia, all quite legal of course, but in conjunction with concealing a weapon in an area within the North Atlantic Defence—'

'Oh for fuck's sake!' Hope jumped up. The chair clattered behind her. 'You'd charge a man with treason for leaving a *bloody air pistol* where the fucking *Russian Army* might find it?'

'Yes,' said Macdonald, pushing her chair and herself backward. 'We would. And if you don't sit down and stop waving your arms around, I'll see to it that you're charged with assaulting a police officer.'

Hope retrieved her chair and sat down. 'Sorry,' she said. 'I wasn't threatening you. I was just – overcome with astonishment.'

'Och, that's quite understandable,' said Macdonald. She pulled herself and the seat forward to the table, propped her elbows, and looked Hope in the eye. 'Now – what was that about an air pistol?'

'Oh, fuck,' said Hope.

'You don't need to say anything,' McKinnon said.

'Indeed you don't,' said Macdonald, cheerfully. 'If you don't mind being charged forthwith, as follows . . .' She looked down at her pad. 'You, Hope Morrison, are hereby—'

'Stop!' Hope cried. 'Stop! I'll tell you everything.'

For a frantic moment, she thought Macdonald would go on reading the charge. Then the policewoman looked up.

'Everything?'

'Yes,' said Hope. 'Everything.'

*

When she'd finished, half an hour later, the policewoman and the lawyer sat back in their chairs and triangulated her with looks of deep bewilderment.

McKinnon spoke first.

'Mrs Morrison,' he said, 'do I take you to be giving me a testimony to deliver to my colleague defending your husband, in support of him urging your husband to enter a plea of *not guilty by reason of insanity*?'

Hope felt as if she was looking up from the bottom of a pit of despair and betrayal, and not sure whether she was seeing a rope to get out or a spade to dig herself in deeper.

'I hadn't thought of that,' she said. 'Do what you like. I've told you the truth.'

'This interview is terminated,' said Macdonald. She stood up. 'Hope, I must ask you to return to the cell.'

Hope had been in the cell for half an hour when the door banged open. Dolina Macdonald stood there.

'Come with me to the front desk, please.'

As she emerged into the reception area, Hope saw Nigel Morrison sitting on a chair at the back, his face grim. He gave her the barest flicker of a smile before she was taken to the desk. Hamish McKinnon stood beside her as her possessions were returned.

'You've been released on bail,' the lawyer told her. 'The bail has been posted by Nigel Morrison. You must remain on Lewis, but as long as you're on the island you can go wherever you like.

The charges are still pending. The child-protection charges, that is – the police haven't said anything more about the other charges Dolina mentioned, and you can be sure I'll be making a complaint about her bringing them up in the interview. Still . . . '

'Yes,' said Hope, in a dull voice. She slid the wedding ring on, then the monitor ring, which immediately began to sting from all the contaminants in the air around her. Alcohol and nicotine molecules in the remaining traces of sick, she guessed. She looked at the fix, still in its carton and bubble, and shoved it in her pocket 'Still. Where's Hugh? If they've charged him, shouldn't he be here?'

McKinnon shook his head. 'Still being held in the military brig at the airbase, I'm afraid. My colleague is making urgent representations about that.'

'Oh please, please, go on doing that and let me know . . . '

'Yes, yes.'

'Did you really take what I said to Hugh's solicitor?'

'Yes,' said McKinnon. 'For whatever good that'll do. I didn't say anything about an insanity defence, of course. That was . . . just my first reaction. Not very professional. Sorry.'

'What about our child? Where is he?'

'I don't know,' said McKinnon. 'You'll have to ask his grand-father.'

'Well, thanks for everything,' said Hope. 'I'm sure I'll see you again.'

'I'm afraid so, yes.'

Hope shook hands with him, stiffly, then walked over to Nigel, who jumped up to meet her.

'Where's Nick?' she asked. 'Is he with Mairi?'

'No,' said Nigel. He took her in his arms. 'They haven't told us where he is.'

He held her until she stopped crying, and then helped her out of the police station and along the street to the car. He carried her rucksack, but she wouldn't let go of Nick's.

24

The Good Cop

Hugh didn't know how long he'd been standing on tiptoe, leaning on his fingertips against the wall. Not knowing the length of time was, he was at some level aware, an intended result, a design feature of the procedure. He could see bright white light through the interweave of the bag over his head, and he could hear white noise through the headphones over his ears. Every so often the white noise would be replaced by jarring, jaunty music, or the sounds of weeping or screaming, and just as he'd got used to these and was beginning to tune them out, the white noise would rush back like incoming breakers. The tiny squares of white light danced and moved in front of his eyes, like pixels in an old low-res video game, and sometimes formed into swooping, attacking space fleets or flying shards of glass.

Every so often, when the pain in his fingers and arms and feet and the back of his legs became unbearable, he would let go and press his palms on the wall or his bare soles on the floor, and enjoy the relief for the second or two before the blow came to the inside of his leg or his groin or the side of his trunk below the ribs or the small of his back.

But it was while he was standing as instructed that he was, without warning, struck hard across the backs of his knees. He fell to the floor, banging his head against the wall on the way down. The phones and hood were snatched off his head while he was still sprawling, dazed, at the foot of the wall. He immediately placed his arms over his head, curled up and pulled up his legs.

'Get up!'

The command came from a metre or two away, and rang like a shout in a public toilet. Hugh rolled to his knees, then to his feet, holding himself up against the wall.

'Open your eyes and step away from the wall.'

Hugh opened his eyes, and closed them tight shut as the light hit them. He stepped away from the wall, swayed, and fell again. This time he didn't bang his head, and the next time he got up he was able to stay on his feet and open his eyes. A man in the uniform of a Royal Marine sergeant stood in front of him, regarding him with a curious detachment. The room was tiled white, with a cork floor and a polystyrene ceiling. The door stood open.

'After you,' the marine said, gesturing to the doorway.

Staggering, cringing from the expected blow, Hugh made for the door. It gave on to a narrow corridor.

'Left,' said the marine.

Hugh walked on until ordered into a room to the side. It looked like a lecture room, with bright overhead lights, a blank white wall screen, and rows of chairs with built-in desks. The marine pushed him, not too hard, towards a desk at the front and told him to sit down. Then he went out. Hugh's head slumped on his arms, across the desk.

'Hello,' said a new voice. Hugh looked up. A shaven-headed man a few years older than him, wearing plain trousers and an open-necked blue shirt, stood over him holding two cans of Coke.

'No coffee, I'm afraid,' the man said, with a light smile. He had a north London accent, clipped to posh. 'Can't risk any hot liquids being slung around, you see. Coke?'

Hugh managed to close his hand on the chilly can. His finger joints hurt. He was still trying to get a fingernail under the tab when the man grabbed a seat, swung it around, and sat down facing him, a metre and a half away. He watched Hugh prise open the can, spill a foamy dribble down his chin, and then force a sip down his throat.

'Good,' he said. 'Don't try to drink too much at once. You've had it rough, haven't you? Those military types ...' He shook his head, sadly. 'Carry on as if they were in a war zone. Never give you a chance to put your side of the story before they pile right in on you with the old routine. You'd almost think they enjoyed it. But they don't, not really. They're very professional. But rough, undeniably rough.'

He popped his own can and continued: 'So, Hugh. This is your chance. Let me hear what you have to say for yourself.

From what I've been told, it doesn't look good for you, but I'm sure, you know, that you have your own version of events, and if it fits in with all the known facts and accounts for them in a different way – well! That's you off the hook! No one would be happier than me – apart from you, of course – if this all turned out to be a ridiculous misunderstanding. Result!' He smacked his palm with his fist, making Hugh wince. 'I'd be absolutely delighted. Walk you to the gate, put you in a taxi back to Stornoway, slap-up dinner with your wife, night in a hotel, all on the taxpayers' tab. Sounds good, yes?'

Hugh nodded.

'On the other hand,' said the man, standing up and pacing about, as if nervously, between the desks and the screen, 'suppose you have something serious to get off your chest. What you've done might look bad to you. Maybe you're afraid to admit it out loud. But even so, you're in a far better position than you might expect if you just spill it all as soon as possible. Names, dates, plans, the lot. The more the better. A full and frank confession makes a good impression on a judge, you know, and I'm sure a smart brief could come up with all sorts of mitigating circumstances. Good Lord! I can reel off half a dozen myself, just off the top of my head. Previous good character. Father of a small child. Local ways, perhaps, about guns and so forth. Seriousness of the offence not realised. Led astray, maybe, by ruthless professionals. All that sort of thing.'

He stopped, by the white screen. Hugh squinted at him, through eyes half-shut against the glare.

'I sometimes think,' mused the man, 'that we make a big

mistake letting so many frightening rumours circulate. They work as a deterrent, I'll give you that, but we seem to forget to balance this against the panic people get into when they're facing charges like those you are. They may think that no matter what they do or say, life as they know it is over. That they're doomed to vanish without trace into the ... parallel detention system. The global gulag, as some very ill-informed journalists so frivolously call it. They really should read the book, you know, before bandying around terms like that.'

He gazed off into the middle distance for a moment. As the room's venetian blinds were closed, this did not strike Hugh as a convincing pose.

'All quite untrue,' the man went on. 'And yet, and yet ...' He sighed. 'I've seen so many cases of people who held out, for days, months, years even, thinking that a confession would make things worse for them. Not true, not true at all. And when you see the state of them when they finally come out ... Sad cases.' He shook his head. 'It makes you wonder what their lawyers were thinking of, it really does. No!'

He turned his head sharply and faced Hugh again.

'No!' he repeated. 'All the grim stuff you've heard of – that only happens to those who don't confess.' He strolled over and resumed his seat. He took a sip of his Coke, and leaned forward.

'So tell me, Hugh,' he began, then jumped to his feet, knocking over the desk, and shoved his face right in front of Hugh's, 'WHERE DID YOU HIDE THAT FUCKING GUN AND WHY DID YOU HIDE IT?'

Hugh recoiled, splashing some of the cola, tipping the desk

almost over. The man picked up his own seat, set it down and sat in it again, leaning forward, knees apart, arms on the desk.

'I really do want to know, you know,' he said. 'Quite apart from the benefits to yourself of telling me, it really is driving me up the wall.' He took another sip, and smiled thoughtfully. 'You trained as an engineer, I understand. I have a smattering of physics myself. The military chaps, of course, all have a very solid scientific education. You see, don't you, how deeply frustrating it is to be told something that violates the law of conservation of mass-energy?'

Hugh tried to speak, but his mouth was too dry. He took a gulp of Coke. His arms felt like they'd been knotted from toy balloons, weak and swollen. They ached like he'd just done a thousand press-ups. His ears rang so much that he strained to hear the man speak. The urge to sleep was almost overpowering.

'Did I say that?' he said. 'I don't remember.'

'Ah,' said the man. 'You were interviewed after your arrest.' He waved a hand, and the screen lit up. Hugh saw an image of himself shouting, in a desperate tone: 'I told you! I told you before! I threw them away in the tunnel!' There was a blur of motion across the screen, and then it went blank again. Hugh felt his hand lift slowly to his face, to meet a bruise over the cheekbone.

'I remember now,' he said.

He had the impression that it had gone on like that for hours, before he'd been made to stand against the wall. That would account for some of the other aches and pains.

'A tad unprofessional,' the man said. 'They're not supposed to leave visible marks, you know. Not when a court appearance is on the cards. But then . . . as I said, the frustration. It can get the better of the best of us.'

He brushed his palms against each other, briskly, twice. 'But luckily for you, I didn't have to listen through all that. I've come to this fresh, so to speak. Think of me as . . . well, supposing you were in a foreign country, and you'd got into trouble with the local police. Beaten up in the back room of the nick, slung into some stinking oubliette, bewildering charges laid against you. Think how pleased you'd be if the British consul turned up! There you are, over a cup of tea, together in private, knowing nothing you say goes beyond these walls. Think how you'd react – you'd tell him, or her, everything.'

He leaned back, opening his arms. 'I'm that British consul, Hugh. I'm here to get you out. Or if that's not possible, to save you from going back to the interrogation cells, and from there to worse places. Far worse. No matter what you've done, you have absolutely nothing to lose by telling me everything.'

'I thought I *had* told them everything,' Hugh said. He raised a hand, painfully. 'Wait, don't . . . don't fly off the handle again. Please . . . bear with me, OK? I want to tell you everything. I'm honestly not sure what I said. I don't even know what I'm accused of. Apart from having an air pistol, which it seems I've already admitted to. OK, I admit it again. I put my hands up to it.' He tried the gesture, and failed. 'Metaphorically, all right?'

The man nodded, looking sympathetic. 'Yes, of course. Go on.'

'I don't know what I'm accused of, or what I'm charged with.'

'Ah!' The man grinned, raising a didactic finger. 'Accused of, charged with. A valid distinction, and an interesting one. What you're charged with are various offences under firearms, child protection, terrorism and so forth, all centred around keeping, carrying and then concealing an illegally held firearm. The terrorism bit comes in because you've stashed it in an area of ongoing military operations, which I take it refers to the aircraft taking off around here to stop the Russians from poking their nose-cones farther into Allied airspace. We're on a Warm War front line, after all. All very much letter-of-the-law stuff, and they've thrown the book at you. If you get sent down for that, you'll be in the regular prison system for decades and your wife gets done as an accomplice, seeing as she didn't shop you when she had the chance, comprendez?'

'Yes,' Hugh croaked.

'Now, I know what you're going to say. This is a heck of a lot to throw at a chap because of an air pistol. Between ourselves, I quite agree. But like it or not, the law is clear on the point: Magnum, Glock, air pistol, replica, or even remotely realistic toy, all equally illegal. Because, you see, it's not what it *can* do, it's what someone might have a reasonable apprehension that it *could* do that turns it into a weapon. An instrument of intimidation, and therefore, potentially, of terrorism. Wave a spud gun around with a political motive, and – bang! You're a terrorist!'

'I understand that, but—'

'Very good. Accused of, let's say suspected of – different

bucket of grief altogether. You've been in touch with two people who've previously confessed to offences under the Acts, you know. Still running around, free as birds. Why, you ask? Well! We're all grown-ups here, nobody's listening, and we're not in the Labour Party. So we don't have to pretend we don't know what these confessions are worth. Not what I'd consider actionable intelligence, let's say, but that's what kicked this whole thing off. That, and the singularly unfortunate fact that the intelligence community has picked up some chatter recently from the Naxals, relating to Stornoway.'

'Naxals in *Stornoway?*' Hugh's voice rose, an intonation he'd meant to sound like scorn and disbelief, but which came out dismayingly like surprise and delight.

The man waved a hand. 'Naxals can pop up anywhere,' he said. 'Just your hard luck that the latest flap happens to be here. Or perhaps not entirely – your trip to Southall to book a flight to Prague didn't help you at all. Throw in the visit and phone call from that woman Geena Fernandez, her friend Joseph Goonwardeene – you know how it is with the security boys. Paranoia is their profession.' He smiled complicitly. 'It isn't mine.'

'What is yours, then?'

The man put his elbows on the desk and wiped his fingers across his closed eyelids, brushing his eyebrows, then slid his hands to his temples and peered across at Hugh. He looked tired, suddenly, as if he'd been awake too long and the night had caught up with him.

'Curiosity,' he said. 'No, seriously, Hugh. My job is getting people like you out of places like this. Do you have any idea of how much false positives cost the taxpayer in accommodation alone? How much of the time of skilled interrogators is wasted in extracting confessions from people who have nothing to confess? The sheer economic loss of taking innocent people out of the workforce? It would make your hair stand on end. And that's leaving aside the cost of what happens when the subjects are cleared, if they ever are. Rehab where possible, compensation, legal costs … Honestly, in ten years of this I've saved HMG the cost of my entire projected lifetime employment plus pension a dozen times over. As for the political fallout – don't get me started.' He shook his head, and sighed. 'Just don't get me started.'

The man stood up and again began pacing around. Hugh eyed him warily, and tensed in his seat.

'Speaking of not getting me started,' the man said, 'you don't need to keep up the evasions. Your wife has given the police a full statement. The suicide box, the tearful conversation, the second sight, the land under the hill, what she saw and what you and the kiddie claimed to see in the tunnel, the lot. And her own troubles with the law and the health system. There's nothing to hide any more, Hugh.'

He stood to the side of the screen, like a lecturer, and waited.

Hugh eased the heels of his hands from the inside edge of the desktop. He laid his arms lightly across it and let his legs stretch a little.

'I didn't mention any of that?' he asked, impressed.

'No,' said the man. 'Despite its being the sort of rigmarole that could have given the chaps pause. Are we, they might have asked themselves, trying to beat the truth out of a lunatic? Well, perhaps they wouldn't have, but the ploy would have been worth a try, one would have thought. Been done, you know, been done. Extraordinary what some people can get up to. Heard of an Indian intelligence bod once, trained by yogis or some such, kept up the most ...' He snapped his fingers. 'One for the memoirs. So, Hugh, no, you didn't mention any of that.'

He tapped the screen, and an image came up, of jagged but approximately rectangular false-colour contours, like a mathematical diagram of some complex equation.

'Let me tell you about the tunnel,' he said. 'Searched from end to end. Scanned with sub-millimetre radar. Police rescue probe plunged into the water at the bottom. Three metres deep, it goes, about two or three steps from where you turned back. No cracks in the concrete wider than a pinkie, through which the water seeps into the peat. Ten centimetres of accumulated detritus at the bottom, then solid rock. Search-and-rescue boys actually found three airgun pellets in the mud, quite easily, that's how thorough the check was.'

He flicked with his middle finger, and another image came up. A big square, with the ghostly shape of a pistol wedged diagonally across it.

'Drone shot of your jacket pocket,' the man said. 'Taken moments before you dropped into the gully. You can practically read the serial number. No question of it having been chucked before you entered the tunnel. No question at all of some piece of misdirection, like, say, one of the coppers picking it up on the way out. Every detail of every one of their movements was logged in real time on their lapel cameras.' He snapped his fingers, and the screen went white. 'Gone. Just like that. So where is it?'

Misdirection, Hugh thought. Like a magic trick. Maybe there was something there he could work with, but first . . .

'Look,' he said, 'I don't want to provoke you or anything, but why does it matter so much? We're talking about a thing that can kill a rabbit, or put an eye out if you're careless. From the way the other guys were shouting, it was like they thought I'd set up some kind of, uh, dead drop, isn't that what you call it? For some terrorist or spy to pick up later. Well, I can see that could be worth doing with explosives or actual guns, but – an air pistol?'

The man clicked his tongue. 'You'd be surprised what can be done with an air pistol. Take what you've just said. Shoot a soldier's eye out from ten paces, get your timing right, and you can relieve him of whatever weapon he has. And you're off. People have built armies that way. And you'd be surprised how important it might be, in some circumstances, to shoot a rabbit. No smoke. No explosive traces to worry about. Very little sound. Stuff like that. Just a thought. But that isn't what's worrying the chaps, and what's worrying me. Proof of concept, that's the worry. If you've found, or been shown, a way to disappear a chunk of metal in full view of half a dozen people, what else is possible?'

Hugh took a deep breath. 'I can see that,' he said. 'I didn't understand that before. Maybe if they'd explained ... but anyway. Can I tell you how it seemed to me, in the culvert?'

'Oh, please do. And do stop cringing. I promise not to hit you, or even yell at you.'

'All right. I didn't see a pool of water. It was like the tunnel ended with an opening on a steep hillside. I saw a landscape, like the real one but at a different time, maybe in an ice age. Or maybe just after one, you know? In the sunshine beyond winter.'

'In the sunshine beyond winter?' The man seemed a little surprised, and to be turning the phrase over in his mind.

'Yes. And when the police came, I threw the air pistol and the box of pellets out of the opening and ... into that landscape. I threw them hard, but it wasn't like ... a good strong fling.'

'Indeed not,' said the man. 'You threw like a girl.'

'I couldn't get my arm back,' Hugh said, defensively. 'I heard them fall, like on scree, not far down the hill. And I'm sure if you have such good images as you say you have of what happened, they'll show how my arm moved, the speed of it, the force. They might even show the trajectory of the gun and the box leaving my hand.'

'As it happens,' said the man, 'they don't. They show the throw. They also show the steep, sloping roof of the culvert right in front of you. They don't actually show the objects bouncing off, but your hand is in the way and the imaging is far from perfect.'

'Do you have these images?' Hugh asked. 'Can you show me them?'

'Of course.' The man snapped with several fingers in succession. The screen lit up with a view, jumpy but clearer than Hugh had expected, of him and Nick and Hope, crowded together and bending over in the low, narrow space, seen from behind. It perturbed Hugh to see the light reflected off the water in front of his feet, and the sloping ceiling a metre and a half or so in front of his face. He saw his struggle to get something out of his pocket, Hope's grab, his throw. No glimpse of what he'd thrown. Then the figures turned around, Hugh first, getting between Nick and the end of the tunnel, Hope momentarily obscuring the view of both of them. They began to move forward. The viewpoint backed off. They remained in view all the way up the tunnel. Then the light, and blurred images as Hope was grabbed.

'That was from one camera?'

'Yes.'

'Show me the others.'

The man did. They were much the same; different angles, different obscurities, each sequence ending with a blur of motion as Nick and then Hugh were grabbed.

'Well, there you are,' Hugh said.

'What?' The man looked at the final still, bright and blurry.

'It's obvious,' said Hugh. 'I don't know about you, but I can just about get my head around the idea of second sight. But not Tir Nan Og.'

The man looked puzzled.

'Call it fairyland,' Hugh explained. 'Or another dimension. Or the past or the future as places you could walk into, or throw things into. Would you agree?'

364

'I'm with you there,' the man said.

'OK. And to be honest, I don't buy the second sight either.' He tapped his forehead, and discovered another bruise. He winced and went on. 'I may get hallucinations, but I'm not crazy. Not now. In there, in the culvert, I maybe was crazy. In some kind of delusional dwam.'

Another puzzled look.

'Altered state of consciousness. I didn't know what I was doing. I don't remember what I did. But think what must have happened. I threw the air pistol and the box hard. They must have hit what was right in front of me and bounced off. They might not have fallen in the water. They might have landed at my feet. The box wasn't strong or tightly closed, so a couple of pellets might have fallen from it, the ones the probe found. Anyway, there I am, stooped over, turning around, behind Nick and Hope. You can't see my arms, you can't see much of me at all in any of these. So I have a moment to kick the pistol and the box forward, snatch them up, maybe stick them in my pocket or up the sleeve of my jacket. I don't know. It's what you said about misdirection that got me thinking this.'

'Misdirection!' the man said, sounding pleased. 'Now that you mention it, what evidence do we have from these images that the pistol and box left your hands at all?'

'Exactly,' said Hugh. 'I might not have let go.'

'So one way or another, you could have had them on you when you came out of the culvert. Then what?'

Hugh shrugged, painfully. 'Ask the guy who grabbed me. Local copper, a Leosach – a Lewis man, I know that from his voice. For all I know, he might know my father. He might even have known me, when we were both kids. Anyway, he'd have seen the gun from the probe images, know how seriously the authorities take that, but still have the Leosach laid-back attitude about guns himself. He might have tried to get me off the hook.'

'Interfering with evidence? Perverting the course of justice? Serious accusations to make against a police officer.'

'I know,' said Hugh. 'And I don't want to get whoever it was into trouble. But the thing is, it does happen sometimes. And things vanishing into thin air ... that doesn't happen, ever.'

He didn't believe a word of it.

The man stared at him for a moment.

'Don't go away,' he said, as if making a joke, and left the room. Hugh didn't watch him go. He could have vanished into thin air. He sipped the remaining Coke, now flat. More than once his head fell forward, jolting him awake.

The man returned, with the marine sergeant.

'Sorry, old chap,' the man said. 'They're not buying it. I did my best, but ...'

He turned to the marine and said, in a quite different tone: 'Let him have some sleep before the next session.'

25

The Unsmoking Gun

Hugh sat on the edge of a narrow metal shelf with a foam mattress and no other bedding, and gazed across at a toilet bowl with no seat a metre or so away, and a tap above a metal bowl fixed in the wall beside it. Two neat stacks, of sheets of toilet paper and of paper towels, lay beside the washstand. After the tiled room, the cell's fittings seemed like scenery. There was no window. One of the panels in the ceiling had a light behind it, silhouetting half a dozen dead flies. Nothing was too good for this cell's residents. Wildlife, even. No expense spared. His body ached all over, even more than it had done in the lecture room with the man. He had drunk some cold water from the tap, he'd pissed, and he'd washed his face and neck and dried them with the scratchy paper towels. His skin itched in various places, mostly over flesh too bruised to scratch. (He'd scratched anyway.) He had no idea what the time was, but he knew he had slept.

He was not even bored. Every minute here was a minute not in the tiled room, or in one of the worse places the man had warned him about. He picked at the edge of the foam mattress. It was about ten centimetres thick and had been quite comfortable to sleep on. He found he couldn't pick away any bits from the edge, but it wasn't clear whether the foam was too strong to tear – perhaps the material was designed that way, so that prisoners couldn't damage it or self-harm with it – or whether his fingers were too weak or too sore to apply enough force to tear it. There must be some way of finding out which it was. This problem occupied his mind for some time.

He was plucking at the front of his shirt and not getting anywhere when the door clanged open. A couple of orderlies in scrubs stepped inside.

Here it comes, he thought. The next session. He brought his knees to his chin and wrapped his arms around his head.

One of the orderlies laughed. 'They learn fast.'

'On your feet, chum,' the other said. 'Come on. Nobody's gonna hurt you. Not unless you stay there.'

Hugh expected this was a trick, but he unfolded his limbs and stood up anyway. They took an arm each and led him out of the cell. Corridor, turn, corridor, door, then double doors and a corridor with carpets and lights and partitions with sounds of office life behind them. They turned him into a cubicle with a desk and three chairs. On the floor beside the rubbish bin were his boots, belt and socks. His jacket and fleece hung from a coat-hanger hooked over the top of a partition.

'Sit down.'

Hugh complied.

'Put your boots and socks on.'

Hugh tried. The socks had been washed and dried. He got them on eventually, and his feet into his boots, but he fumbled the laces. One of the orderlies stooped, tightened the laces a little, and tied them loosely. The boots still felt too tight.

'Stay there.' It didn't sound like a joke.

Hugh nodded. They went away. Hugh stared at the desk, and fumbled his belt through the loops. He kept missing loops and having to go back.

'Ah, good morning,' said a familiar voice. 'Coffee?'

The man came in carrying two plastic cups of coffee and a clutch of sachets.

'Sugar, whitener,' he said, putting them down. He sat behind the desk, and flashed a wink. 'Reckon we can risk hot drinks now, eh?'

Hugh picked up a cup and sipped black coffee, scalding his tongue.

The man leaned sideways and pulled out a drawer of the desk. He took out and placed on the desk a ziplock plastic bag. It contained an air pistol, and a tattered carton from which one or two pellets had spilled in the bag.

'Recognise this?' he said. 'Take your time.'

Hugh stared down at the pistol, through the transparent plastic.

'Pick it up and have a look,' said the man. 'Go on. Just don't do anything impulsive.'

Hugh did, and didn't, as instructed (though he had a wild, vivid momentary daydream of tearing it from the bag and leaping out and contriving a hostage situation; he could feel the heat of a woman's body through a thin blouse, he could smell the hair on the back of her head . . .).

He knew nearly every scratch on the thing. Those he didn't recognise were fresh. He put it down.

'It's mine,' he said.

'The one you said you threw away in the culvert?'

'Yes.'

'The one you might, by sleight of hand, have removed from the culvert?'

'Yes, that one,' said Hugh, irritated.

'Hmm.' The man cupped an elbow and lipped a knuckle. 'Odd. Care to guess where it was found?'

'In the culvert?' Hugh hazarded.

'Don't try my patience,' said the man. 'We've been over that. So to speak.'

'Stornoway Police Station?'

'Much better. It was delivered there earlier this morning. In this evidence bag. By a policeman who has excellent recordings to show that he was called by your father in the wee sma' hours, that he drove to the Old Manse at first light, and was shown to a locked metal safe in the utility meter cupboard.'

'The one under the stairs?'

'Yes. He was handed a key, and he opened the safe himself.

The lock, he said, was very stiff. Inside the safe were these items, along with a very old but still valid firearms licence, naming your father as the responsible owner and you as a permitted user.'

Hugh closed his eyes and opened them. 'How the fuck did these get there?'

'You tell me. Your father claims he was up half the night worrying, suddenly remembered the certificate and wondered if it might be of some help to your defence, searched high and low for the key, found the things in the safe, and immediately rang the police station. He says he'd taken for granted that you took the gun with you when you left home, because you'd always kept it close to hand. Quite gobsmacked to find it there. Swears he hadn't looked in the safe for years.'

'Is he saying it must have been in the safe all along?'

'I've told you what he's saying. The only evidence we have that says anything different is various recordings – the self-surveillance, and the confessions and interrogations – of you and your wife *talking* about it. And we already know that your wife is loyal and you have hallucinations.'

'What about the drone sensor image?'

The man blinked rapidly. 'What image?'

'Oh.'

'I'm talking about the evidence we *have*. Evidence that could be produced in court and backed up by police testimony.' He shifted one shoulder and rubbed the back of his neck. 'I don't think we want to go there.'

The coffee was safe to drink now. Hugh gulped it.

'So what happens now?' he asked.

'You're free to go.'

Hugh stared at him. 'And my wife and my son?'

'Waiting for you at the police station, with your parents. You're all out of trouble. Free and clear.'

Hugh still couldn't believe it.

'And the other people, the people in London, Geena and, uh, Joe? All the conspiracies that got thrown at me between punches?'

'Oh, that,' the man said. 'That stuff only got on your wife's profile because of Islington Social Services, and I don't doubt the audit trail for this whole disgraceful hoo-ha leads straight back to them. That'll go on my report, don't you worry. And I've reset the parameters on your good lady's profile. She'd practically have to starve a kid, beat it and sell it before she gets flagged up as an unfit mother. You needn't expect any more trouble from that quarter. Nor from the police, or the security services, as long as you keep your nose clean. As things stand, there's no evidence that any crime has been committed at all.'

Hugh looked down at the air pistol, still in the bag. 'There might be fingerprints, DNA traces . . .'

'Are you *trying* to get yourself back in trouble?'

'I'm just not sure I'm out of it. I keep expecting a trick.'

'Trust issues,' the man said, nodding. 'You're going to have these, or so the shrinks tell me. No, really, you're free to go. Fingerprints, DNA . . . the local plod didn't have time for that, but we've had a quick look in the lab, and it's all very messy.

You must have let your little pals get their grubby paws all over it when you were a lad.'

Hugh had never let any of his friends know about the air pistol, let alone touch it. He looked the man in the eye and nodded firmly.

'Yeah, 'fraid so. Lesson learned.'

He stood up, slowly, and moved to reach for his jacket and fleece. The man jumped up and held them for him as he put his arms down the sleeves.

'Thanks,' said Hugh.

'No hard feelings, eh?'

The weight of the jacket, or maybe the torch and radio and battery that had been placed in its pockets, was already making Hugh's shoulders ache. He shrugged anyway.

'None at all.'

He stuck out a hand to shake. The man, instead, handed him the bag with the gun.

'Take it,' he said. 'It's yours, and it's legal.'

Hugh put it in his pocket, and the man sat back down at the desk. He put on glasses, and started rattling his fingers on the table, as if he'd forgotten about Hugh and was already busy on another problem.

Hugh hesitated. The man looked up.

'Someone will see you out,' he said.

Hugh saw two Military Police approaching, and he couldn't help but feel for a moment dread rather than relief. Trust issues. He took a grip on himself and stepped firmly out of the cubicle into the aisle to meet them.

'Oi!' the man called out. 'Wait a mo!'

Hugh stood still, feeling as if a huge weight that had been lifted from his shoulders had just crashed down again, then stepped back into the opening of the cubicle.

'One last thing,' the man said, frowning at him over the top of his glasses. 'I almost forgot. Speaking of shrinks. In case you happen to consult one over those hallucinations you've been having, or anything else . . . If I were you, I'd keep my trap shut on any mention of seeing visions of past or future ice ages. *Particularly* future. "The sunshine beyond winter", and all that. Good grief! What were you thinking?' He shook his head, as if in disbelief. 'Not a word, in these or any other circumstances. That kind of loose talk can bring a chap right back up on the radar, flashing bright green. Know what I mean?'

Hugh was still having trust issues when the two Military Police dropped him off from the unmarked car outside the police station, and waited at the kerb, engine running, until he went inside. His legs shook as he stepped over the threshold. He opened the swing door to the reception area with a hand that pushed only with its fingertips.

Sitting on plastic chairs at the side of the room were Nigel, Hope and Nick. Nigel's suit was grubby, and he looked exhausted, his face deeply lined, as if he'd aged five years overnight. Hope was staring straight ahead. Nick saw him first and jumped up and ran to him and hurled himself into Hugh's open arms, and Hugh forgot the pain. He looked over Nick's head, buried in his shoulder, and saw Hope still seated. She gazed at him as if afraid he wasn't there, or as if he might be snatched away at any moment. One of her hands was closed, on her lap, and the other held an open plastic water bottle. Still staring at him, she clapped one hand to her mouth, and followed it with a long swig from the water bottle. She set the bottle down on the floor, and stood up, and walked towards him, smiling like a suicide bomber.

26

The City Burners

It had been a good summer, Hope thought. Not the weather – rainy, damp, or at best a silvery overcast most days, with the occasional glorious breakthrough of deep blue sky and blazing sunshine, though according to the news the year was shaping up to be one of the hottest on record – but how things had gone, and how she felt. This mid-August mid-morning, she sat at the table in the back room of Mairi's shop, sipping coffee and nibbling biscuits and feeling that life was good. Nick, out playing in the wet, in the drysuit that had become like a second skin, was at this moment out of sight. A glance through her glasses showed her where he was, swimming in the shallow water a hundred metres to the left along the shore. He had a wrist phone, which he was so proud of he needed no urging to wear it all the time. He didn't know that its camera and sound and GPS tracker were on constantly, but he didn't need to.

Right now he was laughing and splashing and talking to someone – one of his imaginary friends, or one of the real friends he'd made among the village kids. Hope didn't mind which. He was going to be a much more confident and outgoing boy when he started primary school in a few weeks.

Hope had mixed feelings at the prospect of going back to Islington. On the one hand, they were all having a great time up here. She enjoyed working undisturbed but having at least one person to wander over and talk to whenever she liked, and she'd come to quite welcome the occasional stint behind the counter. The view through the patio doors was often grey, and today the sky was just about black, but it was better than the wall of a basement flat and people's boots going by. Hugh had benefited from working so much in the open air, having a dozen workmates rather than one or two, and banter with folks who shared the same jokes and references as he did, even if their parents or grandparents were English or Polish or Pakistani. The outdoor work and the wider social life had seemed to help him at another level, if the diminishing frequency of the bad dreams and the long silences and the thousand-yard stares was anything to go by. And they all got on well with Nigel and Mairi. Over the past weeks Nigel had become rather careless, as the locals put it, about going to church and keeping the Sabbath and minding his tongue. It had become something of a minor scandal in the parish of Uig, which had very little scandal and made the most of what it could get.

On the other hand, Hope longed to be back in a place of her own, without treading on other people's toes or getting underfoot all the time, kind and laid-back though Nigel and Mairi were about it. She yearned to shop for the baby's arrival, and not in Stornoway. And there were only so many bootees and hats and cardigans that one woman could knit, though try telling Mairi that. 'It'll be a long winter,' she'd say, above a brisk rattle of needles. On top of all that, Hope missed London. She missed the street and the strangers – the strangers more than her friends, come to think of it. She missed meeting people every day who might recognise her and know her name but who didn't know her at all – and above all, who didn't want to know. Unlike everybody here.

Not that they felt isolated, on the island. With glasses and phones and screens they could talk to anyone. They'd taken off the blocks against Maya and Geena and Joe, and had re-established contact. Maya had at first been dismayed and a little disappointed by Hope's decision, but she was still beavering away, like a hacker of legal code, to establish the wish to pass on a non-deleterious gene as an unchallengeable reason to refuse the fix. She'd even persuaded Hope to link up with the Labour Party again, and had fixed her an engagement to speak on civil liberties to the Stornoway branch – which Hope had reluctantly done, and had found the members much more open to her arguments than those in Islington. She still hated the Party, hated it from the very marrow of her bones. She could look at its banners and badges and see behind them cells of hooded, shackled men, and cold bodies covered with cement dust in sudden ruins, and naked people burning under green rainforest canopies. She could see Hugh, his legs kicked from under him, cracking his head against a tiled wall. When she'd stood up to speak in that draughty hall, that hatred had made her tremble, and had tightened her voice. Afterwards, someone had congratulated her on how she'd put so much passion into her argument, despite her evident nervousness about public speaking.

Joe Goonwardeene had become enthusiastic about the possibilities of tachyon detection, and was busy hustling various departments of SynBioTech for money and resources for a project to develop synthetic mutated rhodopsin. His pitch was that even the smallest hint about the future could be of immense value to the company, giving it an edge on its competitors in anticipating promising new ideas. Geena, meanwhile, was already informally observing and recording Joe's efforts with fascinated delight. She'd just about finished her thesis, and was casting about for funding for postdoctoral work on how Joe was going about getting his project funded. And, of course, she was keeping a careful record of her own activities, for possible future use.

'It'll take reflexivity to a whole new level!' she'd said. 'The political economy of the promise of the political economy of the promise of promise!'

Hugh had bought glasses with his first week's wages, and sometimes he shared a virtual space with Hope and Maya and Geena. Sometimes he talked one-to-one with Joe or with Geena, long conversations in the evening – some, like last night, with Geena, continuing long after Hope had gone to bed. Hope wasn't more than slightly jealous. Hugh and Geena, and Joe, shared an experience she was glad she didn't, and talking about it, or indeed about anything, with someone else who'd been through it seemed to help Hugh get to sleep and not wake up shuddering and shouting in the night.

Hope didn't regret her decision to take the fix. There were two reasons why she had taken it. One was that, just after her arrest, she had said she would. She hadn't made any conditions, but it had felt like a bargain: if I get off, if we *all* get out of this, then I'll take the fix. It had not felt like a bargain with the state, whose forces were at that moment holding her down and telling her her rights. She would have had no compunction about breaking a promise to them. No. It had felt like a bargain with God. Hope didn't believe in God, not even in the distant, impersonal, mathematical, indifferent God that Nigel spoke of, but she wouldn't have felt right going back on a bargain with him just because he didn't exist. It would have felt like cheating.

There was another reason why, when she'd seen Hugh walking in, and seen Nick leaping into his arms and proving him real, she'd kept her side of the bargain without a moment of hesitation. It was because it hadn't felt, at that moment, that she'd been finally worn down and defeated. It had felt like a victory. More than that, it had felt like revenge. A revenge on all those who had worn her down and arrested her and tortured her husband and threatened to take her children away.

It had felt like that because she knew the gene was real, and that the bright land was real too; because, in the culvert, she had seen what Hugh and Nick were telling her they saw. She'd seen it faintly, a ghost image, like a double exposure, beyond the water and the wall that she saw too. Maybe that faint refraction was all of the bright land that those without the gene could see. Perhaps those with the gene could do more than see it, in some places or circumstances: they could actually go there. They could even go there and come back, at some cost in lost time as the old tales told, and as Nigel (Hope secretly thought) had done. If any of this was true, she knew that the world contained things stranger even than tachyons. She didn't care. She knew, or at least believed with more surety, that the gene was real and that the fix would neutralise it, and not only did she not care, she was glad. Let it go, let them take it, let them edit it out of the genome.

These people didn't *deserve* to know the future.

At that moment, Hugh, too, was having a tea break. He was a long way off, on a new site up at the north of the island, on the headland of Ness. From where he sat, in the lee of a half-dismantled tower, he could see the lighthouse at the very tip of the island, and on either side the sea, grey and white under the darkening sky. Soon the lighthouse would again be the tallest structure on Lewis, though far older and more obsolete than the wind-farm towers.

He sipped hot black tea from a mug and munched the first of the day's sandwiches, idly scanned the news scrolling on his pad, and without thinking much about it exchanged remarks with the men who sat beside him. He was slightly distracted from all that by the scene straight in front of him, where a gang working for a different contractor was taking no break at all and wasting no time in winding cable out of the conduits in the ground, in lifting reels of the stuff from the winch as one after another the reels filled up, and rolling them to a long low-loading lorry and sticking them along the scaffolding poles that held them in place like spindles, gradually building up to great long cylinders of high-tension cable. The chug of the generator that powered the winch came and went with the freshening breeze. The gang were all of Asian appearance, good old local Stornoway Pakistanis, their accents indistinguishable from his own, and often enough their Gaelic better. He felt a trace of discomfort just from sitting here, watching their unstinting toil. There was something privileged, almost colonial, about the contrast of their work and his rest, while he sat sipping tea from the same subcontinent as their ancestors had come from, and (no doubt) whose current owners the cargo they were loading was ultimately destined to enrich.

There was more than that to his unease. Ever since that moment the first day after their arrival, on the hill above the old school overlooking the bay, he'd felt the same disquiet whenever he'd chanced upon a similar scene. The coiled cable, the generator. Something he couldn't put his finger on. It had troubled Nick too, Hugh recalled. 'Don't like it. Dark.' The boy had said the same, with more obvious justification, a moment before they'd gone into the culvert.

Hugh pushed that memory away. He didn't want to think about it. A few days after his release, a gang of men had gone up the hill behind the house, carrying crowbars and lugging heavy packs. An hour or two later, a series of dull thuds had echoed among the hills, and shortly afterwards the men came down. His father had had a word with them, and he'd told Hugh that they had done a job he'd phoned in to urge the company to do: to dynamite and block up the entrance to the old, unfinished culvert, with its deep and dangerous pool at the far end.

'Should have done it years ago,' Nigel had said. 'That time you and the boys went in it.'

'I'm not sorry you didn't,' Hugh had said. 'And I'm not sure you are, either.'

Nigel had looked at him, grinned, almost winked, and then walked away. It was the closest either of them had come to mentioning anything that had happened the night after Hugh's arrest. The deeper lines that Hugh had noticed in Nigel's face, that morning in the police station, hadn't gone away. Hugh had his suspicions about how the air pistol had got into Nigel's safe, but Nigel had volunteered nothing, and Hugh hadn't asked. It wasn't something you talked about.

But that was manners, or reticence. It wasn't like some other things you didn't mention. Last night, when he'd been speaking to Geena, their conversation had raised and dropped the topic that each of them did and didn't want to talk about, and had ranged off on different matters but always circled back. It was like picking a scab, they agreed; but they also agreed that underneath it all, the scar was healing. In the course of one of these conversational cometary orbits, going far out and then coming back, Geena had touched on the Naxals, and Hugh

383

had said – because it was one of those things that everyone seemed to know and never talk about – 'The Naxals? What the fuck are they about, anyway?'

Geena had explained, and talked about her supervisor's theory of them, and her own analogy with the City Burners, those terrifying folk who'd appeared out of nowhere and burned antiquity to the ground. All the cities and all the records, gone, and then the Burners gone, leaving no trace.

'But how could anyone do that now?' he'd asked. 'Not much point burning books, now we have the net.'

Geena, or her virtual image in his glasses, relayed from the cameras in her front room in Uxbridge, where she sat up while her boyfriend snored in the bedroom behind her, had shrugged. 'Bring down the net?'

'You couldn't do that,' he'd pointed out, 'without some kind of massive virus attack, or electromagnetic pulse bursts, and you'd need supercomputers for the viruses, or nukes for the EMP – all the advanced tech the Naxals don't have and don't want.'

Another shrug. 'I'm sure they're working on it.' A wry smile. 'A low-tech solution, to get us all back to low tech. Meaning millions of us would die without these bastards even having to kill us. God, it terrifies me just thinking about it. It's like, hey guys, you're terrorists, OK? Well, you've got me terrorised! You've made your point. Can you stop now? Maybe negotiate?' She shook her head. 'But that's the thing. They don't *have* demands. There's nothing to negotiate. They just want us dead in the ruins. So I understand why, back home, I mean in the old country, India, the government just bombs them. I can even understand why the cops here . . . '

'Do what they did to us?'

'No, not that, but . . . the death-from-above stuff. The killer drones.' She shuddered. 'Though it's not nice to be in the splatter radius. Ugh!'

And then their talk had moved on. It was odd what they talked about, and what they didn't talk about. Now he came to think of it, even when she was enthusing about the tachyon project, he'd never spoken to her about what he'd seen in the tunnel. Maybe that was a result of the final warning he'd been given by the man. Like Hope, and Geena for that matter, Hugh had become much more reckless and unguarded in what he talked about – they all no longer cared who was watching or listening – but this was one live wire he dared not touch.

Live wire. Something in that thought niggled. The guys around him, by unspoken consensus, began to shift themselves, to splash away dregs of tea or coffee gone cold, to go back to work. We'd better get on with it, Hugh thought, the weather's not going to hold, the wind's picking up, carrying tiny stinging flecks of ice . . . be lucky to get a full day of it at this rate.

He bestirred himself, and as he got to his feet the generator powering the winch ran down, and coughed into silence. An overseer cursed, in loud and fluent Gaelic, and someone hastened to top up the generator's fuel.

Live wire.

Hugh stared across at the cylinders of cable. If the generator had been connected to those reels, and the reels connected to each other, with an iron core through all of them, each cylinder thus connected would have become an enormous electromagnet. And when the generator's fuel ran down, and it stopped, the magnetic field would collapse, resulting in . . .

An electromagnetic pulse.

And that was it, the low-tech solution.

It was so obvious, when you saw it, and its preparation so innocent-seeming and difficult to police or prevent, that Hugh felt sure the Naxals would come up with it sometime, if they hadn't thought of it already. With something like this, they could bring down the net, and more than the net. Power systems, telecoms, machinery, traffic control . . . *air*-traffic control, too. And then what?

With a chill that ran down his chest like a cold shower, Hugh realised that he already knew what would come next. Collapse. And after collapse, barbarism. He had seen the distant consequence already, the barbarians with their gliders over the glens. If that was how the future could be, maybe these visions of his were a warning, of a world that his action or inaction could bring about, and him just the very man to stop it. Or maybe nothing could be done, if his father was right, and the sight never showed you a future you could change.

As Hugh went back to his work on the tower, he thought of shiploads and shiploads of coils and coils of cable, moving into or out of harbours all over the world. Or coils stacked up and generators chugging away, in empty office blocks undergoing renovation or demolition; in dusty warehouses in industrial suburbs; on building sites in central business districts. It would all be a matter of how powerful the electromagnets were, and how strategically they were placed. It would be an interesting exercise, he thought, for this evening, to pull down one of the old physics textbooks and fire up the calculator on his pad and figure out just how many it would take.

And then, and then ... he could take the result to the police, and ask them to take it to the man at the base, to warn the authorities of the danger. That would put him in their good books, for sure.

And then again ...

He thought about the base, and the man, and smiled. He thought about the danger they were in, all unknowing, and smiled.

They'd never see it coming.

He had to knock off work early that day, as the weather broke.

He was still smiling as he drove home, through the first snows of summer.

Acknowledgements

This book owes a good deal to my year as Writer in Residence at the ESRC Genomics Policy and Research Forum at Edinburgh University, whose academic and administrative staff are among the most intellectually stimulating, friendly and helpful people you could hope to meet. In view of this, it's perhaps more than a formality to state that this book's characters, their views and their actions are entirely fictitious, and bear no relation to any living person.

Thanks to Carol, Sharon and Michael for love and support throughout.

Thanks to Darren Nash for the initial brainstorming (and the beer); to Mic Cheetham, Sharon MacLeod, Mairi Ann Cullen, Steve Sturdy and Farah Mendlesohn for reading and commenting on the first draft.

extras

www.orbitbooks.net

about the author

Ken MacLeod graduated with a BSc from Glasgow University in 1976. Following research at Brunel University, he worked in a variety of manual and clerical jobs whilst completing an MPhil thesis. He previously worked as a computer analyst/ programmer in Edinburgh, but is now a full-time writer. He is the author of twelve previous novels, five of which have been nominated for the Arthur C. Clarke Award, and two which have won the BSFA Award. Ken MacLeod is married with two grown-up children and lives in West Lothian.

Find out more about Ken MacLeod and other Orbit authors registering for the free monthly newsletter at www.orbitbooks.net

if you enjoyed

INTRUSION

look out for

EXISTENCE

by

David Brin

1.

I, AMPHORUM

The universe had two great halves.

A hemisphere of glittering stars surrounded Gerald on the right.

Blue-brown Earth took up the other side. *Home,* after this job was done. Cleaning the mess left by another generation.

Like a fetus in its sac, Gerald floated in a crystal shell, perched at the end of a long boom, some distance from the space station *Endurance*. Buffered from its throbbing pulse, this bubble was more space than station.

Here, he could focus on signals coming from a satellite hundreds of kilometers away. A long, narrow ribbon of whirling fiber, far overhead.

The bola. His lariat. His tool in an ongoing chore.
The bola is my arm.
The grabber is my hand.
Magnetic is the lever that I turn.
A planet is my fulcrum.

Most days, the little chant helped Gerald to focus on his job – that of a glorified garbageman. *There are still people who envy me. Millions, down in that film of sea and cloud and shore.*

Some would be looking up right now, as nightfall rushed

faster than sound across teeming Sumatra. Twilight was the best time to glimpse this big old station. It made him feel connected with humanity every time *Endurance* crossed the terminator – whether dawn or dusk – knowing a few people still looked up.

Focus, Gerald. On the job.

Reaching out, extending his right arm fully along the line of his body, he tried again to adjust tension in that far-off, whirling cable, two thousand kilometers overhead, as if it were a languid extension of his own self.

And the cable replied. Feedback signals pulsed along Gerald's neuro-sens suit . . . but they felt wrong.

My fault, Gerald realized. The orders he sent to the slender satellite were too rapid, too impatient. Nearby, little Hachi complained with a screech. The other occupant of this inflated chamber wasn't happy.

'All right.' Gerald grimaced at the little figure, wearing its own neuro-sens outfit. 'Don't get your tail in a knot. I'll fix it.'

Sometimes a monkey has more sense than a man.

Especially a man who looks so raggedy, Gerald thought. A chance glimpse of his reflection revealed how stained his elastic garment had become – from spilled drinks and maintenance fluids. His grizzled cheeks looked gaunt. Infested, even haunted, by bushy, unkempt eyebrows.

If I go home to Houston like this, the family won't even let me in our house. Though, with all my accumulated flight pay . . .

Come on, focus!

Grimly, Gerald clicked down twice on his lower left premolar and three times on the right. His suit responded with another jolt of Slow Juice through a vein in his thigh. Coolness, a lassitude that should help clear thinking, spread through his body—

– and time seemed to crawl.

Feedback signals from the distant bola now had time to catch up. He felt more a *part* of the thirty kilometer strand, as it whirled ponderously in a higher orbit. Pulsing electric currents that throbbed *up there* were translated as a faint tingle *down here*, running from Gerald's wrist, along his arm and shoulder, slanting across his back and then down to his left big toe, where they seemed to *dig* for leverage. When he pushed, the faraway cable-satellite responded, applying force against the planet's magnetic field.

Tele-operation. In an era of ever more sophisticated artificial intelligence, some tasks still needed an old-fashioned human pilot. Even one who floated in a bubble, far below the real action.

Let's increase the current a bit. To notch down our rate of turn. A tingle in his toe represented several hundred amps of electricity, spewing from one end of the whirling tether, increasing magnetic drag. The great cable rotated across the stars a bit slower.

Hachi – linked-in nearby – hooted querulously from his own web of support fibers. This was better, though the capuchin still needed convincing.

'Cut me some slack,' Gerald grumbled. 'I know what I'm doing.'

The computer's dynamical model agreed with Hachi, though. It still forecast no easy grab when the tether's tip reached its brief rendezvous with ... whatever piece of space junk lay in Gerald's sights.

Another tooth-tap command, and night closed in around him more completely, simulating what he would see if he were *up there*, hundreds of klicks higher, at the tether's speeding tip, where stars glittered more clearly. From that greater altitude, Earth seemed a much smaller disc, filling just a quarter of the sky.

Now, everything he heard, felt or saw came from the robotic cable. His lasso. A vine to swing upon, suspended from some distant constellation.

Once an ape ... always an ape.

The tether *became* Gerald's body. An electric tingle along his spine – a sleeting breeze – was the Van Allen radiation wind, caught in magnetic belts that made a lethal sizzle of the middle-orbit heights, from nine hundred kilometers all the way out to thirty thousand or so.

The Bermuda Triangle of outer space. No mere human could

survive in that realm for more than an hour. The Apollo astronauts accumulated half of all their allotted radiation dosage during a few minutes sprinting across the belt, toward the relative calm and safety of the Moon. Expensive communications satellites suffered more damage just passing through those middle altitudes than they would in a decade, higher up in placid geosynchronous orbit.

Ever since that brief time of bold lunar missions – and the even-briefer *Zheng He* era – no astronaut had ventured beyond the radiation belt. Instead, they hunkered in safety, just above the atmosphere, while robots explored the solar system. This made Gerald the Far-Out Guy! With his bola for an arm, and the grabber for a hand, he reached beyond. Just a bit, into the maelstrom. No one else got as high.

Trawling for garbage.

'All right . . .,' he murmured. 'Where are you . . . ?'

Radar had the target pinpointed, about as well as machines could manage amid a crackling fog of charged particles. Position and trajectory kept jittering, evading a fix with slipperiness that seemed almost alive. Worse – though no one believed him – Gerald swore that orbits tended to *shift* in this creepy zone, by up to a few thousandths of a percent, translating into tens of meters. That could make a bola-snatch more artistic guesswork than physics. Computers still had lots to learn, before they took over *this* job from a couple of primates.

Hachi chirped excitedly.

'Yeah, I see it.' Gerald squinted, and optics at the tether-tip automatically magnified a glitter, just ahead. The *target* – probably some piece of space junk, left here by an earlier, wastrel generation. Part of an exploding Russian second stage, perhaps. Or a connector ring from an Apollo flight. Maybe one of those capsules filled with human ashes that used to get fired out here, willy-nilly, during the burial-in-space fad. Or else the remnants of some foolish weapon experiment. Space Command claimed to have all the garbage radar charted and imaged down to a dozen centimeters.

Gerald knew better.

Whatever this thing was, the time had come to bring it home before collision with other debris caused a cascade of secondary impacts – a runaway process that already forced weather and research satellites to be replaced or expensively armored.

Garbage collecting wasn't exactly romantic. Then again, neither was Gerald. Far from the square-jawed, heroic image of a spaceman, he saw only a middle-aged disappointment, on the rare occasions that he looked in a mirror at all, a face lined from squinting in the sharp light of orbit, where sunrise came at you like a wall, every ninety minutes.

At least he was good at achieving a feat of imagination – that he *really* existed far above. That his true body spun out there, thousands of kilometers away.

The illusion felt perfect, at last. Gerald *was* the bola. Thirty kilometers of slender, conducting filament, whirling a slow turn every thirty minutes, or five times during each elongated orbit. At both ends of the pivoting tether were compact clusters of sensors (*my eyes*), cathode emitters (*my muscles*), and grabbers (*my clutching hands*), that felt more part of him, right now, than anything made of flesh. More real than the meaty parts he had been born with, now drifting in a cocoon far below, near the bulky, pitted space station. That distant human body seemed almost imaginary.

Like a hunter with his faithful dog, man and monkey grew silent during final approach, as if sound might spook the prey, glittering in their sights.

It's got an odd shine, he thought, as telemetry showed the distance rapidly narrowing. Only a few kilometers now, till the complex dance of two orbits and the tether's own, gyrating spin converged, like a fielder leaping to snatch a hurtling line drive. Like an acrobat, catching his partner in midair. After which . . .

. . . the bola's natural spin would take over, clasping the seized piece of debris into its whirl, absorbing its old momentum and giving that property new values, new direction. Half a spin later, with this tether-tip at *closest approach* to Earth, the grabber would let go, hurling the debris backward, westward, and *down* to burn in the atmosphere.

The easy part. By then, Gerald would be sipping coffee in the station's shielded crew lounge. Only now—

That's no discarded second stage rocket, he pondered, studying the glimmer. *It's not a cargo faring, or shredded fuel tank, or urine-icicle, dumped by a manned mission.* By now, Gerald knew how all kinds of normal junk reflected sunlight – from archaic launch vehicles and satellites to lost gloves and tools – each playing peekaboo tricks of shadow. But this thing . . .

Even the colors weren't right. Too blue. Too many *kinds* of blue. And light levels remained so steady! As if the thing had no facets or flat surfaces. Hachi's questioning hoot was low and worried. How can you make a firm grab, without knowing where the edges are?

As relative velocity ebbed toward zero, Gerald made adjustments by spewing electrons from cathode emitters at either cable end, creating torque against the planetary field, a trick for maneuvering without rockets or fuel. Ideal for a slow, patient job that had to be done on the cheap.

Now Hachi earned his keep. The little monkey stretched himself like a strand of spaghetti, smoothly taking over final corrections – his instincts honed by a million generations of swinging from jungle branches – while Gerald focused on the grab itself. There would be no second chance.

Slow and patient . . . except at the last, frenetic moment . . . when you wish you had something quicker to work with than magnetism. When you wish—

There it was, ahead. The Whatever.

Rushing toward rendezvous, the bola's camera spied something glittery, vaguely oval in shape, gleaming with a pale blueness that pulsed like something eager.

Gerald's hand *was* the grabber, turning a fielder's mitt of splayed fingers, reaching as the object loomed suddenly.

Don't flinch, he chided ancient intuitions while preparing to snatch whatever this hurtling thing might be.

Relax. It never hurts.
Only this time – in a strange and puzzling way – it did.

A MYRIAD PATHS OF ENTROPY

Does the universe hate us? How many pitfalls lie ahead, waiting to shred our conceited molecule-clusters back into unthinking dust? Shall we count them?

Men and women always felt besieged. By monsters prowling the darkness. By their oppressive rulers, or violent neighbors, or capricious gods. Yet, didn't they most often blame themselves? Bad times were viewed as punishment, brought on by wrong behavior. By unwise belief.

Today, our means of self-destruction seem myriad. (Though *Pandora's Cornucopia* will try to list them all!) We modern folk snort at the superstitions of our ancestors. We know *they* could never really wreck the world, but we can! Zeus or Moloch could not match the destructive power of a nuclear missile exchange, or a dusting of plague bacilli, or some ecological travesty, or ruinous mismanagement of the intricate aiconomy.

Oh, we're mighty. But are we *so* different from our forebears?

Won't our calamity (when it comes) also be blamed on some arrogant mistake? A flaw in judgment? Some obstinate belief? *Culpa nostra.* Won't it be the same old plaint, echoing across the ruin of our hopes?

'We never deserved it all! Our shining towers and golden fields. Our overflowing libraries and full bellies. Our long lives and overindulged children. Our happiness. Whether by God's will or our own hand, we always expected it would come to this.

'To dust.'

—Pandora's Cornucopia

2.

AFICIONADO

Meanwhile, far below, cameras stared across forbidden desert, monitoring disputed territory in a conflict so bitter, antagonists couldn't agree what to call it.

One side named the struggle *righteous war*, with countless innocent lives in peril.

Their opponents claimed there were no victims, at all.

And so, suspicious cameras panned, alert for encroachment. Camouflaged atop hills or under highway culverts or innocuous stones, they probed for a hated adversary. And for some months the guardians succeeded, staving off incursions. Protecting sandy desolation.

Then, technology shifted advantages again.

The enemy's first move? Take out those guarding eyes.

Infiltrators came at dawn, out of the rising sun – several hundred little machines, skimming low on whispering gusts. Each one, resembling a native hummingbird, followed a carefully scouted path toward its target, landing *behind* some camera or sensor, in its blind spot. It then unfolded wings that transformed into holo-displays, depicting perfect false images of the same desert scene to the guardian lens, without even a suspicious flicker. Other spy-machines sniffed out camouflaged seismic sensors and embraced them gently – cushioning to mask approaching tremors.

The robotic attack covered a hundred square kilometers. In eight minutes, the desert lay unwatched, undefended.

Now, from over the horizon, large vehicles converged along multiple roadways toward the same open area – seventeen hybrid-electric rigs, disguised as commercial cargo transports, complete with company hologos. But when their paths inter-sected, crews in dun-colored jumpsuits leaped to unlash cargoes. Generators roared and the air swirled with exotic stench as pun-gent volatiles gushed from storage tanks to fill pressurized vessels. Consoles sprang to life. Hinged panels fell away, reveal-ing long, tapered cylinders on slanted ramps.

Ponderously, each cigar shape raised its nose skyward while fins popped open at the tail. Shouts grew tense as tightly co-ordinated countdowns commenced. Soon the enemy – sophisticated and wary – would pick up enough clues. They would realize . . . and act.

When every missile was aimed, targets acquired, all they lacked were payloads.

A dozen figures emerged from an air-conditioned van, wearing snug suits of shimmering material and garishly painted helmets. Each carried a satchel that hummed and whirred to keep them cool. Several moved with a gait that seemed rubbery with anxious excitement. One skipped a little caper, about every fourth step.

A dour-looking woman awaited them, with badge and uni-form. Holding up a databoard, she confronted the first vacuum-suited figure.

'Name and scan,' she demanded. 'Then affirm your intent.'

The helmet visor, decorated with gilt swirls, swiveled back, revealing heavily tanned features, about thirty years old, with eyes the color of a cold sea – till the official's instrument cast a questioning ray. Then, briefly, one pupil flared retinal red.

'Hacker Sander,' the tall man said, in a voice both taut and restrained. 'I affirm that I'm doing this of my own free will, according to documents on record.'

His clarity of purpose must have satisfied the ai-clipboard, which uttered an approving beep. The inspector nodded. 'Thank you, Mr Sander. Have a safe trip. Next?'

She indicated another would-be rocketeer, who carried his helmet in the crook of one arm, bearing a motif of flames surrounding a screaming mouth.

'What rubbish,' the blond youth snarled, elbowing Hacker as he tried to loom over the bureaucrat. 'Do you have any idea who we are? Who I am?'

'Yes, Lord Smit. Though whether I *care* or not doesn't matter.' She held up the scanner. '*This* matters. It can prevent you from being lasered into tiny fragments by the USSF, while you're passing through controlled airspace.'

'Is that a threat? Why you little . . . *government* . . . pissant. You had better not be trying to—'

'Government *and* guild,' Hacker Sander interrupted, suppressing his own hot anger over that elbow in the ribs. 'Come on, Smitty. We're on a tight schedule.'

The baron whirled on him, tension cracking the normally smooth aristocratic accent. 'I warned you about nicknames, Sander, you third-generation poser. I had to put up with your seniority during pilot training. But just wait until we get back. I'll take you apart!'

'Why wait?' Hacker kept eye contact while reaching up to unlatch his air hose. A quick punch ought to lay this blue-blood out, letting the rest of them get on with it. There were good reasons to hurry. Other forces, more formidable than mere government, were converging right now, eager to prevent what was planned here.

Besides, nobody called a Sander a 'poser.'

The other rocket jockeys intervened before he could use his fist – probably a good thing, at that – grabbing the two men and separating them. Pushed to the end of the queue, Smit stewed and cast deadly looks toward Hacker. But when his turn came again, the nobleman went through ID check with composure, as cold and brittle as some glacier.

'Your permits are in order,' the functionary concluded, unhurriedly addressing Hacker, because he was most experienced. 'Your liability bonds and Rocket Racing League waivers have been accepted. The government won't stand in your way.'

Hacker shrugged, as if the statement was both expected and irrelevant. He flung his visor back down and gave a sign to the other suited figures, who rushed to the ladders that launch personnel braced against each rocket, clambering awkwardly, then squirming into cramped couches and strapping in. Even the novices had practiced countless times.

Hatches slammed, hissing as they sealed. Muffled shouts told of final preparations. Then came a distant chant, familiar, yet always thrilling, counting backward at a steady cadence. A rhythm more than a century old.

Is it really that long, since Robert Goddard came to this same desert? Hacker pondered. *To experiment with the first controllable rockets? Would he be surprised at what we've done with the thing he started? Turning them into weapons of war ... then giant exploration vessels ... and finally playthings of the superrich?*

Oh, there were alternatives, like commercial space tourism. One Japanese orbital hotel and another under construction. Hacker owned stock. There were even multipassenger suborbital jaunts, available to the merely well-off. For the price of maybe twenty college educations.

Hacker felt no shame or regret. *If it weren't for us, there'd be almost nothing left of the dream.*

Countdown approached zero for the first missile.

His.

'Yeeeee-haw!' Hacker Sander shouted ...

... before a violent kick flattened him against the airbed. A mammoth hand seemed to plant itself on his chest and *shoved*, expelling half the contents of his lungs in a moan of sweet agony. Like every other time, the sudden shock brought physical surprise and visceral dread – followed by a sheer ecstatic rush, like nothing else on Earth.

Hell . . . he wasn't even *part* of the Earth! For a little while, at least.

Seconds passed amid brutal shaking as the rocket clawed its way skyward. Friction heat and ionization licked the transparent nose cone only centimeters from his face. Shooting toward heaven at Mach ten, he felt pinned, helplessly immobile . . .

. . . and completely omnipotent.

I'm a freaking god!

At Mach fifteen somehow he drew enough breath for another cry – this time a shout of elated greeting as black space spread before the missile's bubble nose, flecked by a million glittering stars.

Back on the ground, cleanup efforts were even more frenetic than setup. With all rockets away, men and women sprinted across the scorched desert, packing to depart before the enemy arrived. Warning posts had already spotted flying machines, racing this way at high speed.

But the government official moved languidly, tallying damage to vegetation, erodible soils, and tiny animals – all of it localized, without appreciable effect on endangered species. A commercial reconditioning service had already been summoned. Atmospheric pollution was easier to calculate, of course. Harder to ameliorate.

She knew these people had plenty to spend. And nowadays, soaking up excess accumulated wealth was as important as any other process of recycling. Her ai-board printed a bill, which she handed over as the last team member revved his engine, impatient to be off.

'Aw, man!' he complained, reading the total. 'Our club will barely break even on this launch!'

'Then pick a less expensive hobby,' she replied, and stepped back as the driver gunned his truck, roaring away in clouds of dust, incidentally crushing one more barrel cactus en route to the highway. Her vigilant clipboard noted this, adjusting the final tally.

Sitting on the hood of her jeep, she waited for another 'club' whose members were as passionate as the rocketeers. Equally skilled and dedicated, though both groups despised each other. Sensors showed them coming fast, from the west – *radical environmentalists*. The official knew what to expect when they arrived. Frustrated to find their opponents gone and two acres of desert singed, they'd give her a tongue-lashing for being 'even-handed' in a situation where – obviously – you could only choose sides.

Well, she thought. *It takes a thick skin to work in government nowadays. No one thinks you matter much.*

Overhead the contrails were starting to shear, ripped by stratospheric winds, a sight that always tugged the heart. And while her intellectual sympathies lay closer to the eco-activists, not the spoiled rocket jockeys . . .

. . . a part of her still thrilled, whenever she witnessed a launch. So ecstatic – almost orgiastic.

'Go!' she whispered with a touch of secret envy toward those distant glitters, already arcing toward the pinnacle of their brief climb, before starting their long plummet to the Gulf of Mexico.